But ... The Lord Is Silent

Roma Franko

Sonia Morris

Women's Voices in Ukrainian Literature

But ... The Lord Is Silent

Selected Prose Fiction

by

Olha Kobylianska

and

Yevheniya Yaroshynska

Translated by Roma Franko
Edited by Sonia Morris

Language Lanterns Publications
1999

Canadian Cataloguing in Publication Data

Main entry under title:

  Women's voices in Ukrainian literature

  Partial contents: v. 3. But . . . The Lord is silent :
selected prose fiction / by Olha Kobylianska and
Yevheniya Yaroshynska
  ISBN 0-9683899-2-9 (v.3).

1. Short stories, Ukrainian--Women authors--Translations into English.
2. Ukrainian fiction--19th century--Translations into English.
3. Ukrainian fiction--20th century--Translations into English.
I. Franko, Roma Z. II. Morris, Sonia V.

PG3932.5.W65 W65 1998   891.7'93'01089287   C98-920168-6

"All rights reserved. No part of this publication may be reproduced or transmitted in any form or by any means, electronic or mechanical, including photocopy, recording, or any information storage and retrieval system, without permission in writing from the publisher, except for brief passages quoted by a reviewer in a newspaper or magazine."

Series design concept: © Roma Franko and Sonia Morris
Translations: © Roma Franko
Portrait sketches: © Raissa Sonia Choi
Editorial assistance: Paul Cipywnyk
Cover production and technical assistance: Mike Kaweski

This publication has been funded in part by the
Ukrainian Canadian Foundation of Taras Shevchenko

©1999 Language Lanterns Publications
  321- 4th Ave. N., Saskatoon, SK, S7K 2L9
  Web site: www.languagelanterns.com

Printed and bound in Canada by
Hignell Printing Ltd., Winnipeg

Women's Voices in Ukrainian Literature

*Lovingly dedicated to
our mother
Sonia Melnyk Stratychuk
whose indomitable spirit inspired this series*

*This volume is dedicated to
Savella Stechishin
whose leadership role in the Ukrainian women's movement in Canada
was inspired and shaped by the socio-cultural stance of the authors in
this series and her personal association with Olha Kobylianska*

Titles in Print
The Spirit of the Times, 1998
In the Dark of the Night, 1998
But ... The Lord Is Silent, 1999

Forthcoming Titles
From Heart to Heart, 1999
Warm the Children, O Sun, 2000
For a Crust of Bread, 2000

Introduction to the Series

The turn of a century marks a pause in time—a pause that impels us to take stock, assess the extent and significance of societal changes, and make sense of our individual and collective experiences. When the end of a century coincides with the millennium, this need to engage in retrospective analyses is intensified.

The purpose of this series is to make accessible to English readers the selected works of Ukrainian women writers, most of whom have not been previously translated into English, and, in so doing, enhance our understanding of women's slow, difficult, and ongoing trek to political, economic and social equality—a trek on which women in Ukraine embarked over a century ago.

The works selected range from vignettes and sketches to novelettes and novels. Together they constitute an unsystematic but compelling social history of an era during which the mortar of social mores, religious beliefs, and gender distinctions began to crumble as successive political and ideological cataclysms wreaked havoc with time-honoured personal and societal relations.

The authors are not equally talented or skilled. What they have in common is an appreciation of the power of literature, be it as an avenue of self-actualisation or a vehicle of social activism. In addition to national, political, and educational issues, they address matters of gender which cut across ethnic and social divisions, and explore the power and often devastating consequences of social conditioning.

They do not, of course, speak with one voice. For some, women's concerns are overshadowed by larger issues of political freedom, cultural autonomy, and socio-economic reform. Their goals range from group emancipation to individual freedom, with many initially defining their emerging status in terms of a synthesis of traditional female roles, immediate community responsibilities, and more general humanitarian imperatives.

More importantly, whatever the subject matter, they observe and interpret experience from a female perspective. They intuitively understand that women forge their identities in the context of relationships, appreciate the power inherent in this need for connectedness and emotional wholeness, and demonstrate a keen sensitivity to both the promise and the human cost of change.

Their voices are loud and strong, what they have to say is worth hearing, and their impact should not be confined to one time or place. Translating their stories into English permits their message to transcend temporal, geographical, and linguistic boundaries.

The difficulties inherent in the process of translation were compounded by textual variations and vexing problems of transliteration. In the case of the earlier works, there were two other problems: archaic and dialectal language, and nineteenth century stylistic conventions. Ultimately, it was the criterion of readability that informed the many difficult decisions that had to be made.

A biographical note about each author anchors her writings in a social and historical context. No other analyses are provided; the works are allowed to speak for themselves.

Sonia Morris, Editor
Former Assistant Dean of the College of Education,
Former Head of the Department of Educational Psychology,
College of Education, University of Saskatchewan

Roma Franko, Translator
Former Head of the Department of Slavic Studies
and the Department of Modern Languages and Literatures,
College of Arts and Science, University of Saskatchewan

Contents

Introduction to the Series

Olha Kobylianska
(1863-1942)
Biographical Sketch — 2

The Beggar Woman	4
The Aristocratic Woman	7
He and She	12
The Mother of God	37
Time	44
The Peasant Bank	50
The Peasant	54
The Battle	57
Roses	78
What I Loved	80
The Free-Spirited Woman	82
Poets	122
Valse Mélancolique	128
Humility	171
In the Fields	175
Under an Open Sky	183
There, the Stars Shone Through	197
Sadly the Pine Trees Sway	199
I Am Lonely in Rus-Ukraine	204
The Blind Man	205
Across the Sea	207
Beyond the Boundary	212
My Lilies	226
The Thoughts of an Old Man	229
The Cross	240
In the Vale	243

Contents

Spring Accord	247
Old Parents	251
The Moon	261
A Letter to His Wife . . .	288
Judas	295
A Dream . . .	312
He Lost His Mind	319
But . . . The Lord Is Silent	326

Yevheniya Yaroshynska
(1868-1904)
Biographical Sketch	338
The Brothers	340
On the Banks of the Dniester	345
The Linden Tree on the Boundary	431
Her Story	439
The Addressee Is Deceased	454
In the Forest	457
A Woman's Happiness	461
The Guest	466

Olha Kobylianska
1863-1942

Biographical Sketch

Olha Kobylianska was born into the family of a minor government official in a small town in the Ukrainian province of Bukovyna. Despite the modest income of the father, all five sons were able to receive a higher education. The two daughters, however, in keeping with the prevailing view that a woman's place was in the home, were left to their own resources after completing only four years of elementary school.

Fortunately for Olha, the best traits of both her parents were passed on to her. From her father, a self-made man who was orphaned at an early age, she inherited a passion for work and a determination to succeed. Under the guidance of her mother, a kind, gentle woman of Polish-German parentage who was inclined towards the arts, she learned to appreciate beauty, music, and literature.

Growing up amidst the magnificent panoramas of the Carpathian mountains, the sensitive young girl responded intensely to the beauty that surrounded her. Her love of nature was rivalled only by a deep appreciation of music. Both of these passions sustained her during many trying periods in her life and are very much in evidence in her writings.

Olha read voraciously from an early age. Having been schooled in German, the official language imposed on Bukovynians in the Austro-Hungarian Empire, her reading consisted mainly of the works of German authors and world literature translated into German. Encouraged in her literary efforts by her brothers and older sister, young Olha started out by writing poems and stories in German.

In 1884, Kobylianska came under the influence of Nataliya Kobrynska, the leading theoretician of the women's movement in Ukraine, and Sofia Okunevska, the first female physician in Austria-Hungary, who generously shared with Olha the knowledge and perspectives she had acquired abroad. Recognising Olha's talent, these two women encouraged her to read philosophical works, improve her knowledge of Ukrainian, and devote herself to writing in that language.

Fortunately, Kobylianska listened to their advice. Initially however, she wrote her stories in German, and either translated them into Ukrainian herself, or asked established authors to translate them for her. Over time, some of these translations were edited and published in different versions, with significant stylistic and linguistic variations that give rise to unique difficulties in translating her stories into English.

In 1894, Kobylianska's first works appeared in Ukrainian journals and were received most favourably in both Western and Eastern Ukraine. She quickly established herself as a writer of note, and her works were translated into Russian and other languages by writers such as Olena Pchilka. In turn, Kobylianska translated Ukrainian literature into German, including the works of Pchilka, Kobrynska, and Ukrainka—writers featured in other volumes of *Women's Voices in Ukrainian Literature.*

Kobylianska won special acclaim from her contemporaries for her novelette *Tsarivna [The Princess],* written in the form of a diary. This work, published in 1896, is one of the first attempts by a Ukrainian author to write a psychological novel in which events are presented through the inner experiences of the proud, highly moral, intelligent, and sophisticated young woman who is the main character.

This heroine, like many of Kobylianska's protagonists, resembled the author in her philosophy of life, her refined sensibilities, her highly developed aesthetic tastes, and her disdain for the pettiness, vulgarity, and materialism of the society in which she lived. Indeed, it is said that Kobylianska's expectations of people were so high that she had very few close friends, and that she never married because she failed to find her ideal soulmate.

Through her friendship with Kobrynska and Okunevska, Kobylianska became involved in the women's movement in Ukraine, giving speeches and writing articles. In her view, in order to lead harmonious, meaningful, and morally uplifting lives, not only women, but men as well, had to raise themselves spiritually, intellectually, and culturally.

In 1899, after Kobylianska moved to the city of Chernivtsi, she established a close friendship with Yevheniya Yaroshynska, participated actively in Ukrainian literary circles, and developed close ties with a number of prominent Ukrainian writers such as Lesya Ukrainka, Vasyl Stefanyk, and Mykhaylo Kotsiubynsky.

After becoming partially paralysed in 1903, she could no longer participate in community events. Her health failed during the First World War and, in 1925, she travelled to Prague for medical treatment where she was received warmly by Ukrainian expatriates. Her works influenced Ukrainian women's movements in North America and, in later years, when she found herself in straitened circumstances, she received financial assistance from various Ukrainian women's organizations abroad. She lived to see World War II and died under Soviet occupation in 1942.

During her long and productive career, Kobylianska, who always remained true to her principles, created a rich treasury of short stories, prose poems, novelettes, and novels. By the end of the first decade in this century, she was acknowledged as one of the best prose writers of the modernist school in Ukrainian literature.

The Beggar Woman
(1888)

It was a warm, sunny morning in June.
The window of my aesthetically arranged room was opened wide, and I was facing it, seated at my desk.
A wild and indescribably beautiful Carpathian landscape flaunted itself outside my window. A gigantic, densely forested mountain, reaching up like a pyramid to the heavens, was flanked by a dark narrow gorge and intricately patterned formations of forested hills and cliffs. The ceaseless rustling of the pine forest brought to mind the sea, and everything was bathed in sunlight.
There was a superabundance of sunshine everywhere.
The verdure of the forest had never appeared so fresh, so intense. The cloudless, clear sky had never seemed so gentle, so blue. I immersed myself totally in that view . . .
I immersed myself!
Words are so inadequate . . .
I responded to this incredibly magnificent manifestation of the beauty of nature with every nerve. I devoured it with my eyes; I became intoxicated with the essence of its existence. And, in addition, I knew that the creative energies of my soul had been awoken by *her*, by nature, that it was *she* and she alone who had brought them to fruition within me.
Fortunate is he, who can understand her!
I felt an uncontrollable urge to capture on paper an idea that I had long been formulating in my mind. Forcing myself to tear my gaze away from nature, I began to gather my thoughts.
They submitted to me, but they also opposed me, dispersing themselves, mocking me . . . I could not do it!

Not far from my home—perhaps a hundred paces away—a beggar woman has been sitting since early morning, pleading for alms from passersby. She does not beg in the distinctive manner adopted by people of this kind. And she does not sing. She does not even have that beggar's tone which a person becomes accustomed to hearing from such creatures, and which has an impact only as long as they are in view. No, her voice does not have that tone.

She howls—maintaining a steady rhythm and descending down the scale from the highest to the lowest tones. Halfway through each howl there is a barely discernible change, and then it begins all over again: "Take pity on an unfortunate woman, and God will repay you!"

My entire body, from my head to my toes, is assaulted by that howling. I try not to pay attention to it, to turn a deaf ear. It is no use!

"Take pity on an unfortunate woman, and God will repay you!"

The howling has taken root within me, it sticks fast to me, and I listen to it attentively, nervously, indeed, with an avidity bordering on madness.

"Wonderful! Wonderful!" my lips whisper with an indescribable sarcasm. "Wonderful!" And, irritated to the quick, I fling my pen on the table.

Perhaps she will finally stop!

I listen with bated breath for one minute, two, three, and then I hear: "Take pity on an unfortunate woman, and God will repay you!"

It is enough to drive a person mad!

I rush up to the window to take a look at her. It is as if something is forcing me to look at her.

There she is!

She is sitting in front of the little bridge that leads to the market, and she is howling.

"No, let people say what they will," I think, "but it truly is an act of sheer kindness that begging has been forbidden. This curse still exists in small towns, even though there is help for the poor there as well. But I'll put an end to this. I'll fling some money at her to silence her, or to make her leave, or to make her at least beg in a beggar's tone, or to . . . or to . . . Oh! May you be struck dumb!"

"Take pity on an unfortunate woman, and God will repay you!"

I fly into a rage . . . and smile malevolently.

Grabbing my hat, I fly towards her.

She is sitting with her profile turned in the direction from which I am approaching. As soon as she hears my footsteps, she falls silent. Her emaciated, hunched body—with her head lowered to her chest and her hand outstretched—instantly tenses.

I slow my pace, wanting to get a good look at her.

Her face, seen in profile, is wasted and yellow as wax, but young and exceptionally symmetrical. It is buried in her chest, and I still am not able to see the upper part of it well; the lower part is marked by a deep pain that has long since become numb . . .

Now she raises her head to me. It seems to me that she raises it much too high, and I see—she is blind, totally blind. Long, silky, dark eyelashes cover her eyes . . .

Staring at her with horror, with shocked dismay, I hastily place my money in her small, sunburned hand.

Her bloodless, closed lips twist sorrowfully, as if in a smile.

"May God bless you, my dear young man! May God bless you a thousand times! I've been sitting here since the first rays of the sunrise which I can't see, and will never see, and you're the first to take pity on me. May God bless you!"

I reel with an ineffable feeling of shame.

The Aristocratic Woman
(1891)

Some of her eminent, aristocratic relatives laid down their lives as political dissidents in Russia; others were taken away by cholera. And, after long and extraordinary struggles, fate had carried her far beyond the borders of her native land.

For almost fifty years, she lived in a small, impoverished village, at first as the wife of an honourable, widely respected landowner, and later as an impecunious widow, with her son, one of the most besotted and worthless drunkards in the village.

Nothing in the world could ever induce her to leave that place. Even after her husband died, she would not listen to the pleas of her only daughter, now married, to leave the drunken son and move in with her.

"I can't leave him," she replied sadly, but decisively. "Everyone else is abandoning him as it is and, after all, isn't he my son?"

And she did not leave him.

She had given away her daughter in marriage here, and—most importantly—this was where her husband was buried. And she was well-known in the village. Every peasant, every woman knew and respected her, and she had a good word and sage advice for everyone. She was a *babunya [granny]* to every child, and a doctor for the ailing.

While working, she sang—usually sad, mournful songs—in her weak old voice and related stories about her ancestors, the life she had led as a girl in her parents' home, and why she had to live outside the borders of her country.

At moments like that, she seemed to come alive.

Her cloudy eyes became animated, her stooped figure straightened, and her movements reflected a gracious forbearance. It seemed that her own worthiness stood out clearly in her mind, and she involuntarily distinguished herself from her surroundings,

surroundings that were not commensurate with her sense of self-worth. Oh, yes, even when her poverty was most crushing, her destitution most overwhelming, the recollection of her ancestors imbued her with strength, and made her proud and invincible.

Fate scorned and mocked her, but could not break her.

She vested her ego in living out her sad life stoically, with an aristocratic dignity.

"And," she thought more than once, "is this not a sign of noble lineage?"

She continually instructed children, women, and men, and even though she had long since broken off all formal ties with society, she continued to maintain, quite strictly, certain distinctions between herself and her surroundings. The aura of stateliness and superiority inherent in her stance had an ennobling effect even on her. She felt herself to be an uncommon person. But—what about the wider world? Who showed any concern out there, in that clamorous world, about an old, completely indigent woman, the mother of a drunkard?

In contrast to her daughter, whose home was open to everyone, she seemed to be hiding from the world. She sensed that, in her present circumstances, contact with it would bring her only humiliation. As she grew older, her poverty increased, and her problems multiplied. Her son spent more and more money on liquor, and it was not possible for her, despite her best intentions and diligence, despite her subtle attempts at vigilance, to cover all the expenses.

The richer village women, feeling an obligation to come to her assistance, brought her gifts from time to time.

She would not accept them. Thanking them with a graciousness that almost embarrassed them in its meekness—she sent everything back.

When she was in her seventies, her strength failed her completely. The walls of her formerly clean and attractive sitting room were almost bare, and she sat wearily on a sagging, old-fashioned couch, surrounded by her son's hungry and ragged children, who greedily awaited a bite or two of the food that her daughter sent, and which she carefully divided among them, without ever leaving any for herself.

***

It happened at the end of December, during the short, gloomy days of winter.

The ground was covered with knee-high drifts of snow. Frosts alternated with blizzards, and the fields—level as the sea, with snow clouds racing over them—evoked memories of the distant steppes.

It was then that the old woman died.

She was conscious to the very last moment and blessed everyone several times over—her acquaintances, her son's children, and those of her daughter, the latter at a distance, because they were not present. Her daughter's children were her pride and joy, and she always looked at them with a secret pleasure—a pleasure that they did not dare to admit noticing.

She indicated her desire to make a confession and gave instructions as to how she was to be attired for burial.

When the priest entered her room, she told everyone to leave. (Among them were those who were simply waiting for her to die, eager to divide up the rags that covered her body.)

Later they overheard—they were waiting by the door—how the priest berated her for neglecting the church, for not attending for twenty-one years.

And they heard her defend herself with a groan: "You don't want to forgive me, but God will. He is my witness that I did not have the strength to walk to church—and had no other way of getting there."

A moment later, there were more surly, threatening sounds, and then she once again barely managed to moan: "But You'll forgive me, Lord! You know how much I've suffered; You know all the moments of my life, even those in which I was like dust in my humility!"

Then it grew still in the room, and only muffled whispering could be heard. She groaned one last time, as if pleading for mercy—the sound tore at one's heart—and not long after that, the priest walked out of the room.

***

It was an hour before the funeral.

Large snowflakes fell silently, steadily.

It seemed that the sky itself, curving deeply over the ground, was disintegrating into these silvery-white fragments.

The house of the deceased, standing far from the village in the middle of a wide, seemingly boundless field, was a poignantly sad sight—leaning to one side, the walls peeling and dilapidated, the broken windowpanes pasted over with paper. Here and there, a few fruit trees could be seen; on their tips, crows, exchanging places every minute, swayed indifferently.

On either side of the front entrance were propped old church banners, out of which stilted likenesses of saints stared fixedly. Standing next to them, peasants with bared heads peered curiously through the windows.

Toasts were being drunk for the soul of the deceased.

"Drink," the son kept saying in a weepy voice. "The deceased was of noble lineage, and her past . . . Oh, her past!" Wanting to emphasise his words with an energetic stamping of his feet, he succeeded only in lifting them ludicrously, as if in a dance.

The priest was reading a prayer. The daughter and her children had arrived. She wept bitterly, kissing the hands and feet of the deceased over and over again, while the grandchildren turned, time and again, to gaze at their grandmother and her surroundings with a hushed, curious wonderment.

The final scion of a proud family!

She was lying like a beggar amid four bare walls. She, an aristocrat in the full meaning of the word, with a strong spirit, who hated cowardice with all her heart, who preferred to faint from hunger than to humble herself and accept alms, had ended her life in abject poverty.

One of her grandsons, the youngest one, could not take his eyes off her. He was moved to the depths of his young heart, and various memories of her, rising swiftly one after the other in his mind, were choking him. He recalled how he had made two vows to her: first, when he was seven—never to drink, and second, when he was thirteen—to remain true to his people.

"Nothing has ever become great," she had said to him then, "that was not great in its smallest detail and knew how to be strong without the support of others. You have inherited from your ancestors a sovereign right."

He had asked: "What is a 'sovereign right'?"

And she had patted him on the head, smiled, and said: "Guess!"

Only later, did he discover the answer.

Oh, he would keep his word—make it come true. Just as it was true that he marvelled at the determination she had shown, challenging, with her last ounce of strength, the grimness of life, and just as it was true that he was her grandson—and the son of an oppressed nation.

His eyes, turning towards the deceased, ignited and blazed.

If only everyone could feel what he was feeling at this moment; no, not just at this moment, but always, then . . .

But was not everyone feeling this now? The entire oppressed nation on whose strings a most wondrously anarchic melody was being played? And because they do feel it, the sun of elegant freedom is flaming for them, showering its rays among them, transforming them, and permitting them to see clearly what they are taking in their hands and to their lips . . .

Someone standing near him opened the window.

A cold fresh breeze blew over him, and he turned his head toward it. At that very moment, the inebriated son waved his arms and raised a flask to his lips . . .

"She—was my mother!" he called out in a drunkenly proud voice. "My own mother! I must glorify her!"

A hot torrent of shame flooded the tender young features of the grandson. His eyes turned once again to the deceased, and his soul made a mute vow . . .

The soul of his grandmother had reason to be content.

And she too, as she lay here, felt content. She was lying so quietly, so peacefully! Her face was serene, almost ecstatically expectant, and her delicate hands, clad in graceless, large white leather gloves, were draped with a fragment of a fragile, once elegant, lace curtain . . .

He and She
Humoresque
(1892)

> Motto: Der Mensch ist etwas was
> überwunden werden soll.
> *Nietzsche. "Also sprach Zarathustra".*
>
> [Epigraph: Man is something
> that is to be surpassed.
> *Nietzsche. "Thus spake Zarathustra".*]

(He is in his room.) I want nothing to do with womenfolk, absolutely nothing! They're capricious, demanding, full of pretensions and contradictions, and puffed up with egoism. They're limited and childish in their views. Of what use are they to me, these mosaics of feeling? Moreover, one is just like any other.

I have my medicine and my patients, I have my friends and my literature, and I don't need anything else.

(He is lying on the sofa staring thoughtfully into space.) But it seems that I am fated to encounter her every day! And her demeanour never changes! Looking neither to the left, nor the right, she walks through the large park in which fallen leaves are already heaped in layers, and she's always deep in thought. In what is she so absorbed? "Women's issues," "conflicts between a woman and a man!" These are probably the issues that engross her.

I meet others as well, but they have a different air about them. I'm already able to recognize her from afar—by her walk, her slim, delicately built figure, and her snowy white woollen hat. Her hair is black and appears to be modestly styled. Her face—it's pale—assumes an air of severity when I approach her.

(After a few moments, sneeringly.) She probably thinks that someone might take it into his head to address her. Ha-ha! As if I would "address" just anyone! I, a person who is happiest when all of *them* are at least a mile away; who fears them as a sinner fears hell, because before you even know what has happened, they have thrown themselves at you. Well, not one of them will see that happen. My feelings are too manly to fixate on mere women.

I walk through the park every day because it's a shortcut to the hospital where I work as a doctor. But what is her reason? What could she possibly be seeking in the park now? It's autumn, and the park is almost deserted. And those few unexpected guests who do appear in it from time to time are not the kind of company that would prompt a young lady to go for a walk by herself. At least our German women would consider this *extravagant [foolhardy]*.

Who are her parents? What is she like? What sort of person is she?

But really, all this is of very little interest to me.

***

(She, upon returning from the city park.) How sad it is that people are so uncouth when it comes to matters of feelings. Particularly those who are supposedly "educated." To look at someone *that way!* Everyone must be thinking now: "She's adopted this intriguing role in order to draw attention to herself." There can be no doubt about it.

Well, if we all had the "becauses and so ons" written on our foreheads—if for example, it were written on my forehead that I have acute bronchitis and can go for walks only in warm weather; that my mother is ailing; that my father is almost always on the road, and that's why he can't go walking with me; and that, given my melancholy mood, it is more pleasant for me to be alone—if all that were written on my forehead, then . . . But what's the use!

With my foreboding of death and my sad thoughts, the serenity and dignity of nature are most pleasant to me. Autumn suits me.

But how I long to live! I'm tied to this life with all the nerves of my heart. It seems to me that the true beauty of life lies before me, beckoning to me. People laugh in my face when I tell them that I shall die in two or three years.

And I . . . O my God! I don't want to live for my sake! I only want to see how everything is going to turn out. To see and to feel, to a lesser or greater degree, the pulsating life around me. All I want is to be at one with everything. At a distance, in a quiet place. At one with love . . . At one with my dreams . . .

***

(He is at home now, looking out the window.) She pretended to be alarmed when I walked behind her down the short lane! But as everyone knows, they all do that. Well, if she had known that it had occurred to me, at that very moment, to see how she would look at me when I suddenly came up right beside her, she would have been reassured. In any event, she has no need to be concerned. I'm not one of those who goes grey worrying over womenfolk.

I have my research and my patients, I have my friends and my literature, and all this fills my life more than adequately.

How happy I am that I'm going through life alone, that I'm not bound to anyone. Well, perhaps it's going too far to say "bound!" In regard to that, the satanic Nietzsche, that Zarathustra, speaks the truth when he assures us that those who are always together are truly worthy of our respect. *Herr Gott! [Lord!]*

(After a moment.) Does she read? With pleasure? And what? Womenfolk have strange tastes, women's tastes. Their only concern is whether or not the heroes will get married; that's what they consider most important. They read the title of a book, then the ending, and finally—two or three pages in the middle. Just the scene where he proposes to her. After all, this is what matters most to them in life. Tendentiousness, major themes—issues of this kind simply don't exist for them.

I'm a great admirer of Norwegian literature. Take someone like Christiansen, Hansen, or any of the others; they can be truly inspiring . . .

Oh, what the devil! Is someone ringing the doorbell again? It must be that cross-eyed old Jewess bothering me again with her sore finger. She's really trying my patience and, what's more, she's fully convinced that I exist solely to cater to her needs! Well, the next time she comes, I'll squeeze her finger so hard that she'll never come to see me again. She's such an idiot—a simple Jewish woman! And she had to drag herself here just now when I . . . when I would have taken . . . a rest.

Really! It's as if they don't realise that I too am a human being. *Den Kuckuck auch noch einmal!* [*The devil take it!*]

***

(She is in the park.) I'm insulted to the quick! No, it's really strange—to follow me that way! Actually, I shouldn't be bothered by it, but it's my misfortune to be high-strung. This common fellow seems to think that I belong to "the masses" and that I appear here to meet with just anyone at all! But then, it's true, given the way women behave nowadays, it's not surprising that such an idea is uppermost in the minds of men.

Alas! How difficult it is these days for a woman to be a completely free person, to live only for herself, like a flower or a star, like . . . like . . .

Oh, he'd really be surprised if he knew my views on marriage. Yes indeed, my good sir, my nature is not at all compatible with marriage, you see, because how is it possible to have someone *now and forever, to see someone forever,* to be convinced that someone truly *belongs* to us, and that nothing will tear him away from us—none of that enhances love!

Besides, people don't make any effort to maintain in a marriage a mutual love and respect. They don't try to be something special for each other, something always worthy of the highest respect— and all because they already *own* one another. Quite the contrary; they neglect their character and their spiritual growth, and become indolent with respect to both one and the other.

Marriage would be truly beautiful if the people involved would not degrade it. Well, perhaps it will be beautiful some day—for example, when Nietzsche's *Übermenschen*, his supermen, those daring lions, come into existence—but now?

And this common person thinks that someone is paying attention to him!

As for me, I'll never get married, even though I find old maids particularly unpleasant. But I will not become an old maid; I'll simply be an unmarried woman, and that's something quite different . . .

He looks very intelligent, and he's not without dignity. Every time I meet him, I experience the same kind of emotional reaction. I might even say that this feeling forcibly engulfs me whenever I set eyes on him. I can't understand it, or make sense of it, but then, why should any of this matter to me?

The manner in which he walks says to me: "I am going along my own path, and I don't concern myself with the masses," and his whole being gives an impression of decisiveness and mental acuity.

Well, if he only knew how little all of *them* mean to me, he'd probably be furious.

And do I desire anything more from life than simply *to live*? No, I don't ask for anything more.

That old gentleman who greeted him said: "My respects to you, doctor!"

So, he's a doctor. Perhaps he's a throat specialist? But—no, I'm going to continue with the Knaip method of treatment.

An unutterable sadness fills my heart when I think about the hour of my death. And I could succumb at any moment. It's autumn now. This year I feel worse than last year.

How will I feel in the springtime, and next autumn, and then the following spring? Oh, my God, my God! *To exist* no longer! To be forgotten!

This feeling is shattering me.

I desired so much, but not for myself—for others! I no longer think about my personal happiness. I used to think about my country, about its fate . . . about . . . God knows what else I used to think about.

I wanted to translate Goethe's *"Wahlverwandschaften" ["Elective Affinities"],* and once I even thought I might translate Nietzsche's *"Also sprach Zarathustra" ["Thus Spake Zarathustra"]* as well.

Man is something that is to be surpassed—that's what Zarathustra says. I don't know if this is true, but I think so often about that sentence, and then I almost always say to myself: "It's death that will surpass me."

***

(He is at home, happy with himself.) I now know who she is. She's a *Little Russian [Ukrainian]*. Ha-ha-ha! And I'm a German!

She's the daughter of an impoverished landowner, and her name is Sofiya Dobryanovych. What a strange, strange name!

Actually, I should have realized she wasn't German, because she doesn't look German, and they're all emancipated, those Great-White-etc. Russians!

Her calmness and self-assurance are pleasing, but it seems to me she's sad. But from what I've heard about these *Little Russians*, they're all depressed like that; no doubt it's their political situation that makes them that way. Although, they're a nation like . . . hm . . . like . . . *Or* are they not like Bulgarians and Serbs, and is it only now that they're embarking on a period of true development and higher levels of civilisation?

They appeal to me, and perhaps they're not without a future. It is said they come to life only when they talk about the past or lose themselves in their national dances. It is also said that their folk poetry is beautiful and very rich.

Well, we don't know anything about their poets, and they don't make any effort to make us aware of them. They're probably not ambitious.

With the sole exception of the Poles, I find all Slavs appealing. I especially treasure and love Great Russian literature. Consider a writer like Tolstoy. Isn't he a Mohammed of sorts? I wonder whose world will be victorious: his, or that of Nietzsche? It seems to me that Tolstoy's vision will prevail, that it will surpass Nietzsche's and become the order of the day.

She most certainly must know Tolstoy; I wonder if she knows his "Kreutser's Sonata"? Well, this Sonata brings with it a flood of thoughts, but leaves a *tabula rasa [a blank slate]* in one's soul, especially in women. *Den Kuckuck aber auch! [The devil take it!]* To write something like that! A German mind is not capable of creating something similar, even if only because of its bashful women.

I wonder if she knows our young prophet, for example his: *"Also sprach Zarathustra."* She shouldn't be too taken by him, because he does say in one place: "When you go out among women, do not forget to take your whip."

That's what I call speaking "bluntly"! For example, I am to go to her—such a delicate and composed being—and stand before her, whip in hand, like an animal tamer facing beasts gnashing their teeth. No, Zarathustra, your creator is a phenomenal being, but in this instance he has fatally shamed himself.

When all is said and done, women are a tender breed, and if, in many ways, they are naive and immature, it is only we, their masters and defenders, who are to blame.

(He glances at his watch.) It's half-past three already. Why, I should have been on my way to the hospital by now! If my operation there is a success today, I'll truly be proud, as proud as a tsar!

(He looks through the window.) How damp and foggy it is outside, how sad and joyless! It most certainly is going to rain or snow. Will she come today as well? She looks as if she would dare to do something like that. Well, regardless of how things work out, I must go now. If my task goes well for me today, I'll be as proud as a tsar.

I won't meet her in the park now, and I did so want to see her today.

***

(She is at home, pressing her forehead to the windowpane.) Today the weather is so uninviting and wet that it's impossible to go for a walk. But I've become so accustomed to *all of that*. Truly, a person is a miserable creature of habit.

Nevertheless . . . that old park is exceptionally beautiful—those wonderful ancient trees that grow there, and the variegated autumnal colours of the leaves. The golden-yellow mingling with the green, or the yellowish-red with the green, and then the dark-green and, in the distance, the dark-blue as well. There is a great peacefulness in the park—waves of rustling leaves, the fluttering of birds among the leaves and branches, a wonderful play of light, an occasional late-blooming rose, and the fragrance of fading asters.

I love nature in all its everyday aspects, especially where it isn't insulted by onlookers, where one doesn't hear the same thing in many variations: "it's so nice" or "it's so awful."

When I'm in the park I imagine I'm in a forest; I fall into a reverie, and it is only the occasional passerby who reminds me that it isn't a forest.

He . . .

He's punctual, like I am. He's a doctor in a hospital. It's strange how one can sometimes find things out by accident.

Today the postman brought me a registered letter. As I was signing for it, the postman—I like him, that old German—was sorting letters. I accidentally happened to glance at one letter and, without thinking, I read: *"Ernest Ritter, Med. Doktor, Spitalarzt, hier. [Ernest Ritter, a Medical Doctor at the Hospital in this city]."*

"Which doctor is that?" I asked the old postman and, God only knows why, I blushed.

"He's the new one," he replied.

"Is he old?" I asked.

"No, on the contrary, he's young. Actually, he's quite young, and a very nice man. I think he's from Gradtse. But don't you know him?"

"No . . ."

"He's a very famous doctor. He's one of those who still have hearts in their chests, who don't think about the money first and only then weigh a person's life in the balance."

I can't go for a walk today; that is, I can't go to the park! But I do have to leave the house. I have to go to a social at the home of Madam K., the wife of the president. The dear soul has sent me an invitation twice, begging me to come and not absent myself from her select circle this year, as well.

Not absent myself!

It's fine for her to expect this of me, but today's weather is bad for my illness, and most likely she'll plead with me once again to sing for her. And she'll simply expect me to be in the right mood to oblige her.

Oh, my God, dear God! *People* simply won't ever believe someone else!

Ha! I'm supposed to sing! Perhaps something from Schumann or Mendelssohn, or, worst of all, the coquettish mazurkas of Chopin with which she is so "enthralled." No, I can no longer sing these songs; it would have to be something else. For example, a plaintive lament . . .

(Indignantly, after a moment.) What kind of nonsense is this? Why am I thinking about him? I have a feeling he'll also be there. But how in the world would he get there? I'm not aware that someone "new" has joined the group recently. It's true, of course, that I haven't been at one of her soirées for the past three months or so, and I have no way of knowing if they've begun accepting new people again. Besides, I wouldn't have anything against it if *he* were there, as well. It would give me an excellent opportunity to convince him that I don't go to the park just to see him. But then again, I could ignore him in the full meaning of that word.

(Once again, after a few moments.) How silly I'm being! Why, it seems to me that we could converse in a friendly manner, and that I would be happy to get to know him better.

He has offended me with his behaviour, and that's why I've decided to quote him something said by Zarathustra: *Dein Mund ist nicht für meine Ohren! [Your words are not for me!]*

Oh, such boredom and emptiness! How sad I am with a deathly sadness! And I am weary of life. More accurately, I'm despondent, in a mood that makes me highly critical, and my thoughts . . . O God! No matter where I race in my thoughts, I encounter death.

Which dress should I wear? Oh, most certainly not a bright one. Given my morbid frame of mind, that would be ridiculous. I'll wear the black velvet dress; it fits me beautifully and, by choosing it, I will neither profane my sad mood, nor violate the canons of good taste.

***

(He is at home. It is evening, and he is in a foul mood.) What terrible, wet weather! I've ruined my new hat and the gloves I bought the day before yesterday! *Den Kuckuck auch noch einmal!*

Well, it certainly was a strange impulse on my part—to go searching throughout the entire park for some unknown coquette. I'm becoming like all the others, like "the masses." Or, at the very least, I'm behaving like a high school student. If my respected friends, Professor S. and the bookish mummy, could have seen me, they would have stated unhesitatingly and unanimously that I'm a lost soul. But that's what comes of living in this cocoon that is called the capital city, but which in reality is just a hodgepodge of the most ridiculous and most uncultured elements.

So, for the past six weeks, I've had this compelling need to acquaint myself with the *Little Russians*. I've immersed myself in their world to such an extent that I'm beginning to become *involved* in their affairs. I've even asked one of those savages to instruct me in their hieroglyphics.

Ha-ha! And why the devil should I learn their language, when I, a German, can go around the whole world using my own, without finding another Goethe in any other literature!

Oh, I've simply gone mad, and I'm beginning to give in to the mighty force that is threatening us, some time in the dim future—the Slavic force.

I'm experiencing nothing but difficulties and disillusionment, and phases the likes of which I never anticipated. And truly, is there a more serious man in the world than I? There certainly is not, but, nevertheless, today I did not act like a man of science and knowledge, and certainly not like a level-headed German. Just a few days ago I performed an operation so successfully that anyone would be proud of it, but today I am letting my thoughts drift . . . *O satis sapientiae!* [*Nothing more needs to be said!*]

(Later.) It's boredom that is at the root of all this. It is encoded in human nature that a person must have a fulcrum, some passing, insignificant thing, but something that is, nevertheless, "important." Thank God I'm enough of a psychologist to understand that everything that is happening and must happen is *en passant [transitory]*!

This evening, I must tend to some urgent medical matters. They've been lying around for more than a week now, but I've only glanced at them in a perfunctory manner.

All the same . . . Am I my own man? Man is deemed to possess *free will,* yet he is constantly buffeted by fate! Take me, I'm a prisoner of my fellow man, a slave of my foolish . . . nerves. Like now, for example—and I strictly feel like it!—I must jolt myself out of this terrible mood, get dressed, most meticulously of course, and go to the home of Madam K., the president's wife, for the devil only knows what kind of a social gathering. Isn't this ironical?

Oh, if I'd had even the slightest inkling that, after my first visit, she would shower me with attention and drag me into her charmed social circle, then she never would have seen me in her home.

And now I'm asking myself: what, in heaven's name, has all this to do with me? Why do I have to go there? Oh, it's only too true that man is a slave—and what poems one could write about that!

And as the crowning insult, there will be a whole legion of womenfolk there, not too mention all the old crones who frequent these events.

Why do I have to put in an appearance among them? Why me? Ha-ha-ha! How clever she is, that president's wife. But then, I'm no dumbbell either. I'll be reserved with the younger women, because the older ones always hold more appeal for me, even though they persecute me almost to death with their questions about the symptoms of cholera.

(After a short pause.) But what if *she* were to be there as well? What a thought!

But then again, why not? I certainly don't know who all the acquaintances of the old Minerva are because I, praise the Lord, am still a newcomer to her paradise.

But then . . . All of this is of very little concern to me, and, given the mood I'm in today, just let one of them try to make me happy by bestowing her favours upon me . . . Then, by God, as that satanic Zarathustra says somewhere: *"Meine Ohren sind nicht für Ihren Mund! [Your words are not for me]!"*

(He is at home after the social . . . and he is agitated.) She was there, she was there, she was there! *Herr Gott!* Oh, I really like her, and *what a fine person* she is! When I caught sight of her, she was standing in a cluster of womenfolk in the salon; she was almost crushed into a corner, and she wasn't participating in the conversation.

She looked so lovely and elegant in her dark outfit, and her hair was smoothly combed, without those ubiquitous pony-fringe bangs. And her eyes—O my dear God—her eyes! Because of the veil she wears, I hadn't had a good look at them before. Dark blue, they shine, like glistening pools of light, in her white face. And oh, her voice! It's not one of those irritating, tinkly little silver bells. Her voice is charming and soft, and it stroked my soul like velvet; I was conscious of its physical impact.

She was visibly moved when we were introduced. It would appear that she is, by nature, a high-strung person; however, her nervousness suits her, and it reveals, against her wishes, that she is a person with strong emotions. She speaks German with a soft accent, like all the Great and *Little Russians*, and this, of course, appeals to me, just as it appeals to all Germans.

And when her glance fell on me, it was as if the sun were shining on my heart. And how intelligent she is! Well, this impresses a man without antagonising him, and all the while she is "quiet" and "feminine," almost as if she were the epitome of the German ideal of womanhood.

As far as I could tell, she's emancipated, but her emancipation has its own style and does not create as unpleasant an impression as it does in some women, who annoy us to the quick at every step. She's not like that, not like the determined Parcae who see a Lucifer in each and every man, even the most innocent one, and who feel obligated to sing out their sad song about equal rights to everyone, even though no one has placed this obligation upon them. If I had any say in the matter, I would immediately give them their equal rights, just so that they wouldn't paint us in such dark colours and poison innocent souls with their prophesies of a better "future" for women.

Her emancipation is of an attractive and gentle kind; therefore, it goes without saying that the wishes of such a woman are happily granted. She does as she pleases, without any hesitation, and without adhering to the old-fashioned prejudices and mundane virtues that smack of the kitchen; she doesn't try to obtain "protection" by resorting to the hypocritical, commonplace "good tone," under whose guise one tends to find such terrible lies and sins.

She is, in short, a natively intelligent person, and she has remained thus, despite the emancipation of women.

She knows Danish literature, the works of Tolstoy, that northern saint, and is fascinated—this is not in keeping with our tastes—by Heine.

Oh! I could converse with her and listen to her for a whole day and a whole night, and then for another day and night, and I would not take my eyes off her face and lips!

She explained why one is likely to encounter her so frequently in the park. She finds these walks very unpleasant—so she said—but she has to take them because of her ill health. Having said this, she became sad and fell silent. Clever man that I am, I immediately understood why. She truly is ill, but she is keeping this a secret from her overly nervous mother who worries about her to the point of becoming ill herself.

Sometimes she feels very weak, especially on damp days, like today, but she's tired of seeing physicians about her condition, and so she's curing herself according to the Knaip method.

Of course, I immediately offered my services and told her I would come to see her tomorrow to begin treating her. But she became frightened, and asked me not to do this because I had no idea *what* her mother is like—she would be alarmed by my arrival—and it might be better if perhaps . . . if perhaps she herself came to see me.

She seems almost convinced that her illness is incurable, and that she will soon die from it. Well, such thoughts are common in people who are ill, and that is why I drew on all my oratorical skills to reassure her, to convince her that she was wrong.

She gazed at me so nobly and so seriously, so trustingly and so kindly that . . .

Oh, my dear little pretty one! In any event, if I'm unable to help her, then she will be my last patient, and I'll enroll in the Faculty of Philology.

But she really is proud—*den Kuckuck auch noch einmal!* One must follow *her*, because she never casts a look behind. She even managed to put me in my place.

For example: she allowed me to see her home, and it occurred to me, idiot that I am, to give her my arm. She said she wasn't used to walking in pairs and didn't know how to keep in step.

But she did not say this in a pointed manner, or coldly; indeed it in no way resembled those words of Heine: *"Mein Herr, wie können Sie es wagen, mir so etwas in Gesellschaft zu sagen!"* *[How dare you, Sir, say such a thing to me in public!]*

Instead, she said it as if in passing, frankly, delicately . . . And, thankfully, the night was dark, and only I was aware of the flames that suffused my face.

And then she took her farewell of me so properly! Lord!

She almost came out and said: "This is where it ends, my good sir!"

It was her demeanour and her hand that told me this, because all she said was: "Good night, and I thank you kindly."

It goes without saying that I took my leave. That's how they lead all of us around by the nose.

(After a lengthy deliberation.) And that impertinent man . . . Why did *he* stare at her with his ugly eyes during supper, when she was relating something to her neighbour? It was almost as if he couldn't hear and see well. But he, that barbarian, both hears and sees very well. No one needs blind painters; they do not have a reason for existing, nor do they paint any portraits.

When I wanted to help her with her coat, he was there ahead of me. And while assisting her, the dolt gave me a look implying that he was surprised at my intention and was about to say: "And as for you, you German, have you lost something here?"

Well, I controlled myself because she was present, but I was seething with anger.

Even though we Germans are known to be even-tempered, I almost boiled over.

I ask you: what right does he have to her? Is she his fiancée, or what? No, he has no right to her, except perhaps, for one thing—he's a *Muscovite [Russian]*, and she's a *Rusynka [Ukrainian]*. So they're related; but only related, because the *Little*

Russians demonstrate in a variety of ways the independence of their language and literature.

But nothing in a *Muscovite* should surprise anyone. They live by the fist and, despite their Tolstoy, they are the worst of barbarians. They truly are antediluvian dinosaurs.

***

(She is at home, sitting listlessly in an old-fashioned armchair near a window. A little tired and deep in thought, she is looking out at the street as if she were in another world. Some handiwork is lying on her knees.) My ideal man is a man of intellect. I've always said this. Always, even before I read Bruno Ville's *"Philosophie des reinen Mittels"* ["The Philosophy of Pure Means"].

I think he is such a man of intellect. How quickly one can find out what someone is thinking. I, it must be said, felt this. He has something within him that causes the souls of others around him to crystallize. He isn't a slave of any political party; no, he certainly isn't that. He's objectively critical.

He's a true European, who says, despite everything: "I go my own way, and I don't concern myself with the masses."

In addition to that, he seems to have an upright character. He takes delight in Tolstoy's works . . . but he doesn't know much about our poets. He knows nothing at all about Shevchenko. Truly, Germans know nothing about us; this is so painful for me.

When we were talking about the Danish writer Jakobsen, I said something—I forget now what it was—about his excellent novella "Roses Were To Bloom Here."

And he looked at me as if he didn't know what he was doing and said: "I know a face like that, like the one of the older page in that novella. Do you remember him?"

I, of course, did remember him.

"I know exactly the same kind of face, with sadly shining, almost velvety eyes, and lips that have the same grieving, pensive smile."

"Really?"

"Oh, yes! It has the power to change the mood in people . . . and to overpower those who look upon it."

Why was I looking so intently at him? Did I really think I could follow him into his memories? Into those memories of his in which was revived, obviously, the image of some beautiful woman who had played an important role in his life? She has the power—he said—to change the moods of people.

And, as he was saying this and looking at me so unwaveringly, he truly changed.

A wonderful smile crept onto his lips.

(She reclines her head on the back of her chair and smiles sadly.) She must be some beautiful German lady. It is only German women who are so poetic . . . so . . . oh! The girl in the novella is a brunette, but Germans are blondes. But couldn't she, by chance, be a brunette?

Oh, those Germans! One could drown in them; they have a certain beauty and . . . Who else could be the way they are?

I could never be annoyed with him. He has such a strange, kind, and eager nature that it engages and captivates a person; moreover, he probably has a very generous heart. It seems to me he would sooner die than utter a falsehood. I loathe all those who traffic in lies, and in our day everyone does . . . everyone! This is so sad and yet, from the point of view of today's so-called "culture," so insignificant.

It may seem somewhat arrogant, but I sometimes find arrogance most laudable. I especially dislike it when someone kisses the "masses" on the lips. I would never be able to kiss such lips.

In addition, he's very pleasant and, as I already surmised, he must have a good heart. Others, for example, would be happy if their patients gave them some peace, but he simply insisted that he would like to treat me. I truly don't know if I should go to see him, or not.

I want to go to see him, but then again, I don't want to. Some strange feeling prevents me from doing so. It's partly a sense of shame, partly shyness, and partly pride. Should I ask for someone's advice?

(Very proudly.) Oh, no! I could never do that!

I remember ever so well how he looks, and how he talks. And, oh, how his voice quickens my heart!

***

(A week later. He is at home, in a bad mood.) How awful everything is, and how tedious people are! Some kind of dark mood has come over me and, to make things even worse, my patients are tormenting me, driving me to the point of exhaustion.

If I were a writer, I would write only the most tendentious works in order to give my thoughts and feelings free rein. Moreover, if I did write, I would try to convince the world that life and people are decidedly boring, and are of interest only to the extent that they are the reason that a person struggles until he dies.

(After a moment.) Oh, that mastodon, that dinosaur! That *Muscovite* is a horrible barbarian. The old Minerva told me yesterday he is on close terms with the young lady. He is preparing to write something, and she's assisting him with some research. I would really like to know what it is she's researching for him.

(Disparagingly.) Perhaps some psychological notes? For she likes science, and he likes "art," and I—ha-ha-ha!—I'll make her well for him. Yes, I am that god in Nietzsche's "Zarathustra" who looks on with benevolence.

But no, I won't make her better for him, because she still hasn't been in to see me. Knaip will surely cure her! She will rise early to walk over the dew, and then she will dine on herbal tea and rye porridge. How could I compete with the training I have!

She's planning to move to Zurich to study national economics. That's a great idea! In the meantime, he'll paint portraits, and then they will continue their friendship and, under the guise of art and science, proceed to spread socialism.

Something like this has happened before, and I should have realized this about both of them from the very beginning. Because no Russian woman—and no *Rusynka*—is in full possession of her faculties. Take someone like Sofiya Perovska; God have mercy, she's not a woman—she's Satan incarnate! *Herr Gott!*

Well, in any event, all this doesn't matter to me at all.

(After a moment, during which he peers more attentively through the window.) It's she! Oh, God! She's coming here!

(Alone once again.) So, she did come, after all; she was here! Oh, God, how flustered she was—like a child! I had to draw upon all my relaxation techniques to calm her down. I was a true hero, even though I was, *de facto [in fact]*, as excited as a young lad.

And as for her illness, well, praise the Lord, it can be cured. I told her this frankly, and tears welled up in her eyes. She had been convinced she would die.

She didn't say much and was in a hurry to leave. She's supposed to come again in two days, because one should not neglect an illness.

How nice she is! How very nice!

(Greatly agitated, he walks around the room.) What a wonderful girl! It's sheer pleasure to spend time with her; she's so original and so full of a boundless love of justice! And even when she's silent, it's a thoughtful silence. It is this delicate gentleness, this velvet modesty, that appeals to me most of all!

Girls are usually afraid to reveal their thoughts to men; they act hypocritically and bend with the wind. That kind of servile accommodation to a set of circumstances offends me to the point of disdain. Who would guess from the behaviour of today's woman that "matriarchies" once prevailed, and that there existed such proud and independent women as, for example, the Spartans!

It seems so strange to me that she was here. In her confusion, she put her little coat here on top of the books . . . and then placed her white woollen hat here on the desk, almost in the inkwell.

(He gets up, deep in thought, stands in front of his desk, and looks down. Suddenly, he notices a banknote.) What's this? Money?

(He flushes furiously.) Her payment?

(He is visibly and seriously upset.) I . . . No! The Moor has done his duty and may now depart. No, my lady, this time you have erred. This time you have offended the Moor. I don't need your payment. I will cast it at your feet.

Oh! How offended I am by all this! I never expected anything like it. So that's why the immaculate hat found its way to my desk—so the money could be shoved under it!

Oh, you hypocrite! Oh, you wily, velvety hypocrite! Oh, you tigress! So she considers me part of the masses and thinks I simply sell my services. Well, tomorrow we'll meet in the park. I ordered her most sternly to go for walks on bright, warm days.

***

(She, still in her coat and hat, sits deep in thought on a sofa.) Thank God that's finally over! Oh! How difficult it was for me to go there! A human being truly is something that is to be surpassed.

What was it that he said? "We will most certainly cure this illness."

He said this in such a kind manner, and so honestly, that I believe him. I have to keep reminding myself of his words. So, I'm going to live!

(With an emotional gesture, she burrows her face in the pillow on the sofa.) I'm going to live! I'm going to live!

Why am I so agitated? Why is something singing within me, while in the midst of it, forcing its way to the surface, arises the image of . . .

But no, it's just my nerves. Those hateful, ridiculous nerves.

***

(He, the next day.) I did it. I told her what I had to say. She was in the park, and I approached her and turned the conversation in such a direction that I could say whatever I wanted to. Then I said I had one request of her.

"What is it?" she asked in surprise.

A request that she allow me to name my own fee when I completely finished treating her.

She turned white as snow, and it was obvious she had misunderstood me.

I could not accept what she had brought me *(I blundered on)*. And she shouldn't ask why; just chalk it up to my eccentricity etc.

She answered very faintly, and in broken sentences, that she had not wanted to offend me, but that otherwise she could not have come to see me. I understood this. *Kurz und gut [In short],* this matter has been attended to, and I'm completely satisfied.

She's a beautiful person. She possesses such a wealth of pure and noble feelings! I become a different person when I'm with her. She's such an angel! Well, there's no denying: she's an angel who has flown down from heaven—and she's not even German!

It's the truth, so it's not a sin to say it—she is a beautiful person.

She isn't going to Zurich. She can't leave her ill mother alone, and besides, she has no money.

Would any one of our girls state this so frankly and so charmingly? Not on your life. She would probably say: *Mama erlaubt es nicht. [Mother won't permit me to go.]*

When she's completely well, she says, she'll give her trip to in Zurich more thought. It has been her burning desire for the longest time, but right now she doesn't have the strength for it.

Of course, I tried to dissuade her from her intention. *Was zum Kuckuck! [What the devil!]* What's so great about Switzerland? Even she's caught up in it!

Just thinking about it makes me want to jump out of my skin and smash all those ideas about progress to dust.

***

(She is at home, sitting at the piano and leaning against the spine of the chair; she is listening intently to the single notes she is playing with her left hand.) The afternoon was wonderful, gentle . . . a genuinely autumnal sunny afternoon interlaced with poetry. I can't imagine anything more pleasant. I met him in the lane that is thickly planted with linden trees.

I don't know. He's so strange . . . No, not strange, but so . . . You could say . . . he knows everything. I don't lose my composure easily, but I become flustered when I'm with him.

(She smiles sadly.) It's as if I didn't have a clear conscience. Or is it because he seems to peer right into the depths of one's soul? And then there are his eyes! I don't know . . . but they're so impassioned. They burn so terribly . . . Oh, so terribly! No, now I don't know anything any more . . .

He's so gentle and sincere in his behaviour towards me.

(She smiles in the same way again.) As if I were a tiny bird, or something like that. And I'm grateful to him. I would even be submissive with him.

***

(He is at home.) Today we conversed once again, and she was just as pleasant and amiable as always; we talked about her people. And when we did this, her eyes began to shine, and she seemed to come alive.

She briefly told me the history of her nation, its colourful past, before it came under either Polish or Russian oppression. She told me how *Rus [Ukraine]* had its own kings, how the *Ukrainians-Rusyns* were once a free people . . . led by the courageous *kozaks [Cossacks]*.

"Our entire history, our grief, and our happiness"—she related— "is found in our historical songs. But it's all intertwined with the history of the *Muscovites* and the Poles, and that's why the wider world knows so little about us."

She hates the Poles with a passion, and when she was explaining their behaviour towards the *Rusyn [Ukrainian]* nation, her eyes blazed with a hostile fire.

I understood her. But those who know how to hate, also know how to love. To tell the truth, our women do not have the same patriotic feelings that are found among Slavic women.

I understand her hatred of the Poles. It's a known fact that they are intolerant and hypocritical. At the same time, they play the role of martyrs and refer to themselves as "the fallen Greeks." *Schönes Hellenentum das, die "polische Wirtschaft!" [Some Hellenic culture that "Polish Kingdom" is—it's just an unholy mess!],* and that's no lie.

Besides, I don't have any reason to worship them either.

One time, I was travelling with two ladies in a coupé. Both of them were speaking French and enjoying themselves immensely.

I sat without saying anything.

The French woman asked the Polish lady if she spoke any German.

She pouted and answered: "Only dogs speak German!"

If someone had told me this story, I wouldn't have believed it, but I heard it with my own ears. It's too bad it wasn't a man who said that! By God, I would have challenged him to a duel. But what could I do to a woman?

And so I said to my own heart, as Zarathustra says: "Oh, lightning of my wisdom, burn her eyes!"

As I left the coupé, I said a few words to her in French that she will never forget.

***

(He is at home, completely changed, very serious and irritable.) What is this? She came punctually for three weeks, and now she no longer shows up. I can't and won't stand for it! Ha-ha! A doctor can't live without his patient. And what about her? She's better now; her hoarseness is all gone, but she knows she isn't completely well yet.

(After thinking for a moment.) She has something against me. She hardly says anything, and she has completely forgotten about laughter, which she once said Zarathustra called "holy." She's become nervous and lost weight. She's obviously suffering. But what about *me. Herr Gott! Herr Gott!* I was a fool a mere six weeks ago, a mere boy!

(Angrily.) Perhaps the *Muscovite* scarecrow has told her something about me? He has the privilege of visiting her parents' home, and he isn't a doctor.

Or perhaps her mother has taken ill? She lives for her! If that's the case, she simply should have told me. We've become good enough friends for that. During the first week she told me so many things, especially when we walked in the park where I would go to meet her, but now . . .

I haven't seen her there for the past week, even though the weather has never been more pleasant than it is now. If she doesn't come either here or to the park tomorrow, I'll go to her home and tell her everything!

I know now that, for me, life is meaningless without her, that I am nothing without her, that I can't live without her! O

Zarathustra, Zarathustra! As you say: "Man is something that is to be surpassed!"

I *sense* you are speaking the truth. Man is something that is being perfected—only I don't know, is it absolutely necessary that he be surpassed?

* * *

(She is lying motionless on the sofa, her face turned to the wall.) He wanted to cure me, but he's destroying me! I can't go to see him. I love him; I'm well aware of that. I'm afraid of meeting him, because . . . I've discovered the reason why I'm flustered when I'm with him—I love him!

Oh! Now I know from my own experience that *it is possible*—as a German says in a most beautiful song—to be one of those who die of love!

This is no fairy tale. I sense that love is sapping my strength. Some are able to stay healthy and rosy when they fall in love; others cry, sigh, and console themselves; but I become sombre and weary.

He's changed too. Why should that be? He has become quiet and serious, and he fears me.

Whenever I go to his office, he opens the door for me (does he see me approaching?) and becomes terribly agitated. Such agitation can be understood only when it is *seen*.

And that's just the point—there is that *understanding*, that mutual understanding!

Then we both fall silent, and it's difficult to control one's heart. Then one can talk about only trifling matters—and this is called love! It is as solemn as death.

He is always in my heart—and that's wonderful. Now I have neither a future nor a past; there's only the knowledge that I love him!

I am transformed the moment I see him, even from afar. This is the powerful something that's "destroying me."

I turn around and, like a startled doe, flee so swiftly down the path that people make way for me. And it's not timidity, O dear God, it's not that!

(In bitter despair.) It's love! I'm afraid he'll look at me . . .

***

(It is evening, and he is at home. A fire is burning merrily in the fireplace, and he is getting dressed to go to her home.) I met her on a path where I would never have expected to encounter her. She was coming closer and closer . . . And when she looked up and saw me, she turned as white as snow. I felt that I too had blanched.

We stood frozen, face to face, unable to exchange greetings. Her voice was almost inaudible. I became more serious than I've ever been in my life. *We already knew all of each other's thoughts.*

She was on the verge of collapsing, so we sat down on the first bench we came across.

"Why haven't you been coming to see me?" I asked her in a strained voice.

She replied that she couldn't, and then she fell silent.

I too was silent.

Then I took her hand and pressed it to my face.

She must already have known that she had become inexpressibly dear to me, even though I had not told her this in so many words.

"But why? Why haven't you been coming?" I asked again, as I had the first time.

She whispered that she couldn't. Didn't I understand that? She had lost her strength.

But . . . I loved her, I loved her! Didn't she know this?

She knew it—but perhaps it only seemed thus to me.

Oh no, a thousand times no! It was true, so she couldn't help knowing it! It was the truth! I'm simply not capable of doing anything when I don't see her.

She feels the same way.

She admitted this so quietly that I scarcely heard it.

"We already belong to one another," I said to her, and I embraced her.

She was startled, like a turtledove.

"'She doesn't know this for certain," she said, turning and gazing at me searchingly with her innocent, widely opened eyes.

Why couldn't she be sure of this? Didn't she love me?

Oh, she loved me, but . . .

But?

To love someone and to belong to him forever are two quite different things.

"It's one and the same thing," I said. "When two people are in love, they belong to one another, and that's just what I want—I want you to belong to me."

"But that's the crux of the matter," she interjected, "when two people 'belong to one another,' are they capable of always being something that is worthy of respect and love? In a marriage, this is a very great and difficult principle that requires much strength; but people who get married give so little thought to the matter!"

And that's the very thing she's afraid of—that she will not always be capable of being the way she is now, so that I would be able to love and respect her above all others, something that she truly desires. And do I feel within myself the power to remain, above all others, most worthy of her respect and love? Only then would our marriage become the wonderful relationship that human beings are capable of achieving.

Having communicated these feelings, she embraced my shoulder and pressed her face to it.

I will never forget this moment as long as I live.

I promised her everything that she desired.

I sense that if I keep this promise I won't become someone who is worthy only of her "respect."

After all, I understand what she wanted to tell me.

She would like me to become some kind of "higher" being—*Übermensch! [A superman!]*

And so she now is my betrothed.

Her parents already know this, and I am on my way to her home for tea.

The Mother of God
(1894)

Autumn. Nightfall. Stillness.

Raindrops, big as tears and just as transparent, pelt loudly against the window panes, dissolve, and slowly trickle downwards, thickly, densely, unceasingly.

Weary from my day's work, I lie down to rest, and my gaze is drawn to this monotonous image. And all the while, gloomy, dull thoughts, prowling like spiders, weave a web in my mind.

"If someone had as many 'thousands' as there are drops of rain rolling down these windows, how may spines would be bent before him, how many lips would utter words other than the truth—a multitude of colourful lies or declarations of various forms of self-abasement! But, if someone shed as many tears of grief as the raindrops dissolving here, how little attention would be paid to him during his lifetime, and not a single spine would be bent before him!"

It is not the first time that foolish thoughts like these beset my mind. They even lead me to the senseless task of drawing comparisons among "values," examining "morality," creating capital out of human attributes and thoughts—there is a host of them—and building out of them something grand, powerful!

Yes! But, at the same time, I am aware that I too am measuring my "wealth" against the droplets of rain, and that I am a truly impoverished woman, who has nothing that could proudly bear the stamp of something "valuable."

Paupers like me should remain silent and submissive.

Or, better yet—do nothing but think, think, think!

About what?

One could think about "beginnings" and "ends," about "beauty," a beauty with the contours of both love and purity, in whose loveliness "values" would drown, as would contemporary "morality," bent spines, tears of grief, and grief itself . . . Or, one could dream up melodies that would pierce the soul and ravish it with their beauty, laving all evil, washing it as waves wash the shore . . . all the evil that has collected in a mire . . . They would gild what was abandoned, neglected, faded, blackened . . .

Yes, to dream up melodies that would be ravishing in their divine . . . pure . . . beauty . . .

Demented thoughts, anarchical and mocking, overpower me, and while I, subdued and weary, sink insensibly into a dream—they soar away to an unknown land . . .

***

With heavy sorrow I wandered among people, seeking the one for whom my heart yearned. An unknown power pursued me relentlessly and untiringly, pressing me ever forward.

Having lost him, I had to find him again. Here, or there, or over there . . . or, perhaps, there, where a throng of people had crowded together!

Or, perhaps, on that other side, where so many of them were walking in couples?

O perhaps . . . perhaps—over there, on that side.

Time and again I walked down familiar streets on which I had often strolled with him, and, time and again I walked by unknown places in a large, unfamiliar city. And the people around me were all strangers. I did not recognise anyone's face!

This unending search, this hopeless, nerve-racking waiting destroyed both the courage I needed to soar farther and the power of my soul's velocity . . . I felt that the elasticity of my mind was weakening, the alertness of my thoughts was dulling, and I increasingly resembled a musical string that, stretched too tautly, is on the verge of snapping.

Yes, this host of feelings was destroying me, extinguishing my spirit . . .

All at once, it seemed to me that he was emerging from the crowd, breaking through the circle of people that surrounded him, hemming him in, and he was coming straight towards me, cheerfully greeting me . . .

Cheerfully greeting me!

In his eyes shone the light for which I always looked, the light that gilded everything for me.

So, he had tarried there so long? He had made me wait for him so long?

If that was where, then I had already been near him a couple of times.

And my eyes lit up with joy.

Meeting once again after such an oppressive parting demands as much strength as the parting itself.

He was approaching, drawing nearer.

I distinctly felt the charisma of his presence, but, at the same time, something unfamiliar, like an electric current, was passing from me to him.

And was it the light of his being—the light that existed only for me—that struck me now in the eyes, or was it the flaming radiance of the sun that was inclining to the west?

I closed my eyes for a moment and only sensed that someone was standing before me; at the same time, a light hand came to rest gently on my shoulder.

"At last!"

"Yes, at last!"

I opened my eyes.

Before me stood a woman. Dressed in modest dark clothing, her head bound in a black kerchief, she was looking directly at me.

"At last I've chanced upon you."

Astonished, I stared at her, feeling confused and cheated.

"So, again it is not he!"

Who was this? What did she want? Did I know her?

No, she was a stranger to me; but, no—I had seen her once before.

Or was it a few times?

But *when* had I seen her?

Was it recently, or a long time ago?

I did not know exactly.

She had an attractive face with kind, thoughtful eyes that shone with a damp glow; but how weary this face seemed, and what a line of unutterable pain there was near her tender, almost immaculate, girlish lips—the corners of which were set in agony.

"At last I've chanced upon you! I knew you were always with me, and yet . . . But haven't you recognised me? Don't you remember me?"

I could not recognise her.

"But, after all, you've seen me so many times!" and a muted, fleeting smile crossed her face. "They look at me," she said, "but almost always without thinking, deliriously!"

"Deliriously?"

"Yes."

"You saw me once when you were still a child. That was the first time.

"I came to your home with two orphans. They barely supported themselves with paltry earnings from their music, roaming about from one place to another, almost reduced to begging. They sang and played. Your innocent heart broke at the sight of them, even though it did not fully fathom the wretchedness of their situation.

"Still a child, just as they were, you did not have a clear understanding of life, but nevertheless, I could already see your future soul in your eyes. I saw, when you no longer could see me, the bitter tears you shed over them; I saw those tears even a month later. It was then that I placed a kiss on your lips, with the hope that the sense of justice that had awakened in your heart would one day be voiced by your lips.

"And later, I saw you beside a dying, scorned drunkard who did not have the strength to be a complete human being; I saw you there not once, but many times; and I saw how you sat among his rags and made his final moments more pleasant. At that time I saw your face clearly; there were only the two of us beside him; and later . . .

"Don't you remember me?

"Don't you remember the half-mad woman for whom people had neither mercy nor sympathy, and how they jeered her because nature had endowed her so meagrely? And how she evoked only laughter in others? There were times, however, when she had moments of lucidity, and then she was aware of the hopelessness of her situation, and felt keenly the humiliation and scorn that her innate limitations wreaked upon her . . . You visited her when she was ill, lying all alone and abandoned, her poverty having branded human dignity as a wretched bagatelle.

"You don't remember me?

"You don't remember that poor woman who worked in a factory and went blind in her invisible yoke, and then, in her poverty, descended into beastliness? And you, having lost her track, found it, and ran to her to find out how she was getting along, and to bring to her what is owed a human being . . .

"You don't remember me?

"You don't remember the elderly widow whose children had become a curse to her and who, doubled over, had to drive cattle daily in her old age—at the break of dawn, up the steep hill—in order to call death down upon herself, thereby fulfilling the evil wishes of her wicked children?

"You were the one who appeared together with the rising sun and did this task for her, to protect her, in her old age, from contempt and cruelty.

"You don't remember me?

"You don't remember that shunned, fallen woman, that vagrant who could not find refuge anywhere? And, when she died a sudden death, no one accompanied her to the cemetery! She died in full bloom, in the prime of her life. You were the one who walked behind her coffin and who, every year, when spring returned, adorned her grave with flowers, while she, long forgotten, was already turning to dust!

"And you don't remember me?"

Ah! Now . . . I seemed to remember something . . . But I had been so confused at the time—had it been she?

In my life, so much had happened—it was all jammed together; there was so much that was colourful, and I had met such an array of people, that I could not remember. However, it seemed to me that I was detecting, though still vaguely, something I could catch hold of . . .

One time, at dusk, when I was returning, walking slowly, from one of my customary walks, I passed a church that stood on a spot where the road diverged.

Its entrance doors were opened wide, invitingly, and its interior was brightly lit.

I looked at the main icon on the left side of the altar.

It was magnificently illuminated.

Countless candles burning around an icon of the Immaculate Virgin Mary—adorned elegantly with flowers, pearls and veils—shimmered and blazed, as if dissolving in their own light.

And the Mother of God, holding the tiny Baby Jesus, was portrayed so distinctly! Her exquisite silk garments were clearly delineated, as was her serene, comely face—a face aglow with spiritual peace, reflecting infinite contentment.

The devout whispering of those who were kneeling and praying carried through the church; many were prostrating themselves in adoration, striking their breasts, and crossing themselves over and over again. And it was all in her honour.

Now I knew!

Her eyes reminded me of the eyes of *this one* here with me. Her eyes—they were the eyes of the Mother of God! However, this line of anguish—the mark of unutterable grief and pain that *this one* had near her lips—where I had seen it before?

But my memory deserted me.

"And you don't remember me?"

"But you thought of me so often during your darkest and loneliest moments, when, despite your youthfulness and its inherent rights, you lived only with grief; when, because of others, you led a sunless life, as if in a land of fog, a land that has no 'noon.' And while others, losing faith in their own strength, turned to me time and again for assistance, you recalled that I also had stood alone in my most terrible grief, when they nailed my only Son to the cross. And you don't remember me?"

Now I knew her!

In my overwhelming desire to worship her, I wanted to fall on my knees before her, but she stayed me, smiling her muted, fleeting smile, and said: "I have to hurry on in the cause of justice and love, and you are searching for the one for whom your heart is yearning.

"Do you see this narrow street between those tall stone buildings where a funeral procession is making its way, and the corner past which they are going with the coffin, and the spot where the white ribbons are waving as if they are parting for the last time?

"Hasten there! He is taking a roundabout way, but he will come. You must go there to meet him, to wait for him. There, the darkest hour of his life is lying in ambush for him, and only you can avert it. Do you have enough strength and enough love?"

I was left alone.

It is impossible to describe the tormenting sorrow that enveloped me. The foreboding of an indescribable, terrible, future struggle that I was to live through gripped my heart as if it were in convulsions; my courage deserted me completely, and I wilted.

But still, I was the one who could avert it! I wanted to go forward, to be brave; I wanted to speed ahead with flying footsteps so I wouldn't be late, so I wouldn't have loved and suffered in vain . . .

But, what had happened to me? Something heavy was blocking my way, and I could barely take a step forward. Was there lead in my veins? Was I wounded? And what was this darkness that was spreading around me like nightfall, and through which I could see nothing?

A moment of sheer horror!

In frenzied despair, I raised my hands to the sky.

May the heavens not forsake me just this once, this one single time; may God come and help me, take pity on me—just this one time in my life!

And as I waited, I recalled the words: "And, at a time when others, losing faith in their own strength, turned to me again and again for assistance, you recalled that I also had stood alone in my most terrible grief when they nailed my only Son to the cross."

And, casting off the weakness from my limbs, I gathered together all my strength and, with a love I had never before felt for him, sped straight ahead like an arrow.

The sun blazed in the west and defeated the darkness.

The roads revealed themselves brightly and clearly . . .

Time
(1895)

Like a dream of spring, memories and scenes from my native land surface in my mind. The Carpathian mountains, enveloped in bluish mists, and the dense, impenetrable, primeval forests, shimmering blue in the distance, seem like an enchanted, cloistered, isolated world.

Whoever has lived in these mountains, breathed their air, and felt the intoxication of their majestic beauty, will always feel a yearning to return, just as an eagle is drawn to its nest on a solitary cliff. Such a person views with contempt the small-minded, hypocritical careerism and the tense, turbulent lifestyle and values of the lowlands.

A longing for that world has once again stirred within me.

It embraces me strongly, ever more strongly, lifting me high above the dusty, noisy valley and setting me down in a hushed forest high on a hill.

The fragrant scent of resin pervades the fresh forest air, and I lie on the soft moss among the ancient firs, peering through their thickly interwoven branches to catch a glimpse of the azure sky.

The sun's rays, sparkling like living gold on the treetops, strive to penetrate the darkest depths of the forest. It is so pleasant and peaceful in that forest stillness . . . Ha! Peaceful? A human being is like a swift river that continually rushes onwards, knowing neither repose, nor peace.

On a hillside, I came across an old peasant woman sitting by the road, grazing her cow. The animal was nowhere in sight, but its presence was attested to now and again by the sound of its bell.

I initiated a conversation with the woman and, in a short time, heard the entire story of her life. She was a widow, had three sons and a daughter, and now lived with a married son.

"Oh, I've suffered a lot in my time!" she said sadly as we talked.

I observed her silently. She was very small, thin, and stooped with age, but her wrinkled face betrayed no traces of the grief she had experienced.

"Is your daughter still single?" I asked.

"Yes. She turned nineteen on the Feast of St. Illya."

"Is she engaged, perhaps?"

The old woman glanced at me: "Engaged? She's had four suitors, but she's refused all of them!"

"She doesn't love any of them?"

"Love them? One of them is a decent, cheerful young man, and all of them have their own land, cattle, and sheep, but she doesn't want any of them."

"She doesn't love any of them—that's why she doesn't want any of them!" I ventured lightly. "Just you wait and see; one day someone will come along, and she'll fall head over heels in love with him, and then she'll want to get married."

"That's just empty talk!" she stated bluntly, waving her hand impatiently. "Empty talk! People say a lot of things, but everyone knows there's a time for everything. She'll get married when her time comes."

I chuckled softly.

She slowly turned her face in my direction, and her murky eyes slid over me.

"Did you say something?"

"No, I was just thinking."

"What's there to think about? You can think all you want—but there are some things that all the thinking in the world can't change."

"What do you mean, my dear woman?"

Shrugging her shoulders, she muttered, as if to herself: "You can think as much as you want to, but no one has the power to think away the most terrible evil of all!"

"What kind of terrible evil?"

"What kind? Well, of course, for you it's still far away; you're young, like an innocent dove; but I . . . It's death, of course, that is the most terrible evil."

"Death!" I repeated slowly. "That's true; thinking about it can't make it go away."

"That's the way it is, you see!" she stated emphatically and decisively, with a sympathetic smile. "That's how it is. And what else matters?"

"Death is inevitable," I replied, "but it's not the most terrible evil."

"Of course it is! It doesn't turn out well for anyone. But then, there's more than one thing that simply has to be, because God wants it that way!"

"What way, my dear woman?"

"I just said: the way God wants it . . ."

"Wants what?"

"The way it is . . ."

"But people may also want it that way."

She shook her head sadly.

"If your daughter wanted to get married now, she would. After all, you're not standing in her way."

"Why would I? I'm old already. I'm failing—I might die soon. What will she do without me? Will she go into service? What does that kind of work lead to? How will she cope with the young men who chase after her like hawks? She's foolish!"

"She isn't in love," I spoke up again.

"That's a bright thing to say!" she observed testily, in a somewhat mocking tone.

And, resting her head on her scrawny hand, she let her weary gaze wander over the valley.

We were silent for a moment, then I picked up the conversation: "When you're young, you see things one way, but when you're old, you see them differently."

"Yes," she replied sorrowfully. "When you're young, you have strength, and when you're old, you have wisdom. But what good is that? When your time comes, you have to die, if you want to or not. Ah well!" she said with a dismissive gesture of her hand. "It's not that I mind dying; I just don't want to leave her like this."

"Have you forgotten how you felt when you were young?" I asked her with a deliberate cheerfulness. "Or what it was like when you got married? But then, if you really want your daughter to get married, make her do it!"

"It wouldn't be any use. There's a time for everything. When I was young—O dear God, forgive me my sins!—I was mad about a young soldier, and he was mad about me. He flew over the ground to be at my side. My eldest son is his child; nevertheless, we didn't get married. His mother was a nasty Romanian, and furthermore, my time hadn't come yet. I married another man, even though I didn't love or want him. I got married because . . . my time had come! The same thing will happen with Illinka; that's what happens to everybody and with everything . . . everything. But people think they know best; they swim against the tide and want things their own way."

"Is there anything wrong with that, my dear woman?"

"How am I to know! Perhaps it's God's will."

We fell silent.

She sat without moving, looking straight ahead dully and drowsily, and I watched her, thinking how withered and wrinkled she was. She was whispering something to herself, but I could not make out what she was saying. We sat like that for quite some time, until, not far from us, a young woman suddenly came into view.

"Illinka!" the old woman cried out joyfully, and I looked with interest at this Illinka.

She was coming up the path towards us, casually leading a sturdy Hutsulian horse by its mane. She was attractive and slender, like all highlanders. Her face was marked by tranquillity, the kind one sees only in people who live in the deepest solitude and spiritual equilibrium. She moved confidently. Her eyes, cobalt blue and gleaming, seemed to be listless and cold, but when I looked at them more closely, a strange thought flashed through my mind, and I involuntarily thought: "A tigress!"

And truly! Something about her suggested the agility and pent-up strength of that animal. But I could not guess at the source of her strength.

She had come to take the place of the old woman.

I struck up a conversation with her. She smiled at me from time to time and, when she did, her face lit up and became even more beautiful.

"So, you don't want to get married?" I asked her in passing, as if in jest.

She blushed furiously, averted her eyes, and stared into the distance, her lips quivering with mirth and pride.

"She's a fool! She'll wait until her mother dies; then she won't have even a roof over her head," her mother replied for her.

The girl flamed red again and irritably slapped at a fly on the horse's neck.

"If wolves don't devour me, then people won't either," she spoke up. "You're always afraid!"

"Because you're foolish. But you won't always be as young as you are now, and that's why I'm afraid. At your age, I also was foolish: I thought only about foolish things, and I did foolish things!"

"Of what use to you is the wisdom of old age, mother? Does your daughter-in-law treat you with respect when I'm not at your side? It's better to have one full bag than to go begging with two empty ones. Are you planning to die, that you're putting so much pressure on me?"

"Curb your tongue, Illinka! Don't tempt fate!"

"So leave me alone, mother; wait a while!"

"It's fine to say 'wait a while'," the old woman said worriedly, and her glance darted once again to the steep, forested wall across from us. "Am I to wait until the sun sets, until night falls, and I close my eyes forever?"

The girl shrugged her shoulders and got ready to leave.

"Go on home, mother; I'll graze the cow by myself."

And, striking the horse with her palm, she caught hold of its mane and walked off in a calm, almost indolent, manner. A short while later she disappeared from view, and only her singing reverberated through the forest.

The old woman struggled to her feet.

"That's what she's like," she said, troubled and uneasy, gazing for some time in the direction in which the girl had gone. "She's stopped listening to me. She no longer fears me and has a mind of her own now. Who can tell where it will lead her!" And she sighed. "I'm doubled over with worry, but she just laughs at me. Forgive her, O dear God, for that laughter!"

"Farewell," she said, turning towards me. "May God grant you good fortune and a good life, and may you live out your days in happiness!"

Continually whispering something to herself, she laboriously began her descent, clutching anxiously at clumps of bushes to steady herself. In a little while she disappeared, like a phantom, from my view.

And I reclined once again on the soft moss under the ancient fir trees.

As I listened to their rustling, I watched an eagle—a black dot in the blue sky—hovering directly above me, high over the forests.

And all the while, the vibrant, ringing voice of the girl, whose image was imprinted vividly in my mind, resounded in the air. Spreading to the distant reaches of the forest, her song penetrated it like a clarion call to joy and happiness.

And I reflected on her uniqueness.

The ravines reverberated with echoes.

The bold, evocative voice was rebounding from one cliff to another, resonating ever farther and farther . . . ever higher and higher . . .

It seemed that this dauntless call was floating somewhere very far away—into an impenetrable distance . . .

The Peasant Bank
(1895)

I was given the task of informing an impoverished peasant, the father of four young children, that his farm was going to be auctioned off. The small farm that he owned had long been burdened by a debt incurred by his parents at the peasant bank. Some friends of his—simple, ignorant peasants—advised him to take title to the land, prolong the period for paying back the loan, and, in this manner, "save" the property that a certain rich Jew from the same village had been eyeing avariciously for a long time. After listening to their advice, he conscientiously followed their instructions. He asked the bank to wait a few more years, saying that God would reward the bank for waiting and, at the same time, help him pay off both the debt and the interest.

"The interest," he complained, "has multiplied like sin, sucking the last drop of blood out of me."

The final due date came, but he had not made a single payment.

He was an inept manager, and the past few years had been bad ones, with poor crops; he lived only on what he could earn by working for others. All the villagers knew that he would not be able to put together the required sum that, together with the interest, was far greater than the value of his small property, and that consequently—my lips trembled when I explained to him how the matter stood—the farm would have to be auctioned off.

During our conversation, I was haunted by the thought that this poor chap had not had any luck from the day he was born. Occasionally, he drank to excess; it was at those times that he experienced the best moments of his life.

In the end, I had to inform him what was in store for him.

It took some time, but he finally understood me.

The weary smile froze on his lips, turning them white and stiff, and his eyes—eyes that usually looked so good-naturedly at everyone—now turned to me half in alarm and half in shock.

"But I didn't take any money!" he finally groaned in a voice that did not sound like his.

"That doesn't matter, old fellow; you told them to sign over the indebted property to you . . . But didn't you know? This bank doesn't make personal loans; it only lends money against land. If you had at least paid the interest, then the bank would even have waited for your grandchildren to pay off the debt; but you haven't paid anything, either on the interest or the capital, and therefore, you see . . ."

"Oh, my dear God! How can this be?" he cried out in despair. "How can it gobble up my land when I—may my lips wither if I'm not speaking truthfully!—I didn't take or borrow even so much as a *fenyk [penny]*? And the people said that the Kaiser himself permitted the bank to be established to help us peasants."

And he laughed so hard that his eyes filled with tears.

"It's true," he continued, "that I'm neither the first nor the last to have to go begging because of that bank. It's coiled itself like a snake around every second or third household, sucking out their blood. And the Jews, those terrible infidels, rule the banks and control a peasant's fate . . ."

And to this day, I don't know if he said the following with laughter or tears.

"My God! Even today, I worked so hard that by tomorrow these blisters on my palms will turn into wounds, and my wife took her last tiny piece of woven cloth to trade it for a bit of flour. And I'm to move out of my house? Out of the house left to me by my parents—and go begging? O justice, dear justice, where are you? To go begging, begging! I! I, whose grandfather was a wealthy householder, the chief elder of the church, a reeve! The house in which my father died an honest householder, and I . . .

"I'd go even today!" he shouted with inexpressible grief after a pause of almost palpable despair and bitterness. "Whether I have a year more or less of poverty doesn't really matter. I'm almost a cripple as it is; I've wasted all my strength in hard work, and I'm leading a dog's life . . . But my children—my little wrigglers . . . I feel sorry for my little wrigglers!"

And, leaning against the wall, he raised his fingers, misshapen by heavy toil, to cover his face—a face that worry had lined with furrows. A muffled, heart-rending groan tore from his chest.

Then he came to with a start, grabbed his cap, gestured hopelessly—as if giving up on everything—and left.

It was a late autumnal evening, and a sharp cold wind howled and raced over the fields. Far and wide, only freshly ploughed fields could be seen, dotted here and there with small peasant cottages.

He set out.

Lowering his head as if drunk, he stumbled down a narrow path that wound obliquely through a field. This time he was returning home feeling helpless, completely destroyed. No one could help him. He knew that he was too poor to make it worth anyone's while to extend him a helping hand, or to have his fate touch anyone's heart.

The first living creatures to welcome him—and, as always, they welcomed him gladly—were two huge black dogs, the guardians of his cottage and his property.

A short while later, he walked into his house.

It was dark inside.

By the stove, in which a few embers still glowed among the ashes, his wife and children were huddled together, impatiently awaiting his return. He had gone to the village for some kerosene, but he was taking far too long. The children were scared in the dark; it seemed to them that something terrifying was peering through the windows, from the corners, and that it would creep up to them at any moment. His wife felt vaguely unhappy, and her heart was heavy . . .

The door creaked as he entered.

"Daddy's come!" the oldest little boy shouted happily, rushing towards his father. "Daddy's brought some light!"

"Daddy's brought some light!" his younger sister repeated, hurriedly sliding down from the bench.

"He bwought thome wight!" the tiniest lisped in turn. "He bwought thome wight."

But he said nothing.

Tossing a small candle on the table, he did not respond with a single word, as if he did not see or hear them.

His wife looked at him worriedly. What was wrong with him? He was not saying anything; it was almost as if he were mute. He had not even removed his cap . . . Could he be drunk again? He was walking unsteadily . . . Yes, he must be drunk! The damned infidel had once again given him too much to drink, just as he had done the last time; he wanted to cheat him so that he would hoe the corn for next to nothing . . . After all, he was a good worker; why not take advantage of him? And he—may God forgive him—had given in to the snake.

A bitter grief clutched her heart again, and words, harsh and painful, rose to her lips.

She was the first to speak. "You're drunk, again, Petro!" she said in a subdued voice as she lit the light.

"Drunk, Dokiyka . . . Hey, you won't believe how drunk I am! Today I'm drunk with the news that in eight days I, and you, and our children will have to go begging."

Her heart shrieked, and she stared at him in utter disbelief.

His face was pale as death, and his eyes burned with a fierce despair.

"No, today he's not drunk! Oh, would that he were!"

The Peasant
(1895)

Whenever I hear regimental music, I'm reminded of an incident from my younger years. It occurred in a large city, exactly at noon one day, in the month of August.

I was visiting a couple of Polish ladies and admiring the exquisite handmade articles they were showing me—embroideries of garlands of flowers, clusters of grapes, and arabesques stitched densely and aesthetically on a dark velvet background.

I amused them with biting remarks and barbed witticisms, and they "retaliated" in kind.

One of them, Miss Wanda, who had delicate and carefully manicured aristocratic hands that a German would have called *durchgeistigte Hände [ethereal hands],* talked a great deal about enlightenment, humaneness, and feelings; she was almost always sparring with me, and derisively referred to me as "Heine."

To this day, I have no idea what prompted me to waste so much time on her . . .

In the midst of our jokes and laughter, we suddenly heard the sound of military music. Miss Wanda flitted like a butterfly to a French door hidden behind heavy plush drapes, and all three of us stepped out on a balcony from where we looked around with cheerful curiosity.

From a wide side street poured a long dark mass of people—an army—stepping correctly in time to the measured beat of the music.

Their shirts and uniforms, covered with dust, looked grey instead of their usual indigo blue. The faces of the men, burnt by the sun, and weary from hunger and exhaustion, appeared almost black.

This marching—in unison, heavy, mechanical—how typical it is of an army, and how difficult it is to forget! No, at this moment, it was not people who were marching. It was a mechanism, assembled mathematically, with a soul comprised of the dry beat of the music, that moved and pressed ever forward; it was a work of art and compulsion.

There was only one single member of this mechanism, way back in the last row of one division, who was not performing his duty. The man, smaller and weaker than his comrades, did not, or could not, keep pace with them, and limped along, a step behind.

My eyes were drawn to his huge, heavy leather boots, dried out to a dull brick red, and I imagined what a deep wound he must have on his foot. This image instantly evoked within me a host of the most painful memories of my service in the army.

I recalled the oppressiveness and the rigorous physical demands of army life. I recalled the brutality with which some of the officers conducted themselves, a brutality that verged on the incredible, and I also imagined the indescribable suffering of a simple peasant, accustomed to freedom and unschooled in military service, his grief, and his longing for his quiet and simple world.

And I wanted to see the face of this man, so unsuited to being a soldier.

There had to be something carved on it—some suffering, or induced dullness. Or, perhaps, some mute obstinacy? The sun, however, was beating down so strongly that I had to close my eyes momentarily, shielding them with my hand. Even then, I could see nothing but how he struggled to drag along his aching foot.

"What a delightful picture!" the Polish lady standing beside me exclaimed enthusiastically. "Oh, Wanda, look . . . over there. Do you see the officer with the raised sword at the head of the last division? Oh, that's the way all of our soldiers should march against the enemy . . . Oh, Wanda!"

"Yes, I see him, Yadwiga. But haven't you noticed? The entire picture is ruined by the one that's limping in the last row."

Blood rushed to my face, and I turned to look at them. Disdainful smiles lingered on their comely, fresh lips, and Miss Wanda's eyes—large, scintillating stars—were fixed coldly on the scene below.

I happened to be holding a copy of the book *Konrad Wallenrod* that I had forgotten to put back on a table when we rushed out to the balcony. Impulsively, in a fit of sudden, almost insane rage, I flung it at their feet and, bowing to them with a contemptuous smile, turned to the door.

Madam Yadwiga detained me with an aristocratic gesture. "I don't know, sir, what came over you just now," she said haughtily, with icy composure. "But, how dare you forget that you're in *our* company?"

"In *whose* company?" I asked.

"In the company of *Polish ladies!* Don't ever forget this again!"

In reply, I bowed ironically and left.

But never . . . to the day I die—no, never!—will I forget the tone in which the words that followed me out the door were spoken.

"He's just a *khlop [simple peasant],* Yadwiga."

"A *Rusyn [Ukrainian],* Wanda!"

The Battle
(1895)

The Bukovynian Carpathians.

Mountains, clad in forests of fir trees, stand side by side in silent grandeur.

Variously shaped, jutting up into the heavens, they have stood motionless for thousands of years. Conscious of their everlasting durability and deriding every change transpiring before their eyes, they luxuriate in their inherent beauty.

Many mountain chains in the county of Kimpolung are still covered with primeval forests. In the greyish-blue mists, their dark blue greenery shimmers in the distance and, viewed from neighbouring heights, they appear impenetrable.

In the district of Ruska Moldavytsya, two parallel mountain chains have drawn so closely together that the valley dividing them could serve as a suitable playing field for only an arrogant stream. Where the valley grows wider or narrower, or where it disappears completely—no one knows with certainty.

There is no road visible here, no path of any kind, no trace of any human life. Twisting and turning, the valley, with its merrily rushing stream, pushes the mountains apart and, protected on both the right and the left by forested heights, disappears among the mountain walls that, in places, appear to be almost defiantly touching one another.

A mysterious silence prevails. The landscape is dominated by the lush vegetation and the beauty of the multicoloured flora, and the rich abundance of greenery on the mountains is almost oppressive.

Knee-high, greenish-brown moss, untouched by human hands, grows profusely in gentle waves in the moist soil of the ancient forest. Randomly emerging out of it are pine trees—trees whose age can be guessed, but whose beauty and size it is impossible to describe. Their elegant tips caress the clouds and abide only the splendour of the sun above them.

Here and there, giant trees, split by lightning, or weakened and overcome by age, lie on the ground. Having found their final repose in the grass, they are hollow and rotted, and overgrown by moss. Next to them grows a profusion of young trees; these saplings branch out broadly at the bottom but, higher up, they are slender and youthfully supple.

Only rarely does the song of a bird disturb the solitude. More often, a rustling and cracking sound—like the breaking of dry branches—can be heard distinctly in the cloister-like silence; and there is an almost constant sad, far-reaching murmuring.

And only occasionally does the wind succeed in lifting the branches. The tips of the trees scarcely sway during the fiercest whirlwind.

It is as if the rustling has come here from some distant plain and, having become ensnared in the branches, is spreading with heavy sighs through the forest, struggling with the thickly knit branches to free itself and return once again to the open fields.

***

When the whistle of a locomotive first cleaved the air of the valley hidden among the mountain walls, something pierced the centuries-old trees like a lightning bolt.

Along with the locomotive, there appeared a small group of people. It took all their courage to cross through the impregnable edge of the ancient forest and enter its unknown depths.

Things did not look ordinary here.

An unusual silence prevailed.

The air was cold and damp. Resin, oozing through the cracked bark on the trees, hardened in the air and filled it with its fragrance. The tall moss made walking difficult. The hard, unyielding roots of the trees—thick and sinewy, and intertwined with one another—rose out of the moss like snakes and stretched in monstrous coils into the forest's inner recesses which, enveloped in green darkness, exuded hostility.

One of the new arrivals swung an iron broad-axe at an old fir tree on whose trunk mushrooms—as large as swallows' nests—were growing.

The fir tree shuddered. In its long life, it had never felt an axe.

The blow resounded through the forest, and all the trees held their breath. A muted silence—full of tense expectation—descended, and then some words, spoken clearly and deliberately, were heard: "Chop it down!"

The words—"Chop it down! Chop it down!"—raced through the forest as through a church; they rang out close at hand and, at the very same moment, in the most distant reaches of the forest. They echoed like battle cries roused from sleep, stirring up the entire forest and dispersing menacingly to all its corners without dying off . . .

"Chop it down!" The words turned into a rumble. Out of it arose an alarmed whispering, a sighing. Then, a roar—like a whirlwind, like the tumult of the sea—erupted. The terrifying din filled the air far and wide, and soared up to the clouds. And a tempest began to rage.

The sky became overcast, its colour deepened to a threatening black, and a mountain storm broke loose.

Heavy drops of rain began to fall.

At first, the raindrops came down one at a time, and they were so heavy that the leaves trembled and rustled under their weight. Then, they began to fall more and more rapidly, until they streamed obliquely downwards.

Lightning was striking the fir trees and mercilessly splitting the finest trunks, while the thunder was doing its utmost to shatter the mountains. It was jolting them with mighty thunderclaps and crashes, seemingly intent on forcing them to abandon completely their unwavering tranquillity. It was as if gigantic spheres—called forth from time to time by golden flashes of lightning—were hurtling through the mountains . . .

Then it became quiet, and the rain came down without ceasing. It was falling loudly, sobbing mournfully.

***

It grew dark in the forest.

The old trees stood motionless and listened with bated breath to what was happening; the young trees swayed gently, incessantly. From the bushes that grew at the edge of the forest, huge drops of rain fell precipitously into the moss, while in the valley, the agitated muddy stream flung its choppy waves headlong over the stones and, foaming noisily and sweeping away everything in its path—flowers, trout, dry branches, and loosened clumps of earth—it rushed along in a completely unrestrainable and mindless despair, never witnessed before.

***

One cloudy morning, the battle began. In the narrow valley, on a steel track whose rails wound sensuously like silver serpents by the stream that ran alongside them, a freight train came into view.

A hostile hissing and a piercing, penetrating whistle announced its arrival.

Puffing, and fiercely expelling black rings of smoke, it stopped not far from the end of the railroad line.

It brought the enemy.

He stepped down from the train.

Completely unprepossessing in appearance—in tattered, soiled clothing, with a coarse face and ungainly hands deformed by hard work, armed with shiny broadaxes and heavy iron chains—it was thus that he arrived.

An eagle with ruffled feathers, watching all this from his perch on a nearby steep cliff, suddenly spread his wings widely, flapped them angrily and offendedly, and soared upwards. Distraught, he circled for a long time, and then, as if responding to an urgent inner command, plummeted at a precipitous angle like a streak of lightning, paused for a moment, and then lifted himself upwards once again—this time, in a completely leisurely flight—and disappeared in the grey clouds . . . as if vanishing forever.

An unutterable sadness spread over the mountains—a foreboding of the final agony . . .

Everything was waiting; the trees did not stir. The oldest ones, aloof and armed with pride, stood tall, not believing that an attack was possible. After all, they had stood here for so many years—for countless centuries! They had seen many things die, and many things grow; they had lived through more than one spring, more than one winter; they had seen the sunrise so often—the beautiful sun that shone with gold, whose flaming red light had bathed them in the morning and blessed them in the evening; they had withstood more than one whirlwind.

And were they now to die differently than their ancestors who had been struck by lightning, or, in their old age, had lain down of their own accord?

It was ridiculous!

But they did not want to stir; they did not want to betray their incredulity with even the slightest murmuring. It was only the young . . . If only the young were not swayed so easily!

The attack began.

The mercenaries began it with a ferocious cry of: "Hurrah!"

They scrambled up the first mountain with catlike agility; every mercenary wanted to outdo the others, as if being the first to wield an axe against the primeval forest would be the crowning heroic act of his life.

But it was not to be that easy!

They met with resistance.

The deceptive, brownish-green moss gave way under their rapacious hands, and they slid downwards. With the flinty soil crumbling under their feet, they clutched desperately at anything that might break their fall, lacerating and mutilating their hands. From the damp moss, torn up by its roots, loathsome insects crawled out and, trying to avoid the light, skittered up their arms!

In their fervour to do battle, the mercenaries rushed up to a decayed log lying on the ground and tried to roll it into the abyss. They managed only to rock it slightly—and startled snakes slid out from under it, hissed at them, and bit those wearing light footwear.

Thorny wild rose bushes—their long, spindly branches cunningly interwoven with other shrubs and the inextricable ivy, bindweed, and bramble bushes—stood like unassailable walls. Lushly beautiful bright-green ferns fanned out luxuriantly in all directions, and poisonous mushrooms of a reddish hue poked through the underbrush, calling attention to themselves.

The young fir trees huddled together so closely and extended their branches so defensively, that it was almost impossible to make any headway. They clawed the mercenaries' faces, tore at their hair, and grabbed angrily at their clothing.

Ungainly humped-back spiders had spun their webs from one tree to another, and these cobwebs settled on the mercenaries' eyes, clinging to them like repulsive veils. And anthills, covered with dry rusty pine needles, rose up from the ground like barren, grassless hillocks—and the human foot slipped on them like on cupping-glasses.

But the mercenaries continued to force their way forward.

Deep in the forest, where the ground stretched out in an even plain, something shiny flashed at them from the dark-green backdrop. It was surrounded by widely-spreading pines—from which long, snakelike, pale grey moss hung almost to the ground—swamp plants with their lush, circular leaves, and broad-bladed bulrushes.

It was a small, jewel-like mountain pond.

Protected by an overwhelming profusion of greenery, it lay here drowsily, without stirring, with a smooth, serene surface, fathomless, like an eternal mirror of the firmament and the treetops—a spot of pristine beauty.

Lying obliquely across it and half submerged in the water, was a fallen pine. Overgrown in places with moss, it served as a footbridge for light-footed forest animals, and as a place where lizards and dragonflies basked in the sun.

In joyful revelry, these dragonflies circled indefatigably over the water at lightning speed, occasionally skimming its glittering surface wantonly with their transparent blue wings.

***

"Hurrah!"
The forest shuddered.
"Here's where we'll attack the forest!"
An echo resounded: "Attack the fo-o-o-orest!"
"This is where we'll strike!"
A piercing cry of terror reverberated: "We'll stri-i-i-ike!"
Broadaxes flashed in the half-light, and the sound of the blows echoed in unison through the forest.

Not too far away, small birds fearfully fluttered their wings and, for the first time, the still surface of the mountain pond reflected phenomena other than the treetops and the firmament.

***

At first—the younger trees, the ones showing most promise were measured.

Those that were equally sturdy and slender, and of the same height, were chopped down and stripped of their green attire. After they were sawed off at both ends, they were used to build a road in the narrow valley between the mountains, parallel to the stream. There, where railroad tracks could not be run any farther, they were pressed into service.

The tree trunks were placed tightly against one another. In this way, a road was constructed for the corpses that were to follow; Winding for a long distance, in twists and turns between the two mountain ranges, it was a sad and depressing sight, for it was over this road that the ancient giants were to be hauled.

After the young trees were placed in a row on the ground, their heads and feet were bludgeoned by an axe to make them fit tightly and evenly, and serve as a bridge. Their blood flowed . . .

The stream running alongside them worked its way under them, laved them gently, and bore away their blood. In those places where the sun's rays played with the stream's pearly waters, the blood settled on the stones in the stream and stained them forever with a dark reddish hue.

***

A lot of time went by before the mercenaries finished what they were hired to do. They never went down into the lowlands, and they almost never encountered women. Their unkempt beards, shaggy hair, and grimy clothing, soiled with wagon-grease, gave them a fierce, wild, savage-like appearance.

Every week they received their provisions and other necessities of life by rail, and they were protected from the wind and the cold by huts they had woven from branches hacked off the trees—and there was an abundance of these branches.

The bark, stripped off the trees and drying in the sun like huge brown rolls of paper, was soaked through with resin; it was lit every evening on both the left and the right sides of the peaks, and the fires blazed with greedy red tongues—flaming symbols of a servant's life.

This is how they prepared themselves for their battle with the oldest trees.

Finally, the turn came for these trees as well.

On the night before this event—a night intoxicated with light—the moon expanded into a huge, dull-red sphere.

In the silence that merged with the darkness, the mountains, with their dark, endless forests, seemed like a haven for a stoical peace. Moonlight pierced the delicately blue night mists, illuminated the distance, and graced the tips of the trees on the highest mountain tops. The trees were transformed in its glow and appeared to dissolve in it.

A few of them lifted their elegantly attired shoulders up to the heavens, as if pleading for something.

Only a few of them?

As many of them as there were here—and there were so many that no one could have counted them—they all stretched upwards and pleaded for life! The air was heavy with that pleading! It was redolent with a thirst for "still more life"—the breath of thousands and thousands of beings, eager for life.

The fragrance emanating from the depths of the forest was reminiscent of an intoxicating pleasure, of the most exquisite ripeness of maturity, and it bore away with itself those who had thus far been standing in unmoving, hidden expectation, preserving, like a shameful secret, the desire to live in full measure.

Ferns whispered with a prophetic rustle; the chalices of the most immaculate flowers unfolded. The fear that tomorrow they might cease to live awoke in them a desire to display themselves to others one last time, at the peak of their beauty. Tomorrow, perhaps, they would be trampled, their crowns broken, their leaves torn off. Tomorrow, perhaps, no one would know that they had ever existed . . . and that they had been—beautiful!

The forest realm was enlivened by glowworms twinkling on its dark-green canopy like droplets of light, and countless crickets, calling out to and answering one another, did not have the slightest desire to fall silent.

The prevailing mood was one of utter abandonment, and pent-up feelings, muted only by the deep tranquillity of the night, thoughtlessly broke loose from all restraints. The laughter of a joyous, healthy life, blended with heavy tears of grief, was forcibly rending the air, and a gentle longing, like a velvet cloak, enveloped everything, evoking ever intensifying desires and a passion for life.

Truly wondrous were the sounds of the forest in the stillness of this night! More delicate than music, they were, rather, a whispering that merged with the soft darkness of the night. And, amidst this whispering, droplets of rain, that had fallen during the day, rolled down gently from one leaf to another.

***

A long, difficult time—and the centuried ones perished.

They were lying—stretched out, slaughtered—amidst their own greenery.

The remaining stumps and the coiling surface roots protruded, mutilated, from the moss.

The aged ones were still lying on the mountains, but they were not alone. The mountains were strewn with corpses, to the right and to the left. They were lying obliquely, crossways, and in straight lines. Packed closely together, one head next to another, they were lying in groups, or on top of one another, or—just as they had fallen.

From a distance, their appearance created the impression of a mown forest!

The mountains, stripped to near nakedness of their clothing — whose fresh beauty, both in winter and summer, had remained unchanged for countless ages—were now shamefacedly jutting up to the heavens, vainly trying to cover their misshapen limbs with the remnants of their former sartorial splendour.

The betrayed eagles and the orphaned hawks were sadly flying hither and yon. The eagles, ruffling their feathers, rested now and again after a short flight and waited in ambush as they turned their hostile, gleaming dark eyes to the valley; it was then that the hawks orbited in slow, silent circles over the deceased.

As the fallen ones were being pulled down from their heights, a battle of life and death was waged.

Many mercenaries lost their lives; many were maimed and rendered incapable of ever working again; and still others, badly injured, were bedridden for days on end in the valleys.

All in the name of toppling giants!

Giants that had stood in the same place for hundreds of years, whose roots had buried themselves in the innermost depths of the mountain, where they had become interwoven for all eternity with the roots of other plants.

These were the trees they had to bring down—without harming themselves, without destroying the young sprouts, without destroying everything . . .

Like tireless ants, the mercenaries, armed with chains and other tools, forced their way into the most inaccessible thickets.

First, they hewed the bark off the trees.

This task was a difficult one. The bark was firmly imbedded in the body of the tree and had grown so hard that broadaxes rebounded from it; it was only after prolonged chopping that it flew off in splinters and fell on the vast numbers of springy green branches which, after being separated from the tree's body, had been left to dry.

Then, strong hands, disdaining all danger and obstacles, began rolling the ponderous giants. The mercenaries carrying out this work uttered muted, strangled cries intended to buoy up their courage, cries more like the calls of wild birds than sounds issuing from a human throat.

Sweat poured down their foreheads, and blood flowed from their gashed hands. The isolation in which they lived and their consequent descent into savagery filled them with a frenzied disregard for danger. They were obsessed with completing their task, and the hope of a high reward ignited their avaricious eyes with the gleam of victory.

Not far from the foot of the ravaged mountains, bridges were hastily being built out of thick logs. Rolled down from the heights, the giants came to a stop on these bridges. From there, they were once again trundled by the mercenaries and, one after the other, fell with a dull thud to the level ground.

They did not lie there for long. Huge iron hooks were driven into the giants' heads, and horses, harnessed to the hooks, dragged them off at a laborious pace. Their heads lowered, they hauled them down the road paved with the young trees.

After such victories, blood-red fires flamed until midnight on the mountains, and the hero-woodcutters, settling in comfortably around them, smoked their pipes and discussed the obdurate strength of the conquered ones.

***

A special train awaited the fallen ones in the valley.

It consisted of several dozen cars coupled together and a locomotive that snorted impatiently.

From four to six tree trunks were loaded on every car and bound together with chains as thick as an arm. They were chained so tightly, that the iron, eating into their naked bodies, made their blood ooze. This blood was scraped off, rolled into balls, and ignited to provide light in the misty fall evenings as the trees were being transported.

With its cargo of chained tree trunks, the train, racing to the lowlands, rent the air from time to time with a shrill whistle of victory.

The foreman sat on the last car.

Striking his axe into the chest of one of the giants lying on top of the load, he sat with a dull look on his face, his arms folded on his chest.

He had travelled down this road so many times already! His gaze had rested so often on the mountaintops, following the twists and turns in the railroad tracks, that by now these trips had become routine and boring.

The ones he was to watch over did not stir. They silently greeted the district through which they were travelling, and then bade it farewell.

Mountains, still covered with forests, rose on both sides, to their right and their left. These forests sheltered their comrades; they had been their comrades for countless years, but now they were parting from them forever. They would never again hear their murmuring . . .

Later, they tried to guess where they were being taken. They knew they had come down into the lowlands, into the wide valleys from which the mountains were gradually receding, and where the former stream was now racing along as a swiftly flowing river. The train was flying at a furious speed, recklessly snaking its way through narrow passages.

Were they travelling to be among people?

They recalled the tranquil time when they had stood tall and proud, and only the clouds and the eagles had touched their green crowns. Now those crowns were being trampled by human feet. They recalled how they had been attacked one by one, and how they had fallen, one after the other.

So, were they being transported now to those who had *bought* the right to rule over their fate? Or were they being taken once again to the mercenaries who acknowledged neither a holy day nor a Sunday, and did not have the slightest appreciation of beauty? But—no; in addition to the former and the latter, there had to be some other kind of people—perhaps some that were similar to themselves!

Yes, some that were similar to themselves!

***

As they entered the wide valley after their exhausting trip through the virgin forests, they caught their first glimpse of small cottages. At first, these huts appeared sporadically high up in the mountains, and then on the lower slopes, and finally—right alongside the village road that converged with the railroad tracks and did not part from them again. The wooden cottages were small; some were faced with stones, others with shingles.

A tavern came into view along the road, and the engineer brought the train to a stop.

He was supposed to pick up some foreigners and workers waiting for him there.

It was here that the inhabitants of the cottages made their first appearance.

They called themselves Hutsuls.

Tall and strong, with Slavic features, and dressed in picturesque clothing, they were casually sitting and lying about. One of them was a young woman, with a slightly weathered but attractive, almost childlike, face. Dressed in the traditional rich and colourful clothing of her people, she was smoking a pipe and looking languidly straight ahead, not caring one wit that foreigners—a whole group of them—were devouring her with their eyes.

Her companions, very handsome men, slender and supple like fir trees, were sitting around in the building in the most comfortable positions imaginable. And their attire was equally flamboyant—red trousers, white embroidered shirts, and richly embroidered sleeveless jackets. Wide, colourful belts, decorated with iron rings and various shiny baubles, and small black hats, adorned with peacock feathers, completed their outfits.

It was a holiday—so they had gathered here to feast and drink. Two of them were playing a *kolomyika [a fast dance]* on their violins. Another one, stretched out full length on a bench, gazed dreamily into the distance through an open window. He was impervious to the curious looks of the strangers. In fact, all of them seemed oblivious to the stares of strangers, finding their curiosity completely inoffensive—as if they were children.

They themselves did not show the slightest interest, either in the foreign travellers who appeared no more than once a year in their district, or in any other strangers. While the arrival of a train always excited the interest of the inhabitants in neighbouring regions, the Hutsuls scarcely turned their heads in its direction. To them, it was a foreign phenomenon, far removed from their lives. They had nothing in common with it—as if they were from another world—and they had as little contact with it as they had with the clouds in the heavens.

In many ways, they resembled the giants bound in iron chains that were now being transported into the lowlands. Distinctive in their beauty and their customs, they had grown up just as untouched as those Amazons, and just as harmoniously. They lived out their lives in the lofty uplands, on isolated homesteads, without masters and without servants. Their ignorance elicited both amazement and pity; unimpressed by the grandeur of civilization, they greeted its accomplishments with an ingenuous smile.

This is what these children of the forest were like—the ones who resisted the lure of financial gain and would have nothing to do with the toppling of the giants from their heights!

"What kind of heathens are you?" they incredulously asked those who had come to tally the spoils from the battle.

And as they spoke, they frowned threateningly and tightened their grasp on their broadaxes.

They understood weapons.

When they had first seen the train, they had crossed themselves and spit to one side. The evil spirit had to be in it, and they did not want to have anything to do with the people who controlled the whole enterprise. They kept their distance from it and, among the numerous mercenaries who took part in the battle, there was not a single Hutsul to be found.

"Chop down if you will what God has created, but leave us in peace!" one of them replied with abhorrence when he was called to assist with felling the trees.

And they were left in peace.

Their world was the forest and the mountains, and it was only here that they came fully into their own. Like exquisite scarlet flowers they flashed among the greenery of the trees in their beautiful picturesque garments, or flew by on swift, thick-maned horses, whose breeding and care was one of their most beloved occupations.

Their mournful songs echoed through the forests.

These were the people who resembled those giants most closely!

When the train started up again and began to pull away ever more quickly, those who were in the last car could see, through the open windows and the door of the tavern, the women and men dancing in a wide circle with wild abandon. It was an unforgettable scene, fleeting, like a flash of lightning, and just as fiery!

It was the simple melody of the two violins that had whipped them into a state of frenzy. They danced with an unrestrained, boisterous fervour. Their clothing and their kerchiefs flew through the air as they circled, and they cried out from time to time with an impassioned, almost savage ecstasy. It was as if happiness would forsake them after this dance, and they wanted to gorge themselves on it—make it last for the rest of their lives . . .

Others, puffing on short pipes, stood around in small groups in front of the building or stretched out on the ground beside their saddled horses. It seemed as if the building, with its splendid colours and pulsating profusion of life, was flying past the train!

One attractive woman, a widow, galloped wildly up to the others on a young, highly spirited horse. A group of young men sped after her at an equally frenzied pace. Taunting them, she sped away. Giving her horse free rein and glancing back over her shoulder, she laughed loudly, uproariously.

As yet, these people did not dread the monster that, hissing malevolently as it arrived and departed, brought with it enlightenment—but, at the same time, untold woe!

As yet, they did not have any foreboding of the deep, enervating grief, masked by a sickly smile, elicited by education and the strictures of civilisation.

They lived from day to day, unconcerned about the future and its futility; their wishes were simple and unambiguous, and the sole conditions for their happiness—the blue sky and the brilliance of the sun.

***

The lowlands were a hive of activity.

A huge steam sawmill buzzed incessantly.

Brick-red chimneys of wondrous dimensions rose up from the earth and belched black clouds of smoke into the horizon, while the factory was such a hubbub of whistling and droning that all other sounds were completely muffled.

The factory was surrounded by stockpiles of thousands of boards, both narrow and wide, piled crosswise in high stacks, ready for transport. Countless numbers of unplaned tree trunks awaited their death. Dignified old giants, almost several metres in circumference—veritable wonders of antiquity and beauty—lay alongside slender young fir trees.

Fresh trunks, rolling into the factory almost without interruption, were planed a short time later into thin boards and then unceremoniously shoved outside again. The train kept hauling in new sacrificial offerings, and the never-tiring *Molokh [a legendary god demanding sacrifices]* transformed them in a miraculously short time.

And it was the same this time.

The locomotive was uncoupled from the freight cars, which then rolled, together with their victims, a short distance ahead to the warehouse. Here the trunks were freed from their iron chains and unloaded.

As they were rolled past the entrance to the factory, they heard the master of the sawmill speaking with some visitors: "The primeval forests have been purchased by the firm O-ba from the 'Religious Fund.' We've been sawing for seven years already and we still have three years of work ahead of us. We plane seven hundred trunks every day."

Seven hundred trunks a day!

How heartlessly precise this sounded.

Seven hundred of their comrades every day. And each one of them had required dozens of years—no, hundreds of years!—to grow to this glorious circumference!

And mountains of trunks were still lying here, and thousands upon thousands more were lying back there, at home, on the very peaks, from where they would be rolled down at the end of the logging operation. And masses of them were lying at the foot of the mountains, held back by the bridges, and the railroad was bringing sacrificial victims here three times a day. That is why they had to be destroyed in a hurry, why every hour of the day was treasured.

The new arrivals were branded with red-hot iron and then set aside, so that they could have a look around.

They saw that here, in the lowlands, worked the same kind of mercenaries as those who had become half-savage in the mountains. They bustled about in swarms, like indefatigable ants, both inside the factory and outside of it. They cared for the iron *Molokh* and almost sacrificed themselves in their attempt to satisfy him, for he was wonderfully adept at destroying the trunks.

"Yes, yes," they overheard, among other things, one worker—called Kleveta the Muckraker by the authorities—say: "This is the way the foreign antichrists are destroying our wonderful forests, the wealth of our nation. God knows the lords do not protect them adequately, and they will have to answer before Him some day.

"Now this beautiful building material is to be shipped away, perhaps across the sea! And what does our country receive for this? Ask those who manage these fortunes, who live in luxury, indulging their sinful bodies—ask them what our country receives in return!"

And after a moment of fierce silence he continued: "They've begun building a railroad in the opposite direction; I hear that the forests have been sold for another ten years! Yes, this is 'just ten years,' but then—*once again*, for ten more years, and the wealth of our country will be lost! Damn this kind of justice! Why don't I destroy its ugly body instead of this innocent tree? Why don't all these infernal furnaces here, under our feet, swallow their satanic bodies instead?"

His words were cut short by a loud slap on the face by the foreman. "Why don't you watch what your monkey paws are doing instead of flapping a lot of slanderous nonsense, you good-for-nothing mudslinger?"

The reply of the punished man was lost in the deafening din, for freshly arrived trunks were being lowered. Some went under a saw with ten blades, others under a fifteen-blade saw, while still others—those that were hundreds of years old—went under twenty blades.

With an ear-splitting buzz, the trunks were stunned before they were killed, and then the saws tore into their flesh. With their sharp, pointed teeth, they cut through the most magnificent trunks with lightning swiftness. The sawdust burst out of the trees like blood, fell in showers over them, and collected in mounds on the wooden floor.

After the knives had flashed through them for the last time, a loud, harsh hiss spread through the factory, and the proud giants fell apart, fanned out in thin white boards, and ceased to exist.

Workers, pushing huge wheelbarrows, raced back and forth.

They swept up the sawdust lying on the ground, hauled it away, and threw it into the jaws of a furnace in a squat outbuilding. They did this work day after day, without a break. Others pulled away the boards that were falling out from under the saws and threw them so heavily on a pile that, in falling, they sprang up for the last time, like resilient metal sheets.

Still other workers pushed slender fir trees under the buzzing saws that sliced them into narrow laths, while others hammered and sharpened saws, scattering glittering, red-hot sparks.

And all around the factory, many people were rushing about. Some carried boards outside, others took them and passed them farther along. Still others were piling them in stacks, marking them, dividing them into narrow and wide ones, and doing whatever else had to be done.

There was endless movement, noise, shouts, comings and goings—feverish activity calculated with a mathematical precision and controlled by the terrible buzzing of a huge circular saw radiating an almost intolerable heat.

It seemed that the huge black wheels, wound with leather belts, were turning noiselessly; however, the air was filled with their clatter, and the entire region was animated by a demonic energy, right up to the forest . . .

It was only at night that a deathly silence prevailed. The black chimney stood like a sentry and gazed sternly at the entire encampment.

Countless naked trunks, illuminated by the gentle light of the moon, lay like corpses. Tiers of boards, piled to majestic heights, shimmered with a silvery glow and, viewed from the side, looked like finely drawn lines.

Wherever one looked, there were tree trunks lying on the ground—and more tree trunks, and wood, and boards, and waste material; and, among all this, huge dogs, casting large, grotesque shadows, silently made their rounds. From the time that the factory had gone up in flames after being set on fire by an arsonist, the dogs had been set to act as guards.

But no one crept onto the premises; no one disturbed the tranquillity of the fallen ones.

Here, the muffled murmuring of the mountain stream, glistening in the darkness of the forest, echoed gently but insistently, while the forest created an impenetrable wall around the valley, from beyond which only the moon could rise.

And every night it did rise over that wall.

White, silent, and still, as if completely depleted by sorrow, it seemed to find relief only when it diffused its rays in the bluish transparent mists of the night or bathed them in the dark depths of the water . . .

The sad murmuring of the river evoked a sorrowful mood in the moon—a mood that it could not repress .

"Where to? Where to? Where to?" the waves murmured tirelessly every night, and they sorrowfully washed the banks and splashed ingratiatingly and gently against the great rocks that peered out immovably from out of the water.

But they did not receive a reply.

Everything in the camp remained silent.

The tree trunks lay without souls, and the boards were laid out like corpses . . .

But the moon could see the reply. Wherever it turned its benign face—it could read it.

On the boards and tree trunks destined to be transported, black letters spelled out the words: "To Batum." "To Batum." "To Batum."

***

Summer.

The inflamed rays of the sun were searing, and the air was oppressively hot.

Solitary dark clouds dispersed and vanished in the azure firmament. A gentle breeze stirred occasionally, widening and elongating the clouds, creating menacing shadows. It appeared to be urging them to fly away from here, and it seemed that the power of the sun might destroy them; however, exactly at noon, they stopped short in their flight and hung pendulously in greyish black masses over the mountains.

The battle was over.

A heartless silence descended.

As far as the eye could see there stretched an unimaginable devastation, and the repugnant barrenness of the mountain tops evoked profound feelings of grief.

White, decaying stumps, pressing closely together, stood like skeletons in the yellowed grass. Trees that were of no value lay crippled in large numbers everywhere, and denuded tree trunks that had been deemed unfit, were rotting, untouched.

Large, razed, burned-out areas silently bore witness to the wounds caused by huge conflagrations and attested to the victory of the flames that had gleamed so often in the night, greedily gobbling up everything around them. Piles of spruce bark lay half-rotted in dark brown rolls and fragments, and masses of splinters smothered the grass.

Old fir trees, survivors of thunderbolts, had remained untouched, and they stood dolefully, like enfeebled patriarchs, stretching out their half-withered arms and striving in vain to hold back the wind with their branches.

From time to time a poignant, grievous creaking drifted through the air. It originated with the solitary, healthy young fir trees that had been left and which, youthfully slender and exceptionally tall, stood branchless, topped with green crowns that bowed to the ground, as if pulled down by a hundredweight suspended from their tips. Abandoned to the whims of the wind and bereft of all protection and defence, they creaked, swaying mournfully . . .

Young spruce trees, once a shiny, vibrant green, were broken and scarred forever. Ferns dropped their torn serrated leaves and, deprived of life-giving shade, wilted, withering slowly and painfully in the blazing sun.

Tall moss, yanked out, shredded, and exposed by its roots to the sun, dried up, and the trampled grass died the same kind of agonising death. Many of the forest bushes—raspberries, junipers, and other strong, resilient plants—and flowers that once had grown luxuriantly in great profusion, had been partially uprooted and were now pressed deep into the ground. Thousands upon thousands of giants had been rolled and dragged over them!

The occasional elderberry bush—crushed, but not completely bereft of its strength—gave birth to countless red berries which glowed garishly against the dull green canopy, like gory puddles of blood . . .

The once wild stream flowed hesitantly among the rocks in the valley. Masses of shorn branches, bark, and splinters had dulled its merry gurgling for a long time to come. Eagles and hawks abandoned their nests and swooped overhead only rarely. It was only once or twice in the spring that they flew over what was once their proud fatherland.

And the cuckoo stopped singing here. Waiting in vain for an echo to its call—an echo which once had sped through the dignified, silent forests, as if it were racing against the call itself— the cuckoo now remained stubbornly silent, as if it had forgotten how to sing its distinctive song.

The mountains—devastated, abandoned, plundered of all their native beauty and former wealth—were a mockery of their former selves; they could not prevent the searing rays of the sun from mercilessly scorching the remaining undergrowth that required the very deepest shadows for its survival.

Young fir trees and pines—seedlings that barely reached above the ground and had not been accidentally mutilated—stood forlorn and forsaken. Fierce storms and the blazing sun alternated over tender young crowns that, for a long time yet, would not be ready to withstand the merciless blows of the inconstant weather.

The centuried trees had protected them from the elements with their broad shoulders—but now? And even if they did manage to withstand it all—the heat of the sun that so greedily drank their youthful sap, the storms that strove to tear off their crowns, the chilling frosts, and all the other destructive forces of nature—what then?

Would the same murderous hand not stretch out after them just when they stood in their most proud beauty?

They chose to die . . .

Roses
(1896)

They were in a finely cut, transparent glass filled to the brim with fresh water.

A dark-red one, encircled by listlessly drooping leaves, flamed with a deep purple hue. Blooming luxuriously, she was intoxicated with her own beauty; alluring in her loveliness, she waited uneasily.

Immediately beside her, under the protection of tiny, hardy, dark green sepals, nestled *a pale pink rose* that was only half open.

Just a few short moments ago, she had been a tender bud, but now, as if roused by the animating breath of a morning breeze, had begun to unfold, preening as if her exquisite beauty was of her own making—even though she was not yet in full bloom.

She was saturated with poetic feeling—a rose smiled at by the southern sun and its multicoloured butterflies . . .

Her outer petals were brimming with a dark rose hue, but the centre ones were only slightly tinged with a wisp of pink. Delicate and fragrant, and indescribably pure, she leaned against the dark-red rose and, nestling up to her, innocently demanded to be taken into her embrace.

Next to them stood *a white rose.*

Encircled by her fresh green calyx, she was drowning in herself, yet felt that she was living. Scarcely aware of her colourful surroundings, she radiated innocence and purity, and had such a wondrous fragrance that the green sepals held their breath and ecstatically imbibed her sweetness.

By this rose and the French ones, a single, opaquely yellowish bud concealed itself.

Did buds look like *that*?

. . . That rose was leaning over the edge of the glass.

And her large shiny leaves bent tenderly towards her, pressing in as closely as possible. But the rose, deeply troubled and depressed by an unappeased grief, did not so much as glance at them. She looked down, her head lowered, as if fearing a sudden illuminating flash or a ray of the sun determined to glance into her closed heart—something she could not endure.

Her large leaves had curled at the tips, darkened slightly, and withered before their time . . .

Beside her, there were two thick-necked wild roses with bright green leaves.

The table on which the glass stood was made of white marble.

The base was a burnished gold.

There was also a lit, shaded lamp.

The air was sultry.

Were they dreaming?

Hardly. They appeared to be waiting for something new, something wonderful . . .

. . . Across from the table, a tall, narrow gothic window is opened wide and, beyond it, giant trees drown in the darkness, while above them stretch the heavens, covered by threatening clouds that partially conceal the moon.

Among the trees there is a soft rustling.

At first tender and gentle, and then, growing stronger, it becomes a secret, passionate whispering—and finally, a fresh, lively breeze flits in through the window.

Flying directly to the spot where the roses are standing, it touches them boldly, as if kissing them, and causes the robust flame of the lamp to flare and tremble . . .

Then silence descends once again.

The petals of the dark red rose fall almost audibly on the white surface of the marble.

First one petal, then three, four, and then a few more, and finally, almost all of them.

. . . Out of their falling, the prevailing silence, absorbing everything, composes a fairy tale about the fate of roses . . .

What I Loved
(1896)

These were the small, slim hands of a woman.

There was something more of the aristocrat in them than of the intelligentsia, and it was this that first caught my attention.

The slender fingertips and the delicately convex fingernails were proof to me that their ancestors were not tradespeople and had not engaged in heavy work. Their beauty was not accidental. When in motion, they reminded me of tiny birds—but why, I do not know.

They peered so assuredly, so elegantly from under white silk lace, and assumed such an air of importance! The very thought that *they* too might want to do something made one smile, for they never did anything.

Work is not at all suited to gentility. It belongs to the masses, and her hands were not typical of the masses.

I would have clad them—those small, tender, sprightly little birds—in the finest gloves, so that they would not come into contact too often with coarse realia, thus losing the quality of purity that I, a son of the Muses, especially adored.

And in my most serene moments, I dreamt of caring for them. But not as ordinary creations of that ilk are cared for; I dreamt about something better. I wanted to care for them as I care for the precious gems on some of my favourite rings which—after they have glittered opulently, and I have delighted in their pristine beauty to my heart's content—have to return to the expensive *étui [jewellery box]* lined with silk and velvet to await the moment when my hand will once again reach for them.

I dreamt about this in my most tranquil moments, and also when my heart wove such rash plans for the future that I almost became alarmed myself, and my mind chided my foolhardy boldness!

Was I not ashamed?

Truly, both alarmed and ashamed, I behaved in a cool and aloof manner, as if I were not the least concerned about any tiny birds.

But in my soul, and when I was alone, I always kept a watchful eye on them, taking care that nothing touched them, that they did not strain themselves or strike any hard, solid objects, that they would not be irritated by the fierce cold of winter, and that the arrogant, radiant rays of the spring sun—those seductively alluring rays—would not shine on them for too long or become overly friendly with them.

But one day brought forth an evil hour.

Those small feminine hands fell to dreaming in the bright rays of the spring sun, became ill and, mustering all their strength, inherited perhaps from their noble ancestors, formed a fist and struck me in the chest so powerfully that I toppled backwards.

And now I cannot summon my former strength and my former daring in order to approach them once more, take them in my hands, and press them sincerely—those tiny, animated birds that do not bear the characteristics of the masses. Those treasures!

The Free-Spirited Woman
A Novella
(1896)

The cottage of the free-spirited woman nestled at the foot of the woman-mountain "Mahgurah."

Densely overgrown with fir trees from foot to tip, Mahgurah's forbidding impenetrable greenery and the steepness of her walls shielded her from summer visitors. Standing alone, day in and day out, she listened to the harmonious murmuring of her own fir trees, or, gazing out at the peaks of neighbouring mountains, contemplated her nearest neighbour . . .

This neighbour was "Rhungh," the man-mountain. He was separated from her by a narrow valley that harboured a stream.

Rhungh was a splendid giant, tall and stalwart. His north side, overgrown with a young forest, sloped gently upwards. His west side, however, the side that stood close to Mahgurah, equalled her in steepness and was similarly adorned with thick stands of ancient fir trees.

It seemed that Rhungh and Mahgurah were separated forever. In the valley dividing them lay vast numbers of sharp-edged rocks, and the stream, avidly growing bigger after every heavy downpour, delighted in the sheer green walls of Rhungh and Mahgurah, splashing them with pearls of cold water, as if reminding them that it was still there, that it existed and would continue to exist, dividing them forever.

On summer days, when the midday sun was flaming hot, and the sky dissolved into a delicate blueness, one or two hawks lifted up from the depths of Rhungh's forests and, after floating over his tip in dreamy flight, sank in Mahgurah's lush, dark-green woodlands.

Pausing here and there on the thickly knit branches of Mahgurah's fir trees, they called out, in voices that echoed into the distance, that they were from Rhungh; and Mahgurah, catching the sounds, absorbed them and then gave voice to them as a far-reaching murmur.

At sunset, the side of Mahgurah that faced the sun was flooded with golden light. The fir trees in which she was attired bathed in the sun's rays and, basking in their splendour, she smiled at Rhungh.

Rhungh also glittered, but from the cold. The side that he turned to Mahgurah was a steep and almost gloomy slope, proudly clad in fir trees from the ground to his peak. Clear, cold droplets of dew glistened on the branches of the trees, and a fine silvery net of dewdrops covered the ground.

The stream running between them pressed closely to Mahgurah to warm itself. And then, excited by the heat, it turned to Rhungh's frigid wall to cool its ardour . . . but only so that it could once again wind its way around Mahgurah.

Did the broad beams of the morning light not reach Rhungh? Was it only Mahgurah's shadow that was cast upon him? An occasional ray of sunlight did reach Rhungh as well and, sinking in colourful, slanted, transparently colourful beams among the trees, they warmed his cold, dark green depths.

Where their sides looked to the south, both mountains, sloping gently and almost merging, bathed in the sun. Here, among the rocks, grew the tall, splendid arnica, its face, like that of the sunflower, turned forever to the sun. And slender pale violet harebells and pink thistles flowered in lush profusion.

The water tried to cool down the air. But the air, sultry and intoxicatingly heavy with the resinous aroma of the trees, heated it instead. And the water, weakened to the point of softness and transformed into shimmering gold, spilled sensuously, almost silently, over the stones.

A dense, primeval forest spread itself broadly here, and Rhungh and Mahgurah, mutually enraptured by their beauty, dipped and sank into its dark depths.

The penetrating, reverberating clangour of gypsies crushing rocks in the valley sped furiously after the receding mountains, but the dignified murmuring of the ancient forest repelled it.

It was there that the paradise of the two mountains lay . . .

***

And it was here that Paraska, an older *Hutsul woman [a highlander living in the eastern Carpathian mountains]* came to steal wood.

She knew every hiding place and could have squirrelled herself away if anyone were following her, but no one was on her trail, so she serenely cracked and gathered dry branches, confident of her booty and in no hurry to get home. After stacking her brushwood into piles, she would sit down to rest on any available rock, fill her pipe, and smoke. She could sit like that for an hour or more and, sinking into a reverie, often lost track of time.

She did not know what it meant to feel lonely. It was true that it was quiet in the mountains, but the silence was not like the silence in her cottage; here, it seemed to be alive. In front of her—no, almost at her feet, a stream trickled; high up in a fir tree above her head, a squirrel dashed about like a flash of lightning; in the forest, the abrupt cry of a hawk occasionally pierced the silence; and the air was full of swirling flies, butterflies, and God knows what kind of insects.

The lush greenness of the mountain walls attracted her eyes and absorbed her loneliness. Once in a while, catching sight of a silky black and gold snake among the small white pebbles, she would stare at it intently, and then spit in disgust. Such a tiny thing, but so ugly! Worse than a ravenous wolf . . .

Here, between Rhungh and Mahgurah, she felt at home. There was even someone to talk to. It was here, between the two mountain walls, that a family of gypsies crushed rocks. Their arms dark and sinewy, they worked from the cool dawn until the setting of the sun, breaking apart the jagged boulders. An old gypsy, a gypsy woman, and a youth.

They lived as comfortably here as if they were in their own home. Not far from them burned a fire. On sunny days, the colourful flames, greedily rising upwards, blended with the splendour of the sun's rays, and only greyish smoke attested to the presence of a fire. It was here they cooked their food.

Whenever she entered the forest or came out of it with her load of brushwood, she had to pass by their camp. Seating herself near them, she would light up her pipe and share her tobacco with them; after that the conversation flowed easily. They knew the most intimate details of her life, and she knew theirs. Every summer they came here to crush rocks, supporting themselves almost entirely with this work, while she made her trips all year round between Rhungh and Mahgurah.

"So, you're off to the forest again, Paraska?" the dark gypsy calls out to her, flashing his eyes at her from under his hat. "What are you looking for?"

She laughs.

"Gold!" she says.

"Just gold? Not a golden man?"

"Oh, a golden man, a golden man! I've forgotten all that, old fellow," and she laughs still harder.

"Uh-oh, watch out," he says. "Our Hutsul woman is going to go mad."

And, spitting, as if cursing a woman's nature—because there is as much peace of mind with a woman as with a devil—he pretends to flee.

"Hey you, shut up!" his wife calls out.

With her dishevelled hair, fiery eyes, and a shirt unbuttoned down the front, she looks fierce, like a sorceress.

"The poor thing will soon be all stooped over from the gold she hauls almost daily on her back, just to have some firewood," she adds.

"Then let her find herself a golden man, and he'll do the hauling for her! Wouldn't that be better, Paraska?"

"May he break his legs before he finds his way to my cottage," Paraska pretends to lay a curse and, coming up closer, settles in beside the gypsy family.

"Oh, sure! But just yesterday you said that if a man came along, you'd take him into your home right away. Isn't that so?"

"So, it's so! That's what I said—and I didn't lie!" she retorts abruptly.

"And what is he supposed to be like? Maybe like me?" the gypsy jokes merrily.

"Phooey! You ugly old gypsy!" And she spits.

The gypsies roar with laughter.

"Well then, like who, my dear little Paraska?"

"Leave me alone—am I a soothsayer? Let him be whatever he's like—it's not up to me to decide . . . Oh, just shut up!"

Smoking her pipe, she leans coquettishly against her pile of brushwood, puffs away, and waits for more quips from the gypsies.

She was a widow, in her forties. Dark-complexioned and still quite attractive, she was slender, almost delicately built, lively and agile. She seemed much younger than her age and, looking at her tiny hands, no one would guess that she was as strong as a man.

She liked to talk at great length about her physical prowess.

"Now, my strength is beginning to fade," she would say, "but when I was younger . . .! At one time I'd pick up a *korets' [100 kilograms]* of corncobs and heave it on a horse so hard that his back would sag. Or I'd gather brushwood in the forest, pile it up so that only my feet could be seen from under it, and then I'd run, not walk, home. Once there, I'd slam it to the ground with such a whack that the house rang out; and I'd have enough to burn for four weeks! People were amazed, but I just laughed. Can you believe it? Or the stacks that I could pile . . . hey, hey!"

She relishes what she is saying. Her unusually lively, intelligent eyes blaze with an inner fire, and her whole face takes on a youthful appearance.

"But I'm growing weaker now; it's all over for me."

She does not say this sadly. She does not say it in a whining voice as if asking for sympathy; she speaks with dignity, thoughtfully.

As there was a beginning, so there has to be an end, and, as for grief—let the winds scatter it where they may!

"Where did you stack hay?" the gypsy asks.

"Where did I stack hay? I worked for the late Lord Kubah, the father of our present lord who owns the mountain beyond the river. You don't happen to know him, do you?"

"Yes, we do. He's a Romanian. He's the one who bought people beer when he wanted them to elect him as mayor, and told them he was their brother."

"Their brother?" she asks, narrowing her eyes. "And why isn't he their brother now, after they elected someone else? Oh, he's a bad man, not like his father used to be. He takes after his mother;

indeed, he even says he's Romanian. She's from Moldava, but his father spoke Ukrainian to us. Oh, it was good back then, when his father was still alive and had a fortune. I stacked hay for him in the mountains."

And after a moment of animated thought, she continues.

"There used to be two people by every stack, but I did mine myself. Can you believe it? I'd pile them myself, trample them down by myself, and make them as wide and as splendid as cottages.

"Lord Kubah would come up, stand to one side, and watch me. He'd watch for an hour or more. When he saw that I was good and tired, he'd come over and give me some tobacco, saying: 'Have a smoke, Paraska; you're my best worker.'"

"And what did you do, Paraska?"

"I'd sit down under the stack, laugh, and have a smoke."

"Ey, Paraska, Paraska . . ."

She glances up at the gypsy and admonishes him with her head and her eyes.

"Ey, come on, old fellow! I'm not one of those!" And, spitting once again, she clambers to her feet and sets out for home with her load of brushwood.

Her house is an ordinary peasant cottage with a *pryz'ba [an earthen embankment abutting the cottage]* and whitewash around the windows. Near the house there is a garden with all manner of things in it—fruit trees, vegetables, flowers, basil, and two rows of yellow cloves. Their strong scent makes you giddy.

She lives alone. Never having had any children, she delights in every flower individually.

"I like to have a lot of everything—it's more cheerful that way," she says whenever anyone expresses amazement at the size of the garden.

And even though there is nothing very special about it, it is like paradise to her. On Sunday afternoons, she likes to lie under the pear tree with a dog, a cat, and two or three chickens at her side, and smoke or sleep. She does not seek out company, nor does she like to talk with just anyone at all; she rarely visits her neighbours and, when she does drop in, she first looks closely at everything before she sits down or has anything to eat.

"Paraska is very *dzhingash [delicate]*," her Romanian women neighbours say in an offended tone. "She looks around like a lady when she walks into a house. But she'd do better to look closely at her own hovel—she's more likely to find something dirty there."

But she does not care what they say. And so, even though Romanian cottages are kept very clean, even the slightest hint of slovenliness disgusts her, and she does not try to hide her feelings.

If they start preparing something for her to eat—she immediately heads for the door.

"I forgot to gather the chicks back into the yard," she says by way of an excuse, "and something might happen to them."

And she hurries home.

"If you had a child," a neighbour would say to her, "you would be happier."

"Maybe I would be happier," she would reply. "But if it were an ugly child . . . O God! No, I don't want to so much as lay eyes on children that are ugly or dirty."

"But it's sad for you like this . . ."

"I'm not sad."

And she spoke the truth. She never feels dejected.

Even in the winter, when she is alone for weeks at a time without seeing anyone, she does not become depressed. She spins and smokes; talks to the cat, the dog, and her pet chickens; tells fortunes with cards and with corn—and does not experience any melancholy. In the evenings, when the snow pelts her tiny windows, and the wind hums with its mournful voice, she huddles by her clay oven, nurses her pipe, and listens.

A loud noise whooshes through the air. It rushes in from Rhungh and Mahgurah like clouds of birds, and the wind scatters it everywhere. But she is not afraid.

If someone knocks on the door, she does not budge from her spot.

"Who is it?" she asks in a calm, bold voice, refusing to open the door until she finds out exactly who has come and why.

It is not that she is alarmed in any way—she just feels too lazy to get up from her warm, comfortable niche.

Her thoughts—in her view—are dreams.

Everything that she thinks of, she explains by saying: "God sent me this dream . . ."

She has an older sister, Teklya, who, like she, is an attractive, childless widow. But Paraska does not like her. And they do not live together. Teklya had tried to steal the affections of Malyna's son and, since that time, Paraska has not liked her.

Moreover, this sister . . .

If one of the men or youths jokes with her, she immediately reaches for his leather belt and starts poking around for his purse or some tobacco . . . She's utterly shameless!

There were a few times that Lord Kubah gave *her*—Paraska— tobacco, oh, yes, yes indeed! She could have gone far in life if she had wanted to. But she has a sense of shame . . .

Paraska's cottage is untidy and marked by poverty.

There is a long oak bench, a bed knocked together out of boards darkened by age, a table of the same vintage, a heavy, awkward trunk, a few things hanging on a clothes-rack, and not much else. But the walls are covered with colourful pictures, bright papers, ribbons, wooden crosses, cups, and dried flowers. And, on the windowsill, spindly scarlet flowers press themselves in vain to the grimy glass, reaching for a bit of sunlight.

In the midst of all this, she is always active. She either sits and spins, or carves something out of wood—crosses, spoons, dishes, or other small articles—whatever comes to mind.

"Who taught you to carve?" people often ask her.

"Who!" she says in astonishment. "I do it on my own! I can't sit without doing something. When I take a piece of wood in my hands, it takes shape all by itself."

One time, a lady sought shelter in her cottage. Seeing how well she spun, and finding out that she spun for others, she began bringing work and money to her cottage. From time to time, she gave her some tobacco, having observed that such a gift put her in a talkative mood. Paraska became attached to her, like a child.

One day, after the lady had not come to her cottage for quite some time, Paraska ran into her on the road and, out of sheer joy, kissed her right on the lips—much to the surprise of the lady.

"I feel so much better now that I've seen you again," she said joyfully. "Come to my place for some cherries. They've just turned ripe," she invited her warmly.

"And should I bring you some tobacco? Or have you, perhaps, stopped smoking?" the lady pretended to ask her seriously.

"Oh, no, I haven't stopped!" she replied, almost in alarm. "I've grown to like it even more."

"Really? Well then, I'll come and bring you a package, and you prepare a big bunch of yellow cloves for me . . . They must be blooming in your garden by now."

"And how!" Paraska bragged. "They're so big, and their heads are so splendid . . . that . . . O God!"

The next day, when the lady was returning from her walk, she stepped in to see Paraska. She found her at her sewing.

After listening to her for a while, she asked: "Why don't I ever see you in an embroidered shirt, Paraska? I thought that Hutsul women always embroidered their clothing."

Paraska was a little embarrassed. "I have a few things somewhere," she replied, glancing around the cottage in a way that made it clear there were no such articles.

Then she added with a smile: "Well, I've deceived you this time. I don't have any embroidered shirts. I don't like to embroider—and that's that. And I didn't do it even when I was younger. I used to launder my shirt really well, so that it was white as snow, and I'd wear it like that. I never liked women's work and, to tell the truth, I still don't like it, even now. Can you believe it?"

One look around the house provided ample proof of that!

"So what did you like to do?" the lady asked.

"I'll tell you what! The work that menservants do. If a rake needed to be made—I made it. If firewood had to be chopped—I chopped it. If the horses had to be taken to the blacksmith—I took them. If a wooden bucket had to be made—I made it. And there were quite a few times that I caught horses for Lord Kubah in the highland meadow . . . hey, hey! Yes indeed!"

And she laughed merrily.

"Why are you laughing?"

"Because I remembered how it used to be. I was quite a prankster in my time!" Her eyes changed and blazed, and she looked even younger than she usually did—or, at least, no older.

"You must have caused the young men's heads to spin, right?"

The corners of her mouth quivered wantonly.

"They were crazy about me!" she replied, and then she started relating part of her life story.

How attractive she must have been!

And not just her facial features, that even now attested to a former, almost intelligent beauty that was exceptional among these simple people; but also another kind of loveliness—an inner beauty filled with a wild, untrained feeling for art, and an eternal youthfulness that even now showed through strongly in every word, every glance of her wise, shining eyes, every movement of her slim figure and, most of all, in the animated motions of her hands and head, on which she always wore an eye-catching, flowered red kerchief.

She did not exhibit any of the coarseness synonymous with the word "peasant," which no refined feelings can ever come to terms with, or accept.

"You made their heads spin!" the lady repeated. "But in the end, you married an old man, a widower. Isn't that so, Paraska? Wasn't your husband a widower?"

She gazed piercingly at the lady. "So, it's so! Isn't a widower a man?"

"Well," she added, "I married him, but it was the will of God and the Fates!"

"And not yours?" the lady teased her.

"How am I to know? We came together from opposite ends of the earth to get married here. He was a forty-year-old man, and I was a girl of nineteen. I was lucky, and that's that. Not everyone has luck; some people have such bad luck that you have to give them wide berth so that you don't catch it. But I had good luck, right from the time I was a child."

"You've never told me about your luck, Paraska," the lady said, smiling.

"I didn't tell you, because you didn't ask."

"Well, have a smoke and let your hands rest for a while. I'm listening."

"It's no big deal to talk!" she replied indifferently, and then, filling her stubby pipe, she began her story.

From the age of nine, she lived with her godmother. She hired herself out to work in her village and, never afraid of work, lived well no matter where she went.

She buried her parents when she was fifteen. Her father had been a superb craftsman—he built churches—and all of her kin were renowned woodworkers.

Two sons of an uncle were especially famous. They were both handsome, and always stuck together, making a name for themselves by carving violins, saddles, flasks and the like out of wood. Once, when they went into the forest to fell trees, a tree toppled over and killed them both. On the spot. And so they were buried together in the same grave.

And the son of another uncle's son—his name was Andriy, and she was his aunt—was the most famous of all. Some of the things that he carved were taken away by the Kaiser's son. That was the kind of family she came from—she was not like the Hutsuls from the province of Bukovyna.

And she continued with her narration . . .

One day my godmother advised me that during Lent, on a Sunday night before Monday, I should put under my pillow everything I had worn that day—that is, on Sunday—and that if I did this, I would see in my dreams the man God had destined for me.

I did so.

I crammed under my pillow everything that I had worn that day and went to sleep.

And I had a dream.

I dreamt that I was going uphill carrying some sacks, and in the sacks there was some hay. I was walking on a high mountain, through grass up to my knees, to a forest, and the forest was all dried up. It was so dried up, to the last tiniest twig, that it had turned rusty in colour. It was all so sad, so quiet . . . I looked around—and a gate appeared from somewhere, right in front of me. A man, neither old nor young, walked out of it, carrying the moon and twirling it.

He stood before me, placed his hands on my head, and said: "My child! If you have an idea, stick to it. You will walk for seven miles and seven hours—and you'll find the one destined for you." And he vanished! That's what I dreamt.

Time went by. I didn't sit around. I worked, and served, and toiled—because I had the strength to do it. Hey, was I ever strong!

And I lived without a care. But I couldn't stay in one place for any length of time. I always felt an urge to move on; I always felt like going somewhere else, and I got the idea of going to Bukovyna. Oh yes indeed, to go to Bukovyna to work there for the haying season.

Summer came, and I asked my sister Teklya to go with me, but she didn't want to. Once she hired herself out someplace, she'd stay there as if rooted to the spot. But I was always thinking about going to Bukovyna; it must have been fated for me by the soothsayers.

So I went.

I managed to convince my sister, and we went with other Hutsuls to make hay in Vyzhnystya and Ispas. Hahvrisahn, a wealthy Romanian farmer who looked after Lord Kubah's enclosures and meadows in the mountains, came there from Bryaza and, wouldn't you know it—he began convincing us, all of us who were there, to do the haying on the lord's holdings in Bukovyna, in Bryaza.

I was so anxious to go that I could feel the ground burning beneath my feet. Some said they'd go, others said they wouldn't, and still others were mulling things over. My sister refused to go. But I . . . O God! I would have gone that very moment. Can you believe it?

Hahvrisahn turned to me and looked me over from head to foot.

"What about you?"

"I'll go," I said.

"Good!"

All of us who agreed to go left the very next day, and those who didn't agree went home. My sister went back with them, but later she came here and took a liking to this place.

We were haying far away in the mountains—mowing, raking, and piling the hay; some were making piles, others—stacks. I stacked the hay so quickly that Hahvrisahn just stood and gaped! Others worked in pairs on a stack, but I did it all myself. Hey, but I was fast. The sun was scorching, as if it wanted to melt the earth . . . The searing heat was beating down so hard, it was impossible to look at the sky, but my hands did not wilt. I was so hot and flushed that blood was almost bursting from my face, but I didn't stop until I finished.

Lord Kubah would ride up—he always rode on horseback—and, letting the horse graze, would lie down at the edge of the forest, or on the ground in the shade of a stack, toss his hat from his head, and watch me. He didn't stay by anyone as long as he stayed by me. Then he'd pull out his tobacco, pass me some, and say: "Have a smoke, Paraska."

I'd smoke, and we'd talk. He asked questions, and I answered. He was a good lord; he liked the way I laughed.

After we finished our work there, we were anxious to get home; in fact, we were on our way already, all packed together in a big wagon, singing as we went along. And then we saw someone riding horseback, trying to catch up to us.

It was Hahvrisahn.

"Leave Paraska here!" he shouted. "Bring Paraska back! The lord said so . . ."

We had to stop.

When I decided to stay behind in the lord's fields, a young man who always tried to sit beside me poked me in the ribs and said: "Go, go and split your sides laughing!"

"Are you jealous?" I asked him; then I laughed and everyone else joined me. He probably burst from anger before he got home.

And I liked it at Hahvrisahn's.

I did my work, and I was happy, so happy . . . O God!

"Worry doesn't fancy you," Hahvrisahn said to me.

"And I won't be worry's servant," I said to him. "I don't know how to be sad . . ."

"And, you know, to this very day I haven't learned how to be sad. Can you believe it?"

It was impossible not to believe her!

Her dark eyes flashed an untamed exuberance, and her voice and movements revealed an untrammelled love of life, humour and, at the same time, a childlike innocence.

"I make my own happiness. Nothing bothers me—I used to feel strong enough to move mountains, but now . . . But even now I won't give up, even though my hands are no longer what they used to be; but even now, if someone came . . . No, just let him come!" With a swift movement, she raised her tiny clenched fist and brandished it threateningly.

"Oh sure, Paraska. As if someone would be afraid of your fist!" the lady said.

"He may or may not be afraid, but I certainly wouldn't be."

And she began reminiscing once again.

When I was younger, everyone knew my fist, even at Hahvrisahn's. No one could pry it open; two of them would even try at the same time, but they still couldn't. Not any youth, nor any man. I always bet a ring on it.

One young shepherd, a powerful, handsome Romanian, was determined to pry open my fist—for a ring. He almost went mad, she added in a softer voice, smiling coyly. And then she spat.

"You'll pry open my fist when a hen begins to crow," I said to him.

But he just said: "Uh-huh." And nothing else.

Some time later, I was carrying some salt to the *styna*. Do you know what a *styna* is? It's a hut where shepherds spend the summer, living with the sheep, milking them, and making cheese. It's a shanty thrown together out of rough boards on a mountain pasture.

Well, I was running down the mountain—all by myself; the forest surrounded me, and the grass was so tall that it choked me. I was running down, singing loudly ... All at once I heard a loud echo, a prolonged shout: "He-e-e-y!"

I looked at the mountain opposite me where, next to the forest, a meadow stretched endlessly ... and, on it, a flock of white sheep was grazing. And then I saw a young shepherd racing down the mountain like a bullet, his long black hair bouncing on his neck and flying down his back.

He had recognised me. He bellowed—excuse me for using such a word in your presence—like a bull; in a word, he'd gone mad.

I waved my fist at him and took off.

"Run," I thought. "You'll have to hop on your head if you want to catch me."

But he did catch up to me! I hid behind a fir tree, exploding with laughter.

He stopped and glared all around like a ravenous wolf.

"Hey, you fool!" I suddenly shouted as I came out from behind the tree. "I'm over here, you blind dolt!"

He dashed up to me—like a real wolf!

"Now you'll have to open your fist," he said, glaring like the devil.

Sparks flew from his eyes, and his face first flushed and then paled.

"I won't," I said.

"You will!"

"I won't!"

"We'll see."

"Yes, we will . . ."

He lunged at me like a crazy man and began ripping the shirt on my chest.

"We'll see," he said, "who'll crow like a rooster," and he tried to knock me to the ground.

Then I . . . God forbid! "Just you wait!" I shrieked, beginning to fight. I was fighting for my life!

He was strong, enraged, and kept pushing me down, but I wouldn't give in!

"You will crow, you will!" he snarled, grabbing me by the throat to throw me down.

"You'll do the crowing," I said, sinking my teeth into his arm so hard that he howled.

He kept howling, and I jumped to my feet and rushed at him.

He came at me . . . with a terrifying expression on his face. I think he wanted to kill me, but I didn't wait to find out. I pounded his face, and then I was no longer afraid.

"Do you see my fist? Do you see it?" I yelled. "And do you see my teeth? I'll rip you to pieces, chew you up, and pull you apart—like the cruelest cutthroat! Just you wait and see!"

And I walked up closer, shaking with anger, and stared him down.

He was standing there, white as death; his cap had flown off, and he didn't say a word.

"You bandit," I said, brandishing both fists at him, "you think I'm one of those? What a fool you are!" I spat and walked away.

And he picked up his cap and staggered back to his mountain. When I had gone quite far—I was on the crest of the next mountain—he began to play the *trembita [a long mountain horn]*. He played so mournfully. And later he told Hahvrisahn that he had cried.

"That's the kind of fists I had," she concluded.

"And you weren't afraid, Paraska?"

She glanced at the lady with eyes that were still flaming, "Why?" she asked. "Let this thing be afraid!" she exclaimed and, grabbing a little dog that was sleeping cuddled up to her, pressed it vehemently to herself. "Let it be afraid when I yell at it when it yaps too much; but not me!"

And she laughed in a softer tone now.

"Who would be stupid enough to be afraid!"

And she continued her story.

At Hahvrisahn's I took care of the animals.

I liked horses and oxen, but I couldn't care less about housework.

Not long after my fight with the shepherd, Lord Kubah sent a message from here, from this town, that I was to come here to serve in his home.

I didn't want to.

"I'm not a town servant," I said, "I'm a field worker. I'll go back where I came from. I'm not afraid of the open road."

"Have Paraska come here!" he said. "There's a widower here from her part of the country—Yuriy, a servant-farmer. He'll marry her, and they can both work for me."

"Let him marry who he wants!" I said. "I won't go."

And I didn't go.

He sent for me again.

"No,' I said. "I won't go. Who does he think I am that I have to marry him? Aren't I well off as it is?"

And I had peace of mind after that. They no longer sent for me, or asked for me. And life was good. The days flitted by like birds. I had no worries. God certainly gave me a lot of luck. The Fates turned sorrow away from me, and it's said that they gild the soul of the one they love. I was happy!

"Or you made your own happiness!" the lady added, as if speaking to herself.

"How would I know? I was happy!" she responded.

And she went on.

"Paraska, will you ever cry?" Hahvrisahn asked me more than once, shaking his head.

"I'll cry when dry rain begins to fall," I said, "but in the meantime, give me some money for tobacco."

And he'd laugh and give me some.

He was good man, that Hahvrisahn. I would have married him, but he had a wife. She strutted around in a kerchief and skirt, and what a fine housekeeper she was! She knew how to do absolutely everything, and she grieved for wasted time as you'd grieve for a child.

"She'll cry when she marries trouble," Hahvrisahn's wife said.

"I didn't agree to marry any of the young men who courted me," I said, "and there must have been fifteen of them, both rich and poor—and I'm going to marry someone who brings me trouble? Hey, hey, I won't let trouble gobble me up!"

"I guess life to you is nothing but sunshine!"

"Well," I said, "it may not always be sunny, but neither is it filled with sorrow."

One time I had a dream. I was sitting by a house, spinning white wool. The wool was white as snow, but the yarn that came out of it was silver, and the ball of yarn was so silvery that I'd never seen anything like it. I continued spinning. Suddenly, a Jewish woman came up to me and filled my lap with buns. That's what I dreamed.

And now, listen to this. On that same night, from Friday to Saturday, Yuriy was dreaming, at Lord Kubah's home in town, that I came to him, gave him one bun, and kept one for myself. Can you believe it? And that's when he insisted on coming to see me. The dream affected him so powerfully.

Lord Kubah himself told me all about it later.

He said: "If you take her as a wife, she'll stick with you as long as she lives; the girl's like lightning, and you'll live well in my home."

Another time, he once again tried to drum it into his head: "Marry Paraska, because someone else will pluck her right from under your nose, like a hawk grabs a chicken!"

And so Yuriy set out to see me.

He took with him a friend who had come once before to Bryaza to see us at Hahvrisahn's, and knew me.

At the time, I was in the hut on the mountain tending to some work. His friend came to me—Yuriy stayed behind at Hahvrisahn's in the village—stood at the foot of the mountain, and thundered: "Paraska, he-e-e-y!" until an echo raced through the forest.

"Hey!" I called back.

"Come here."

"What do you want?"

"Give me a light for my pipe."

"And where's your flint?"

"I lost it . . ."

"And mine fell into the water!"

He cursed, and I burst out laughing.

"Aren't you coming?"

"You need a light?"

"You'll give it to me in the house. Yuriy has come for you. Get a move on, charmer!"

"I'll charm you for news like that," I thought, and then I became confused. "He's here! What will come of this?"

And I don't even remember running down the mountain.

I only know that I felt so bewildered that I lost my pipe—the one Lord Kubah had given me. I felt shy, so shy that . . . O God! But I went.

I walked into the house, and he was sitting on the spot where the benches are joined together. When I saw that, I shivered all over. Because if a young man really wants to win a girl, he's careful, when he enters a house, to choose the best place to sit—where the benches are joined together; if he does so, then no one can take her from him. At that time, I walked about the house as if my knees were dragging on the floor.

And I couldn't see what he was like. If he was old, or young, or handsome, or ugly! Something came over my eyes . . . I felt so strange—as if I might die.

But he was devouring me with his eyes. And he insisted that I go with him. Well, if I'm to go, then I'll go! He had already talked with Hahvrisahn and his wife, and the Romanian shepherd I had fought with was, by this time, bawling in his hut; he had told everyone that he had come for me and was only waiting for me to go away with him.

And I went. Can you believe it?

"On whose word are you going?" Hahvrisahn's wife asked me.

"On God's," I replied.

"She wanders from place to place like fair weather," Hahvrisahn muttered, unhappy to see me go. 'First here, then there, and she doesn't stay anywhere long enough to warm a spot."

"I'll warm a spot where I want to. What's it to anyone?" I retorted.

"And what if you fall on bad times?"

"I won't. I know what I'm doing—it's not as if I carry my head around in a sack. If I don't like it there, I'll come back."

"You'd be better off marrying that shepherd Ilya," Hahvrisahn's wife scolded me. "At least he's a young man, like a bear, and he's good at everything; but this one's a *Boyko [a man from the Boyko uplands in Western Ukraine]*."

"But who said I'm marrying him?" I said. "I'm just going with him."

Hahvrisahn spat.

"The girl's gone mad," he said.

"But hey, aren't you afraid?"

"Why should I be? The world belongs to God, not to him."

And I wasn't afraid. "Why shouldn't I go?" I thought. "I'll go and look at the town; I've never been there. Lord Kubah lives there. Maybe he'll give me another pipe, and he's sure to give me some tobacco! And if I don't want to, I won't stay at this man's place."

And he kept asking me every minute: "Are you coming, Paraska? Come along; leave your work here."

And so we went.

When we were passing the mountain where Lord Kubah's and Hahvrisahn's sheep were grazing, the shepherd was playing on his *trembita*. It was such a melancholy song that . . . O God! I looked up at the mountain—and I'll never forget him.

This big bear of a man, with his shaggy black hair, was standing there surrounded by white and black sheep dwarfed by the grass. He stood there all alone, pouring his sorrow into his *trembita*. He played as long as he could see us, and when we passed out of sight his "He-e-e-ey" rang through the mountains and reverberated in my heart.

That's the last time I saw him.

"What's going on?' Yuriy asked, looking askance at me.

"The shepherd is weeping for Paraska!" his friend said. "He fell in love with her."

"Why didn't you marry him?' he then asked, turning swiftly towards me and grimacing at Yuriy.

"Are you sad I didn't?" I asked.

"Lizard!"

"I didn't feel like it."

And we continued on our way.

I was walking after them like a blind man trails behind those who can see. And so we went along . . . They walked ahead of me, and I followed them. I listened and heard them talking in Romanian—so that I wouldn't understand them. But I understood everything—I couldn't speak Romanian, but I could understand it from hearing the shepherd speak.

They were saying: "Instead of walking on the road, let's take her across the mountain tops and through the narrow gorges, so she can't run away and go back . . ."

And so I raised my head and took a good look around.

"That's fine, just fine," I thought. "I'm not blind, and my feet are better than yours. If I don't want to stay, I'll find a way out!"

And I made a point of remembering where they were leading me . . .

In the evening we reached the town and came to a house. Here Yuriy's friend parted with us and went on his way.

Yuriy opened the door.

"So, aren't we going to Lord Kubah's?" I asked.

"What for? Do you suppose," he said, "that I brought you here for Lord Kubah? I know that he wants it that way, but I don't. He'll find himself another servant; you don't have to worry about that."

"Why should I worry about him?" I replied, thinking about my pipe—he would have given me another one.

Then Yuriy said: "We're home now. Happy housekeeping! Cook us something to eat!"

And he gave me some eggs, butter, and milk.

"You won't live to see the day," I thought, "that I'm going to cook for you!"

But then I got up, took off my outer garments, and cooked a meal.

There were only the two of us at the supper table. There wasn't another living soul in sight—not even a dog, or a cat, or a chicken. The food wouldn't go into my mouth; I felt so shy, so ashamed, that . . . O God!

I ate, trying not to look at him. During supper, he said that it was God Himself who made the first couple.

I didn't say anything. Let it be so, for all I cared; what did it have to do with me?

Then we went to sleep.

He said that he was tired, and I—well, to tell you the truth, it was a long and difficult night for me. I dreamt of Hahvrisahn's wife who kept scolding me: 'On whose word are you going?'

And then I dreamt about the shepherd, standing on the mountain at the forest's edge, among his white and black sheep, sorrowfully playing on his *trembita* . . . And then I recalled how he tried to pry open my fist and pressed me to the ground . . .

When I got up in the morning, I was not myself.

Then his brother came, and his relatives, and his friends—a whole crowd of them.

His brother took one look at me and said: "You did well to bring home this girl!"

All the others surrounded me, persuading me to marry him.

One woman, who—excuse me for saying this to you—knew him very well, was all decked out in strings of coral beads and silver coins; her head was wrapped in a snow-white cloth from under which black curls peeked out on her forehead, and she kept saying to me: "Marry Yuriy, and we'll live like sisters."

I just said: "I won't live with him unless we're married in church."

As soon as he heard this, Yuriy grabbed his cap and went to see the priest.

He went, and I walked through the house and the yard, thinking: "Should I run away, or should I marry him? Hahvrisahn will take me back, because I'm like his right hand man when it comes to the cattle; but the shepherd is there . . . He'll say something nasty, and I'll be ashamed, embarrassed. I guess I'll stay here. And why wouldn't I? It wasn't my idea to come here; it's the will of the

Fates . . . And it's not all that bad here. There's a house, money, a cow, and a real shortage of girls!"

That's what I thought, and I did marry him.

For the wedding, I prepared everything nicely: meat—a whole ram—*holubtsi [cabbage rolls]*, a bucket of whiskey, and everything that was needed; then I went to get married. I walked to the church as if my legs had been cut off at the knees. Why? I don't know.

We came back from the ceremony—and found that all the pots were empty!

The guests had eaten everything! The ones who had remained at home had eaten everything and, maybe, even stolen a thing or two; God alone knows. And so I rolled up my sleeves and prepared another dinner, and only then did things go right.

And I lived with Yuriy for seventeen years. He was a good man—he never beat me. It was only the last three years that were difficult. He drank and hated to work. If I did the work, it got done, and if I didn't, it didn't. Then he died. This cottage that I now have, the two of us earned together. And it's a good thing that it's here.

She fell silent and shook the ashes out of her pipe.

"Now you're all alone, Paraska," the lady said, after a lengthy pause.

"Yes, I'm alone." And she shrugged her shoulders indifferently.

"But don't you feel bored, always sitting all alone like this?"

"No, I'm not bored. I do my work—in the house, in the yard—and I smoke, and I'm never bored. Oh, not at all!" she added, as if she were laughing at something.

"And in the winter?"

"In the winter as well; I go for wood, spin, tear feathers. I have my cards, and I tell fortunes. I always tell fortunes on Sunday afternoon; and in the evening too, if there's time."

"Who taught you how to tell fortunes?"

"I learned by myself. I sit and think about one thing or another. My dreams tell me some things, and I think of others myself, and it's good enough for me. If it weren't for the firewood, I wouldn't know what hardship is; it's only because of it that I find life hard. It's hard work, carrying brushwood."

She had a bad leg and walked with a limp.

"What happened to your foot, Paraska?" the lady asked, her interest aroused by the Hutsul woman's story.

She wrinkled her brow for a moment before she responded.

"It's that damned man who's to blame," she said, without raising her gloomy eyes.

"Who?"

"Why, Malyna's son, and my sister, of course . . ."

"What do you mean, Paraska?"

"Just that."

"Well, tell me about it."

"There's nothing worth listening to . . ."

But a moment later, she started talking.

From her words, which this time were strung together rather abruptly, it turned out that she had lived with "Malyna's son" and loved him, even though the word "love" did not cross her lips

Her sister Teklya, in an effort to lure away the handsome young Romanian, slandered her with all sorts of trumped-up stories, and, trying to win his favour, kept dragging him to the tavern. She bought him whiskey, gave him money, sneaked his laundry away to wash it, and, yes indeed, sometimes did not even let him go home to spend the night.

It reached the point that Teklya and the young man decided to do away with her in order to inherit her cottage and set up house together. He was a poorly paid worker, and her sister did not have a house; she rented a dilapidated old shack, earned what she could, and then spent it thoughtlessly.

So, he, the son of old Malyna—who, you had to admit, was a good woman, as she had given her the cards she now used to tell fortunes—together with Teklya, came up with a plan to ship her off into the next world. He sent her to the *moara dracului [the devil's mill]* near the Shandro pasture and asked her to find out on what days they ground flour free of charge, so that later, either he or she could take some corn there to be milled.

There was supposed to be a very good mill there that, on certain days, ground flour for poor people without charging anything. The road to the mill was bad, and that was why the miller agreed to work for nothing, just to have people come to his mill. It was about four miles from the town, or maybe even farther . . .

And she went.

She went as he had told her to go, setting out down a road that cut through beautiful meadows and pastures, as cheerful and green as paradise itself. Then she took a worse, narrower road through the mountains.

She walked for a long time through a deserted area—there was not a cottage or a sign of human life anywhere.

And then . . . And then she reached the place he had sent her to.

Coming out of the mountains without meeting a single soul, she suddenly found herself in a forest. And this forest was not cheerful and inviting like the one that covered Mahgurah or Rhungh. Seeded by the hand of God at the time that He created the world, it was ancient, dense as a sieve, and dark . . .

O God! Its thrumming filled the air and was so loud it made you fall to your knees and pray that some evil spirit would not grab you.

And there was no road, no path through the forest, only a stream. She was to make her way to the mill by following the stream.

She walked in the water.

The stones in the stream were big and jagged—it was impossible to walk on them; the water, deep and swift, was foaming, and so cold that it penetrated to the bone and made your feet ache. But, when she crawled out of it to take a few steps along the edge of the forest to warm her feet—because the sun never reached the water—she hastily jumped back into the stream, for, on the swampy ground where the forest met the stream, grew something that was beyond human comprehension; and it was so tall, and so large, and so strong . . . And she was barefoot!

Well!

Someone, only God knows who, had toppled a log, thick as half a house into the stream. She wanted to cross over it, but it cracked under her feet, and she sank up to her waist in the water . . . It had rotted! Old, and having outlived its time, it had crashed to the ground and was disintegrating, untouched by human hands; untouched by the sun's rays, as well . . .

Hey, hey, hey—it was some road! But she pushed on, and she would rather not say for how long. She walked out of the forest as out of a dark night and found herself between two huge stone walls that seemed to be lying in wait for a human soul in order to crush it. They were that close together. She herself, and maybe one other person like her, could go through it side by side, but no one else.

It was so cold here . . . It was like winter, no doubt about it. What was going on? It was cold in the water, cold above the water, and the sun had disappeared . . .

What kind of ill-luck was this? Was she lost? Had she not gone the way she should have? What Unclean Spirit was leading her on?

He had said the road was bad, but that it would get better; she should just keep going and not stop anywhere . . . And once she reached the mill, she could rest there for the night.

Well, if she must go on, then she must go on. A bad road is no big deal; she wasn't scared of a bad road, but it was frightening here . . . Still, what was to be done? The end must be near. She wanted to come to the end; she could not have any peace of mind until she saw the mill.

She felt strange and weary, and she had not met anyone, nor even seen a human footprint . . . As if there could be a human footprint in a place like this!

She would have liked to smoke to ease her soul—because something dreadful was settling in her heart—but she had lost her pipe. She had fallen a few times, and the pipe had slipped out of the bosom of her shirt.

Hey, she kept on going, poor thing, she kept on going! Maybe the sun would shine at least once, or some warmth would blow in from somewhere—she was frozen right through. To be frozen to the bone in the middle of a summer's day—can you believe it?

What damned soul had built a mill in such a place? What good was it to anyone? Who would travel on such a road? You could not get there with a sleigh, or a wagon, or with oxen, or horses. It was the end of the world, and a paradise only for wild birds and bears . . .

Damn it all to hell!

The walls of stone came to an end.

She walked out of them as out of a gate. She walked out and stood dumbfounded.

What was this in front of her?

It was a forest again. The same forest she had just passed by—dark, wide, growing for all ages, and quiet! No, it must be a cursed forest. Why else would there be this thrumming in the air? She had walked through many forests, but never had she heard such a strange sound. It choked you, poured into your ears, and roared, but at the same time—it was quiet . . . O God! The stillness sucked out your soul . . .

And not too far away from the forest, rising grandly upwards, stood two high cliffs . . . Rahryv *[Pietrele doamnei—The Stone Lady]!*

She stood and stared.

She saw the mountaintops, the gilded cliffs, the sun that was setting, the night already hovering over the forest, and nothing else, except more forest . . . Her mind went blank, and then a light flashed through it, as if she had been struck by an evil thunderbolt, and a knife had been plunged into her heart . . .

This was the devil's mill; it was *its* noise that flooded the air when it was milling!

She shrieked.

He had duped her. He had sent her here to get lost, to break her neck, to have a wild animal tear her to pieces, or for the Unclean One to seize her . . .

Hey, just you wait! Just you wait!

Anger raged within her, distending her heart, and she almost lost consciousness.

Where was he, so that she could kill him and smash him into dust against those cliffs over there, so the birds flying on high could pluck out his eyes. With her very own hands she would kill him, choke him like a snake . . .

And, standing as she was, beside an ancient, thick-girthed fir tree, she banged her head against it. Let her die, let her die right now, if it had come to this.

Then she looked around. And she did not know if the world had darkened in her eyes, or if night was already falling.

Night was falling . . .

O God!

And she cursed him. And she cursed him in a good hour; it must have been either God or the Unclean One who placed that curse on her lips, because it reached him. She pressed her hands to her head to stop herself from losing her mind—but maybe she had already lost it? And she knew—and did not know—what was happening to her.

What should she do now? Spend the night here, or go on?

She now knew that there was no mill, and that everything that she saw and heard was "the devil's mill."

To spend the night, or to go on—it made no difference. Death awaited her both here and there. How could she spend the night in that hell where devils mill in the daytime?

Suddenly, her hair stood on end. Midnight would come, and she would die without a candle!

Oh, how heavy her heart was! Her blood was boiling in her chest; her poor soul was seething with anger, grief, and fear. She was surrounded by darkness, and something like a cloud descended and enveloped her; it was terrifying . . . From the forest only blackness breathed . . . death!

But if something was to be, then let it be. It was better to return. If hours and days still lay ahead of her, then she would live through everything. She had always been lucky. Surely, luck would not forsake her now!

Her feet throbbed, she was shaking from the cold, and all that was warming her was her fervent desire to kill him. But now she had to step once more into the water. If only the moon would shine! But would she even be able to see it between the stone walls that she had to pass through again?

When she stepped out of the passageway, the moon was shining. Leaving the walls of stone behind, she re-entered the forest. It was terrifying during the day, but at night—well, it was better not to say anything.

And once again she walked in the water; she walked blindly.

The places that she avoided during the day were all the same to her now. She only knew that if she stayed in the water, she would not get lost, and her heart felt lighter when she could hear the gurgling of the stream. Occasionally, the moon's light stole through the branches—they were as dense as a net—and flickered on the water, and that's all the light there was. Then she realised that she was crawling along a sharp rock that seemed to be waiting, like an ignorant blockhead, for her to hurt herself. But what did it matter to her feet now! She could no longer feel them. They were so badly injured that, in the light of day, she might have seen her blood colouring the water.

Then she sank once again up to her waist among rotted trees. She gashed her arm—she still had the scar—and when she dug her way out of one tree, something icy and slimy slid swiftly over her hand—it still makes her shudder.

There was only one thing that she did not remember—she was walking as if she were unconscious. Was the forest murmuring? And did it sound the same as beyond the gate of cliffs? She did not think so.

And she figured out that when she finally got out of this terrifying forest, it would be midnight. Then, she would either die, or live.

She did not look around; it seemed to her that she was carrying something terribly heavy on her back and that, at any moment now, it would tickle her until she laughed. And maybe she had carried something—how would she know?

Near the very edge of the water, where the trees thinned out, something grotesque pressed in from the forest—horrifying, transparent white shapes. They rose out of the ground and slithered through the branches. Crowding in on her breast, they tried to choke her, but, sizing up the situation in a flash, she pummelled them with her fists . . . And then she felt better.

When she came out of the forest—God forbid that anyone live to endure something like that—and looked back for the first time into its depths, something tickled her so mightily that she roared with laughter. No! She bellowed. And holy God saw to it that her laughter, losing itself at first in the forest and then returning to her, brought her back to her senses.

Something was trying to drive her mad—the thing that had sat on her back and tickled her; the thing she had carried through the entire forest . . .

Could anyone believe this?

Well, after that, she ran as if possessed!

Fleeing in a wild panic, she tore frantically down the road that stretched between the mountains until she came to the pastures and meadows. There were barns here in which cattle, bunched together, were sleeping, and she found this reassuring.

The moon shone brightly; it was like daylight, and she could finally see where she was.

She saw the mountains as she had seen them at noon, and she saw the sky sown with holy stars. And once, a dog, spending the night with the cattle, barked, and this barking calmed her down, like a human voice . . .

It was quiet everywhere . . . The horrible thrumming had disappeared—it was clear that God's power reigned here . . .

But now she could no longer run. The strength had vanished from her legs, as if she had left it behind somewhere, and she could barely drag herself along.

She did not want to spend the night anywhere near here. How would she make her way home in the morning, past the houses of women she knew? How could she explain her bloodied legs, her soaked, tattered clothing, and the fact that she was returning, like an unmarried woman, without a kerchief? And as for her splendid red kerchief—hey, hey, who knew where it was! Maybe it was now in the devil's hands!

And, dragging herself slowly, every so slowly and painfully, like a blind or beaten woman, or one decrepit with age, she finally made it home.

Limping up to the gates, she saw a light in the cottage. He was at home.

Stepping up to the window, she looked inside, and saw her sister Teklya, dishevelled and repulsive, sprawled on the bed sleeping. He was sitting by the stove, mending something.

She went into shock . . . Her legs began to shake . . . Something from her heart rose to her head, something terrible. She wanted to set fire to the house or do something to kill the two of them.

But then the feeling passed, as if someone's hand had swept it away, and she no longer felt either grief or pain. Weak and utterly exhausted, she felt completely indifferent; her whole body ached, and as for her feet . . . Pain was pounding them like a hammer.

Her head was buzzing . . . That awful forest thrumming, penetrated by a strange clanging, had crept into her head.

Stumbling numbly to a shed attached to the cottage and screened by a spreading cherry tree, she took off her cloak and fur vest, threw them to the ground, slumped down on them, crossed herself, and went to sleep . . .

When she got up in the morning, the house was empty—both he and her sister were gone. She slept for a day and a night, and when she got up the following morning, she felt as healthy and serene as on the day that she had set out on the road to meet her death.

"What happened when he came home, Paraska?" the lady asked.

"When he came home," she said, "I was feeding the chickens. He took one look at me and spat."

"Well," he said, "were you at the *moara dracului*? When are they going to be milling there?"

"May your sins mill you!" she replied, and she did not say another word.

And for five days she did not speak to him; she did not tell him to leave, and she did not tell him to stay. She did not cook for him or light the lamp when he came home in the evening, and on Sunday, when he said that he had no clean clothes, she just said: "I'm not here."

"And what about Teklya?" the lady wanted to know.

When Teklya came, she felt as if the tongues of a hundred snakes had pricked her in the ribs. She leapt to her feet and grabbed a broad-axe.

"Will you get out of my house, bitch?" she yelled.

"What's got into you? Have you gone mad?" her sister asked, staring at her with bulging eyes.

"Get out! Get out!" she kept on shouting. "Or it will be the death of both of us!"

And she could feel her arm rising to slam the axe into Teklya's head. But God turned sin away from her and willed her sister to leave. She flung the axe on the firewood near the stove and wiped the sweat from her forehead . . . O God!

On the fifth day, she set out for town.

He caught up with her.

"Give me some money," he said.

"I won't."

"Really!" he said, laughing at her.

She did not say anything.

"Hey, won't you give me any?"

"No."

He spat and pushed his cap back on his head.

"You won't?"

"No."

He struck her in the face—whack! "This is for you!"

The world began to spin and turned dark, ever so dark. Sparks flew before her eyes, and she fell to the ground.

He grabbed her by the legs, flung her over his shoulder like a sack, and carried her home. Then, slamming her down on the *pryz'ba,* he left her there.

"Die!" he shouted, and turned on his heel.

When she regained consciousness and tried to get up, she saw that she could not. Her foot was swollen, and it ached—if you've never felt pain like that, may you never know it. And she cursed him a second time. And she cursed him in a good hour. Either God or the Unclean One placed the curse on her lips, because it reached him.

In a week he came back.

From where? She did not know. She did not ask. She no longer felt anything for him in her heart and was only waiting for the curse to take effect.

"Good evening . . ."

"Good evening."

And nothing more. She walked around the house—no, now she limped, leaning on a cane.

He was looking for a bit of milk, but she did not say a word to him.

"Paraska, is there anything to eat?" he asked, collapsing wearily on the bed.

"Eat what you've prepared for yourself!" she said to him.

And he lay there, and lay there . . . and then he began to cry. He howled like a wounded wolf.

But she said nothing.

"Cry," she thought, "until you put out the hellfire raging within you; I no longer feel anything for you in my heart."

He cried the whole night. And he cried the next day. He walked around, gathered up his clothing, and chopped some firewood for her—crying all the while.

The day ended.

In the evening he said: "Paraska, I'm going to Dornah-Vatrah to work in the sawmill; goodbye and stay healthy."

"Go in good health," she replied. "May God help you."

And he went.

He went, and to this day he has not returned.

"What happened to him, Paraska?"

"Well, what!" she replied. "He didn't go to Dornah-Vatrah. He robbed a certain Jew here, the one who runs the tavern where he used to drink with Teklya, and fled to Moldava. And, as he was fleeing, he broke his arm and lost all the money."

" 'That's God's doing,' I said, when I heard about it. 'God did it for me; you broke my leg, and God broke your arm!' "

Old Malyna cried and said he was crippled forever and had to go begging!

Well, he had it coming to him!

"Oh, Paraska, you didn't know what kind of a person you had in your home," the lady said. "He could have killed you!"

She shook her head and smiled.

"What would he have taken from me? I'm poor, and he could not have traded my body for money. Before he could have killed me, I would have choked him to death. I'm not afraid!" she said.

"You're not afraid! But all the same, he duped you and crippled your leg."

"Well," she said, shrugging her shoulders, "it must be the Fates that willed it. God punished him for what he did to me. One thing leads to another."

"And what about Teklya? Did you make up with her?"

She spat and began to pack her pipe. "Well, what was I supposed to do with her? She wheedled her way back into my house. She's a sister, no matter what. Whether she's good or bad, she's still a sister. I let her live with me, so people wouldn't think badly of me, but I no longer feel anything for her in my heart.

"A week to the day after I was going to kill her, she took a blind child—a three-year-old girl—as her own. It seems her conscience was troubling her because of me, or maybe God told her in a dream to take in the child. And she did the right thing when she listened to God's will; maybe she'll have a better fate in the next world because of it. The poor thing can't see, but it keeps smiling at her; it's so pitiful that . . . O God! And it pretends to spin along with her . . ."

"And since then you've lived alone, Paraska?"

"Well, more or less," she said. "One time I accepted a carpenter into my home, also a Romanian. He was neither old, nor young—a widower. I accepted him into my home, thinking that if he was good, it would work out well for him as well; but if he turned out to be bad, there's always a door in the house."

"How can you accept a strange man into your house just like that?" the lady asked in alarm. "Aren't you scared? A woman all alone like you, and not so strong any more . . ."

Her eyes flashed, and a cheerful smile flitted across her face.

"Hey, hey, a woman all alone! Did I come into this world with a partner that I should now be afraid to be alone?" she responded. "Who was with me when I married Yuriy? Did I know him? He came, and I went with him. But even then, I didn't know if I'd like it at his place. I just went! I was lucky. I've never been afraid. It's God's doing that I'm never afraid; I always think—what is to be, will be."

"Well, what happened with the carpenter?"

"Nothing. Everything was fine for a while. He went to work early and came home in the evening. After supper, he'd chop me some firewood . . . And he helped me with my work both in the house and in the yard, and everything was fine. I thought I'd have someone to leave the house to when I died.

"But it didn't turn out that way. He started coming home drunk. Once, twice, and then a third time. I could see that things weren't going too well.

"Instead of sleeping at night, he'd talk and carry on. It was frightening. He'd get up, yell, rattle on about something, lie down again, get up again . . . O God! When he was on the bed, I was on the bench in the corner, huddling by the door . . . I didn't sleep for nights on end. And God kept sending me a dream: 'He'll hack you to death!'

"'What am I to do?' I thought.

"Misfortune found me and made itself at home in my house—may it drop dead! I worried, couldn't sleep, and he kept on doing the same things. And even that wasn't enough for him, oh, no! He began to beat my head with his fists.

"That's when I became furious, more furious than he'd ever seen me before. I showed him what kind of stock I came from—and threw him out the door! For about a week he'd come by in the evening, knocking on the door and trying to get into the house, but I wouldn't let him in.

"'May your head be knocked in,' I thought, without stirring from my bed atop the clay oven. 'Why should I keep you in my house if you're not to my liking? Aren't there other people in the world? I'll end my days alone, and if I choose not to . . . I'm not worried that I won't find someone; I'll find a man if I want to!'

"He went away. And since then, whenever he meets me, he treats me to some tobacco and says: 'Sweetheart, my heart aches for you.'

"And I reply: 'Your heart may ache for me, old fellow, but mine doesn't ache for you!'

"And that's that. Now I'm alone again, and I take life as it comes—sometimes it's good, and sometimes it's bad; whatever life brings me—I've no choice in that. And despite everything, I'm still lucky. I have enough money for tobacco, maybe just a *kreytsar [dollar]* or maybe two—but I have it."

"Oh, luck!" the lady interjected in a scornful voice.

She looked at the lady with her lively, intelligent eyes. "It's whatever befalls one!" she said. "I don't grieve, because God did not give me anything to grieve about, and so I wouldn't know how. I do whatever comes to mind. I have enough to eat . . . I'm happy. Things are going well for me now, and maybe they'll get even better. One *moshnyagh [old man]* told me that I have great luck on my side. It was back when Yuriy was still alive."

And she launched into another story.

One day, we were picking cherries. It was a Saturday, and I was up in the tree, and Yuriy was down below, picking up whatever fell to the ground. The *moshnyagh* came along and asked us for anything that we might be able to give him.

"Bring him a bowl of flour," Yuriy said to me.

I quickly got down from the tree and brought it to him.

"Well," he said, "since you're so kind and took pity on me, then carry it to my house; it's not far from here. And in return I'll read you your fate from the writings that I have."

I carried it for him, and he pulled out a thick, really old book from his small trunk and began reading. He read everything—how things used to be, and how they would be. That I was not from here, and about Yuriy, and about sickness, what causes it, and everything, just everything . . .

"You have the kind of luck," he said, "that will never desert you. God has placed luck in your soul, so that it can never abandon you; and it will be thus until you die—luck, happiness, joy. There is no sorrow. Live out your allotted time in good health."

And that's why I say that I have good luck.

After thinking for a moment, she added: "If something good happens, and I find someone to leave the house to, or if he appeals to me—I'll take him in. If it doesn't happen, I'll rely on God's will."

"Take your sister in."

"My sister? O God! Then I truly would die without a candle. No, I don't feel anything for her. I'll stay alone. The sun will shine into my home!"

And she's still alone.

She looks after her property, busying herself around her house and garden, followed around by her dog, cat, chickens, and two tame pigs that she has named Ivan and Paraska.

Occasionally, she hires herself out to farmers to help with the haying. She likes this work best of all.

On Sunday she dresses herself attractively and goes to church. After dinner, if no one comes to visit her, she stretches out comfortably on the *pryz'ba* and, surrounded by her usual retinue of followers, puffs contentedly on her pipe.

"Come on, let's go to town!" her acquaintances shout at her as they pass by her cottage.

She shrugs her shoulders and laughs.

"I lost my purse, and I've no money to buy liquor."

"Come on, just have a look!"

"I'm afraid that someone may give me the evil eye. Go by yourselves in good health . . . I have to look after my children," and she caresses whatever is closest to her—the cat, the dog, or one of the chicks . . .

Offended, they continue on their way.

"How *dzhingash* she is."

But they like her nevertheless. She's a good neighbour, knows a lot about herbs, and has a healing touch. If she gives you something, it will be helpful—you cannot be annoyed with her for long.

***

One morning, while picking raspberries, she clambered all the way up to the top of Mahgurah. When her bucket was full, she turned to go down the southern slope; it was easier to go down that side because the forest was interspersed with huge meadows, and the mountain itself was not so steep.

She sat down to rest.

She was satisfied. She would get at least six *shistky [a coin worth six or ten pennies]* and could buy herself something with the money. What exactly? She was not sure. But it was good that she would have the money.

Wiping the sweat from her forehead—the kerchief that hung down her back was heavy and made her very hot—she pulled out her pipe, packed it with tobacco, and lit it.

She was surrounded by greenery. Mahgurah was a tall mountain, so from it you could see the tops of other mountains over a wide area, and the sky was clear, blue, and so bright that your eyelids involuntarily covered your eyes.

Mount Rahryv rose high above the other peaks. It was encircled by a dark green forest shrouded by a translucent mist, and from this forest emerged two identical parallel stone walls that led, like a trellis, to the magnificent cliff.

That was the *moara dracului.*

She gazed at it for a long time—suddenly recognised it, and spat. That was where she had been! She had lost her kerchief then—a beautiful red one, like worsted yarn—and a brand new pipe. Hey, what a pipe that had been! Only Lord Kubah bought pipes like that.

And then her heart bubbled with youthful laughter.

What a scare she had experienced back then in that horrible mill; she had almost lost her mind; but she had luck, and everything had turned out well. But if it had happened to someone else . . . O God!

She kept thinking and remembering. And when she finished smoking, she recalled that it was time to go home.

Tomorrow was Sunday . . . She wanted to go to Rhungh to pick mushrooms. Wonderful mushrooms grew on that mountain; she would plait herself a few mushroom braids, and they would last her a good while. But she also had work at home that had to be done today and tomorrow. And she had to see the gypsies.

The old gypsy had begged her to lend him two *shistky*, promising to bring her two loads of brushwood in return. She hoped to God that he wasn't lying—because every second word of his was a lie. And she had told him that she would give them to him on her way back.

It must be time to be getting back already. They would be watching for her, because they knew which road she had taken and on which one she would be returning. They knew this territory like the back of their hand—they knew everything here, just like the black crows.

She still felt tired and did not want to budge; however, if she did not finish her work today, she could not go mushroom picking tomorrow.

But her final hour had not yet struck! And what if there were no mushrooms this year? And what if it rained tomorrow morning? And, her eyes twinkling, she made up excuses like this to trick herself, just so she could sit a while longer. It was so good to sit here!

Then, far off in the distance, she spotted a hut and some animals. Was there anyone in the hut? Was it empty? Her youthful curiosity returned, and she got the urge to find out more about it, to hear human voices here in this solitude. And she shouted with all her might in a clear, ringing voice: "Hey, hey!"

A man walked out of the hut and looked around. Could he see her? She did not know. But the sad, prolonged, reverberating "hey, hey" returned to her and reminded her of years gone by, those distant years when she worked for Hahvrisahn.

An indistinct feeling of joy, a joy she had once known, enveloped her, transforming itself into the thought: "Hahvrisahn was a *good man*."

Then, without giving it any more thought, she flung herself down on the grass. Yes, she would have a little nap; she had risen before dawn, and now it was noon. She would spend the noon hour lying here. What reason did she have to hurry home? It did not matter if she finished her work or not; it was just for herself that she was doing it, not for someone else!

Besides, if she tarried too long, the gypsies would come and wake her. The old gypsy would not forget about the *shistky*. Damn him anyway! But still, she liked them. No matter when she stopped to talk with them, they were always cheerful. And their schemes were . . . well, like gypsy schemes!

She made herself comfortable in a partly shady spot at the edge of the forest. Placing the bucket with raspberries close by, she tucked her fist under her head and half closed her eyes.

Above her and near her, countless tiny insects, circling restlessly through the air and over the flowers growing riotously in the grass, buzz in peaceful harmony. Not far from her feet, red ants bustle and scurry, and farther on, maybe three steps from her head, a half-coiled snake, pushed out by the mountain, sunbathes on a big stone as if it were its home, flaunting itself in the sun and narrowing its tiny eyes.

And the midday silence lords over everything.

All sounds drown in it like in an invisible sea; the murmuring of the ancient forest joining Mahgurah and Rhungh spreads into the distance. The stillness thirstily imbibes every fresh wave of sound and is refreshed by it . . .

It is so good to lie here! God alone knows why it is so good! A kaleidoscope of colours flashes before her closed eyes. Yellowish, reddish—all so marvellous!

Snippets of unclear thoughts pass through her mind; then one idea comes through clearly: "I guess I'll take him back." She fixes her attention on what has been preoccupying her very actively for the last while—the carpenter that she threw out of her house.

Time and again he keeps beating a path to Malyna's door, pleading with her to persuade Paraska to take him back. He can't live without her, he says. He doesn't know if she has cast a spell on him or what. He's always drawn to her. He won't drink any more, no matter what; as long as she takes him back.

And old Malyna tells her all this and tries to convince her to take him back.

But she does not want to hear of it. Was she suffering without him? It was only the firewood that made life hard . . .

But he keeps crawling back. Not so long ago, she came home from town—she had gone to get some grain for her chicks—and saw a pile of chopped wood in front of her house. She knew right away that he had chopped it.

A few days later she came back from work and saw that his sheepskin coat and a pair of his boots were on the *pryz'ba*. What was she to do? She could not throw them out beyond the gate; someone could steal them.

Everything would be fine if he did not drink, because, in truth, he was a good man. He never hit her, and he was a capable worker. He had good clothes—two sheepskin coats, two wool coats . . .

"Take him back; maybe he'll settle down," her dream tells her over and over again. "It will be easier for you; a fence doesn't stand by itself—it has to be supported. And you can't support it with just one post!"

These thoughts swirl in her head. She'll take him back; she'll try one more time to live with him. Who knows? If he wants to come back so badly, maybe it will turn out to the good. There's many a time a person thinks that things will be bad, but they turn out well. After all, it's not she who is asking him to come back; it's he who wants to. And if he ever again creates a ruckus in her home, she'll take care of it.

Her fists are still strong, and she can still knock a drunk man to the ground. But if she has to knock him down even once . . . Well! He'll remember that day! She's kind as long as she's kind, but if she gets angry . . . You'd better watch out!

A broad beam of sunlight creeps up stealthily, and playfully caresses her face; she is already half asleep. She seems to hear a strange, yet familiar ringing, like the tinkling of bells worn by sheep and goats, and the whistles and calls of shepherds that herd them.

Suddenly, she is on Hahvrisahn's farm.

She is walking with Yuriy and his friend, and they are passing the mountain where the flocks of Lord Kubah and Hahvrisahn graze. The bear of a shepherd is there. With his straggly black hair, he stands in the meadow at the edge of the forest, all alone among his white and black sheep that are dwarfed by the grass, and he is pouring his grief into his *trembita*.

Hey! How grievously he weeps! The voice of the *trembita* spreads mournfully among the mountains, so sorrowful . . . so lingering . . . so . . . O God!

And she is strangely troubled, and her heart feels as if she is going to her death.

Then the *trembita* falls silent; its voice is lost . . . and a black darkness falls on everything around her.

Terrified, she seizes Yuriy's friend by the shoulder . . . "Uncle, save me!"

And he says: "Now your luck is abandoning you; now you will have to live in this world without it!"

She shrieks with fear and wakes up . . .

No! There is no darkness! It is broad daylight, and the bright noon sun is shining.

She sits up and rubs her eyes, straining to hear . . . No, there is no *trembita* to be heard anywhere . . . It is quiet—there is only the rustling of the forest.

Not only was it was a bad dream, but a false one. Her luck could never abandon her.

The *moshnyagh* had said: "You have luck, such great good luck that it will never desert you. God has placed your luck in your soul, so that it could never abandon you!"

An old man like that—he would not lie!

Poets
A Fantasy
(1897)

I once had an auroral soul. This is as significant as happiness, as the rays of the sun, as spring . . . This is the essence of everything that is greatest and best within a person, that which makes it possible to look upon life with a smile and to endure its trials with equanimity.

I had the poets to thank for this. They fashioned me in such a way that I was ever sensitive to art and beauty. This is a great blessing, is it not? When one can open one's eyes and perceive everything! Beginning with the rose that sways in the garden, and ending with what is known as the distance—that which stretches far off into the sun's radiance, drawing our sadness away with itself! There is no one more blessed than poets and artists!

Or how did my auroral soul phrase it?

"God," she said, "could not engage in poetry Himself, and that is why He created poets."

As for poetry—it is the source of all greatness, of all beauty.

When you send your soul on a tranquil voyage, and it compares "here" and "there," and takes away with itself everything that is the finest . . .

It is poets and artists who cultivate auroral souls!

Above all else, my auroral soul loved poets and artists: the high priests of beauty, the singers of love, the gods of the earth. My auroral soul worshipped poets above all else.

May poets, the creators of auroral souls, live forever.

* * *

I have a sizeable host of souls within me . . . It consists of the most select audience that I invite into my home and protect diligently. In my home, into which the sun peeks all day long with a smile, gilding everything that is in it, kissing and exuberantly warming the choicest flowers with its breath, and sweeping out with its rays all the dogs of gloominess that bring illness into the soul . . .

It is a select company to which great deeds, refined gestures, and highly cultured manners are equally sacred. And the essence of intelligence as well. All these are not trifles to them, nor fleeting embellishments, but the basis and foundation on which is built a clean, holy dwelling, full of joy and happiness. And shut tight with a heavy, oaken door—*for protection* from ugly sounds and the lowbrow masses.

It is poets and artists who are within me—people of good breeding. I would say—the very best. For is there a finer breed than this? Oh, if there were, I would open wide the door of my house to those of still finer breeding, and I would let them enter, and I would spread the floor with costly rugs to cushion their steps . . . as befits people of the very best breeding.

O favourites of my auroral soul! O flowers of humanity!

***

Their sublime souls stroll about freely within me and conduct themselves as if they were in their own home. They converse about everything; they reach up into the heights and down into the depths, and always succeed in coming up with something new. New treasures, new values, new forms . . . of women and of men, after whom one can fashion oneself, as on a pattern.

At the same time as they graft one thing onto life, they pull out something else from under heaps and ruins, and reveal beauties that are ever fresh. They discover loveliness in all of its hiding places. They solve the conundrums of souls and pose enigmas that are ever new. At the same time, they are decorous and polite, and they know how to love.

It seems to me that they love me and always gaze at me most kindly . . . No, I can actually feel their love.

The love of a poet affords us a very special feeling, a very special pleasure, a very special delight. It reminds us of the fragrance of violets and the happiness that lies bewitched in ancient fairy tales . . .

But the masses cannot even imagine all of this. I consider the masses, the unenlightened masses, to be all those who do not respect and honour the poet, who do not spread the most costly rugs under his feet, who do not strew his path with flowers and gold . . . The ignorant, coarse masses! They are not worthy of having beauty pass even once through their dwellings, to have it fully turn its wonderful face upon them even once and show them something that is masterfully wrought!

I spit on the dimwitted masses that do not honour their chosen ones . . . the gods of the earth . . . the beloved of my auroral soul!

It has already been stated. My soul was not an ordinary kiosk overflowing with merchandise. No, she was a true lady. Through her long association with those selected by the spirit, she took on refined manners and tender feelings. Her instincts were delicate, like the pollen dust of the lily.

In the morning, when the sun flamed in all its glory in the heavens, when the air was clear, and the eye could accurately distinguish all the forms of nature and of art, she would set off on her quiet wanderings. Her wise eyes examined every figure, and her ears were filled with the melody of the day.

In the evening, whether she was in a joyous mood or a sad one, she related everything that her prolonged observations had seized upon. She painted in the manner that artists had instructed her to paint—with only a few strokes, but accurately and boldly, so that the figure stood out clearly before me.

She loved the distance, as much as we love the future—that to which we are pulled by yearning. This was why she flew beyond the borders of her own country.

When she returned home, there was no end to her stories; there was no end to her adoration and wonder. Intoxicated with beauty, she was wide-eyed, amazed by the unending marvel of it all, and she herself became a part of that beauty.

For what she had seen was splendid in its perfection, in its greatness. It spoke of culture and power, about the proud self-knowledge of still prouder peoples, and about guarantees for the future. And about a broad world view. No, it spoke about a thousand proofs of a capacity for a vigorous life! And it was all true.

Finally, and above all else, she rejoiced; she truly knew how to rejoice. She rejoiced just as little children take delight in multicoloured coral beads in the golden splendour of the sun's light. She rejoiced in *poets and artists* and in knowing that, over there, costly rugs are spread for them; flowers and gold are scattered at their feet; and they are caressed like precious gems, and looked after by men, women, and girls. They are able to devote themselves, single-mindedly and without impediments, to the muses . . .

Then, happy and contented, she would lie down to sleep and dream about her loved ones and their carefree good fortune. At that time, in the evening quiet, she always greeted the one whom her heart had chosen: *"You are the beginning and the end of my life!"*

This is how she would greet him, and then she would fall asleep.

***

One day, she did not go beyond the borders of *her own country*. She remained where she was, and she went on a quiet journey. In the evening, she did not return. Nor did she return on the second day, or the third.

It was only on the fifth evening that she came back. Much later than she usually returned. She approached, dragging her feet, her eyes fixed on the ground. Her face was reminiscent of the chalky paleness of a corpse.

She was silent. She did not even answer my questions. Even my question about what she had seen in her native land, what tones had fallen on her ears. I was waiting for the smile that usually brightened her face before she began her stories, but there was no smile.

On a dark night, stars are not seen.

O my auroral Soul! O my sweet Soul!

***

The following morning she did not want any food. When I spoke to her and began asking her questions, she turned her face aside and slowly closed her eyes. Then I heard sobbing—and I understood. Just as she knew how to rejoice, so too did she know how to suffer.

Then the souls of the poets came to her—all the ones with whom she loved to converse—and they asked her in worried tones what was troubling her. They asked her what it was she desired and gave her all of their treasures in abundance. They told her to look them over and to take whichever was the finest. Whatever she wanted—gold, flowers, or precious artifacts. Or an attentive solicitude in the form of a huge expensive pearl set in gold, and other costly things that are found only in the treasure houses of poets and artists.

But she remained silent. She remained silent and shut her eyes tightly before all of them, as if the sight of them caused her pain, or even blinded her, like the brightest splendour of noon. Heavy tears rolled down her cheeks.

In solitude—it was in solitude that it was easiest to divine her and, sometimes, even hear her—I pondered over what could have happened to her. I felt that she would soon be carried away into the great sea of eternal silence . . .

I wept and recalled the quite recent time that she, as happy as the first morning in May, her eyes brimming with joy, filled me with happiness as well.

O my Soul!

I was willing to call out to her a thousand times: "Remain with me, O my auroral Soul!"

***

The windows and doors were opened wide. Solitude and silence had settled in all around, and only the flowers—her beloved, fragrant flowers—basked in the light of the setting sun.

There was the sound of approaching footsteps.

It was the one—the one and only to whom she sent her greeting every evening before she fell asleep: "You are the beginning and the end of my life!"

This is how she always greeted him.

He drew near. Cautiously and quietly, he seated himself on the edge of her bed.

He sat and spoke for a long time.

I could guess what he was saying to her, what he was pleading for. I held my breath so I could tear from the greedy silence what was bound to happen. Eventually she gave in to his pleading, for she loved him, and a great love makes everything possible . . .

She sat up in bed and looked around, amazed and fearful—more fearful than I had never seen her before . . .

"Is there no one here? *Absolutely no one?*"

"There is no one. Just the flowers. But flowers do not hear anything; all they can do is bloom and perfume the air."

Then, covering her face, on which all the shame of her being was flaming, she whispered: "In my country . . ."

He solemnly repeated her words: "In my country . . ."

"*poets . . .*"

"*poets . . .*"

"*are beggars!*"

"*are beggars!*"

***

Then she flew away. My auroral soul flew away. She flew away, like day fleeing from night.

And she left behind—a beggar . . .

Valse Mélancolique
[Melancholy Waltz]
A Fragment
(1897)

I

I cannot abide melancholy music.

And least of all the kind that initially attracts your soul with dazzling, polished sounds that beckon you to dance, and then, imperceptibly renouncing them, pours forth in a vast stream of inexorable grief! I dissolve then into a flood of emotions, and am unable to stave off a sombre mood that, like a black mourning veil, is not at all easy for me to cast off. However, when uplifting music in all its splendour resounds, I feel doubly alive.

At times like that, I feel like embracing the whole world, proclaiming far and wide that music is being played!

And I love classical music with a passion.

I was taught to understand it and to uncover its motifs by one of my friends—a girl whose soul seemed to be composed of musical sounds, and who herself was music personified.

She was always in search of harmony.

In people, in their feelings, in their relationships with each other and with nature . . .

***

Three of us girls lived together.

At first there were only two of us. An artist and I. She had almost completed her studies and was working on a painting she wanted to sell before going to Italy to study the artistic masterpieces there and find her own path in art.

A Germanized Pole who was twenty-something, she took her work very seriously. Irritable and capricious while painting, she was a most charming person in everyday life.

She was popular with her fellow students, and even the professors, who often were sharply critical of their students—to the point of rudeness—had a fatherly affection for her and proffered their remarks and suggestions in the most gentle manner, so as not to hurt her feelings. *"Das schönste Glückskind [Fate's most beautiful Favourite]"* they called her, and she always referred to herself as *"Ich—das Glückskind [I'm Fate's Favourite]."*

I wanted to be a teacher and was preparing for my final examinations.

I studied music, languages, various types of handiwork and, if the truth be told, everything that I could possibly absorb, in the hope that it would serve as a capital reserve and stand me in good stead one day. I possessed no wealth, and life, as capricious as a young woman, makes its own demands.

Having been friends from our earliest years, we lived together.

We had two large rooms that were furnished elegantly, almost luxuriously, because my friend came from a good family and, even though she did not have large sums of money at her disposal, was pampered and pretentious.

"I can't give up everything like you can," she said irritably to me one time when I suggested that she should manage her money more carefully and deny herself some pleasures.

"You shouldn't talk!' she fumed. "You don't understand. I'm an artist, and I live according to artistic laws that are more demanding than the laws of a rigidly programmed person like you. You can confine yourself to your area because you must; it's narrow, whereas my field is expansive, boundless, and that's why I live as I do. It's not exactly the way I'll live someday when I'll be completely on my own—then I'll soar to the heavens on my wings. That's what artistic feelings compel one to do.

"I view everything from the standpoint of art. And you should do likewise; and so should everyone, all of society. If all people were trained and enlightened artists in all respects—from their feelings to the way they dressed—there wouldn't be as much ugliness and wickedness in the world as there is now; there would be only beauty and harmony. But the way things are, what do we see around us? It is only we, the artists—the chosen few—who uphold beauty in life. Do you understand?"

"I understand."

"I understand! You aren't capable of understanding me. I really don't know why I love you." She would then proceed to apologise to me more or less *en passant [in passing]:* "You're overly critical of me. You constantly attack me with your philistine mind, your constraining, domestically practical views, and your old-fashioned outbursts of femininity. Wrench yourself free, once and for all, from a foundation of obsolete fragments and transform yourself into a new type of person, one from whom I could occasionally draw some invigorating strength . . . something new!"

"That's enough, my little dove; I'll remain an old-fashioned type," I would respond calmly.

I knew her pure and candid nature far too well to be provoked by her hastily flung words. On the contrary, I resolved for the hundredth time not to tear myself away "from a foundation of old fragments" and to remain the same as I had always been, in order to stay on guard over her. For she, in her heady pursuit of beauty, ignored the malicious conspiratorial whisperings of life's obstacles and would have come to grief more than once, if it had not been for me . . .

And even though I never was a new "type" and had no pretensions to the title of "a chosen being" or "a person of breeding," I did understand her and knew when to restrain her truly artistic nature, as well as when to encourage her flights of creativity and support her abiding faith in the future.

"If we remain unmarried women," she said—she hated the term 'old maid'—"we'll continue living together. We'll accept a third member for company—because two isn't enough to set out a program or draw up statutes—and we'll go on living like that.

"We'll try out a third companion, determine what this person is like in terms of temperament, level of education, and orientation towards the past and future, and then we'll make a decision. And then those bugaboos that are used to frighten unmarried women—such as loneliness, helplessness, queerness and the like—can draw as near to us as they want to. We won't be alone. We won't appear ridiculous, and we won't be, so to say, pitiful.

"We'll have our own little group, including men, of course—because life without men is monotonous—and we'll live as we wish. Then the masses will be convinced that an unmarried woman is not an object of ridicule and pity, but a being that has developed organically. This means, for example, that we won't be the wives of men, or mothers, but just women. Do you understand? We'll be human beings who, having chosen not to become either wives or mothers, develop fully on their own.

"I'm not saying that I'm committing myself to this ideal. I live for art, and it satisfies my soul completely; it may be that I will get married. I don't know. But if I don't marry, then I most certainly won't be a timid little bird that begs forgiveness from the entire world for not having a 'husband.' What about you?"

"I feel the same way, Hannusya."

And I truly did agree with her. Why shouldn't two or three unmarried women live together if their characters were compatible, if their intellectual needs were better met together than if they lived by themselves? This was another of the new ideas that I, with my "inartistic, philistine mind," could not have articulated myself.

She treated me like her subject, and even though I could have opposed her and taken control of my own will as fully as she took control of hers, I never did so.

I was not at all pained by my subjugation to her power; feelings of resistance never stirred within me. On the contrary, when she had to leave our home for a while to attend to some of her own matters, I even missed her—her and that power that emanated from her and endowed our surroundings with character and life.

She was attractive in appearance—almost an ash blond, with refined facial features and very animated, sparkling eyes. Her figure was stunning. And because she was quick and firm in her decisions, I loved her wholeheartedly, adapted myself to her unhesitatingly, and flowed calmly, like a river in a river bed of her making, so that, like a river, I might lose myself, perhaps with others like me, in the sea of life.

This was probably why she loved me and called me her "*zhinka [woman* or *wife].*" And the two of us lived together in harmony for a long time.

I studied diligently for my various examinations, and she painted. The painting on which she was working so indefatigably, her cheeks flaming, engrossed her to the depths of her soul. It was a large copy of Correggio's painting—"The Inconstant Woman."

She was painting it with arrogant certainty, fully convinced that it would be a successful reproduction. It was this belief in herself that fuelled her talent and led to the attainment of her goal.

One time, we found ourselves in straitened circumstances, and, to make matters even worse, our landlord raised our rent.

The artist was enraged.

She flung objects to the floor and ripped up her sketches, cursing her fate, that seemed to be a tattered wench, and swearing that she would rather go blind this instant than continue being a painter.

I calmly followed her around, picking up after her, gently taking her paintings away from her and unobtrusively hiding them, so that they would not find their way into her hands again; and all the while I was trying to think of ways of solving our problem.

"I'll take on another hour of tutoring in English, and everything will be fine," I tried to calm her, but she wept, railing all the while against her parents who, in her view, sent her too little money.

"I won't agree to that," she interrupted me. "You're working hard enough as it is. You've already lost all sense of freedom and turned yourself into a machine from slaving over texts and exercise books . . . Oh, how abhorrent this life is! Why did it have to pick us to persecute and humiliate?"

"Why shouldn't I take on another hour?" I protested. "I'm free from six to seven in the evening. Instead of attending lectures of dubious quality on 'harmony,' I'll tutor someone in either French or English, and our problem will be solved. Listen to me, Hannusya," I pleaded with her, "and consent to this . . ."

"I don't want to! I'd rather sell all my paintings! This one, and this one, and that one over there . . ."

Now it was I who could not agree to her plan.

I knew only too well what each painting meant to her, how attached she was to every single one of them, and what destiny she had in mind for each and every one of them. Every painting contained, as she often said, a fragment of her soul, and now they were to be treated like ordinary merchandise? No, I could not consent to that.

I came up with another plan. As soon as I thought of it, I told her about it. We could accept a third companion into our home, and our situation would immediately improve.

She looked at me for a long moment, her flashing eyes inflamed with crying, and then retorted that she would not agree to such an idea. It was impossible to take in a stranger just now, when she was completing her painting—a process that demanded the most favourable conditions.

Would I never understand what "art" meant and what "creativity" was? Did it simply mean turning an organ handle, sewing with a machine, or knitting a stocking? Had all those mediocre lectures made me completely insensitive—that inane jabbering devised for the express purpose of systematically stifling the most noble stirrings towards the uninhibited development of individuality? The idea of taking a stranger into our home who, at best, would be talkative, ugly, and, it went without saying, without a shred of artistic education, and with God knows what kind of vulgar manners.

Oh, she was in utter despair!

"Why should this person be the worst possible creature?" I asked, somewhat exasperated by her histrionic outbursts. "We'll select our third companion ourselves; if we don't like her, we won't accept her!"

"Oh sure, I'm certain you won't accept her—you with your saintly heart that instructs you to love your fellow man more than you love yourself."

"Hannusya, be good!" I begged her. "Your perpetual opposition is driving me to distraction. What are we to do, since there's no other way out? If you can think of something better, then tell me about it, and I'll go along with you; but if you can't, then agree to what I'm suggesting."

Realising that she had cut me to the quick, she instantly retreated.

Pausing in front of her large painting and smiling bitterly, she said: "When do I ever oppose anything? I just listen mutely to my talent, and it's people like you, Marta, people like you, who comprise that great force that oppresses people like me. As a throng, you oppress creative individuals like me, and, because of you, we perish like seedless flowers. But you, as an individual, are unaware of this, and that's why you can't understand it . . ."

Then she took a few steps towards me. "Are you angry with me, Marta dear?"

I did not respond.

"But I say to you, Marta, that, all this notwithstanding, you shall inherit the earth."

"Oh, come now . . ."

"But I say to you, Marta, that, all this notwithstanding, you shall inherit the earth." And, flinging her arms impetuously around my neck, she searched, with damp eyes, for traces of anger on my face.

I could never stay annoyed with her for very long. I knew only too well that if I were truly angry with her, she would not be appeased until I reassured her several times: "I'm not angry."

She had an exceptionally kind heart; at one moment, she could be ranting, raging, and arguing, and the next, she would be the soul of graciousness. The circle in which she moved and her admiring girlfriends spoiled her, giving in to her every whim, and worshipping her for her beauty, her talent, and the originality of her thoughts. She belonged to various organizations, did not begrudge anyone anything, and never accepted repayment of money that she lent her friends.

She valued elegance above all else, calling it the third most important commandment for the attainment of happiness; because of this, she was often unjust in her judgement of people—but then she was drawn to elegance as a child to a flower.

"You can rely on me," I said, "not to bring an unsuitable creature into our home that might offend you and your artistic milieu either with its appearance or its behaviour. I'll make sure of that. I also understand a thing or two!"

"Oho!" she smiled. "So 'you' also understand a thing or two? You understand perfectly how to serve tea; you have all the attributes of a good hostess, mother, and wife; you're an excellent bookkeeper and the future pillar of your family! But, you do not understand the psychology, the colours, and the nuances of art. And this is why I'm terribly concerned that you'll bring an elephant into our home.

"Judging by your kind heart, you'd be willing to take in the first seamstress you came across, as long as she shows herself to be an exemplar of morality—the philistine kind, of course—and has a pious appearance . . ."

"You needn't worry," I responded. "I've learned from you how to appreciate the artistic in life, and, as for the invisible refinements in people, my instinct will sense them. It has always been my best guide."

"I'll see."

"You'll see."

"But remember! If her appearance is 'impossible,' that is, if she's both ugly and ill-mannered, I won't sit at the same table with her."

"Oh, I think you will."

"Do you have someone in mind already, that you're so confident you'll be able to satisfy me?"

"No. But I'm sure that I'll find someone suitable."

"Well, do as you please."

I had said "no," denying that I had someone in mind, and I truly did not. In fact, I did not have so much as a clue or feeling as to who would be the most appropriate person to join our household, and yet . . . and yet, at the very moment that I said "no," a girl's face appeared momentarily in my mind, passing through it like an icon—a gaunt face with sorrowful eyes—and, for a second, it pierced me tenderly, tenderly and fleetingly, with an unimaginable sadness, an ineffable grief, and then, before it could assume a shape, it was gone . . .

Did I know anyone like that?

No!

Had I seen her somewhere?

Probably not. Unless, perhaps, I had caught a glimpse of her on the street at some time.

Perhaps . . .

***

We posted a notice about the room and waited for a new partner.

One day—it was in December—we both returned home in the afternoon, and the servant woman who came in to work for us gave us a visiting card from some unknown "lady" who had come to inquire about the suite.

Hannusya lunged eagerly at the card, almost tearing it from the hands of the old serving woman. "Sofiya Doroshenko," she read aloud through the thick black veil that covered her fresh, rosy cheeks. And then she curiously examined both sides of the card.

It was long, narrow, and edged in gold. There was nothing else written on it, but it carried a faint fragrance of violets.

"Who is this?' she turned inquisitively towards me.

I shrugged my shoulders and, taking the card from her, I too read aloud: "Sofiya Doroshenko," and examined the otherwise blank card from all angles.

"How was she dressed?" Hannusya asked. "Elegantly?"

The old woman shrugged her shoulders. "How am I to know? I didn't pay any attention. I think she was dressed in something black, and I don't think it was very elegant . . . She was wearing a little hat draped with a black silk shawl—the kind that you young ladies wear to the theatre, only it was black, but then again . . . it wasn't at all like what you wear, my dear young lady."

And with a gesture that was almost worshipful, she lovingly stroked the sleeve of Hannusya's outfit—an exquisite dark-blue suit, trimmed with real Crimean lamb's fur, with a matching hat and muff.

"There, you see? Didn't I say she would turn out to be a seamstress?" Hannusya turned to me.

"Was she pretty?" I asked, feeling a need to defend myself.

"How am I to know? She wasn't too bad looking. But she wasn't pretty. Her face was thin, and she had sad eyes . . ."

"Did you hear that?" Hannusya tugged at my sleeve. "She must be a seamstress who continually suffers toothaches and wraps her head in a shawl. What did she say, Kateryna?"

"What was she supposed to say? She didn't say anything," the old woman replied. "She asked if these rooms were rented together, and if she could have a look at them."

"And what did you say, Kateryna?"

"I said she could, and showed her the rooms."

"And what did she say?"

"She looked at the rooms carefully and thoughtfully, and asked if the apartment was warm, because she has a piano, and when she plays she can't stand the cold."

"So-o-o-o!" Hannusya cried. "She has a piano, and she can't stand the cold! She must be a governess! And she thinks that I'll accept her and her piano? Oh, of course, at once! I'm going to be painting here, absorbed in my work and, instead of being immersed in blessed silence, I'm going to have to listen to stupid exercises and scales. No, *danke schön [thank you very much]* for such harmony. Perhaps you'll be so kind as to understand that it's absolutely impossible to go into a partnership with *two* objects.

"She must be a teacher who slaves all day long with children, and then bangs away on the piano all evening to revivify her dulled nerves. I just know it. The shawl draped over the hat, the thin face and sad eyes, the black clothing . . . Oh, we know this type!" Saying this, she opened wide the door and, feigning anger, sailed haughtily into the adjoining room.

I remained in the kitchen with the old woman a little while longer, gazing mindlessly at the card.

A moment later, the artist reappeared. "Why are you standing here?" she asked. "What more do you want to find out?"

"Why, nothing," I replied.

I felt annoyed and wanted to challenge her. For the first time in my life I seriously wanted to stand up to her, but could not. Who was the unknown young lady? What was her family background? The fact that she played the piano did not speak in her favour. Who could know how she played and how much she played! And Hannusya truly did require peace and quiet. What should I do?

"Did she say anything else?" I addressed the old woman.

"She said she would come in two days time to talk with the young ladies."

"And nothing more?"

"No. Oh, yes, she also said; 'It's beautiful here; it speaks to one's soul.'"

Hannusya's eyes flew wide open: "It speaks to one's soul!" she repeated. "You see, you see . . . the artistic atmosphere moved her, but she . . . How was she dressed, my dear little Katie?" And she smiled waggishly at the old woman.

"How am I supposed to know?" Kateryna replied impatiently. "I saw that she was all in black, one of her coat buttons was dangling by a thread, and her gloves were either ripped or torn. But then, why should I examine everyone!"

"*Zhinka*," Hannusya, now very serious, turned to face me. "I won't accept her into our partnership! This is my final word." And, turning on her heel, she stalked out of the kitchen.

I tucked away the card and followed her. We did not discuss the matter any further.

After dinner, Hannusya slung her ice-skates over her shoulder and rushed off to the rink, while I went to my English-language conversation circle.

Twice a week, a group of young people met in the home of an old English woman—a teacher—to practise speaking English. These were the most wonderful hours of my life . . .

While I was there, it occurred to me to inquire if anyone knew this Sofiya Doroshenko.

They did know her. A German girl and a male student knew her. The German girl assured me that "Sophie" was a lady who was *"höchst anständig and fein [very proper and nice]"*, and the student said that she played the piano and was preparing to enter the conservatory.

Where was she from? They did not know. Obviously she was not a local girl, but her deportment bespoke intelligence and attested to her good lineage.

"But haven't you seen her?" the German girl asked me. "At our harmony lessons, she always sits in the second row, directly in front of you."

"No, I haven't seen her."

"She stands out—you can't miss her. Her posture is perfect, and she's thin and has sad eyes. But it's her hair that makes her easily identifiable. She combs herself *antique [in a classical style]* and wraps her head twice around with black velvet, like a diadem. And her profile is truly *type antique [classical]*. Her forehead and nose have the same sweep . . . You must have seen her."

"No, I haven't."

"Well then, take a look tomorrow; you'll see her."

When I returned home, I told Hannusya everything I had found out about her.

"Perhaps we should accept her?" I asked.

Hannusya wrinkled her forehead, obviously wanting to oppose me, as she usually did. But, after thinking for a moment, she said: "Take a good look at her tomorrow, and then, if she makes a favourable impression when she comes here the day after tomorrow, we may accept her."

The next day at my harmony lecture, I looked for our "partner."

I finally saw her.

Not long after had I settled into my usual spot, she appeared and seated herself in the second row, directly in front of me. I could not get a good look at her face, but I could see her smooth, shiny, thick black hair—carefully arranged into a heavy knot and wrapped around twice with velvet—and a bit of her profile, which truly was strictly classical. Her forehead and nose flowed in a gentle line . . . and her sloping shoulders gave her an air of elegance and assurance.

I do not know why, but I could not take my eyes off her. I seemed to be drawn to her, as if I were being compelled to offer myself completely to her service, or, even more—to endow her with all the radiance of my soul, to inspire her with it . . . I really cannot say what it was that attracted me to her.

"If only she'd turn around! If only she'd turn around!" I kept thinking. "Haven't I seen her before? I must have seen her if she sits in front of me in the second row. If only she'd turn around!"

She turned around. At that very moment she turned around for the first time that evening and looked me in the face—with a full, astonished, and almost inquiring expression . . .

Embarrassed, I lowered my eyes.

She did not turn around again that evening.

After the lecture was over, she left before I did and disappeared from view.

***

Around six o'clock the next evening, Hannusya and I were sitting silently in the twilight. It was quiet in the room; the logs in the fireplace were crackling, and the light from the flames fell in a reddish shadow in front of the fireplace and on the ottoman on which Hannusya was lying stretched out full length.

She was extremely upset.

She had applied for a scholarship and had been confident she would receive it; as it turned out, however, she did not. At first, she simply could not believe it. She, *"das Glückskind,"* had not attained what she desired!

When she finally accepted the inexorable truth, she wept violently and passionately until she completely exhausted herself, and her face turned ashen. Then, mocking both herself and the refusal, she fell into an irritable mood, interrupting the silence from time to time with words that were neither monologues nor questions.

I sat quietly by the window, looking out at the street.

I was also feeling very depressed.

A certain young professor who was a member of the English conversation circle had begun to dance attention upon the German girl. It was as if he had completely forgotten that he talked only to me, that we were the best of friends, and that, starting out our conversations in English, we inevitably ended up speaking in our maternal tongue because we had so much to say to each other that we simply could not find the English words quickly enough. And the hour passed by like a minute.

Why was he such an ingrate? The German girl did not speak English as well as I did! Of course, she was always inviting him to her home and promising him God knows what kind of things on behalf of her father, the president of the university, whereas I, who was such an insignificant person compared to her, and who blushed furiously when he was still fifty paces away, could never do anything like that. What would he think? What would Hannusya say?

Oh, Hannusya!

She would not laugh, as she often did, at my inadvertent clumsiness; instead, curving her lips, she would simply say: "So you feel *aroused*? Well, of course, you're over twenty—*ergo [therefore],* you must shove your head under a married woman's headdress, the sooner the better."

No matter how much we liked each other and how much we agreed on things—*that* was something we could not agree upon. She had a lot of admirers, but had never fallen in love with any of them. She would talk for hours about them, admire what was beautiful in them, analyse virtually all the attributes of their beings, but love never touched her; on the contrary, she would often laugh at all of them, as if they were little boys. And once she began working on a project, there was no use even talking to her about anything like that.

I don't know if that kind of behaviour is demanded by the laws of higher art or by something else, but I am not able to function that way. Even the slightest hint of beauty moves my soul, and I readily succumb to it. She—an artist—demands God knows what, but her turn will come as well. And when it comes . . . Hannusya, O Hannusya! Your weeping alone will destroy you!

Art is a great force; but I would say that love is greater. The professor who attends the English conversation circle . . .

"*Zhinka!*"

I came to with a start . . .

"What is it Hannusya?"

"Why are you so determined to stay silent?"

"What am I to say? You aren't asking me anything."

"I'm not asking, but you can still talk. It seems to me that you rush off all too eagerly to your English conversation circles and return home much too animated. You've probably been blinded by someone, haven't you? I can read you like a book. Shame on you . . . You're right in the middle of your studies, and you've let your emotions run away with you!"

Completely taken aback, I felt as if I'd been scalded. She knew!

"Hannusya . . ."

"Isn't it true? Even a blind person could see what's going on, let alone me! But I was right in saying that you shall inherit the earth."

Then she laughed mockingly. "I'd like to be like you—to be governed by my emotions and blinded by even the most inferior 'object'; it would make my life easier. But no! I'll get married without all that. If what happened to me with this scholarship today ever happens again, I'm prepared to accept the first rich man who comes along, who happens to cross my path, just so that I can devote myself more wholeheartedly to my art."

"Hannusya!"

"What?" she asked frostily.

"Are you're saying . . . without being in love? You, an artist, would marry without being in love?"

"Precisely because I am an artist. Precisely because, in addition to my heart, I carry within me another force . . .

"O Marta!" she suddenly exclaimed in a choked voice, impassionedly tearing at her hair. "You have no idea how much one can love what people call art—what lives within us and fills our soul; it appears in us of its own free will, grows and develops, and masters us, giving us no peace, and making our beings its servants and statisticians.

"This force is something so great, so powerful, that our individual happiness appears paltry beside it and, unable to hold its own, cannot co-exist with it in a a state of equilibrium. With its demanding nature, this artistic impulse destroys our being at the very moment that it pledges us its fidelity.

"Is one to stifle that inner world and live only for one's husband, for one's children? That's impossible . . . moreover, love is also inconstant . . . It's impossible for me . . . it's impossible for anyone with the soul of a true artist!"

"But what if you fall in love, Hannusya?"

"What if I do!" she dismissed the idea disdainfully. "Then I'll love. Is it the worst thing that can happen in this world? I'll love *a living image.* One, and then a second, and a third! So long as they are handsome enough, exciting enough, and worthy of my love and my being! As long as they are filled with great, overpowering, original, aspirations . . . And as for loving them— it means nothing! I'm waiting for the flowering of a soul . . . And maybe I'll create a great painting . . . in his honour."

Then she turned to the wall and, a moment later, I could hear her crying again.

I became alarmed.

I always greatly feared such scenes.

There were many things in life that she simply accepted, without thought, scarcely grazing them with the wings of her demanding soul, while others, burdened with their own importance, fell to the ground; but in art she was serious and deep—like the sea.

And it was difficult to win an argument with her. She defeated me with statements that would not have been generally accepted as valid but were, nevertheless, not completely unreasonable.

I went up to her and began to calm her down.

"With what do you intend to soothe me?" she asked, looking me straight in the eye, her mien caustic and severe. "With sentiments? Will you try to influence my mind with heartfelt phrases? Let's not put masks on our souls. Both you and I know that I must go abroad for the good of my art . . . I must, I must!"

After a few moments, she rose briskly from the ottoman and began pacing the room, all the while nervously rubbing her hands, a sign that she was suffering the greatest despair. It seemed that at any moment she would beat her head against a wall . . .

I lit the big lamp that hung over the table in the middle of the room, and the light seemed to defuse the critical situation. It gently illuminated all the objects in the large, attractive room, leaving half-shadows only in the corners, where ferns, plush armchairs, huge bouquets, and white busts stood motionless.

There was a knock at the door.

She stopped in alarm and, turning her head angrily and haughtily, looked over her shoulder at the door, as if asking: "Who dares to come at such a moment?"

I issued an invitation.

The door opened, and a woman entered.

Dressed in black, with a dark shawl draped over her hat, and standing straight and tall—it was she!

"Sofiya Doroshenko," she said to me.

"I'm very pleased to meet you. You've been here already?"

Yes, she had been, but had not found anyone at home, so she had left a message with the servant that she would come another time. She apologised for coming at a somewhat late hour, but she was busy during the day; she also feared that if she came any earlier, she would not find me here, and it was important to her that I be at home . . . She liked the suite, and if I had nothing against the fact that she played the piano—she was preparing to enter the conservatory—she would gladly agree to any conditions that I might put forward, and she could move in either tomorrow or the day after.

She spoke very gently and, without waiting for me to invite her to be seated, pulled a chair out from the table and sat down, her movements calm and confident. The light fell in a pale wide stream on her face. A gaunt face with large, sad eyes . . .

I turned towards Hannusya. Did she not see Hannusya?

It appeared that she did not. She spoke as if she did not see her at all, or as if she were deliberately ignoring her.

The artist was standing by the fireplace—tall, proud, aloof, and intensely irritated—and her large eyes, flaming with her inner pain, rested greedily on the girl's thin face. No, they were not resting; they were maliciously searching for something— something they could destroy the very next minute, thereby easing the pain that was devouring her . . . At that moment she was filled with malevolence.

I presented her to the young woman. The visitor bowed slightly, but the artist barely inclined her head.

"Whether or not you can live with us will be decided by my companion," I said, giving Hannusya a chance to speak.

And Hannusya, without changing her pose, asked coldly: "Do you play well?"

Alarmed, I glanced first at her and then at our visitor, who smiled almost imperceptibly, and then, rubbing her forehead with a somewhat weary gesture, said: "I don't know; I play as my soul tells me to . . ."

A pout settled on Hannusya's lips, and she said nothing more.

I found myself in an awkward position. For some reason, I wanted to accept this young woman who, even though I did not know her, evoked in me feelings of trust and rapport. It was her gentleness, her self-assurance, and most of all, the look in her eyes—so calm and, at the same time, so melancholy! The confidence in her movements and the self-assurance in her voice had to have some other basis—either "a good upbringing," or "a good family."

"So, what do you think, Hannusya?" I hesitantly asked the distraught artist.

She shrugged her shoulders and willed my eyes to turn and look at the two buttons dangling more loosely than the others on the visitor's coat and at her ripped or chewed gloves—or rather, at her fingertips, for, at that very moment, she raised them to her lips and started chewing nervously. She did this unconsciously; it obviously was an engrained habit.

The blood rushed to my face; I felt embarrassed and angry. Never before had I felt so keenly any pain that Hannusya had caused me as I did at this moment when faced by a stranger who, as could be seen from her bearing, had placed her faith in me; at the same time, Hannusya and I were acting stupidly and compromising ourselves in front of her.

After a moment of painful silence from which anyone could guess the artist's answer and her present mood, the visitor rose slowly from her chair. Gently stroking her muff, she turned her large, brilliant eyes anxiously at the artist.

"You can't quite muster up the courage to refuse me, can you, madam?" she asked. "You find it difficult, right? That's the way it is sometimes. But you're not to blame for this, madam! It is I who am to blame for appearing here before you. No, it is you who are to blame," she corrected herself, turning to me with an indescribably charming smile. "You've awoken in me an affinity for you that you probably did not dream of, even though I know you only by sight, from seeing you at our harmony lectures.

"While I was searching for a suite, I came upon this street quite by chance. I read the notice posted in the window, found out that it was you who lived here, and immediately decided to move in with you. That's why I'm here.

"But I can see that it's no use. I would never be able to play if I were convinced that someone in my immediate surroundings was displeased with my playing and, by extension, with me! Oh, no, never! My 'profession' is demanding and requires an unfettered freedom. And as I am accustomed to devoting to music the most boundless, liberated feelings, my soul would be distressed by the continual uneasiness, the suspicion that I might unsettle someone's nerves and have a negative effect on my surroundings; I would never want that!

"I require the tranquillity that flows from an appreciation of music and of harmony in relationships—harmony above all! Now it is I who must beg your forgiveness for withdrawing my request," she added a trifle shyly, while her gaze once again glided over the artist, "but I truly can't help it. It's obvious that here," she added, looking around, "a finer beauty reigns, but I must seek out lovers of music."

Hannusya stirred.

Glancing at her, I knew immediately that she had undergone a profound change, and that the kind-hearted side of her nature had won out. She was smiling now, as if she had not been angry, no, infuriated, a moment earlier.

Raising her eyebrows in astonishment, she asked: "Who told you, madam, that we don't like music? We do like music—genuine music that flows from the soul, that is not simply the result of training and a profanation of what is known as talent, but an outpouring of music from the strings of a gifted soul, the kind that you have just described." And, extending her hand warmly to her, she continued. "We invite you to live with us and to pass on your affinity for music to others—to those who are not as terrible as they seem when they are all clouded over . . . Isn't that so, my dear Marta?"

I smiled, nodding my head. I could have hugged her then and there for being so gracious.

"And as for harmony in relationships, we truly know how to value it. Harmony plays a very important role in our lives, and if you should agree to settle in with us, we would be a perfect trio. *Zhinka!*" she turned to me. "Confirm what I've said and put in a good word for me."

And I, delighted with such a gratifying swing in her mood, confirmed what she had said, put in a good word for her, and issued my own invitation for the young woman to settle in with us.

She thanked us.

It was evident that she was happy, even though she did not say so. It seemed that she was unable to express her emotions, and it was only her eyes that revealed how pleased she was. Those eyes spoke eloquently to us with a damp, grateful glow, and then she quickly lowered them, as if embarrassed by the emotional display that the sincere words of the artist had evoked in her.

I invited her to stay to tea, but she refused and excused herself, saying that she had work to attend to at home if she was to move the day after tomorrow. Then, reaching into her pocket, she immediately paid us three months rent.

She stayed only a little while longer and made her farewells.

Three days later, she moved in.

The artist looked on curiously, with eyes that avidly devoured every object as it was carried into the house. It was as if she wanted to divine the young woman's character from her belongings, to sense the milieu from which they came, and to see if it was worthwhile "to be on kissing terms" with her.

But she did not have many belongings.

Her finest possession was her grand piano.

It was black, shiny like a mirror, built of expensive wood, and decorated with arabesques inlaid with mother-of-pearl.

When it was being carried in, she came with the movers, picked the spot for it herself, and put in place the heavy glass coasters on which it was to stand.

In the evening, after everything was in order, all three of us sat around a hissing samovar at the table and looked contentedly into the room where her beloved instrument stood. She seemed to be exchanging smiles with it, as if both she and her piano were happy that she had found such a good spot for it.

"The ceilings in these rooms are high, and it should sound wonderful here," she said all at once. "It has an excellent sounding board, a fine wooden resonator, but it requires a spacious room, and only then you can fully appreciate its sound. I know my instrument well . . . I will truly enjoy living here!"

The room in which it was standing was not lit, and her door was wide open . . .

It stood wide open, and something emanated from it, something swathed in darkness, with a character completely foreign to me. Her eyes, turning in that direction as if drawn by a dark, secret power, were radiant with delight, as if her soul were succumbing, without even a hint of resistance, to an entity stronger than she, one that she loved passionately, and that totally overpowered her.

Then she played for us.

She raised the top of the grand piano completely, so that the resonator could breathe in fully "the artistic atmosphere." And she played. Not compositions by various composers—but one piece only, the entire evening.

"It seems analogous to me," she explained to us, "to someone reading several authors at the same time, instead of immersing himself in the writings of one. In playing the works of a composer, you have to divine the essence of his being if you want to understand the motif of his composition. Otherwise, the playing has no character. First—it does not capture the composer's soul; second—it fails to reflect the player's soul if, failing to find the strings that bind him to the composition, he simply gropes in the darkness. What is commonly understood to be good playing is no more than a harmony of sounds shaded by nuances that are the result of sheer practice."

She played one of Chopin's études, opus 21 or 24.

Several times, over and over again.

And there must have been some truth in what she had said. I had heard this étude more than once; I heard it and promptly forgot it, but when she played it several times, it was as if I had been given a new sense of hearing.

My soul became fit to understand music.

Our room appeared to change.

One after the other, the sounds flowed continuously into it in gentle, even waves. Sounds and more sounds . . . Agitating one to greater and lesser degrees, rising high and falling once again, filling the entire expanse.

As they were repeated, they were transformed imperceptibly into an incandescent beauty that swept you away. Not with a clamorous, overwhelming power, but tenderly, gently. It engulfed you, alluring you with colourful sounds, and you abandoned your feelings to it, drowning in it without regret . . .

***

The artist was sitting opposite the piano, leaning back against the spine of her chair. Her restless hands were lying idle in her lap, her intensely emotional response to the music had turned her face ashen, and her eyes were virtually illuminating the player.

I saw, for the first time, an external force gain mastery over her, and witnessed how she succumbed to it.

The young woman who was playing sat like a statue, with her classical profile turned towards us; her body was not moving; only her hands flashed over the keyboard like white petals . . .

When she stopped playing, Hannusya rushed up to her with enthusiastic compliments. "You're a born artist," she said over and over again, shaking her hand warmly. "And I feel truly fortunate that you're staying with us."

Sofiya smiled but did not reply. She probably was accustomed to similar words of praise.

But I could not manage to come up with even an approximation of them. I felt so petty and insignificant compared to her that I could not find the words to describe my inferiority.

There is no denying that love is a potent force—but music is no less so!

As for her, she remained quiet and modest, visibly rejecting all the attention showered upon her, as if it were a troublesome obstacle in her path.

***

She was very pleasant in her behaviour, easy-going and unobtrusive, but also silent and very serious. The smile that only rarely appeared on her lips seemed to be darkened by constant sorrow.

In answer to Hannusya's question about her family, she told us that her father had been a director in one of the bigger banks and, having lost his wealth, died a sudden death; her mother—who had been confined by a painful illness to a wheelchair for several years now—lived with her brother, an old bachelor.

Sofiya was concerned that this uncle might get married—he occasionally threatened to do so—because then she would not be able to enter the conservatory, and this would be like death to her. He supported both her and her mother, and even though she could earn money in Vienna—she did so now by giving music lessons—she did not want to have to do this when abroad, as she wanted to devote herself entirely to her music. We could find out nothing more from her.

"I still can't characterise this *type antique* of yours," Hannusya said to me once when we happened to be home alone, a week or two later.

"From Sofiya's interests," she continued, "I discern a refined nature, concerned with beauty and art in the truest meaning of these words. But, in other ways—she remains an enigma to me. She's indifferent, like a block of wood, to most other things.

"For example, tell me, if you please, what kind of a person is she? Have you noticed her linens? They're beautiful and delicate like those of a countess, and her bed clothes are even finer. She sleeps like a queen, and when she washes she never forgets to sprinkle a few drops of the finest perfume into the water. But then consider her outer garments—they smack of 'the masses.' I'm curious how long those two buttons are going to dangle on her coat, when she'll sew on the fragment of lace that she's pinned up hastily on her dress, and when she'll mend her gloves!"

"She's chewed them up, Hannusya."

"It's a strange habit—chewing gloves."

"She chews her fingernails as well."

"There is no doubt in my mind that she is high-strung. Only people whose nerves are on edge, whose souls overflow with emotion, seek solace in such diversions. But then she's probably placed a strong harness on her feelings. She's always cool and composed, like marble. From the contours of her refined lips I deduce that she's not passionate; from her wide temples—that she's loyal; and from her eyebrows that grow together between her eyes—that she knows how to keep a secret . . ."

"What a Lafater you've turned out to be!" I laughed at her.

"But am I wrong in my surmising? Let me do an analysis of you. From your lips I can tell that you'd kiss any young man as long as he's the slightest bit handsome and considered 'decent' by parents and old aunts, and that you're as talkative as a magpie; from your twinkling eyes—that you would embrace the whole world and immediately be on 'intimate terms' with everyone; and from your hands—that, in a case of dire necessity, you'd even chop firewood . . ."

I burst out laughing.

"When it comes to my hands, you're right," I said.

"You're saying you wouldn't embrace the whole world?"

"Maybe I would. It's a good thing that I have so much warmth that I can share it with others. That's why God gave us a heart."

"Oh, of course! You must hurry and shove your head under a married woman's headdress. I'm telling you—you truly shall inherit the earth."

And with these words she concluded her criticism of me.

After some time, during which she painted most diligently, she spoke up again: "Sofiya must be in the throes of a tragic love. Tragic love can often change a person's nature to the core."

"You're always going on about the same thing!" I protested, even though in my heart I had long ago come to the same conclusion.

"What could have played a more important role in her life than love?" Hannusya continued in the same vein. "All sorts of strengths can grow on its foundation; but if she's sensitive—and it seems to me that she is—and also faithful, then everything is ripe for a metamorphosis. Oh, I have a keen eye, and I can tell right away who has experienced unhappiness."

"She herself admits that she's nervous, Hannusya; she said that she became that way after the death of her father. She was alone with him when he suffered a heart attack, and he died almost in her arms. She was ill for a long time after that. For a while, the doctors even forbade her to continue with her music, but because, as she says, there is no life for her without music, she disobeyed their orders and played—and continued playing—as much as she wanted to.

"She said: 'I know without their telling me that I've inherited my father's nervous system and his illness, but what's one day more or less to me! I have no fear of death! When it comes, all the music in my distraught soul will fall silent, as will that which has stifled its resonance.'"

"You see, Marta?" the artist cried, triumphantly flourishing her paintbrush. "There's something concealed behind all this, and I'm determined to find out what it is. I'm terribly curious. What misadventure was it that stifled the 'music' of her soul?"

I shrugged my shoulders. "But even so, she plays enchantingly."

And truly—she did play enchantingly.

***

She soon held sway over both of us.

The artist fell in love with her like a man, and almost smothered her with sincere feelings that were—to Sofiya's way of thinking—too tempestuous, too loud, and too obvious.

And I quietly worshipped her.

Every day, Hannusya uncovered a new beauty in her, and took charge of her outward appearance as a mother cares for her child. She combed Sofiya's long, silky hair, arranging it in her own *antique* style, and dreamt up special collars and other clothing to enhance her classical profile.

I loved her without any "motives."

No, I loved both of them.

Neither of them demanded this love from me as something higher, holier in life, but I offered it to them myself. And, in offering it to them, I found happiness. Neither of them expected any "out-of-the-ordinary" work to be done for them, or any special favours, but I offered these to them on my own—to the one and to the other. The first—Hannusya—accepted them as if they were her due, but the second—Sofiya—bowed gratefully to me as a flower inclines to the sun.

"Hannusya is right to call you '*zhinka*,'" Sofiya once said to me when I had done her still another favour. "You are a *born* wife and mother, whereas in the case of both Hannusya and me, only love could effect such a transformation, and it would have to occur as a further development of our beings.

"As for you—you are the primordial woman, untouched by the new spirit of the times, who reminds us of Cain's wife Ada, or other biblical women overflowing with humility and love. Not a *tutored* humility and love, but pure humility and love, as it is found in nature. Even without any training, you would be the same as you are now. You would sacrifice yourself under the pressure of innate goodness, instinctively, and without thought of gratitude. You—you are one of the thousands of ordinary ants who work untiringly and die without a reward, but who are born to maintain harmony in the world with their love . . ."

Embarrassed by her kind words, I covered my face with my hands . . . I felt that I was on a level that was inferior, very inferior, to her; that, in comparison to her, I was just a simple worker.

And she, as if sensing this and wishing to elevate me, said: "You will be a wonderful mother, Marta!"

"So will you," I assured her, kissing her beautiful white hands.

She wrinkled her brow, and her lips quivered: "I? No!" she replied curtly and morosely, as if I had offended her.

"Oh, you most certainly will be! You possess so much beauty and tenderness . . ."

"I would destroy everyone with my love—my children and my husband," she said in a trembling voice, hastily dropping her gaze to the floor. "I'm not one of those who love temperately."

And, smiling a woeful smile, she changed the topic to Hannusya.

"She's an artist. Unruly and changeable, like the sea, but also as beautiful as the sea. Who could ever have the power to bind her to himself forever!"

"Her turn will come as well," I spoke up.

"No, her turn will never come. She's an artist to the core—even though her painting may not gain her a European reputation. There is no cure for her. Neither a husband nor children will cure her; and furthermore, she's beautiful—she's beauty incarnate, and it would be a pity to force her artistically fashioned spirit into the standard mould of the average woman's soul. She should live life to the fullest, just as she is."

But she did not become as attached to her as she did to me.

They often spent entire evenings discussing a variety of topics; they agreed in their views about the most important things in life, about art and literature, and many other issues; but the very manner in which the artist expressed her feelings offended, it seemed, the pianist's exceptionally refined sensibilities.

Occasionally, there were moments when Sofiya withdrew from Hannusya as if she were being pushed away by a premonition of pain that the strong character of the latter might cause her.

But the artist did not notice this. She loved Sofiya passionately and assured her that she was an angel, an angel sent down from heaven especially for her, to be immortalized on canvas by her talent and skill.

And to me she said that she wanted to set on fire this *type antique* and shake it out of its classical composure.

Occasionally, a group of girls gathered in Hannusya's room, and she taught them drawing. After a while, the girls would begin to talk in earnest and, at times, express their thoughts and feelings too freely.

Then "the musician"—this is what we often called Sofiya—would begin to examine her hands minutely, as if she had discovered a spot on them, rise to her feet and, as if noticing something that had to be mended on her dress, slowly leave the clamorous room.

The girls were glad to see her go. Her presence hampered them. First, because she was older than the rest of them, and second, because there was something about her that demanded refinement in their thoughts and behaviour, and limited their freedom.

***

We scrupulously shared our household duties, rotating our tasks weekly.

When it was Sofiya's turn to prepare the tea or do some other chore of this nature, we were simply delighted. The artist would stretch out comfortably on her ottoman, and I would be in the best possible humour.

She took her duties very seriously.

"It is necessary to look at the bright side of things, even in matters such as these, and then they will never become a burden," she said.

When she lowered the window shades in the evening, she fearfully stopped up even the smallest crack, so that no one could peek in, even though she was convinced that it was impossible to see into our suite because our windows were high, and the blinds were opaque and new. Then she would light the samovar and begin her preparations.

If she was certain that no stranger could see her, she became lively and animated, and changed into a different being—warm, approachable, and incomparable in her creative ideas on how "to enhance domestic living . . ."

However, if someone dropped in unexpectedly at such a time, she would hide herself away in her room and, sitting there like a shadow, remain silent for the duration.

***

One day, our neighbours *vis-a-vis [from across the way]* moved out, and a young technician and his wife moved in.

From the belongings that were being carried in for them, it was evident that they were well-to-do. Seeing this, Sofiya underwent a drastic change. Indescribably intense hatred distorted her usually tranquil face, and her eyes sparked with malice.

I instinctively felt that the reason for this lay in the new neighbours, but I did not have the courage to inquire about it, and she did not volunteer any information.

Turning on her heel, she strode to the piano, controlling herself as if she were the strongest of men.

Then she played.

It was twilight, and she played from memory.

Beginning with a few lilting notes, she began playing a waltz lightly and gracefully.

The first movement was happy, delicate, elegant.

The second movement was different.

It began with a searching among the notes, a restlessness, a desperate urgency. She dwelled time and again on bass notes—moving from lower ones to higher ones—and then, abandoning them, crossed over in an excruciatingly rapid run to the higher register. From there she fled weepingly to the bass clef again—and once more there was a searching among the notes, filled with anguish and turbulence . . . Everything was repeated, and then there was another swift succession of sounds descending to the depths.

The happy harmony was lost; there remained only maddening pain deranged with brighter sounds, fleeting laughter that tugged insanely at the emotions. She played for more than half an hour, then she broke off with a chord of frenzied grief in the middle of a soaring run.

The moon was shining, lighting up the entire wall and the spot where she was sitting.

After she finished playing, she folded her arms on the music ledge and lowered her head.

There was a dead silence.

But I sensed that the waltz she had just played was being replayed in her heart, and that she could not free herself of the impressions it had left on her. Those agonizing runs and the futile searching in the lower register . . .

I was afraid to break the silence.

And it was not an ordinary silence. It was a silence fraught with tension and stifled grief, and out of it something was coming alive and assuming the shapes of malevolent shadows.

All at once she lifted her head and began playing the same composition . . . The airy, elegant beginning, and then the second movement.

She played determinedly, as if struggling mightily with something, and stopped once again with frantic anguish in the middle of a run.

Pressing her fingers to her temples, she sighed.

I broke the silence.

"Is it a waltz, Sofiya?" I asked timidly.
"Yes."
"It's beautiful."
"Yes! It's the *Valse Mélancolique*."
"Whose composition is it?"
"Mine."
"Do you have the notes for it?"
"No, it's in my heart . . ."
And she fell silent.

I wanted to ask her what motif she had used in composing it, but I could not bring myself to put the question to her.

The tone of her voice when she said: "No, it's in my heart," dismissed all questions before they were even asked.

After falling silent, her heart continued to communicate her feelings in the stillness.

Every movement, look, and smile—which she did not indulge in needlessly or often—took on meaning and became an extension of her inner life. It seemed that an extraordinary power was compressed into a classical form of stoical peace—and this is why, even though her thinking was thoroughly modern, her bearing called to mind classical figures whose forms and movements embody a perfected beauty.

***

There was a time when I felt very unhappy.

The hours that I spent in the English conversation circles were becoming increasingly unpleasant for me.

The young professor visited the German girl's family, and even though I could not accuse him of insincerity in his behaviour towards me, the very fact that he frequented her home made me most unhappy.

I lost my desire to speak during these hours, and my entire conversation consisted of brief responses to questions addressed to me.

Life became unbearable, for I realised, beyond a shadow of a doubt, that I had fallen in love with him.

Hannusya was not home, so I flung myself on the sofa, burrowed my head in a pillow, and wept.

I do not know how long I cried, but I suddenly felt someone firmly shaking my shoulder, and Sofiya's voice rang out above me: "*Zhinka!*"

I sat up.

Tall and calm, she was standing before me, her large, sad eyes brimming with sympathy. "Why are you crying?"

I told her everything.

She raised her eyebrows and asked: "And that's why you're weeping?"

"But isn't it enough to make one die of grief?" I replied.

She shrugged her shoulders as if to say: "Well, for you it may be enough."

But she did not reply.

When I tried, unsuccessfully, to quell my tears, she said: "You should strive to develop more pride—the pride with which nature endows our hearts. It is the only weapon that can truly help a woman remain in control of life. You'll be a mother one day . . ."

"What meaning does pride have in comparison to love?" I asked.

Then, with an impassioned gesture, she hid her face in her hands and groaned in despair: "It's the same everywhere! It's the same everywhere!"

Lifting her head, she asked: "And what does *the abasement of yourself* before an unworthy person mean? Do you hear me?"

And her eyes ignited with the same hatred as when she found out that the young technician had moved to our street.

I sensed great sorrow in her voice and, burying my face in her lap, I asked very quietly: "Musician, you have loved?"

"Yes . . ."

Silence.

"You've been in love, musician!"

"Yes . . ."

"Very much in love?"

"There is a kind of love found in women," she spoke with a trembling voice, as if she were afraid to speak, "that a man can never understand. It is too all-encompassing for him to understand. It was such an encompassing love—a love that was to bring me to completion, no, into full bloom—that I gave to him. Not just from today until tomorrow, but for all time. I needed his every movement and his every look; my soul needed his voice; I needed all his virtues . . . and his faults.

"I needed him to become complete and to awaken much that was still sleeping within me. He was to become my sun, and I was to unfold fully in his light and his warmth; I was to become a different person—exactly what kind, I really can't say . . .

"All I needed for my soul to blossom were a few words of love from him; we never talked about our love for each other—it existed between us like mute music. Yes, all I needed were a few words of love from him . . . just as a flower often requires only a breeze, a light puff of air, to fully unfold, regardless of what will happen later. But he did not speak them. He had them in his heart. He bore them in his voice, his eyes, but . . . he never spoke them.

"And I searched for a reason for that silence, a silence which was killing me. I searched . . . no! I'm still searching even now—but I can't find it. I scattered all the lilies of my soul at his feet, but he did not recognise them for what they were. He thought they were flowers that wilt and come alive again when they are placed in water. But it is lilies, only lilies, that do not revive in water.

"He did not understand me. He did not understand the nature of my love.

"'God could not be everywhere himself, and that is why he created mothers,' says an Arabian proverb; mothers could not be everywhere, and so they created daughters and sons. The sons for the daughters, and the daughters for the sons. He was the son for whom my mother created me. But when the time came that I revealed my soul to him, he thought . . . no . . . no!" She suddenly stopped talking, hiding her face in her hands. "I can't utter those words!"

"One day," she continued after taking a deep breath, "we parted, just until 'tomorrow.' I had a smile on my lips and the sun in my heart, because we were to see each other soon.

"But we never saw each other again.

"He went away, or, I should say—he fled.

"Did you, Marta, as a child, ever lose your mother in a big city? I got lost one time, when I was seven years old—and the despair, the sorrow, and the fear that I felt back then, I relived for a second time when I suddenly realised he was no longer with me. I didn't know what had happened to him, because he never came to our home; I searched for him where I was accustomed to seeing him. But I never saw him there either. With despair in my breast, I ran through the streets searching for him—and I was almost on the verge of asking every passer-by: 'Have you seen him?' He was—and then he was no more . . .

"He was, and then he was no more.

"But no one had seen him.

"From that time, I no longer laughed in my heart.

"Later, I found out that he had been transferred to another position and had gone away. He did not bid me farewell, because—as he said—he did not have the 'courage' to break my heart. I was one to be loved, he said, but not one to be taken as a wife.

"You should know, Marta," she spoke now in a voice that was completely calm, "that this is not a fantasy—it is the truth; and he loved me . . . He later married the daughter of a rich brewer and he lives right here . . .

"But he no longer is who he once was; he no longer has the same spirit! She holds sway over him so completely that he has lost the original nature of his being. He has become an unfeeling machine, and all the colour and the resonance of his soul have vanished.

"It's as if he has been left without a character . . ."

"And you never met with him again?" I asked.

"No. I came across him only three times. As we passed by each other, he fixed his eyes on me as if he wanted to bind me to himself forever with his look, forever! A look, Marta, that kissed my feet."

Then she started laughing, softly, but so mockingly, that chills ran down my spine.

"He grieves for me, Marta," she added in a lowered voice, "he grieves and says that he is persecuted by a poignant foreboding, that he hears my weeping—my quiet, stifled weeping that makes one's body shudder, because it is secret weeping.

"But I don't weep. I never did weep.

"I don't grieve for him. He taught me how to hate, and deadened my entire being, from my head to my feet, with humiliation. He was the first to make me experience the ugliness of self-abasement.

Occasionally, I still feel that dirty stain on my soul, and I'll probably never wash it off. I gave him my heart, spreading it before him like a fan, but he—he was a peasant . . ."

She uttered these words with indescribable disdain. If he had heard this word and the tone in which it was said, he most likely would have killed her.

"I never loved anyone again in all my life.

"But it's just as well," she added, casting a radiant glance into the other room where her beloved instrument stood, "because I can devote my entire soul to my piano's sounding board, its resonator. And I do devote it to him—to my resonator!

"When I sit down to play, I find equilibrium for my soul; my resonator returns to me my pride and the feeling that I am elevated, standing high, way up high! And in return, I play exquisite music for him that he will not hear from anyone else; and I'll continue to play for him until I draw my last breath.

"I know he will remain faithful to me. He is not a peasant; he is not made from the trees that grow on the open road, but from those that grow on lofty mountaintops. I am his musician."

She rose to her feet and opened her arms wide as if she wanted to embrace him, and her eyes—her large, sad eyes—shone with a wondrous glow.

Then she dropped her arms.

"Just wait and see," she said, "how I'll play for him when I go to the conservatory, and how he will respond. Our music will take everyone's breath away. Now I'm still just an ordinary musician, and I can't do it yet, but later . . . later, both he and I will begin to live fully . . ."

A controlled joy quivered in her voice and, as if exhausted by a strong emotion, she leaned back against the divan, bringing into sharp relief her delicate, classical profile.

At that moment, she looked very beautiful and elated, but it was at that very moment, as my gaze rested upon her that, for the first time in our acquaintance, her secret, enigmatic happiness was openly revealed—and I was seized by an unutterable grief. I was overcome with pity for her . . .

Then my glance, as if pulled by an invisible force, glided to the wide open door of her room where her instrument—this world of hers—stood.

I dropped my head in her lap once again and, pressing my lips to her hand, asked her quietly if she would play the *Valse Mélancolique* for me.

I wanted to hear it.

She went to the piano and began to play.

I do not know . . . these sounds broke one's heart—those graceful sounds, holding out the promise of the greatest happiness, and ending in sorrow and frenzied unrest. The searching in the lower register, the rushing and storming among the notes for something—for happiness, perhaps?—but all in vain! She interrupted the middle of a run unexpectedly with a mournful chord, leaving in the soul of the listener a riot of unresolved feelings . . . as if in derision . . .

I wept.

What good was that pride that she was telling me had to be fostered in order to control one's life—of what use was it to me?

And where was I to get it, if it did not arise of its own accord in my heart? No, I was not capable of doing what she had done. Neither in love, nor in grief, nor in conquering myself, and even less so in the cultivation of pride.

I was a simple worker—a born servant whom nature intentionally did not endow with proud grief—content to be servile.

And that is why, to this very day, I cater to others and humble myself, fully aware that I belong to those thousands who are born to die without a reward!

***

Two days later, she left to see her seriously ill mother who had telephoned her, asking her to come home.

I told the artist what she had revealed to me about her love.

"It's a story completely without any striking elements," she observed, raising her eyebrows in surprise. "To tell the truth, I expected something more dramatic."

"Well," I said, "not everyone is given to momentous melodrama; still, I don't know, it all seems so very sad and pointless . . ."

"Nevertheless, she still expects something from life," the artist said.

"Oh, no, she no longer expects anything!"

"No? But then what is the *Valse Mélancolique* saying? What is it continually in search of? It's not with words, not with acts, and certainly not with her eyes, or her hands that she's searching—it's with these sounds. And I know what she's searching for."

"For what, Hannusya?"

"Oh, you wouldn't understand . . ."

"Happiness, Hannusya?"

"Oh, happiness! There is no such thing. She's searching for harmony; she wants to live her life in complete harmony. She's seeking equilibrium. Do you understand what this means? Not to be weighed down too heavily and not to rise too high—to find the right balance. But you wouldn't understand that."

And, after a moment, glancing straight ahead into the distance with her piercing, thoughtful look, she said slowly, with a bitter smile: "But I'm telling you, Marta, as I've said many a time, and will often say again—you shall inherit the earth . . ."

***

When Sofiya returned from visiting her mother, the artist flung herself at her with a love that was twice as strong; it seemed that she had once again uncovered a new "beauty" in her.

But Sofiya returned dejected. She had to go back home immediately—her mother was bedridden and very ill—and her only reason for returning was to ask her music pupils' parents for a two-week leave of absence.

And so, after taking care of this matter, she departed again, entrusting her beloved instrument to our care, "so that none of the artist's pupils would play on it and irritate the resonator with discordant chords."

She came back before the two weeks were up.

Her mother had died, and Sofiya returned after the funeral.

She returned pale and quiet—as if both her body and soul were frozen.

When she entered the suite, such a long trail of cold air followed her, that Hannusya raised her shoulders in response.

"It's death's chill that's still on me," she justified herself when she saw Hannusya's reaction.

Then she complained that she could not get warm . . .

Later she settled into her armchair by the fireplace.

I am unable to forget her . . . how she sat there . . .

Her long, black cape, trimmed with fur from around the neck down to her feet, was flung over her shoulders, and she held it together casually on her chest with a hand that looked like a white brooch. The dark knot of her hair, bound twice with velvet, had slipped down on her neck, and her head was resting against the background of the rich red spine of the chair. Her fine-featured face, with its large sad eyes, looked like sculpted marble.

No, no, I'll never forget her!

Hannusya brought her some tea to warm her, and she drank it while telling us what she had just lived through.

After the death of her father, her mother was very unhappy. First, there was her loss, and second, there was her serious illness that confined her to a wheelchair, threw her at both the mercy and the unmercifulness of the servants, and poisoned her life with the knowledge that she was a burden to her brother. She prayed to God to let her die, and her only consolation was the Bible that she read from morning until night. For a long time, she had been prepared to die, and she made Sofiya swear that she would not grieve for her, because this would deprive her of the peace that she so much desired to have in her grave.

And Sofiya had made her this promise.

When her mother was being buried, she struggled desperately to maintain her self-control, so that she would not break her word.

After all, she had never yet broken her word; but just at the moment when her grief was almost overcoming her, and she was struggling valiantly to fight it off, she was undone by the singing of the funeral service—that terribly dark music that was composed especially to depress one, to fight off any bolder and brighter feelings of the spirit, and to turn one into a powerless, humble slave—and so, despite all her efforts, she had wailed as if she were demented!

And she could not rid herself of death's lingering chill that had seized her during that singing by the grave. She could not warm her heart.

But the morning that her mother was buried had been wonderful. The sun had turned the snow rosy with its golden rays, and the weather was bright and sunny, as if it had cleared up on purpose for that holy day when someone returns to the bosom of nature.

She would have liked to have heard a symphony accompany her mother to the grave—a splendid, grand symphony that attunes the soul to a broad flight and, with its very nature, appeases the tumultuous grief in one's breast. But the way it was . . . her nerves were unstrung by the dark music, and she had succumbed to its oppressive sorrow.

And truly, she was profoundly depressed.

It was not in vain, however, that Hannusya determined to warm this *type antique* with her love. She could not do enough for her. She was tender and caring; she was kind to her as I had never before seen her be kind to anyone—and all this was not without results.

"Between the two of you, I'm losing my feeling of aloneness," she said in response to our ministering, her gentle smile expressing her gratitude.

And this was sufficient reward for our efforts.

The artist, spouting witticisms as if she were scattering sparks, was carried away with herself; her mood broke the sadness of the young woman and, slowly, very slowly, she became her former self.

It seemed that she had come to terms with life.

She returned to her music with a doubled enthusiasm.

In the fall, she was to travel to the conservatory in Vienna, where she had been accepted into the third year of the program. And truly, her talent and her passion for music prophesied a brilliant future for her.

***

It was the month of May.

Everything was flourishing.

Trees were white with blossoms whose fragrance drifted far and wide through the air, and the evenings were filled with an inexpressibly soft, alluring beauty.

Hannusya and I were waiting for Sofiya, who was to come home momentarily from her lesson to have supper with us and, as was our custom, go for a walk.

Sitting in an unlit room, we were both engrossed in our own thoughts.

Hannusya had sold her large painting of Correggio's "The Inconstant Woman" and was dreaming about her trip to Rome. And I was no less content.

I had passed my written examinations, was looking forward to doing equally well in my orals and, most importantly—I was engaged to a professor, the one from my English conversation circle. My suspicions about his feelings for the German girl had proven groundless—he had simply been putting in a good word for a friend.

The door to the room where Sofiya's instrument stood was open.

Moonlight poured in cheerful streams through our windows, but a gloomy darkness drifted in through that open door.

Thinking about nothing in particular, my glance kept falling on the tall, dark, narrow opening, and the funereal silence that reigned there seemed to be creeping up on us.

"If only someone would gently close the door." This thought flashed through my mind, but I was reluctant to get up and do it.

Then my eye was led to Sofiya's dark red armchair by the fireplace, not far from Hannusya's ottoman. It was her favourite chair, and she liked to stretch out comfortably in it. Straight and wooden, it was standing in the shadow cast by the door

Hannusya was lying on the ottoman and, like me, was saying nothing.

Then all at once, she spoke: "Marta, shut the door to Sofiya's room."

"You shut it."

"I'm too comfortable . . ."

"Then let's shut it together," I pleaded uncertainly, rising resolutely from my chair.

"Let's!"

As if led by a single feeling, we walked up to one another and, with a hurried, energetic movement, shut the door . . . No, Hannusya slammed the door and the lock.

"Darkness offends me," she muttered apologetically, grabbing me by the hand and pulling me to the ottoman. "Sit here!"

I sat silently, unable to force myself to say a word. Something was sealing my lips, impeding the flow of my thoughts, and a discomforting uneasiness enveloped me. My whole being was waiting for something.

Hannusya maintained her mute silence.

After a while, footsteps—light but slow—could be heard on the stairs.

Sofiya was approaching. She came nearer and nearer . . . and finally—she walked in. She did not greet us as was her custom. It was as if she did not see us. She went directly to the door that we had closed a minute earlier, opened it, and walked into the other room.

We heard her open the window and, after a moment or two, the top of the piano . . . and on it, completely out of character, she placed her hat and parasol. Only then did she come in to see us.

Like a shadow, she drew closer, her steps slow and rhythmical, dragging another shadow after her through the door that was once more ajar . . .

Then she sat down next to us in her armchair.

She was silent.

"I'm glad you've come, musician," Hannusya spoke up. "We've been waiting for you a long time."

She did not respond. She sat motionless, like a statue.

"Did you hear, Sofiya?" I asked.

"Yes. Please, light the lamp!" she said in an altered voice. I stared at her in the darkness—it was quite unlike her to speak in that way. I lit the large lamp hanging over the table and glanced at her in alarm.

She was pale as death; she turned towards me, and her eyes, exceptionally wide and staring, glowed with a phosphorescent light.

The artist also noticed the change in her.

"Sofiya, my dear, are you ill?" she asked, rushing up to her.

"Oh, no, no!" she said, hastily lowering her eyes and forcing herself to speak normally.

"But I can see that you're not yourself, my precious! Come, let's have something to eat. Then we'll go for a walk."

"I'm not hungry," she replied, "but you two go ahead and eat. I'll play for a bit. I'll play while you're eating."

"But you're tired! Do come and eat with us," we both pleaded, coming up to her.

"I won't; I can't!" She looked at us with large, pleading eyes. "I received a letter from my uncle . . . And I can't! Read it. I'm going to play now. I have to play!"

And, rising to her feet, she reached into her pocket and tossed a letter on the table. Then, with the same measured step as before, she went to her room.

We rushed to read the letter. Her uncle informed her that he had married and could not support her in Vienna.

We turned numb.

Hannusya's eyes filled with tears, and I was pierced with pain—an irrational, deep pain!

"This is terrible, Marta . . . Oh, what a villain he is!"

I nodded and sat down. I sat at the table without thinking, but my eyes were turned to where she was.

She was playing there, in her unlit room, and the door was standing open, as it had been previously.

She was playing her waltz, but she played it as never before.

In all likelihood, it had never before deserved the title *Valse Mélancolique* as it did now. The first part was filled with happiness and gracefulness, with a call to dance, but the second . . . Oh, that run! That agitating run that we knew so well! It sped in furious flight from the bright sounds to the dark ones, and once there—there was the unrest, the searching, a despairing rummaging time and again, a crowding of tones, a struggling—and then another flight downwards . . . and then, in the very middle of a run, a mournful chord . . . and it was over.

Hannusya wept. And I also wept.

We both knew that a life had been broken.

When she finished playing, she came to us.

"Now give me something to eat," she said and, stopping at the table directly under the light, she placed her arms behind her head and stretched as was her custom after a long, exhausting session at the piano.

Gladdened by her words, we rose to our feet.

However, just as she was at the height of her stretch, there was a terrible cracking sound in the room where her instrument stood, followed by the mournful wail of a string . . .

She was shaken.

"The resonator cracked!" Hannusya shouted.

"It's just a string!" I cried.

"The resonator!" Sofiya shrieked insanely and flew to her room.

Before we could dash in after her with a light, she already knew what had happened.

"Was it the resonator?" Hannusya asked.

"A string . . ."

"So—it's a string!"

And in fact—it was only a string.

The instrument was wide open, and we leaned over it and saw the string. Among the straight, taut strings, one of the bass ones, gleaming like dark gold in the light, lay coiled from the release of the strong tension.

"And I thought it was the resonator that had betrayed you!" Hannusya said in her usual unworried tone.

But Sofiya did not reply. She fell face forward on the strings in a dead faint . . .

We carried her to the other room, revived her, and Hannusya ran for a doctor.

Before she returned, Sofiya spoke: "Why did she say the resonator cracked?

"Why?" she kept asking despairingly, just as little children ask when they do not understand the reason for their grief, and do not comprehend what is happening to them.

I tried to calm her down.

"Why? Why?"

"But why did she say that?" she kept demanding, and large tears rolled from her eyes. "Why did she say that? It did not betray me!"

***

The doctor arrived at her bedside just as she suffered a massive heart attack.

He could not help her.

Her physical strength could not withstand the series of aggravations that she had sustained, one after the other. They vanquished her.

***

They carried out our musician.

The month of May claimed her.

Hannusya never found out how her thoughtlessly uttered words contributed to Sofiya's death; but even so, she could not find peace for several weeks. She shunned everything colourful, tore up a beautiful painting she had begun in which her "musician" was supposed to serve as a motif and, every so often, was overcome with violent, passionate weeping. After six weeks, however, she began yearning for colours once again and, bidding farewell to everyone, set out for Rome.

I took the "musician's" piano, and my little son plays on it now. But even though I look after the piano carefully, wiping off even the slightest bit of dust, it seems to me that it is gloomy, feels orphaned, and longs for the slender white hands that stroked its gleaming black surface with a gesture filled with love and tenderness, and flashed over its keys like white petals . . .

Hannusya tries to convince me that my son will never be an artist—and she may be right. But her son will most certainly be an artist, if not by profession, then at least in his heart.

She returned after three years in Italy and brought back with her a handsome two-year old boy, dark as bronze, and with her eyes.

"Where is your husband?" I asked her when, looking as elegant as a queen, she paid me a visit.

She raised her eyebrows and glanced at me in amazement. "My husband? I don't have a 'husband.' The father of my son is still there, where he was. When he refused to understand my way of thinking, I left him. But the boy is mine. I support him myself, and he's mine. No one else has any right to him besides me. I bought that right with my good name. But—you wouldn't understand that."

And perhaps I truly do not understand that. But . . . what is it about her that made her do what she did? Perhaps she is to blame . . . although . . . examining carefully her eccentric character, I am unable to cast a stone at her. And I am convinced that even our "musician," that pure, *antique type,* would not have turned away from her. She herself said that it would be a shame to spoil that thoroughly artistic individuality, and that an artist should be allowed to live life to the fullest!

It was only she—whose life was cut short—who could not live life to the fullest.

Even though she opposed the pressure of destructive forces with an almost classical equilibrium of her strong soul—she could not oppose *music* itself. And her "finale" had always been there, hidden in her music. Its sorrow and melancholy, agitatingly beautiful, were discernible whenever she played her compositions and fantasies, whenever she revelled in music, her natural element.

To this very day, I am unable to dispel the thought that it was music that ended her life.

It killed her with a single, slender string!

Humility
(1898)

The day was overflowing with the vibrant greenery of May—and the laughter of the sun.

The quadrangular garden, enclosed by silent, stately buildings, blazed with colour.

Spring flowers were in bloom. In the grey light of the early morning, beneath cool droplets of dew, they had unfolded for the day.

And now they were fully displayed.

Turkish lilacs . . . white lilacs . . . full-blown, rounded tulips, narcissi—clinging to green stems like white butterflies . . .

Verdant shrubs, their branches arching thickly and bending to the ground, resembling wreaths sprinkled with tiny, yellow, star-shaped blossoms . . .

Pungently aromatic nasturtiums flaunting their intense, dark red hues.

And pansies. A riot of the most varied pansies—and other flowers as well.

Paths, strewn with white sand, sensuously winding their way and encircling flower beds and arabesques before disappearing from view in the dense shrubbery bordering the cold brick walls . . .

Around ten in the morning, an artist, preparing to go out, was about to lower a blind over an open window.

At that moment, a young gypsy woman—about twenty years old, with two little girls aged four or five in tow—stepped up to the window, begging for alms.

She intoned pious, humble words, and the little ones imitated her, stretching their tiny hands towards him as well. Their eyes were fixed on him sorrowfully but, at the same time, greedily. They were large, anxious eyes, smouldering with the unconscious passion of southern races.

He tossed a coin through the window, and they skilfully caught it.

They remained standing there.

They wanted something else. The mother continued pleading. Some unneeded, worn-out clothing . . . an old kerchief . . . or something else. It didn't matter what, just anything at all. They had nothing. They had come here from far away and had still farther to go . . . a long way . . . a terribly long way!

And once again, just as before, their eyes turned towards him. Large eyes, with an avid, expectant expression.

The mother folded her arms across her chest and bowed humbly to the ground.

Someone called him from within the house. A resonant, even, female voice, ordering him to shut the window immediately . . .

A few minutes went by.

Had they gone?

They had.

She, leaving behind a vestige of her humility here, in front of the window, was walking down a wide, white path that, in the golden splendour of the sun, wound its way among the spring flowers, among the bushes covered with tiny, yellow blossoms, to other inhabited buildings.

She was walking slowly . . . hesitantly . . . with her arms at her sides . . . through the garden . . . upright, as if she were carrying a full jug on her head. And yet . . . how rhythmical her even gait, how elegant the lines of her body, how slender and delicate her figure—a figure whose loveliness even the shabby clothing could not diminish, and whose every movement betrayed grace and beauty.

He—the artist— gazed after her.

Catching sight of an inhabitant on a porch of a nearby mansion, she now folded her arms across her chest *there*—just as she had formerly done before him—and her humility returned. In a manner that was both modest and refined, she bowed down—quietly, deeply, and respectfully—to the ground.

He was overcome by shame.

What had happened? A moment before, by begging for something he could not give, she had left behind, all in vain, a vestige of her humility.

What had happened?
He felt ashamed.
Then he found something and ran down the stairs with it.
She had entered the porch over there, but the little ones had remained in the garden.

He beckoned to them with his hand, waving the gift up high, luring them with it.

They flew to him.

They flew like birds—with a delighted, joyous chirping.

Lovely, dark-blue baby swallows—all aflutter in this moment of joy.

The older one snatched the gift excitedly and, laughing joyfully, clutched his hand and pressed it to her lips. But not where one's hand is usually kissed, but slightly higher, almost under his sleeve.

At that moment, the mother was coming down the stairs, and she saw everything. Folding her arms across her chest, she bowed deeply . . .

He hurried back into the house—with a secret happiness in his heart . . .

He did not like kissing. But he could feel this kiss from the child's lips in his very soul. It lay on his hand as if a pansy were clinging to it—one of those velvety-soft ones with dark eyes, so many of which were blooming right over there, amidst the greenness in the sunlight. Or, better still, it had left behind *the distinctive trace of southern warmth* . . .

And he, the artist, forgot everything else.

The moment passed. Time went by, and autumn came.

Everything in nature was moving towards its masterful finale. Here and there one could see in it the last traces of luminous beauty. In the forest . . . on the meadows . . . in the park, but most of all, among the proud, autumnal flowers, bereft of scent.

The weeks went by, but the little gypsy child stood before his soul.

He saw her as she had stood then . . . in her shabby clothing, with her head bound in the manner of a matron . . . in a kerchief of nondescript colour . . . her swarthy face, her dark eyes etched with sadness . . . her wondrously beautiful eyes—fleetingly touched with happiness—they were *unique!*

And he wanted the child to come again.

But not now—in May.

When everything would be suffused with golden sunlight, when everything would be revelling in the fresh foliage and the flowers, in the fragrance and the beauty, in the newness and the joy, and when the swallows returned—that's when he wanted the child to come.

And he would lift her up high and give her some alms.

And let the child kiss him for that. But not on his hand, near his sleeve—on his lips. Let her kiss him with her warm, innocent, tiny lips. With those pure, velvety-soft pansies . . . once, and a second time, and a third . . . and then let her continue on her way . . .

But the child would not come.

She had floated somewhere far away, roaming under the open sky—and she would not come . . .

And, like her mother, she would grow up to resemble a palm tree—tall, dignified . . . with sadly etched eyes. And she would bow down low.

She would learn to fold her arms across her chest and, begging at every house and at every threshold for used clothing, to leave behind a vestige of her humility . . .

In the Fields
A Sketch
(1898)

Spring came so seasonably and so gently!

It came with its warm breezes, sunny rays, and gleaming rain, and the snow receded from the ground almost imperceptibly, leaving it without a coverlet.

And the earth was glad of it.

In all its black nakedness, it spread out far and wide in the sun, bathing in the damp, fragrant breath of spring. In places where water collected, it covered itself with a film of hoarfrost and, where winter wheat rested in its bosom, it adorned itself in a vivid, cheerful green.

Under the canopy of the sky, meadowlarks sang light-heartedly, and their trills glided like pearls in the heights and, like pearls, rolled downwards to the earth . . .

"The only time that spring came as early and as gently as it did this year, was when our Vasyl was born," the peasant woman Mariya said to her husband.

He was lying near the house, warming himself in the sun and grazing his two splendid young oxen. Well, no, not exactly grazing them; he was only letting them sniff the grass, for it was still too delicate and mossy for their coarse mouths to pluck.

"Yes. It was back then, when we had nothing yet, but now that God has helped us get some land, we're about to lose him."

She did not reply; heaving a sigh, she continued spinning.

And between that *then* and *now*, there had been only work.

From the grey dawn until late night—only work.

It was always present, always waiting. Morose and inexorable, it consumed everything. Time, thought, pleasure, strength, health, youth, and even that small crumb of enthusiasm for life when, in unguarded moments, it wanted to break and gild the grey, unvarying tone of their mundane existence. It was always insatiable and discontented, barely leaving a drop of blood in a man's veins; even on the seventh day—it was off to church in the morning, and into the fields in the afternoon.

The fields! After almost twenty years of struggling, they finally owned a few *morgy [acres]* of land.

Every lump of it was drenched with their worry and their toil, but also with their love—the anxious, fearful love that every peasant has for his land.

It was referred to as if it were a living being.

Whoever fed it—would be fed by it.

Whoever neglected it—was neglected by it. No one understood the land better than the peasant. And that is why God made peasants when He created the earth.

And as long as the earth will last—there will be peasants.

They had two grown sons.

In a few weeks, the older one, Vasyl, was to be drafted. From the moment he was called up, everyone walked around as if weighed down by a heavy burden. Would he be drafted? Or would they exempt him? If they took him—may such an evil hour never befall anyone—it would be the end of everything. Without his youthful vigour, the fields would yield poorly.

The two of them had grown old before their time, and their younger son had not turned out well. He avoided work and cared nothing about the land. Carefree, and interested in girls, he swooped down like a hawk among them and created havoc wherever there was dancing. In addition, he stole, lied, and drowned his conscience in whiskey.

Finally, falling in love with a young gypsy woman who knew how to concoct magic potions, he forgot all about his father and mother.

Even shame turned away from him in tears.

That was what the younger son was like.

God alone knew what would happen now. The parents peered into the future as into a dark night. Up to now, their older son had been their only joy.

And he already had a betrothed—an unassuming young woman who wept with love for him.

"Did you go to see the priest?" she broke into the silence. "Maybe he could tell us what to do, so we don't lose our child."

"Oh, the priest! He was very irritable again today. The day before, his wife came drunk to church during the liturgy and began quarrelling with him because he had rented a piece of their field to a peasant without telling her. Afterwards, they started fighting, right in church. She threw a cross at him. Now he's so furious that he weighs his words in gold."

"What did he say?"

"He said: 'Pay for a divine liturgy. It will be as God wills.'"

"We'd better do it," his wife responded.

"Yes, I'll do it," he replied piously, "but we'll have to sell something."

"What?"

He had not thought things through yet. Maybe the wheat he had been safeguarding so carefully in the loft for seed, and which he wanted to use now for the seeding, or maybe a beehive? He had four of them.

"You should have a talk with the teacher," Mariya continued. "Maybe he could give us some advice."

"Oh! What can he tell us! All he knows is how to rattle on about his poverty and complain that he and his children are dying of hunger. Just imagine, Mariya, he told me that Vasyl should marry his daughter."

"Has he gone mad? Why would Vasyl want a young lady?"

"It's because they're so desperately poor. He has a lot of children."

"But he also has the wages of a Kaiser."

"I told him that; and he said: 'The pay is too big to let us die, but too small to let us live.'"

"That's bad . . ."

They both fell silent.

Worry spread on her prematurely old but delicate face. She began spinning even more diligently.

He kept looking at the oxen. Vasyl had raised them. And now everyone tended them with the utmost care. And they were truly handsome . . . The entire village delighted in them. Even the village chief did not have oxen like these. They were both blood-red, heavy-set, and sleek, and their craws hung to their knees. In addition, they had small horns, white like a new moon. And they were so smart and obedient—they were Vasyl's hope and joy!

In the autumn, he wanted to plough his land and then sell them. With the money, he planned to build a cottage for himself and his wife-to-be. Or buy a small parcel of land and a few head of cattle. Or a horse and some farming equipment—a wagon, and a few other necessities like that. Or build a barn, even a small one, like those the German farmers built. Or pay the taxes and other community dues. Or . . . Oh, there was so much that he *wanted* to do.

All the things that were needed came to a man's mind so often, pressed in so closely . . . piling higher and higher, one after the other, and adding to his despair—that *everything* was not yet his. And everything that he wanted seemed to be vested in those two fine, gentle oxen that were looked after by the family as if they were one of them, eating and sleeping with them under the same roof.

On rainy days, when it was impossible to go out into the fields, they played the *sopilka [shepherd's flute]* for them. All sorts of songs—both sad and happy ones. The oxen stood quietly, chewing their cud and looking straight ahead ever so intelligently with their large, gentle eyes. And if the playing stopped, the animals turned their dignified heads towards the departing player and lowed mournfully. And then, you could not help yourself—you had to go back and pet them . . .

Splendid, wise animals . . .

Mariya and her husband recognised the former tavern owner Ben'yamin from afar as he walked down a narrow path towards them. He had come to the village more than twenty-five years ago as a poor Jew with a wife and nine little children.

For the last three years now, he had been living in the district capital. Moving there after becoming wealthy, he now lived in an imposing brick house and always wore a watch with a thick gold chain and a large hat that gleamed in the sun. And he had married his daughters off to rich dealers who worked for the lords.

But he did not shun the peaceful village that, lying with its thatched cottages among wide green fields of clover and rye, resembled a pile of seashells in the midst of all the greenery.

Every spring he came to the village, asked the people how they were getting along, and inquired about their health. He knew all about their dealings and their concerns. He had grown old with them, knew the way they lived, and could not make a permanent break with this small corner of the region.

In the springtime, in addition to the usual problems that peasants feel most keenly at this time of the year, there was the great worry about their sons, who were being called up to the army. Like a fog, sorrow settled on the minds of both the young and the old.

They exchanged greetings.

He extended his hand, clad in a red leather glove, and they talked about a variety of things—mostly about the economic conditions in the village and the sowing of the crops.

Then Ben'yamin turned his attention to the two handsome oxen grazing nearby.

"What splendid animals!" he said, and his eyes smiled.

The old peasant's heart lifted in joy. "Yes, aren't they?"

He knew what the other man was thinking.

Mariya stopped spinning and stared him straight in the eye. "They belong to our Vasyl," she said. "You don't know, Mr. Ben'yamin, but our Vasyl is such a good farmer that he has no equal in the village. You never see him at dances or in the tavern. If it weren't for Vasyl, we would have been done for a long time ago. If you only knew how obedient he is . . . if you only knew."

But he knew everything, and he added his praise to theirs.

"And these oxen, Mr. Ben'yamin . . ."

She wanted to say something about the animals, but he interrupted her.

"Eh, what do the oxen matter! An ox is an ox. But how do things stand with the draft?"

The peasant couple sighed and began bemoaning their fate.

He spoke resignedly, with restraint, and with his head sadly lowered on his chest; but she spoke garrulously, heatedly, and with threatening gestures.

She had already cursed more than a hundred times those who attacked sons like ravenous wolves. May they never find rest in their graves or a single bright corner in the next world!

And Ben'yamin laughed.

How *stupid* she was! Did she not know that it could not be otherwise?

She knew! What comfort could that bring her?

Ben'yamin toyed with the gold chain of his watch and thought for a while.

Then he said that perhaps things could be turned around for the better, and the lad could remain at home. That it truly was doubtful whether he would be released from the draft, but . . . but . . . Without finishing what he was saying, he shook his head worriedly.

But what?

But it would cost a great deal.

God!

Yes indeed. It would cost a great deal . . . Maybe even more than these two dumb animals . . .

Jesus Christ!

Well, what of it? Was it so terrible? If you considered that everything depended on this . . . that their son could work at home for three years instead of running around and working for nothing, cleaning rifles, being the servant of others, exposed to all sorts of dangers and—even worse—to death, then what did two stupid oxen mean when compared to all that? In the course of those three years, they could once again have such a "treasure."

They both conceded that he was right, but they did not stop lamenting—a pair of oxen like *these!*

"I've already given the matter some thought," the peasant spoke up, "even though I haven't said anything about it. For example, I could sell these handsome oxen and go to see the gentlemen with the money . . ."

"What would you want for them?" Ben'yamin almost shrieked.

"I'll go, as I said, to the gentlemen, bow to them, put the money on the table and say: 'Release my child. I don't expect you to do so for nothing. Here is what I've earned with my work; I'm giving it gladly . . . to the Emperor . . . or whoever needs it. In return, release my child.'"

Ben'yamin burst out laughing, as he had earlier.

"What a simple peasant *you are!*"

"It's true that I'm simple, but you don't need many brains to do something like that . . ."

"No? You don't need many brains? Just try doing it, and you'll see what will happen to you and your Vasyl. Just try!"

The woman began to weep.

"Yes, yes, he's right, old man! You sit here, out in these fields, and you understand as much about these matters as your oxen. I'm saying this to you because there's no getting away from it. We aren't even *allowed* to see the gentlemen; and even if you, a peasant, do get to see them, and even if you bow a hundred times, everything you say would still be said *as a peasant!* You have to know how to talk to gentlemen. You don't know how to do that. Just leave things alone if you don't want to make matters worse."

The frightened peasant did not want *to make matters worse.*

Ben'yamin would take matters into his own hands. Not very willingly, but out of pity for them. He knew all about their circumstances, how they hovered anxiously over their son, and what a pillar of strength he was to them. That was the only reason he would do it. And because the old man was not a bad peasant like the others, because he was always good and honest, and because the lad did not want to go to the army, despite the fact that he was strong and healthy, like a bear . . .

And all the while, Vasyl's youthful voice was drifting in to them from afar in soft, gentle waves. He was singing as he worked, and his songs, in turn happy and mournful, contributed unwittingly to the bitter decision they were making.

They decided to sell their beloved animals and use the money to obtain their son's release. Ben'yamin was to look after the matter for them.

The old couple saw Ben'yamin off to the edge of the village. Before they set out, Mariya brought out a present for Ben'yamin's wife—a colourful rug she had made herself to cover the bench of honour at Vasyl's wedding. It was the finest piece of handiwork in her trunk.

Afterwards, they both returned home.

It was a cold, rainy day in October when Vasyl parted from his parents and his native land.

Nothing had helped, even though they had sold the oxen, and even though Ben'yamin had taken care of the money himself.

The day before he left, black crows kept circling the thatched cottage, as if a corpse were lying there, as if it had been awaiting them for a long time . . .

Then autumn set in.

Muffled in fog, accompanied by cold winds, mournful grey evenings, and the incessant sobbing of the rain . . .

It was still and deserted everywhere, but there was a feeling of unease in the air.

There was something that tormented . . . gnawed . . . something that, eating away at itself, spread without any rest or peace.

It was a yearning.

A yearning for a youthful, healthy, spirited vigour that had dragged itself off somewhere, leaving behind, like summer, traces of itself here and there.

The barn stood empty.

The handsome animals with their wide gentle eyes and pungent warm breath had left the peasant couple with a painful emptiness that could not be eased. Everything that they still needed—and had never had—grew in importance and assailed their eyes; indifferent and persistent, it assumed ever greater proportions and foreshadowed an interminable existence . . .

The land lay forlorn.

Without youthful vigour, it could not produce anything sturdy and strong. It had to wait.

And from the outset, from the very first moment that he went away—everything waited . . .

Through the gloomy fog interwoven with corrosive yearning—an oppressive mass that settled ever more heavily on everything, spread out in heavy waves as far as the eye could see, and caused all colours to fade—a solitary voice strove to make itself heard.

Unheeded by anyone, it repeated endlessly: *"We need light! The light of knowledge! Light!"*

Under an Open Sky
A Sketch
(1900)

The dead of winter.

The sky was muffled in a dreary greyness; dismal snow clouds huddled under it and, merging with it, formed a cupola over the endless whiteness of the level fields. Black jackdaws, tumbling out of the heavens in great masses, strung themselves together in long rows along white ridges and, strutting pompously, conferred in a dignified manner. After an hour, they divided into three flocks, lifted off apprehensively, one after the other, and, forming a black cross, sailed off into the distance.

Flying slowly and rhythmically, they soared ever higher and higher. Occasionally looping back, they circled dejectedly, lamenting over the fields, and then set out unhurriedly for a distant hill, where the towers of a city peered through the fog. Finally, making one last loop, they vanished like dwindling dots in the hazy distance.

***

The white plain was left deserted.

Boundless and expansive, like the steppe, it cloaked itself in a thick layer of snow and gazed dully into the grey heavenly cupola.

Through the plain, a road winding into the distance gradually disappeared in the whiteness. The eye ached from its silvered surface.

Into this unbroken smoothness headed a small sleigh.

The deep silence covering the broad, frozen sea of snow was broken along the roadway by the tinkling of tiny bells that rang out like children's voices, sprinkling the stillness with uniform droplets of sound.

The small sleigh was pulled by an unkempt roan mare.

She was homely and ungainly. The long hair of her coat was neither brushed nor curried, and her ungroomed mane grew wildly. Her legs were slim but tough, like musical strings, and her chest and nostrils were wide—a sign of endurance when pulling and running.

She was moving forward with precision. From the care with which she stepped, it was evident that she was an intelligent and reliable animal, one of those that would sooner collapse from fatigue than give up on a difficult task.

And she liked to do her duty. She was born into the world that way—to complete whatever work was demanded of her—and the world never gave her a moment's rest.

She hated the whip. Her brief acquaintance with it deeply affronted her and, the few times that she was struck with it, she drew her ears back and kicked madly with her hind legs, breaking either the shaft or the whiffletree, or ripping the halter. From then on, instead of being whipped, she was only threatened with a fist.

And it was strange! Even though her master sat behind her, and she could not see what was happening there, she sensed when he raised his fist and, in conjunction with his coarse, admonishing shouts, waved it intimidatingly. At those times, she flew like mad over the broad plain, driven by a desperate fear that at any moment the black, tattered banners that were pursuing her through the air would fall on her back and, like a thunderbolt, strike her dead.

Harnessed in a halter and ropes that were painstakingly tied and tacked together, she trotted at a fast and steady clip, her shaggy head bent downwards as if she were fully conscious of her responsibilities. First, she had to arrive home in good time to avoid spending the night on the white sea and meeting full face the blizzard blustering so wilfully and menacingly on the horizon; second, she knew who it was she was hauling.

She was hauling a family of idiots.

Having begun to pull them when the morning was still darkened by the opaque veil of gloomy night, she had to wade through this entire solidified sea of snow by evening.

Could she do it in time?

She did not know.

The snow was heaped in heavy drifts, the road was not well-travelled and, way up high in the air, tiny white flurries, boding evil, swirled and rose in spires. It was not yet possible to tell just when they would break up to fill the air with their silent flight, burying the already white plain.

The wind took on a slightly mocking tone. Joining forces with the sharp, almost burning cold, it indulged in noisy revelry. At first, it danced lightly, touching down only occasionally. Then it changed its tempo, leapt up abruptly and, just as suddenly, grew calm again. It crouched on the ground, holding its breath, then sprang up madly and, soaring upwards on wide wings, seized clouds of tender snowflakes in its embrace. And, running amuck with them, it charged capriciously over the rigid sea.

Pausing occasionally in its flight, it whirled with savage, frenetic wantonness and flung masses of snow, like columns of smoke, high into the air . . .

The droplets of sounds from the tiny bells began to weep.

***

He sat at the front of the sleigh, holding the reins.

Dressed in a grimy old sheepskin coat, he—as the head of the family—was sitting on a small makeshift seat.

His head, covered with a cheap, well-worn cap, sat on a short, stubby neck and ended in a chin covered with a small, black goatee—the feature that constituted the main and most visible part of his face. He was snub-nosed, and his eyes, small as peppercorns, dull, but idiotically thoughtful and vapidly preoccupied, peered straight ahead from under his low forehead.

Not too far behind him, his wife sat on corncob husks strewn on the floor of the sleigh. Her head, wrapped in a dark kerchief, was tied around the forehead with a white, narrow cloth—a sure sign that she was on a long trip.

Her head, like her husband's, also sat squarely on her body as if she had no neck. But her face . . . God, that face of hers! Round and flat, it was almost always turned upwards. A pug nose and thick, broad lips flaunted themselves repulsively on her face, and her wide eyes, blue like the sky, bore a perpetually vacant expression.

It was evident that never, in her entire life, had a thought furrowed her brow. She had never experienced deep emotion; her soul was always serene. An unending, unchanging, obtuse, and blank serenity that drove one to despair.

An unrelenting, vacuous serenity.

It was clear, from *the way* she sat behind him, that he was in charge and steered their lives, while she, with unruffled, trusting obedience, accepted everything he said and did without ever reflecting on it.

He knew what he was doing.

How had he come across her? And how had she found him?

Many people had walked and shuffled past them—they were born in different locales—but *each had waited unknowingly for the other*. No one had wanted him, until she met him, and everyone had laughed at her, until he reached an understanding with her.

Afterwards, there arose between them an amazingly wonderful harmony, both bizarre and comical. And, despite his limitations, he managed to organise a world of his own where he alone was the master, where he ruled and held sway over everything, where, as it turned out, he could be the despot if he so desired, and where he was just that, in all his idiotic self-importance.

He was sitting now, looking in his mind's eye at his cottage, his face taut from the mental strain.

His hut was small and low, with a thatched roof and slanted windows; near it stood a shed and a stack of straw. Almost completely surrounded by the forest, it stood in a deep silence like an old, rotting mushroom untouched by human hands.

In this cottage he had left his dying mother. For long stretches around the forest there was not a living soul to be found—there was only the pale, mute, level plain.

They had left home yesterday morning. They had needed to go to the city. Now they were returning . . .

Between the two of them *it* sat. Bearing traces of both him and her, it was the single divine spark in their impoverished souls, the focus of their love. It linked them closely together and bound them to the small cottage wedged under the forest. Tiny and sickly, the very fact of its existence immediately gave them a purpose in life and unexpectedly forced them to think and work more actively. They understood. They had to start doing something. It existed. And it looked to them for everything.

Wrapped in the warmest clothing and a kerchief, it sat, staring fixedly ahead like a turtle, its eyes bulging and transparent. Its ugliness called to mind a bald nestling gaping out of a nest, its eyes popping out of its sockets.

And between them lay a silent and benign vacuity.

***

During the summer, they occasionally took small brooms made of green oak leaves to a large bathhouse in the city, where they were paid two gold coins per hundred. They tied these little brooms all summer long.

Everything they did, they did together. The little one brought them the tiny branches, prepared beforehand, and the parents tied them silently and mechanically. In the summer, no matter where you looked, these little brooms were everywhere. The cottage was muffled in them, and the *pryz'ba [earthen embankment abutting the cottage]* was smothered with layer upon layer of these riches.

It seemed that their entire life, their future, was vested in the green oak forest that year after year renewed itself in the spring and extended to them its thick, bushy branches; they clung to those green twigs and relied on them for their livelihood.

In the wintertime, she spun thread or tore feathers for a Jewess she knew in the city. He played the dulcimer at weddings and, from time to time, hired himself out to haul something with his old roan mare. The latter happened infrequently. His cottage was a long way from the city, and people rarely called on him. Occasionally, he hauled coal into the city.

Things were wretched in their home during the winter.

They slept through most of it. The only living creatures that gave rise to some activity were the mare and the dog. Someone had to feed and look after them.

The mare, like a good housekeeper, roamed freely all day long around the cottage, looking things over here and there, poking at this or that, either near the *pryz'ba* or by the forest, and, once in a while, glancing with her intelligent, shining eyes through the window into the cottage.

As for the dog, he raised a ruckus over even the slightest rustling of the trees. His barking tore savagely into the gloomy depths of the oak forest, drove timid does into a frenzy, and lingered like a threatening echo in the stillness of the forest.

Late in the autumn, the man's elderly mother, who spent her summers begging and her winters with him, had wearily made her way to the cottage. She had fallen ill recently, suffered a stroke, and could move only one hand. She was waiting for death to claim her, and a candle burned by her side almost continuously.

Now, lying all alone in the cottage, she was waiting for them to return.

They had gone to the city to get an advance on their brooms. The money would be needed to pay for the mother's funeral. A coffin had to be built, the priest had to be paid, a funeral dinner had to be served . . .

Promising to tie a thousand small brooms, they managed to secure fifteen gold coins. Ordinarily, they would have been paid twenty, but this time they got less, because it was still winter, and the money was given in advance.

And now, they were on their way home. They were halfway there, in the middle of the boundless plain.

They were returning happy and contented. He felt as if he had completed a difficult task and struck it rich. He had so much money now! Never before had he had so much all at one time . ..

But his mother was dying—or maybe she had already died? He would bury her properly, as a good householder should, so that people would not laugh at him—because, for some reason, they were always poking fun at him. But that did not matter; everything would be fine now. And he felt important and could almost see the funeral.

He saw the church banners by his cottage, and a lot of men with bared heads. One man was carrying a cross. Beyond that, he did not see anything, nor, at the moment, could he think of anything more.

Yes. His mother had died.

And he did not want anyone to say that he had not given her a proper burial. His own, dear mother . . .

He was also bringing back twenty or so candles, a chunk of meat for the funeral dinner, some flour . . . and a flagon of whiskey.

***

Back at the cottage, the dog, plaintively howling with hunger, was leaping up and lunging in all directions, almost snapping the worn rope that held him; but no living being appeared. At times, he stared unwaveringly at the cottage door, hoping it would open and someone would throw him something to eat; but the door seemed to be shut for all eternity, and the dog wailed with impatience and grief.

A flock of ravens, like a black cloud, perched themselves on the branches of the trees surrounding the cottage and wearily bristled their feathers. Ferocious, muted blasts of wind screamed through the forest, and dry branches cracked, as if jarred by an unknown intruder . . .

Then night drew near—a menacing night, unlike any other.

The violent gale was not abating. The cold, like searing flames, destroyed everything, and the wind churned the snow mercilessly.

A white squall blew in from beyond the forest and flung itself at the cottage. It tore at the walls, shook them, and tried to break open the door or a window. Did no one in the cottage hear it? Was there no one inside?

The snow had blown in from the wide endless fields and was seeking succour. Dreadful things were happening out there . . . on the open plain.

It was quiet and dark in the cottage; the candle had gone out.

Darkness, having risen in columns, stood motionless in the corners, and twilight settled in the middle of the room.

Lying on the sleeping area atop the clay oven, the old woman did not move her gleaming dark eyes from the window.

She heard everything.

The window was nailed down, and she could not open it; barely clinging to life and straining to cross herself with her one good hand, she called to the cloud of snow: "I hear you," she said, "but I can't help you; go back."

The snow cloud raced off, leaving behind a deathly silence in the cottage; a moment later, another squall blew in.

Everything repeated itself. The shaking, the groaning, and the roaring in the chimney. Fistfuls of snow flung themselves at the windows, and a wave of pandemonium careened around the cottage. Even if it burst in its fury, it was determined to claim the living being inside . . . The cold, striving to freeze everything for all eternity, pressed itself tightly around the panes, and the wind, whistling shrilly, urged it on. A moment later, there was a loud crash followed by a mournful tinkling. On the side of the cottage facing the forest, a window broke loose, smashed to the ground, and shattered into tiny fragments . . .

***

The fields were fraught with peril.

An unparalleled struggle erupted in the air. Snow clouds, swirling madly and shattering into fragments, lunged at each other like dragons; sheets of snow zigzagged erratically, spreading wide their wings and opposing the pressure of the violent wind. But the wind, powerful and enraged, swept them up on its way, flung them to the ground, and then, with a triumphant whistle, lifted them up once again and scattered them over the immense plain.

The small mare struggled mightily amid the white swarms of snow. Step by step, she hauled her heavy burden, no longer sure where the road was. It was blown over—and she suddenly found herself confronted by an unending sea of whiteness.

Her coat and mane were stiff with frost. Breathing heavily, she plodded on with a lowered head, afraid she might drop at any moment. From time to time she halted, caught her breath, and then, as if sensing a menacing fist behind her, spasmodically jerked forward again. But the wind pressed in on her from all sides, and just when she was about to set out, sheets of snow turned her back in the other direction. She could not see where she was going.

The bells encouraged her, and she listened to them. Coming at her in waves, they sounded like the quiet buzzing of flies in the summer, swarming lazily in the air in the sun's radiance, or annoying her by alighting near her eyes when she grazed at the edge of the forest.

She bolted forward, and it seemed to her that, having increased her pace, she would soon stop near the green forest and the young shoots of tender grass that she grazed on with such pleasure. But no! It was not summer; it was winter—a winter as fierce as fire.

Coarse shouts flew over her head more feebly and less frequently. They seemed to be drifting away. No one, it seemed, was holding the reins.

And, in fact, her master was not holding them. He pulled out the whiskey he was bringing home for the funeral dinner, and all three of them warmed themselves with it. All they had to sit on was a few rags and a heap of corncob husks, and they were frozen to the bone.

The weather had been calm when they left home.

Blowing repeatedly on her numb hands, the woman greedily drank the warming whiskey that he passed her, and the little one, after taking a few gulps, fell asleep. The man pressed the bottle to his lips the longest. After that, he yelled at the mare in a heavy and menacing voice; at times, as if he had suddenly thought of something, his wild, terrified eyes scanned the horizon.

The dreadful blizzard, worse by far than any he could remember, was raging all around him, and he could see nothing. Whenever he stuck his face out anxiously to see what lay ahead, it was pelted by tiny, frozen needles, and his eyes closed involuntarily. His cheeks were flaming from the cold; his ears were numb.

A few times, a thought struck him: "Am I going the wrong way?"

But each time he quickly calmed himself. That could not happen. This mare never lost her way. It was the fourth winter he was driving her. One time, when he and another man, having had a few drinks too many, had fallen asleep in the wagon, she made it home all by herself.

And there was no possibility of getting lost. There was only one road leading through the fields; people rarely travelled over it in the winter—they used it more in the summer when the grain was lying out on the fields—and so they did not have to go off it to get out of someone's way.

There was only one problem—the blizzard was roaring viciously and covering the road with snow. But the mare knew everything; she would get there without a problem. She was always anxious to get home. All cattle were like that.

If only the cold would let up a little . . . His cheeks were aching from it. Something grabbed at his cap and almost knocked it off his head. He barely managed to hang on to it. Pulling it down more tightly on his forehead, he took another swig from the bottle, passed it to his wife, and then, hiding it at his feet, threw the reins around his neck, tucked his hands in his sleeves and, hunching over to shield himself from the wind, sat motionless, giving in to his gloomy thoughts.

Everything behind him in the sleigh also fell silent. His wife lay down to protect herself from the wind and shield her sleeping child—so there could be no conversation. Moreover, the wind stole their words and kept them for itself. They rode like this for a long time.

Once in a while, as if awakening from a dream, he shouted at the roan mare: "Hey, you cripple, why have you stopped?" Or he threatened her in a furious voice.

In his mind's eye, the huge oak forest stood before him like a sombre stone wall, and at the edge of this forest stood his cottage. Then he saw his mother on the bed atop the clay oven. A candle was burning beside her.

He had placed it there himself . . . and it continued to burn.

Then he saw the funeral . . . the church banners . . . the men with their bared heads, and the funeral dinner. He had prepared a funeral dinner because his mother had died.

He is walking among the people, inviting them to eat and drink, and pouring them shot glasses of whiskey. They drink. He continues pouring, and they continue drinking. Let them drink, so that they would not speak ill of him later; as it is, they always laughed at him—but just this once, let them know that he knew what to do. *He was burying his mother.* He had prepared a funeral dinner.

Outdoors there is a blizzard; it is impossible to open one's eyes, but that does not matter. It is warm in the cottage, and he feels warm all over. Warmth is flowing through his entire body, but the blizzard is raging and storming so furiously—it is terrifying . . . The forest is humming . . .

And it keeps on humming and rustling; it never stops. It is a giant forest, and it is its leaves that are rustling . . . the leaves of those precious oak trees!

Oh, that forest, that forest, that forest! Who could tell what kind of a forest it was—who could tell in the springtime . . . So huge and so green! It was his father and mother, and it fed him like its own child. Its branches were broad and green, its leaves were dark and shiny—it was so pleasant to tie those brooms.

They all tie them—he, and his wife, and the little one. But the little one does the least work. It carries the twigs, and, carrying them, plays with them, strewing the path with green leaves. It throws the leaves up over itself, and they flutter down like green butterflies around its head. What does work mean to it? What does it know? All it cares about is to have everything it needs and to be warm. For the sun to warm it. And the sun shone and sent down its warmth . . . so much warmth, that it was a sheer delight.

It flooded your whole body with its warmth . . .

"Hey, cripple, why have you stopped?"

Had she imagined this, or had the wind carried off these words, only to return them now to her ears?

Suddenly, the little bells rang out loudly, as if they had been jolted, as if a handful of them had been thrown in terror to the ground.

And then it began all over again. The heavy gasping that was almost a groan—and her slim legs waded once more through the frozen sea.

It seemed there was no sky.

A dark, gloomy mass hung over the earth. Squalls of snow tumbled over the white plain; others, as if possessed by an indescribable terror, rushed about aimlessly in a mad race, chased by the frenzied blizzard. And the blizzard itself, invisible but fierce, careened about wilfully and erratically, searching for someone, chasing after someone, and blustering in an unutterable rage.

A chase like no other was taking place on the vast plain.

The little bells shook, and then fell silent.

The roan mare halted, as if struck dumb. Not too far ahead of her, a huge black dragon, muffled in sheets of snow, its flame-red eyes blazing with fire, roared loudly, breathing heavily as it sped across the field and then disappeared, leaving behind it columns of smoke. Its groaning and clattering could be heard for a long time afterwards, and then everything fell silent again.

Almost without knowing what she was doing, the mare turned around. Her whole body was shaking with fear. She looked around for help, but there was only the mute wind and the dance of the frenzied snow sweeping into her eyes.

Inching forward a few steps, she hit her head against a tall slim pole. She came to a stop again. Above her head a wondrous harmony poured forth, a bold stream of sounds that did not fall silent. It strummed incessantly, caught up in an unvarying, unconcerned flight across the entire boundless expanse . . .

She cocked her ears and listened. What was it? It was pleasant and appealing, and she had never heard it before, even though this was not her first time down this road. It hummed so loudly and evenly, and it had nothing in common with this blizzard. It did not fear the storm, and flew ever so calmly and boldly through the tempest to its goal . . .

Then she came to with a start.

She had halted once again; in a moment, the voice would thunder at her, and the fist would be raised. She had not sensed it over her for some time. So, any minute now, he would get up, raising those menacing black banners that she feared as she feared thunderbolts.

She lunged forward. The bells came alive and sprinkled her steps with tinkling sounds. She ran a short distance . . .

What was it? She banged her head on the same kind of pole as she had a moment ago, and from it, as before, the same pleasant music flowed forth. A stream of sounds that flowed without interruption, all by itself, in an even unbroken hum across this sea, into infinity . . .

But she was no longer standing still. Straining with all her might, she was pulling once more. At times she stumbled, but forced herself up again. She was seized by a naked terror. It seemed quite clear to her that, instead of a fist, a black, unmoving, conical heap had settled in the sleigh behind her, and, as it steadily became heavier, it stared fixedly at her spine.

She felt something alien on the sleigh, and it was this something that she had to pull. The lucid instinct that had guided her up to now abandoned her. Her eyes sparked, her nostrils flared, her long mane bristled and, leaping suddenly to one side, she fled in a mindless panic.

A frenzied energy possessed her, and she ran; her haunches were almost dragging on the ground, while her chest was breaking its way through the snow. The little bells did not desert her. They struck against her neck and begged her desperately not to stop anywhere, not for even a moment. And when her chest felt as if it would burst, and she slowed down to recoup her strength, the tiny bells fell silent fearfully, as if they were suddenly hiding in the snow. This exacerbated her panic, and she fled mindlessly once again.

The black heap on the sleigh behind her grew larger, flanked on both sides by sheets of snow. Continually changing places, they nestled up to the sleigh and, silently settling on it, covered it completely with their tender whiteness. Only a black tip peeked out from under it—becoming a source of incessant fear for the roan mare.

***

The struggle ended towards morning.

A dull silence reigned.

The wide snowy wings of the clouds fell in white silver to the ground and did not rise up from it again. The gale-force winds vanished. The sky turned a dark slate grey and sank into a sorrowful meditation.

With a crippled gait and a scarcely audible trembling of her bells, the mare dragged herself home.

She came to a stop before the very door.

The dog was lunging at the end of his rope. He had heard the sleigh from afar and welcomed it with wild, furious howls. Now he dragged himself abjectly over the ground as far as his rope would allow him. He whined and whimpered, and his eyes sparked with a strange light. He raised his head and told them his story.

He had waited two days . . . without eating . . . without seeing a living soul. The door over there had not opened after they closed it when they left, and now . . . and now . . .

His barking became even more agitated, painful, and irritating, and he went into a frenzy again, stretching his paws to the roan mare.

"What's happening? What's going on?"

She shook him off with all her strength and dragged herself and her heavy burden to the stack of straw. Her little bells slipped off her neck and fell to the ground, and the sound hurriedly dispersed and then vanished.

***

Night.
A deep, endless sky, serene, but animated. Stars twinkle, shimmer, and sparkle, flying here and there in an arched flight, changing places in the sky.

Among them, the moon remains tranquil.

Its bright, magical light flows gently all around it. The deserted plain, flooded with moonlight, appears silver, and the tall, slim poles, cutting across it in a straight unbroken line, cast slender shadows on it, seemingly holding hands so as not to get lost in the unvarying wilderness.

The far-flung oak forest, adorned with hoarfrost, formed a crystal wall at the edge of the plain, with the tips of the trees, transparent in the moonlight, almost dissolving in it.

At midnight, it stood in petrified immobility and turned completely white.

It saw a mist, an almost invisible silver gossamer, float stealthily past the cottage, assume a most marvellously formed figure, and pass silently over the crystal tips into the empty, illuminated plain.

The moon penetrated it with its gentle light, and then, after glancing into its phosphorescent immortal eyes, hid for a moment behind a cloud . . .

The misty figure vanished . . .

***

A stream of melodious, soothing music flows swiftly along a straight thread far into the white plain; it flows untiringly, without a pause, as if into eternity . . .

Where will it snap?

It is indifferent.

It fears nothing.

There, the Stars Shone Through
Poetry in Prose
(1900)

At the very edge of the forest flowed a deep, narrow river. It laved the roots of the ancient oaks, cooled the banks covered with lush grasses and dense, wild shrubbery—and, on occasion, receded from the shore as if to attest to its vitality.

The dense oak forest imbued it with a distinctive hue. Its water was profoundly green as it flowed along, and only there, where it pressed up against the flat level plain on its left bank, did it glisten from afar with a greyish silvery tone.

On its surface, water lilies flourished, and their wide green leaves spread out luxuriantly.

The level plain that pressed up closely to its left bank was the wide steppe. The Ukrainian steppe. And over it shimmered a lofty, boundless grief and an immutable sorrow.

Where had it come from?

It did not know. It had existed for a long time now. There was ample room for it here, and it spread its sorrowful wings and dominated that empty sea like a tsar.

The river flowed on imperceptibly. It was only when the wind arose and raged over the steppe that its smooth surface wrinkled in pain.

"Why are you suffering?" the verdant oak forest, rustling softly, inquired.

"I am being provoked, but I am unable to overflow my banks," the river whispered painfully in reply.

"Spill over your banks, swirl about, and flood the whole wide steppe, so it will realize that you too are strong," the giant advised it.

"There is too little of me to engulf the whole wide steppe," the river replied sadly. "At most, I would be transformed into dewdrops upon it, and those droplets would beautify it as though they were crystal. I prefer it this way."

"This way? Crammed into this trough and continually guarded by a rocky bank?"

. . . In the bright, moonlit night, a smile swept fleetingly over the river's smooth surface.

"I am deep. Infinitely deep. The narrower I am, the deeper I am. Those broad leaves that, reaching towards the radiant light, rise up on an invisible stem from my muddy bottom and float on the water—they can tell you how deep I am. This is my strength and my wealth . . ."

The oak forest fell deep into thought.

The river was talking about its wealth and smiling, but it was almost indiscernible in that wide steppe.

The forest was its eternal adornment. Full of ancient, silent poetry. During magical moonlit nights, nymphs roamed about on its shore. In its dark, noiseless depths, timorous nightingales sang . . . and, here and there, a mighty, giant oak rose up to the heights from the dense thicket and gazed out far into the empty, grey steppe . . . Was the sunrise still far away?

Not too far away.

But the night was still in its glory.

And well-suited to that night were the steppe's vast sadness and its far-flung sorrow . . .

Sorrow for what?

That the stars did not shine through it. That all the splendour, the opulence that, high up in the heavens, flourished and trembled with an eternally silver glow—the paradise blooming in the indigo sky—did not bend down to it and was not mirrored even once in its mighty, far-reaching expanse . . .

But, at the edge of the forest, in a dark, quiet spot, where the river was the narrowest and the deepest, where it moved forward with its luminous, mysteriously dark surface—there the heavenly light sparkled.

There, the stars shone through . . .

Sadly the Pine Trees Sway
A Fantasy
(1901)

A long time ago, they say, tsars held sway over the forests and mountains.

And perhaps they rule them even now.

In the dark, ancient mountains, inaccessible to humans, and known only to timorous birds, bears, and eagles with a hostile disposition—it is there that they still may dwell. Strolling in their magnificent, costly, sweeping garments and silver crowns, they count the pines and oak trees in their kingdom . . . assigning them their life span, and pausing to rest by large calm ponds that glisten like silvery green mirrors in the thick forest grass; and that is all they have to do.

One such tsar, they say, loved one of the little ponds more than all the others.

He called it "the eye of the sea," even thought it was quite small . . . and hidden in the depths of the forest . . . as if it shimmered, in the midst of the greenery, intentionally and exclusively for him.

On moonlit nights he lingered by it, gazing with pleasure into its depths.

Where the bottom of the pond lay—how deep it reached—probably only he knew. On the surface, it was placid and still, concealing, with this stillness, its profundity.

The tsar saw marvels on the bed of the pond. He bathed his royal image in the mirror of its silvery surface whenever he counted the precious stones in his crown. He immersed himself in the harmonious flow of music that, evoking the strumming of golden strings, reached him from its mysterious depths. And tarrying, he searched for wonders on its fathomless emerald floor.

A magical golden harp lay there and, on moonlit nights, it serenaded him with its wondrous melodies.

For long years it played an exquisite, tender song that could be heard not only by him, but by wild white doves, ferns not yet unfurled, the tips of the ancient fir trees and, on spring nights—the entire forest.

Young does and harts, coming to the pond for water . . . and hearing the marvellous music . . . became entranced . . . and stood transfixed . . .

One day, the tsar's favourite nymph betrayed him.

Amoral from birth, she rushed off in an amorous flight with a forest spirit, abandoning the tsar forever . . .

The forest tsar grieved for her.

In his grief, he agitatedly paced the length and breadth of his kingdom, searching for peace of mind. In this search, his former trust in all things living faded, and he could not dispel the disillusionment gripping his soul.

One day when he came to visit his pond, he glanced at its surface and, pausing in thought for a moment, menacingly wrinkled his noble brow.

It seemed to him that the silvery surface did not reflect his royal figure as clearly as before; his crown appeared to have lost its unique, glittering beauty, and the tips of the tall elegant fir trees and pines were reflected more distinctly in the water than he, in all his regal pride.

"*You have no depth,*" he shouted haughtily, and he stamped his foot.

"You are not 'the eye of the sea,' the eternal 'mirror' of the forest truth, but just a contemptible puddle, like all the others that glimmer with a false, alluring light. From this day forth, I do not want to set eyes on you!"

He shouted this angrily and arrogantly.

Then, with a swift movement of his powerful hand, he broke off a slab from a nearby cliff and, raising it—instead of a stone—hurled it furiously, with all his royal might, into the still, placid, shiny depths . . .

The harsh sound of the slab striking the water echoed dully through the forest.

The silvery surface shuddered and began to churn in its bottomless cauldron and, simultaneously, an agonised wail surged violently from the depths. After a brief, hidden underwater struggle—the agitated bottom cast up a golden magical harp. Its golden strings, broken by the jagged rock heaved by the tsar, and throbbing with sudden, unexpected pain, sprang loose and coiled themselves around the harp; then, after floating aimlessly over the turbulent surface, the sorrowing threads and the harp sank forever in the watery abyss . . .

That night, an invisible forest power transformed the tsar into an eagle.

He sits all alone on a high rugged cliff and, on moonlit nights, his eyes are drawn involuntarily and yearningly to the serene surface of "the eye of the sea."

Since *that* moment, a deathly silence reigns over it.

It neither wrinkles its surface nor shudders . . . And its once serene, radiant mirror has lost its innate gleam and, as if undermined by oozing slime, has faded to a muddy green, and no longer reflects the emerald crowns of the tallest fir trees.

The wondrous music that issued from its depths at midnight and, carried by spring waters, floated delicately through the dense forest like the dulcet tones of a dream . . . is lost. And in its deepest recesses lies the marvellous harp, shrouded by its severed golden strings.

And it awaits the day . . . they say . . . when the tsar's hand will reach into the affronted depths of its bed, raise it up and, with his royal touch, repair its strings for the revivifying song of the Resurrection.

It was created to be played.

And the bewitched forest tsar, in the form of an eagle, sits alone on a steep cliff and, mute in the manner of eagles, yearns for the song of the harp—the harp that his pride sank forever . . .

The green fir trees, having lowered their boughs dejectedly to the ground in mourning, have not lifted them to this day, as they too wait in vain for the enchanting music . . . that seems to have disappeared forever . . . vanished . . . . in the distance . . .

The forest is sad without it.

And they both wait.

He on the steep high cliff, and the harp in the forest's watery depths.

And for countless days and nights, they wait for the magical hour of that special wonder-working *midnight* that might bring with it with the miracle of a resurrection—turning the eagle into a tsar again, and breathing life into the harp and its golden strings, so that, as before, its enchanting melodies might blend with the rustling of the forest.

But the hour does not come.

And people say that, in the flight of time, there is a night that is marked by the blossoming of the fern and the union of tsars and nymphs . . .

It is the night when the tiny heads of the forest harebells ring out and call together all the flowers, known and unknown, to celebrate the splendid holiday of the forest's rebirth; when the sound of water, once muted, but now splashing enticingly on its banks, echoes through the forest, and everything *is resurrected*.

And they say that on that wondrous night, the cursed silent eagle will awaken on his sorrowful heights and, assuming the guise of the tsar he once was, will descend into the deep verdure of the forest, his former kingdom.

And when he passes the overgrown bank of his "eye of the sea," the silenced magical harp will resound once more in its murky waters.

And then, they say, the tsar will relinquish his splendid crown to the fathomless pond, thereby returning the power of song to the golden strings he once so unjustly broke. And then the harp will play for him as it played before, enlivening, as in the past, the still waters and the hushed ancient forest.

Others, however, say something different.

The tsar awoke one night in his former shape and walked with an even gait to his tranquil pond.

He waited there, bending over the lifeless surface, but the harp did not respond.

Then he cast his crown into the depths—but it still did not respond . . .

"Have you turned silent forever?" he called out in grief.

There was no reply.

"Forever?"

Silence.

"Forever?"

Instead of the harp, the pines rustled with a muffled sound and, when he strained to catch the murmuring of the fir trees, to delight once more in the marvellous playing of the harp, he heard only the sorrowful whispering of the pines . . .

"*A magical harp plays only once—it will not play for you again. Depart from us forever!*"

The tsar's crown lay on the muddy floor of the pond alongside the broken harp . . .

The tsar abandoned the forest . . .

As he left, he was followed by a rustling sound.

The moon peeked out from beyond the mountains, glanced into the water, and came to rest on its sleek surface.

Here and there . . . in the greenery on the banks, droplets of water gleamed in the moonlight . . . like golden tears . . .

The eternal sorrowful rustling of the swaying pines gently lulled the forest and, to this day, wherever firs and pine trees grow, they murmur and sadly sway.

I Am Lonely in Rus-Ukraine
A Fragment
(1901)

I am lonely in *Rus-Ukraine.*

I have no soulmates, neither women nor men. I had one unfortunate white bear—just one, only one—and they begrudged me even him.

But there is a mounted figure of him, far away from here. It stands motionless in a Museum of Natural History in Vienna, in the seventeenth room, under clear, clean glass. A giant white bear from the polar sea . . . with huge thick paws and bared claws.

And around him they placed monkeys and chimpanzees, and more monkeys, and more chimpanzees.

And to prevent him from catching sight of his sea and grieving for it, they removed his eyes and replaced them with glass ones; and, with his glass eyes, he gazes continually at those monkeys and chimpanzees. And he's condemned to look, for as long as he lives, at the monkeys and chimpanzees. And, in the end, he'll become accustomed to it.

"There is no sea," he'll say. "There are only monkeys and chimpanzees, monkeys and chimpanzees."

And all of them, as befits monkeys and chimpanzees, call out with him: "There is no sea; there are only monkeys and chimpanzees, monkeys and chimpanzees . . ."

And white seagulls will fly over the deserted sea. Together with the cold sea, they will await the great bear.

I am lonely in *Rus-Ukraine.*

I have no soulmates, neither women nor men. I had an unfortunate white bear—just one, only one—and they turned even him away from me. And they left me only monkeys and chimpanzees, monkeys and chimpanzees . . .

The Blind Man
(1902)

I went blind.

How it happened does not matter. What does matter—and it is a most dreadful thing—is that I went blind.

And with me in the hospital there was another man who, like I, was blind. We felt comfortable when we were left alone together.

"Do you see at least a tiny sliver of the sun?" I sometimes asked my unfortunate friend.

"No," he replied. "And what about you?"

"Me neither."

After this, a silence would descend. Our souls rose within us and mutually sank into one another.

And why was it that we liked to be together in our grief?

Then, my friend was given his freedom. One day, he saw the sun, and they let him out. The people quickly took him into their midst, but I was released only because they decided that I would never again behold the sun; and they gave me—my friends gave me—a pilgrim's staff for the rest of my life.

And I walk about the world.

That is, I meant to say that I move from one place to another. And even though I know that never in my life will I see the sun again, I nevertheless strive to see it.

I open my eyes very wide . . . so very wide, my dear friends, in the hope that I will see at least an illusory likeness . . . at least the tiniest speck . . . that at least . . . at least—oh, what's the use!—that I will see at least a faint flickering ray of the holy sun—but I do not!

I do not see it.

As I go from place to place, I stretch my arms out in front of myself, spread my fingers apart, raise my head . . . It seems to me that, at any moment now, I will catch the sun. Even though I know that the sun will not allow itself to be caught, for it is the sun! I think—any moment now, I'll touch the sun.

But suddenly it is alms that I touch.

I shut my eyes tightly, for tears are welling up in them.

I shut my eyes tightly, for tears are welling up in them—sincere, grateful, humble tears, for the alms.

They welled up by themselves. I did not call them forth. My soul is already dark, even though it is opened wide like my eyes . . . I strain my ears; it seems to me . . . something sunny will break through for me from the bustle of life that surrounds me.

I lower my head helplessly to my chest, immersing myself in my soul in order to grasp the sun and the light with my hearing, even though I know that no blind man has caught the light with his soul, and that I too will not catch it!

O Sun . . .

Now I am calling out to you. Bear in mind that it is not a human voice that is calling—it is the voice of *a blind man*. Scarcely audible . . . as if it were not pleading at all . . . as if it were speaking casually . . . for how can I plead with words, crying: *"O dear Sun, you are my divine, my holy Sun!"* and then add: "I am blind . . ."

It shines on everything.

A tree, people. And over there somewhere, there may be a puddle, and its rays will glance on it as well.

But the sun has an age-old habit—it never shines for the blind.

Then I drown in the depths of my soul.

It is as deep now, as it is dark. As sad as my eyes. But I am opening my eyes before you, my friends. And you see me—but I do not see *you*! I am unable to see you now, and as long as I live I will never see you again. And I am content with the fact, my friends, that I—listen to me—that I will *never*, never in my life, *see* you . . .

It is only my *eyes* that are incapable of seeing the sun, but you, my friends—you have never illuminated either my soul or my eyes.

Across the Sea
A Sketch
(1902)

The day has been clear since early morning.

It is so clear and sunny that the sky—usually an intense blue on days that are fine—is reflected as pure azure in the sea. And this is why the sea is blue, and its surface, glittering with silver, is serene and proud. Its waves chase each other to the shore, splash merrily, and conspire noisily to rush about just as merrily all day long, every day.

On the shore, two white seagulls are sitting and arguing. A larger one and a smaller one.

"I must fly across the sea!" declares the larger male seagull. "I simply have to fly across it! I must alight on the tall cliff on the opposite shore. They say the view from there is unlike anything we have from here, from the sea. And they also say that once you have flown there, you can never return. This means you have to make an irrevocable decision—either you stay here, or there. And I want to go there."

"I also want to go there!" the smaller female seagull cries.

"No," he says. "You stay here!"

Offended, she ruffles her feathers in anger. "I want to fly across the sea with you and alight on the same cliff as you! I'm a seagull too, just like you!"

"So what if you're a seagull?" And the larger seagull, overcome with anger, flaps his wings fiercely.

"You pitiful creature!" he exclaims. "Just look at your wings! You aren't capable of flying across this terrible sea! Do you think it will always be as calm as it is now? Do you think the sun will always be shining as it's shining now, and that the flight across the sea will be just like one of your sea games in which you fly as long as you want to above the sea and then simply turn back?

"No! You must understand—once you have made up your mind to fly across it, there is no turning back. You must also understand that you'll be facing death every minute of the way. I don't want to travel in your company! You will most certainly perish in mid-flight, and what good will that do you? Seek out another companion for yourself, and I'll go on alone. Farewell!"

And, lifting off, he flies away.

The smaller seagull, troubled and dejected, remains on the shore. Examining her wings sadly and anxiously, she sees that they truly are ever so much weaker and smaller than those of the larger seagull.

She looks out at the sea—it is wide, endless, and empty. Then, peering far off into the distance, where the larger seagull is glistening like a silver arrow in flight, she spreads her wings mournfully and widely, and sets out to follow the larger seagull in his flight across the sea.

They are flying . . .

A vast expanse stretches between them, and below them there is the sea. It roars and roars . . . It roars threateningly, and there is nothing amusing in its roar.

"Are you following me?" the larger seagull calls out.

"I'm following you."

"You're flying to the cliff?"

"I'm flying to the cliff."

"That's disastrous! But you have to understand," he reminds her, "I will not be your companion there; I'm flying to the cliff *alone*."

"No, no," she says. "I'm not your companion; I'm flying to the cliff on my own, of my own free will."

They continue flying . . .

The stronger one flies smoothly, high above the sea, as if attached to a thread in the boundless sky, speeding swiftly forward like a silver arrow. Vibrant, tireless, and strong, he bathes his chest in the invigorating air. With a sharp eye he gazes far ahead and into the heights, measuring the distance to the spot where the cliff was to emerge mistily from afar.

But the weaker seagull flies unevenly. Lower . . . higher. Faster . . . slower. Too low over the depths to look up into the heights, and, even when she does lift her head, it is only to see which way the larger seagull is turning. Then her gaze once again plumbs the depths. Once in a while, the arrogant waves splash her with cold droplets of foam, reminding her that she is flying over water.

From time to time, the larger seagull turns to her and calls out, admonishing her: "Remember, over there I won't be *your* companion; I'm flying to the cliff *alone!*"

"No, no," she says. "I'm not your companion; I'm flying to the cliff on my own, of my own free will."

And they continue flying. The larger seagull in the lead, and the weaker one a long way behind him.

The sun rises and sets, days alternate with nights, and below them the rhythms of the sea also change.

"Are you still following me?" the larger seagull, flying on, calls out to the smaller one.

"I'm following you."

"You're not turning back?"

"I'm not turning back."

"Then you must know, I don't *see* you. The expanse before me is so great that it will *certainly* devour your strength; even now it is increasingly taking possession of me and my mind. And ever so far away in the distance, the cliff to which I'm rushing is rising out of the mist as out of a dream."

"As for me, I see the depths," replies the weaker one. "And in the depths I see death. And alongside death, I see the sky. And between death and the sky, I see you."

"So you're not turning back?"

"I'm not turning back."

He flaps his wings.

"You must remember," he says to her. "No matter what, I am not your companion; I'm flying to the cliff *alone.*"

And they continue flying onwards.

Whoever thought that the sea is always calm, sparkling, and unthreatening, that it never assumes a terrifying appearance, is badly mistaken, for the sea is continually changing. On the calm, sparkling surface that glistens at times with silver and changes in hue from blue to green, a terrible storm blew up. The sky darkened, the wind turned into a furious gale, and the sea, raging with the roar of a giant, went berserk. The waves rose in mountainous crests. They clambered over one another, rolled, and crashed. Time and again they crested, and then receded to the depths. Over here, they died away, while over there, they rose up again. And the infuriated white froth seethed on the backs of the frenzied waves and ripped itself apart.

Tumult . . . groaning . . . an inferno under the blackened sky.

And above it all, the seagulls.

They do not see one another, or hear one another. They do not meet one another. The vast expanse separates them, and below them lies disaster.

The larger one is using all his strength to cut through the air, but he is scarcely able to stay his course in the heights. This storm is more than terrifying. He had never experienced a storm like this. It is only now that he realizes fully what a storm at sea is truly like. But what has happened to the unfortunate creature following him? Probably drowned . . .

"Where are you?" he cries pityingly. "Are you drowning? Or have you *already* drowned? And it will look as if I'm to blame for your misfortune! But I distinctly told you: 'I won't be your companion there; I'm flying to the cliff *alone*!'"

He listens, but there is no reply.

"Where are you?" he calls out again.

Once again, there is no reply . . .

Down below, the sea is churning, the water is swirling, and the foam is being dashed about as it rolls in a thick mane on every wave; however, it seems that from among the frenzied waves, right from the midst of the inferno, there issues forth a faint hint of a sound: "I'm here!"

"Way down there, right over the sea? Because I'm way up here, in the heights, far above that inferno!"

"No, I'm flying over the very depths. I'm coming to know the inferno. My wings are already covered with a mortal sweat, and it may well be that I'll soon perish. I am no longer flying with my own strength; the whirlwind is carrying me along!"

"What did I tell you? I am not to blame! I am not your companion; I'm flying to the cliff independently, alone!"

"No, no," she calls. "I am not your companion; I am flying through the inferno on my own, of my own free will!"

Then there is silence . . .

The ferocious storm bends their feeble wings and toys with their strength. At times, it throws them high above the depths and then carries them downwards, just above the foam. Finally, it calms down and stops its savage sport.

The stronger seagull reaches the cliff. He alights on the summit and sees that the cliff to which he has flown is the cliff of death. And his powerful wings wilt instantly, and he shudders in his death throes . . .

A few minutes later, as is to be expected of someone weaker, the smaller seagull flies up. She arrives just as the stronger seagull is in his final agony.

"It is good that you have flown here," he says, "for now on *this* side I won't die alone!"

"It is good that I did not remain there," she says, "for now on *that* side I won't die alone!"

"But you must understand," he says to her, "I am not your companion, but neither will I take you to your death!"

"No, no," she says. "I am not your companion, and I will meet my death alone!"

Beyond the Boundary
A Sketch of Village Life
(1902)

Winter.

The elderly priest from the village of D. trudged slowly and wearily down a village road skirting a forest. The going was difficult, for the road was badly drifted with snow. For the past few days, the snow had fallen continuously, as if it were being strewn by an invisible hand, and layer after layer piled into white drifts.

No matter where one looked—it reigned supreme. Beyond the small village huts, huge white mounds sculpted by the wind rose upwards and glistened with a cold, crystalline sheen under the moon's glow.

The frost stung and burned, and only those who had to ventured outdoors.

And the elderly priest had to.

Two householders from the village, one young, and the other old, had stopped by his home and asked: "What's to be done about a stranger, a poor man who has drifted in from heaven knows where and is now lying half dead on the forest road not far from the cottage of Gloomy Magdalena? Some sickness must have struck him down just beyond the village. It's obvious that he was ill when he collapsed in the middle of the deserted road near the forest."

That is why he had to go and have a look at the poor fellow. Perhaps his tracks would show where he had come from, or perhaps he might still be able to say something . . . Perhaps he might even be able to rise to his feet and continue on his way.

A stranger like this, who appears from out of nowhere, is nothing but trouble for a village. He could die, and then one would have to bury him without getting paid for it; one would have to go to a lot of trouble for only God knows what kind of sins . . .

He did not like to work without getting paid. He was old now and, even more to the point, of what benefit was it to him—that was the point!

"Whew! What a road, what a terrible road! This is God's punishment coming down on us, God's punishment!" he grumbled, wheezing and leaning heavily on his sturdy, iron-tipped cane. His long white beard was frozen stiff.

"But it's Holy God Himself who has given us the snow," the young man ventured. "Maybe it will do the earth some good in the spring?"

"Oh sure, 'it will do some good,' you fool! You sin, and drink, and rob, and steal, and bear false witness against one another; you don't give offerings to the church—and you think that fate and bitter cold are going to bring you some *good*? It would be better if you didn't prattle such nonsense!"

The young man fell silent.

He crossed his hands and shoved them up his sleeves, lowered his head, and tried to lean into the sharp, stinging wind burning his face. He had no desire to talk; the truth was, he was afraid of the priest.

His companion—a garrulous old fellow who was the village watchman—glanced obliquely at the priest and then spoke up: "What were we supposed to do, Father? We couldn't consult the bailiff, because he wasn't at home. And as we live close to you, we stopped in for your sage advice.

"He isn't one of ours, Father. He's a stranger. One can't drag just any old stranger—and a sick one at that—into one's home. One can drag in a lot of trouble. The two of us, I and this young fellow, were on our way to the forest. And we saw a man lying not far from Gloomy Magdalena's orchard . . . almost on the village boundary. We drew nearer . . . looked . . . and saw he was *not* from our village."

"And not from the neighbouring one!" the young man added pointedly.

"And not from the neighbouring one!" the older man repeated. "Instead of a fur cap, he was wearing a straw one, and instead of a wool coat—a cloth one."

"From *Galicia [Halychyna, Western Ukraine]!*" the young man once again interjected tersely.

The older man picked up the story: "I said, 'That's right.' Then this young fellow said, 'Perhaps he's frozen to death!' 'Or maybe he got sick,' I said, 'and dropped dead'."

"Or got drunk, or got drunk!" the priest cried out in an exasperated voice as he stopped to catch his breath, for the road was beginning to wind uphill between the fields.

Both of the village men burst out laughing.

"Maybe he wanted to get warm," suggested the older man, "and the whiskey rushed to his feet and knocked him over!"

After a longer period of silence, the priest asked: "Is it much farther to where he is?"

"Well, it's not too far. It's close to Magdalena's cottage, by her small garden, near the *boundary* . . ."

"Which Magdalena?"

"Why, *the gloomy one*, Father, the gloomy one . . ."

"Ah, yes . . . yes!" the priest spoke in a drawn-out voice. *"The gloomy one . . ."* And he fell silent.

He knew her all too well. He had crossed the threshold of her cottage thirteen times. It was that Magdalena—the one who had buried *thirteen* children.

"She has to work hard now both for herself and for her husband, because his hands and feet are all twisted," the old watchman began to elaborate.

"How did they become twisted?" the priest inquired.

"Who knows . . . He went away to work, and ever since he came back—it will be two years on the Feast of St. Nicholas—all he does is lie in bed. He just lies there . . . And his hands and feet are all twisted. She's certainly had her share of bad luck! May the Lord preserve one from a fate like that!

"And to make matters worse, her children keep dying. As for this last one, the one that's still with her—she's on the verge of losing her as well. All that's left of the child is her staring eyes. She's all wasted away and yellow . . . And she coughs and coughs, both day and night. It's terrible!"

"My, my!" exclaimed the priest, and he took another short rest. After catching his breath, he added: "It's still quite far to her place. They built their cottage a long way off from the village—as if distancing themselves from enemies. So, you were saying . . . Her little one is ill?"

"Yes, very ill. She's tried everything, and she's gone everywhere for medicine, but the child still isn't like other children. She even went on a pilgrimage to St. John, the Miracle-Worker of Suchava. It looks as if this child of hers won't live to grow up either."

"Well, if that's how things are, then it most likely won't. But she's a pious woman; she doesn't forget about God. She gives offerings to have masses served . . . and she's a good worker. Whenever one sends for her, she comes immediately. She finds time for everything."

"Yes, she's a good woman, that's true," the men agreed. "It's just that she doesn't have any luck. The children grow up, claw their way out of the worst possible poverty, and then, just as if someone whistled for them—they're gone. She's so worn out from the worry and the expense of it all, that she's becoming gloomier and gloomier. It's no wonder she's called *gloomy*. All she does is christen and bury, christen and bury. I don't know how the earth can bear her weight—her soul is that heavy with grief.

"And her fingers are just as twisted as her husband's, but hers are twisted from work. Death and illness have devoured everything in that home. If it weren't for the child with the staring eyes, she would lie down in the ground as well; it's her child and her work that keep her alive. And that seems to be her lot in life."

"That's some fate!" the younger man sang out.

And once again there was a brief period of silence; all that could be heard was the laboured breathing of the priest and the thumping of his iron-tipped cane on the frozen road.

"Why is it that some people have no luck from the time they're children—like Magdalena, for example?" the older man once again took over the conversation. "Just think: she was left an orphan and had to hire herself out when she was ever so little. And after she married, death began pouncing greedily on her children; then, for some unknown reason, her husband's hands and feet got twisted. Why is that? She's *pitiful,* and that's all there's to it. And they say her children are as wise as adults—that they 'know' everything."

"Because they're meant to die!" the young man commented impatiently. "Ask any woman whose child has died, what it was like while it was still alive. And listen to what she tells you. It was thus and thus—it knew this and it knew that, and it saw this, and heard that . . . while an ordinary man grows old and wastes away, and he still doesn't know all that!"

"It's the power of God!" the watchman replied piously.

"Hey there! Can you see Magdalena's cottage yet?" the priest called out suddenly from behind the conversationalists.

This unwelcome trek was making him irritable.

"Yes, we can! We can see it!" the village men hastened to inform him.

And truly, the thatched roof of a little cottage, partially covered with snow, seemed to spring up like a mushroom at the edge of the forest.

"Well, it looks as if we're finally there!"

"Magdalena's house faces the forest," commented the younger man.

"That's because the boundary with the neighbouring village is just beyond her garden. You see, the fierce storm that's lying in ambush at our very backs is actually in another village," the older one responded. "The fallow land that extends up to this point belongs to the other village. Her house stands right at the crossroads. She listens to the wolves howling in the forest and to fate roaming about at night.

"You know," he explained further, "that's why she's plagued by so many misfortunes. They say that good luck shuns those who live on a boundary; it pulls either in one direction or in the other, but gives nothing to the one who is on the boundary.

"Oh look, the poor fellow who's lying over there can be seen now. Praise God we finally got here, for the priest would not have wanted to go any farther."

They came to a standstill.

It is quiet all around, except for the hum of the forest . . . The dark giant breathes with an icy coldness, immovable—like a wall. A narrow village road runs past it and, by the edge of the road, stands Magdalena's cottage "with its face turned towards it." Beyond the cottage, there is a wretched little orchard that backs up to the fallow land of the next village.

At that moment, however, Magdalena's cottage does not interest anyone. It is still a good two hundred paces from the three wayfarers.

The three men turn their attention to the stranger in the white cloth coat lying motionless on the roadside at the edge of the forest. His face is yellow, contorted with pain, and seems to be numb. His hands are clenched.

It is a pitiful sight.

"Lord Jesus Christ!" the young man exclaimed, and he crossed himself.

"His soul is ready to take flight!" the other man said.

"Hey, hurry up there! Shake him, so we can find out if he's alive or not . . ." the priest ordered impatiently.

Now that he had seen the stranger, he understood everything. A destitute peasant wayfarer had fallen ill while travelling and had toppled over in this spot. His shabby clothing, the worn bag at his side, and his emaciated face, yellow as wax, told him everything he needed to know.

"Is he moving?"

The older man touched the stranger gingerly and exclaimed: "He's alive!"

Then he called out: "He's moving!"

There was a moment of tense silence.

The priest was deep in thought, and the men said nothing. They looked with curious eyes at the poor stranger lying there, his groans barely audible. It was quite extraordinary.

Where was he coming from? Who was he? He was neither old nor young . . . it was possible he was returning home from some job. His hands were smeared with wagon grease, as if he traded in it. And this was what lay in store for the poor fellow on his journey . . .

Suddenly, without saying a single word, the priest rapped his cane testily. The men looked questioningly at him, and then the older one bent over the stranger once again.

"He's alive, Father, he's alive," he assured him once more. "But he's not far from death. His lips have turned blue . . . What should we do?"

"What should we do?"

"We should bring a candle, so he won't die without one!" the younger one interjected solemnly.

"You fool!" the priest rebuked him.

Then he twisted his old lips in disdain.

"They wander off someplace," he spoke through clenched teeth, "they wander off the straight and narrow, waste their lives, and in the end they become a burden on others. *Who will assume responsibility for him?* Who will conduct his funeral? Who will take on all the expenses?"

The men gazed at him, their eyes bulging in fear, and did not utter a word.

The priest's eyes blazed with an angry light; his long white beard shook . . . He bent over even lower and, raising his hand high in the air, pointed his long cane at the fallow, drifted field of the neighbouring village.

"*Beyond the boundary*," he whispered in a cold voice brimming with shrewdness. "*Drag him beyond the boundary* . . . Let the *neighbouring* village rack its brains over what to do with him."

And, turning away from everyone with an exasperated movement, he trotted back down the white road at a good clip.

The men stayed behind.

They stood for a good minute in silence, with an indecisive look on their faces; then the older one came to his senses.

"Shall we lug him away?" he asked

"No!" the younger one replied. "He isn't lying on my land."

"Nor on mine—that's the first point; and the second one is—who knows what kind of fellow he is?"

* * *

At that moment, Gloomy Magdalena was in her house, weaving. From time to time, she fastened her worried gaze on her thirteen-year-old daughter, clad only in a long shirt. The girl was sitting on the ledge of the oven, tearing feathers and breaking the silence with prolonged spells of coughing. The man on the bed was lying silently, his face to the wall.

For some time now, in a little lean-to by the small shed where the family's single treasure—a cow—was housed, a dog had been howling nonstop, seemingly unable to settle down.

"It's howling as if it's caught the scent of wolves," the invalid observed from the bed.

He spoke in a manner which assumed that the others were thinking the same thing he was.

"Go and have a look at how it's holding its head," he said to his wife. "If it's raised—it smells wolves nearby; if it's lowered—it smells death."

The woman, who was not expecting death, glanced at him and then turned to look at their child. Even though the young girl was ill, and even though she was coughing day and night, the mother was not expecting death. Lord Jesus Christ, what would they do if the child died!

She set her work aside and stood up. Tall and dark, her entire figure was submissively stooped, as if she carried the sins of several generations on her shoulders and was asking forgiveness for them.

At one time she had been beautiful. Her black hair, sweeping over her young back and chest, had shimmered like silk; her gentle, dusky face had radiated youthful energy, and her eyes—her wonderful, beautiful, dark eyes—had burned with the flames of strength and hope. They were flaming now as well, but with the fire of inextinguishable grief.

"Mummy, I'll go outside with you!" the young girl called out animatedly from her perch.

She lifted her head, and her eyes—dark stars like those that flamed in her mother's face—shone on her mother.

"Why, my daughter?" the mother asked gently. "What for? You can see how cold it is. The wind will strangle your chest and make you cough more. I'll go myself. I have to run to the village for salt anyway. There's no salt, and no coal oil. You stay in the house and take care of daddy. I'll go myself, and I'll come back right away; listen to me, my little daughter."

She threw a long black wool coat on her back and, winding a white cloth carefully around her head and her doleful face, walked out of the house.

When she was by the shed, she glanced at the dog, and it seemed to her that it had calmed down. Then she set out for the forest road that led to the village.

Having gone barely a few hundred paces from the house, she almost stumbled on the unfortunate stranger and, stopping dead in her tracks, called out in fright. But she stayed where she was. One glance at the man's clothing, at his emaciated yellow face and, like the priest a short while ago, she immediately guessed the stranger's situation.

Various thoughts swarmed in her head. "Who is he? Where was he coming from? What was wrong with him? Had he collapsed from hunger? Had he become ill?"

And then it occurred to her: "Was he dead? *Truly* dead?"

At that moment, a powerful feeling swept over her soul, took control of her feelings, and commanded her to do one thing: to get the unfortunate man into her house. To get him there as quickly as possible.

She did not think about the consequences. Bending down over him, she stared at him with her large eyes, worn out from worry, and as she did so, she held her breath. He couldn't be dead. God is magnanimous.

Then a bitter smile contorted her lips—his chest was rattling like a boiling kettle . . .

She glanced around in despair. Was there any chance that someone might show up to help her? She wanted to drag him into her house as quickly as possible. Evening was approaching, the frost was stinging bitterly, and the stranger was fading . . . growing numb.

She could not see a soul.

It was quiet everywhere; over here, there was the dark gloomy forest, and over there—the drifted fields and the fallow land.

O Lord, save him!

"My dear man . . . uncle, " she pleaded in a voice filled with indescribable tenderness. "Lift yourself up a little. I want to take you to my home. To my warm home, uncle, and I'll give you some warm food. Just raise yourself a little . . . just a wee little bit . . . Just raise yourself, my dear uncle!"

She tried to lift the sick man and carry him herself, but she could not. He was dead weight in her arms, almost chained to the spot.

She looked around once again.

Her wide dark eyes, fixed on the village road, pleaded desperately: "Hurry and help me, my good people! This poor man is dying! Come quickly and help me save him! Come, for the love of God!"

All she needed was a tiny bit of help, and she would be able to drag him home. She would lift him by his back, under his shoulders, and if someone took his feet, they could get him to the house. Just a tiny bit of help! He would come to, say something, and everything would be fine.

"Oh, do hurry, do come, my good people!" And she looked around again and again. It was impossible for her to drag away the sick man who was already parting with this world. This was a sin! It was bad enough that he was dying as a stranger on the road, like some wild animal.

Suddenly, something that was white against the background of the snow stirred not far from her cottage. It stirred, and then it grew bigger and flung itself towards her. Spreading its little arms as if it were in flight, it rushed right at her.

"Mummy . . . mummy! I'm coming!"

The mother cried out in surprise. Her child was flying to her like an angel. And then she grew numb with sudden fear. The child was just in her shirt; she had only thrown a kerchief on her head. This was her only child . . .

"Run back to the house and bundle up!" she shouted.

But the little one did not listen. She ran straight to her mother and came to a stop beside her.

With the help of her child, the woman was able to drag the stranger to her cottage and place him on her own bed.

* * *

Three days later, in the morning, a small group of people from the neighbouring village were going down the distant fallow field to market.

"That's how things are . . ." said one man when they approached the boundary not far from Magdalena's cottage. "Magdalena had a funeral again."

"What are you saying, old fellow? What funeral?" one woman cried out. "Did she bury a child?"

"No, not a child this time."

"Lord Jesus Christ, so now she's buried her husband as well?"

"No, not her husband! She buried a stranger. Didn't you hear?"

"How could I have heard? What was I to hear? What happened, old fellow?"

"Oh," the man's voice rang out, and he pushed his cap to one side. "Well, you'll regret you didn't hear about it, for you could have dropped in to Magdalena's for the funeral dinner; but, as it is, you missed it. And the funeral dinner was really something. She buried the poor stranger so beautifully . . . And, my goodness, she went all out for the funeral dinner! She didn't stint on anything!"

"What stranger? What kind of a stranger? Tell me, old fellow, because for some reason I didn't hear anything about it."

"Well, if you didn't hear anything, then it's your loss," came the quiet response. "They say she ran out of the house to look at the dog that wouldn't stop howling, to see if its head was raised or lowered. But when the dog saw her, it ran into its lean-to, as if it didn't want its mistress to see that it was foretelling a funeral in her home.

"Then she set out for the village to get some salt and coal oil, because they didn't have any left in the house. And, on the road not far from her cottage, she came across a sick stranger who was lying there, close to death.

"Well, she took the poor fellow into her home. They say she cared for him just as she would have cared for her own father. She tended to him, warmed him, and fed him, but he didn't say so much as a word to her. He just groaned and groaned. And then, when he fell asleep on the third night—at about midnight, they say—he didn't wake up again. He crossed over into that other world."

"O my God!"

"That's how it was."

"And he didn't say what his name was?"

"No."

"Nor where he'd come from?"

"No."

"Nor where he was going?"

"He didn't say anything. He died as if he were groping his way to death. And he didn't leave so much as a single word behind him when he died. Figure it out, if you can!"

The woman sang out in astonishment. Then she sighed and crossed herself.

"It would be terrible to have a man like that in the house!" she added in a frightened voice. "May God forbid! I'd die of fear. Who knows what kind of a fellow he was? Or what he had in his soul? There are lots of people roaming around—both good ones, and bad ones. No," she added vehemently. "I wouldn't have taken someone like that into my home. Who ever heard of such a thing—to take a stranger in from the road. Especially from the road!"

"Well," the man replied, "you see, she did take him in, and she had a funeral for him, and a funeral dinner . . . And she gave an offering for a mass for him, and she paid the priest all by herself. She paid him despite the fact that she's so poor. They say she took her last quilt to the Jew to pay the priest for the funeral! They say that, after that funeral, her house is as empty as a beehive. She didn't have much to begin with, and now, even what she did have has gone for the dead man."

"God!"

Silence.

* * *

When they were returning in the evening, a woman stopped them not far from the cottage of Gloomy Magdalena.

"My good people!" she said. "Even though you're strangers, don't pass by Magdalena's cottage without saying a prayer. Go and step in to see her and say the *Lord's Prayer* for the soul of the departed. Magdalena's little girl, Nastunya, is no longer alive. She died at noon today."

The people stood as if they had been turned to stone.

"What are you saying, my good woman?"

"At noon today. The other day, right after the funeral, she got a fever, and she ached and burned with it until Holy God took pity upon her."

Shocked, the people cried out in sympathy, and one woman wrung her hands.

"May God forbid! This was her very last one. If you had seen how the woman lamented, how she carried on! You would . . ." the woman broke off her story and burst into tears. "Her grief was raw, like an open wound. She went mad—pounded her head against the wall and screamed. Her screaming made your hair stand on end. And her husband trailed off quietly to the shed and is still lying there. It's all over now."

With these words, the woman finished her story and rushed off.

The people who had been to the market were left in stunned silence.

They walked on without saying a word to each other. They did not step in to Magdalena's house. It was as if they did not have the courage. Every one of them glanced fearfully and curiously at the cottage and at the small windows, filled with light, and then they continued on their way.

"I'll go tomorrow!" they all said to themselves.

It was only after a lengthy period of silence that one person spoke up. It was a white-haired man, the oldest one in the group.

"I'm telling you, my good people, that there's something strange about this Magdalena," he said. "I've known her for a long time, ever since she was a little girl. I'm telling you—she's been bruised and bloodied this horribly for some *sins*. And don't you go and think that it's for her own sins. Nor that it's for the sins of her father or mother. No. From the looks of things, this has been going on since those ancient times that neither we nor she can remember. She's suffering *for the sins of others*.

"And, you know, she's been carrying that burden since she was a child. And that's because she took it over from her mother. Her mother wasn't from these parts, and she left her when she was just a little tyke."

The neighbours sighed without saying a word.

"And it always turned out," the white-haired man continued explaining, "that everything was different at her place. Just look! She even built her cottage near the forest, far away from other people, as if she didn't want to belong to a community. She was alone, on the boundary.

"And the poor man who married her—he was a good man, and wise—well, you know what happened to his hands and feet when he grew old. They became twisted. And take even this trouble with the stranger—it was her lot to have to deal with it. He had to collapse right by her cottage. She had to come outside and find him. She, and no one else, and she had to take him into her home."

"May the Lord forbid!"

There was another silence. This time, a pious one . . . A resigned silence filled with fear.

"But how will she be able to have a funeral now, old man?" a female acquaintance of his inquired. "They say that everything she had in her home went to take care of the stranger. The priest won't bury someone for nothing!"

"She'll sell the cow," the white-haired man replied.

"Why sell the cow, when she'll manage to do it without any money?" one man who had remained silent up to now spoke up.

"How will she do it without any money?"

"Well, it's like this. She'll have to pay people back for it. All the people will give her something . . . The priest will wait . . . And when the spring comes—she'll work off her debt. Don't worry—it's not the first child she's burying."

The woman looked askance at him.

"You haven't figured things out very well, old fellow, if you're saying something like that," she responded. "After the death of this child, Magdalena will no longer go out in the fields to hoe! She may have had the strength and the will to do so at one time but, after the death of her fourteenth child, it's all over for her. She lived and breathed for that child, but now it's all over . . ."

"The deceased will be buried one way or another, never fear!" the man replied, a faint note of derision in his voice. "Even though her house is as empty as a hive after the death of the stranger, the child will still be buried somehow."

The wind rose up with a sudden violent blast from the fallow field and roared in a wide current. No matter which way the even field stretched, it tore down it in a crazed flight and continued roaring: *"Beyond the boundary! Beyond the boundary!"*

My Lilies
Prose Poems
(1903)

Give me a desert!

A distant, boundless desert with a searing sun . . . without tumult and without life—let me weep.

There I will not have to look into anyone's eyes.

Neither the eyes of a mother with a prophetic heart . . . nor those of a father, ever ready to do battle for the happiness of his child . . . nor the eyes of the brutal, vapid, prying mob . . .

I will not encounter anyone.

I will bury my face in the scorched earth and refresh it with my tears . . . until they cease to flow . . . and drown my mortal grief, and me.

And the sun will drink of them, imbibe them without end . . . the sun, avid for pain.

***

Trust?

It is a little child with candid, innocent eyes, who, gathering thoughts and feelings into its shirttails, runs to the one who calls it.

The child does not repress its words. It laughs and cries artlessly—it does not know how to do otherwise; this is the essence of its existence, its entire beauty, its wealth!

And it waits.

Its large eyes look trustingly, without any hint of sorrow, directly into the eyes of the one who calls it. It waits eagerly. It does not know for what. Perhaps for a moment of happiness. Or for something else, something lovely and holy like its soul, brimming with genuine pearls.

But no.

The mighty hand of disillusionment rises and falls like a heavy stone on its bright head . . . on the one guided only by honesty, and justice, and faith in its own sunny perceptions.

There are three kinds of love.

The one that feeds on caresses, the one that feeds on kisses, and the one that, grim as death, nourishes both itself and others. It nourishes itself with tears, and grief, and sorrow, and loneliness, and, beyond the grave, with the golden shadow of memory—recollections about its holy, immortal power.

***

Solitude—is empty?

Who can prove this?

Just listen what a cloud of tears rises from it, swirling madly!

And how many countless white marble hands cut across its expanse in convulsive pain; and the veils of torn dreams that sway back and forth, back and forth; and the swarms of thoughts that surge into it with brutal strength, scourging themselves mercilessly, rushing to get somewhere, faster and faster . . .

Where?

God Almighty! Where?

Listen!

Shut the doors, huddle together, hold your breath—and listen!

A doe is running through the forest.

Through the cheery, lush green forest—in search of something.

She runs, crushing and trampling flowers under her feet. Rustling the leaves on trees, she whispers something. The sombre branches of the trees in the ancient forest sway imperceptibly.

But now she has stopped.

Has she arrived where she was going? She does not know.

She thinks she has. Startled into headlong flight, she had bounded ahead with high, erratic leaps, but now she has stopped.

Her eyes are opened wide.

She waits, so taut that she trembles.

What is this?

A shot rings through the forest.

Something begins to crack, to collapse silently—and it is collapsing on her, always on her.

Wide-eyed, she suddenly sees what she has not seen before and hears what she has not heard before.

The quiet forest is filled with something she has not known until now.

And the blood drains out of her.

That is why she had to race through the green forest.

Listen!

The Thoughts of An Old Man
(1903)

My dearest children!
You take no notice of me, but I keep watch over all of you. I am left among you like a solitary, ancient oak tree in a young forest, able to see all its treetops, its agitated movements during a storm, and its slight stirrings in times of fair weather.

I am saying: I see you doubly. I see what lies ahead of you and what is happening to you now, and—what is more—I can see the footprints you are leaving behind you.

I am chained to a chair by a lengthy illness, and my one and only activity is *to watch* you, to think about you. About your past, your present, and your future. To watch you grow, and to contemplate the results of your growth.

You, my seven sons—a Biblical number—and my three daughters, embarked on life a long time ago, and now you are exactly at the midpoint of your lives. But I have outlived seven of you. I have outlived you down here. Up there, however, where we shall all meet one day, I am always with you. This is why I have all of you in mind when I am talking to you.

My dearest children!
You take no notice of me, but I keep watch over all of you. It is true, that recently I have been watching over you with only my own eyes, but until not so long ago, I also watched over you with the eyes of your mother. Together, the two of us observed your growth, and we rejoiced and wept over you.

Your mother was like a figure from the Holy Scriptures, with a soul that was pure, like that of Mary, Martha's sister, about whom Christ once said that she had chosen "the better part," as she attended His holy teachings; but she also had the hands of Martha, who never rested, rushing about from morning until evening, tending to the work in their home. She was a spotless white flower that I plucked along with her roots from her family's home and transplanted into my garden which was strewn with stones. She put it all in order with her own hands, so that you, my dearest children, would have wide open paths on which to grow and develop—that is what she was like. Delicate but energetic, kind but firm, gentle but severe, and as wily as a snake.

You grew.

At first—like flowers that we lovingly tended, and then—like birds. Later, you gathered together in small groups to be on your own. But we still observed you, and we saw how you continued growing and how you lived.

My dearest children, do not say that old age sees nothing and cannot understand the young! That its spirit lives only in the past, is indifferent to the present, and has no comprehension of the future!

My dearest children! A person should strive not only to continue the family line, but to improve it as well. *This was our goal when we were rearing you.*

You, our seven sons and our three daughters.

And so, in every one of you, we implanted a feeling of national pride, and then we proceeded to carve and form your characters. We intended to make you exemplary models, commendable patterns for *your* progeny. This was the most difficult undertaking of our life, the one requiring the most skill. As we raised you, we had to transform ourselves variously into children, philosophers, and artists, and, at times, cast ourselves in the moulds of saints and martyrs.

Your descendants were supposed to be better than you. Whatever was lacking in you was to be perfected in them by you and your life's companions, who were to have a cultural level commensurate with yours.

We were still "biblical" and primitive.

We submitted to the saints, feared *God's wrath*, believed in miracles, *in fate*—our souls had a childlike quality, naive at times, to the point of being ludicrous.

We knew only the Holy Scriptures . . . But, you were already more informed . . .

My dearest children!

You take no notice of me, but I always watch over you. Without erudition, without affectation, without a newly conceptualized individuality, a newly espoused philosophy—with just our "unaffected" eyes *that learned, over countless years, to discriminate* among all manifestations and shades of human character and life.

I shall begin with you, my eldest son.
O my first-born son! I want to say just a few words to you, and to recall your mother while doing so.
Her life revolved around you, and she trembled over you before you first set eyes on God's world.
In this world, it is only a mother who can understand maternal feelings, so what *else* can I tell you about her?
It seems that in this world, there was no child more beautiful under the sun, than you. This is what she always told me.
Once, when you were a small boy, you ran out of the house into the street, and she ran after you, just as playfully, to catch you and, at the same time, to act as your guardian angel, there on that wide road.
Just then, a lord she did not know drove up with an expensive team of four horses, and you rushed towards him. She screamed like an insane woman, and the carriage stopped. The lord stepped down from the carriage and picked you up in his arms. He gazed in wonderment at your little face, at your eyes, clear as the sky. And your mother, half-petrified with fear, could not move from her spot.
Then the lord led you up to her and said: "I do not know who you are, my good woman. But if I had a child like this I would be as proud as a tsar. But I am a beggar. My only child has died. *Raise him so that he brings glory to you . . .*"
And he drove off.
And we tried to raise you to bring us glory.

I was like a "tsar" among all of you. Stern, but, I think, kind. I kept an ear and an eye open for all of you, and for each of you individually. I had a hand that rewarded, and a hand that meted out punishment. And I used my head both day and night. And all I thought about was the future.
I fashioned your upbringing for the future, I prepared your minds for the future; you were to become "quintessential human

beings," I often said smilingly, "to become models for your future great grandchildren. Examples for your nation!"

Everything—for the future. Do you think, my dearest children, that it was only for yourselves? Oh, no! For your fatherland and for your nation. For this unfortunate nation that is always demanding its fate, but cannot exact it . . .

You became a musician when you were still a young boy. You learned how to become one somewhere outside of our home. We were poor! There were more and more of you . . . We exerted ourselves and worked with all our strength . . . We lived for you, as I have already said, so that later you could live for others. You worked for yourselves with your tiny, childish strength, and we laboured with our mature, untiring, conscious strength.

Did you follow in your parents' footsteps, my son? Did you develop the inclination to strive for what was good, for everything that is better and finer, to give up advantages, comfort, and a trouble-free existence in the cause of noble qualities and benevolent ideas? I think you did.

This is why you struggled until you attained your goal. And when you completed your preparation for manhood, you became a dignified, noble, and serene man. You also attained material wealth, but this is a matter of secondary importance. I am interested in your psychic life.

You wanted to gain the world with an instrument under your arm. You were ruled by the great and holy sounds of music.

What did you want to become in the field of music, my son? A reformer of our folk music? Did you want to direct the attention of other nations to our great, innate musicality and the rich treasure house of our melodies?

Oh, my son! I feel like screaming aloud in pain when I see what has become of you after all of our joint efforts, after all my hopes.

I can still see how you, as a young lad, used to gaze clearly and lovingly into my eyes, your own eyes smiling and full of thoughts and dreams, and you would talk about the future as your father talked. And now I shall only repeat my earlier words: "My dearest children! You take no notice of me, but I always watch over you."

I saw you when you stopped seeing me, and life, the eager life that prods and pulls one to action, that gives one no peace and drives one on to goals, conclusions, accomplishments, carried you away. You did not have the time to look after me, but I watched over you. And I saw. A *woman* came to you.

My son! *How many eyes did she have? How many lips? And she had seven heads and a beautiful body.* And you had only two eyes and a weak, male body . . .

My son! You never faint from hunger and cold. Untroubled, you enter your opulent house, and your eye comes to rest appreciatively on the gleamingly pristine objects in your home—and so for a short while you satisfy your physical needs; but, my son, why is your violin silent? Why has it fallen asleep in its dark coffin, why are its strings broken, and why has the horsehair grown slack on its bow? Why do the walls of your home never hear a good word about your neighbour? Why does no question *about the fate of your nation* never fly through it? Why does not so much as a word of your *native language* ring in your home? And why does the spirit of unselfish altruism, the spirit of inner life, tender beauty, and noble ideas stand with lowered eyes, its wings drooping hopelessly?

And you are content, my son! Oh, my son . . . *You are content!*

I would fall to your feet with my arms outstretched like a cross, and I would plead: has your soul—formerly so vibrant and so sensitive to the pain of humanity, so idealistic, so full of awareness of life's emotions—gone blind?

If it has gone blind . . . then . . . O Lord Jesus Christ, heal it.

But the Messiah no longer treads upon the earth. It is not possible to touch the dear holy garments in order to be healed; it is a fellow man who must awaken a man's soul from its deathlike state.

Oh, my son! I, your white-haired father, am lying outstretched like a cross before you, and I am calling to you: "O my son . . . Awaken! It cannot be true that your beautiful soul has died, and that *seven heads, and seven lips, and seven eyes* have sucked the life and the consciousness out of it . . ."

Perhaps it is my old eyes that have gone blind and no longer see well. Perhaps it is they who are fooling me and whispering that my grandchildren, your *children*, shrug off indifferently the songs of their grandfather and great grandfather, and do not want to hear the stories about justice and injustice, and even less—prophesies about the future! That their souls, like young saplings, have been bent to one side by an unknown hand, that they have willingly allowed their crooked tips to be twisted to the ground, as if they did not see the heavens above them and were avoiding all heights! This is why an elegant crown will never unfold on their heads, and eagles will not fly over their tips . . .

Perhaps I am wrong, my son, perhaps I have gone blind. But if I have gone blind, my soul has not, and *it alone* has known you well and *will know you well*, even after everyone else has forgotten *what you once were like*. My pain for you is red, like blood.

You have drowned.

I pray for your dead soul . . .

II

My daughter!

Your father and mother told you: do not marry that man. Death has imprinted its mark on him and is just biding its time to take him away.

But you answered decisively and calmly: "It may well be that I shall live only *one* year with him, but I cannot give him up—I will not forsake him. *For I love him!*"

You wrought a miracle with your words . . . You married him, and the Lord was kind enough to grant him five years of life. In other words, five times as long as you expected. Then his time was up, and death came silently, unannounced, and took him away.

Your insane cry, when he left you, burns in my memory. Your shriek was so visceral that he must have heard you with his spirit; and it must have been so, for how else could he have visited you! You told me afterwards that, in those moments when you are alone, you always feel his presence in your home . . .

What I am saying is that your soul has been augmented through your suffering, and this is why you can sense him.

Your life together was pure and harmonious, and even though you took no notice of me, my children, I always watched over you.

Your minds were nurtured to the same degree, your inner beauty was developed to the same degree and tuned in the same key.

But then . . . You adhered, through some kind of wonderful instinct, to a secret rule that can perhaps be expressed in the following way: you always maintained that it was necessary *to do something more in order to love one another reciprocally*, to understand each other reciprocally, to merit one another reciprocally. You did not regard yourself as being married, you did not think that you had "fully understood" each other, that you were already completely deserving and worthy of one another. No. *You always left something between yourselves, something that was unattainable, still to be understood.*

You knew that harmony cannot exist, cannot stay alive, unless people who want to live *harmoniously* together allow an element of mystery to remain between them.

You never allowed frankness and forbearance to be effaced between you, but at the same time you always left something behind in the place where your thoughts and feelings resided, something that manifested itself in your constant reciprocal longing for each other's company.

Because of this, you maintained that often inexplicable "inner beauty" that we call "delight" or "charm"; for you both retained the *pure instinct* to remain forever appealing to each other. I saw this, my dearest children. Now this harmony is reflected in your children.

You were left alone with your children. My dearest children! You take no notice of me, but I always watch over you.

I see how you, having been left all alone, strive to do your best, be it with your younger or grown children. I would say that you gaze at them with two sets of eyes. One—your husband's, and the other—your own.

Your husband's—so that through his spirit you would be a companion and an educator of his children; and your own—so that they would draw spiritual nourishment and moral values from your character.

I see how you are straining yourself to mould the little ones, and to sink, with your entire soul, into the inner being of the older ones in order to comprehend them fully and secure their future. And I can see from afar how their future is being put in order, because it has behind it an entire array of past events. And you are doing well to accumulate tenderness and refinement from the outside and inculcate these qualities in them, so that they will be beautiful and healthy.

My dear grandchildren!

I see you and I love you. But you do not remind me of my childhood. In some ways you are more perfected, more mature, and clearer in your feelings and thoughts. You are, in some ways, more complex, but also more sure of who you are. Your soul has been augmented by your mother.

But at the same time, I see a distancing of your mother from me, and of you from your mother! *Look behind you, and do not sever the golden skein that binds her to me, and you to her—and, in this way, to our people*, in the way that my unfortunate son has lost sight of it, and because of which the stamp of our people has vanished from the face and the soul of *his* children.

Sing the songs that I sang as a child, that I transmitted to your mother, and she passed on to you, and when fate arrogantly scatters you—you will come to know yourselves through these songs, and your mother will come alive to you, and your grandfather, and your great grandfather, and all those who belong to you . . .

Do you understand?

And what else did I wish to say to you?

I do not know. Perhaps I have already said everything. But listen.

For a long time now, people have striven to unlock the secrets of nature. Now they are attempting to discover the *laws of the soul*, and later—but by then there will be no trace or memory left of me—they will discover the laws of society.

Your grandfather suppressed his feelings and feared becoming overly tender—you, his grandchildren, are striving to temper this bashfulness and point to the finest, tiniest note in your souls . . .

But, perhaps, it is good to do it this way. Perhaps this is why your soul has become augmented . . .

I remain like a giant oak tree in a young forest, and I can see how the forest is unfolding, and into *what* the tips are unfolding.

My dearest children! You take no notice of me, but I always watch over you. You are so preoccupied with *yourselves* that you have forgotten the words of God: "Love your neighbour as you love yourself." You love your neighbour only *through your individuality*. Your heightened individuality conceals the wider horizon from you with a veil, the veil that Christ drew back with His love . . .

My dearest children!

I think about you as my soul is inclining towards its departure. Everyone crossing over into eternity is a prophet . . .

Do not lose sight of the golden skein behind you . . . So that you do not lose your mother, and your father, and your grandfather, and your great grandfather . . . And your future will be intact.

I see your future in golden contours, veiled in the mist; I see how your souls are being augmented, and how you . . . like those tiny ants, move diligently towards it . . .

I pray for you and for your augmented souls.

III

My white dove!

You fly about the green forest, but you have no place of your own. You encounter people here and there, but you have not alighted anywhere in order to give your pure white wings a chance to rest.

But I cannot say that my soul is wilting with grief for you. You are flying—because you are strong; you are flying alone—because you fill your aloneness with yourself.

You, my youngest, have remained *alone* without a life's companion. Who is to blame? No one. You were assigned this fate when you were still a child.

It is said . . . that there is no fate, that everything is a matter of chance. But I—whose eyes have been open for so many years, and who has followed more than one fate in its journey—I am telling you that fate does exist. Yes, it does. *It exists in one's character.*

You searched, above all, for a soul similar to your own, but you did not find it. You brushed by it here and there with your soul, but you could not blend into a complete harmony with it. *It was in this that your fate lay.*

It seems to me that your soul is of a future type. It is not the power of your mind, but your feelings, that alienate you from the present.

And I see farther.

The period of a woman's youthfulness is a matter of perception, and at some point the time will come when her youthfulness, those "years of grace," will become lengthened of their own accord. The inner beauty of the soul, which up to now has been kept in bonds, is increasingly becoming the real power that prevails in love.

Until recently, the unattractive face of a girl could not expect anything from a man other than a bullet in the forehead. But how many of them are there nowadays, these unattractive but intelligent heads that live and blossom *now* on the foundation of their inner spiritual beauty and goodness? And many women themselves stood in the way and did not permit men to discover the soul in a woman!

But this is not what I wanted to say. What it was is this: I am no longer able to protect you with my love. My strength has faded, the black angel awaits me, and I want to hand you over to the care of *those closest to you.*

My brethren!

I am handing my youngest child over to you, to your care. Do not forget these words of mine—*I am leaving her to you.*

Take care of her in such a way that she will not feel that she has been orphaned, *left without a father and a mother,* and without a male companion.

Take care of her without scorn, without cruelty, without the present and past heartlessness that honours only youthfulness in a woman and does not see the soul.

Respect her with the kind of love preached by Apostle John— a love that is patient, independent, that does not proceed immodestly, that is not self-aggrandising, that is not selfish, that does not turn bitter, that has no evil thoughts, that does not rejoice at injustice, but delights in the truth. A love that withstands everything, believes in everything, that hopes for everything, tolerates everything; that never ceases, even if all predictions cease.

For truly, if you spread all your wealth at her feet and even presented your body to be burned as a sacrificial offering, but did not proffer her love—all your efforts would come to naught . . .

It is with these words that I am making my request to you, my brethren—that you care for my youngest, solitary daughter.

My dear white dove!

Come to rest wherever your strength permits you to.

Do not act against your better judgement, and do not shutter your soul, but let it remain open to those close to you, for otherwise the laws of your soul and its turmoil will remain an eternal mystery, in the broadest meaning of that word—and you will become a slave of narrow traditions that limit your life to one plane, and, if you should gain a son, a one-sided mother.

My dearest children!

You take no notice of me, but I always watch over you. Like an oak, an ancient giant in a young forest, thus do I remain among you, and I see your every movement and, as I put each one in place, I am able to envision your future.

Recall your ancestors, keep our history alive, and do not sever the golden skein . . .

I pray for you . . .

The Cross
A Sketch
(1905)

I died.

All those who respected and loved me, appreciated and hated me, wronged and defended me, were now seized with the same grief for me. And so they came. They filled the rooms, placed wreaths at my feet, and whispered sadly among themselves. As always, women and men—*they* are everywhere.

But that is the way it is.

I was interested in the ones preparing orations to declaim over my grave, and in the girls and boys. The former were thinking only of themselves, wondering what kind of an impression their speech would make on those gathered here and forgetting completely about the deceased. The youthful boys and girls were eyeing one another.

Some of them were mournful, and their eyes were damp with tears. Sensitive girls! The gravity of the moment attuned them in this way, and they immediately succumbed.

But, if the truth be told, no one here was thinking about me. I had left behind neither a wife, nor children, nor a sister, nor a brother—and I had buried my parents a long time ago. I had lived alone—and died a rich man.

But still—my funeral did distinguish itself in a number of ways.

A large throng of people walked behind my coffin.

And everything was black—all black. The hearse that carried me was swaying, weighed down by the prevailing sadly respectful mood and the costly wreaths. I'm saying *costly*, because the money spent on them would have shod several dozen tiny bare feet and brought joy to more than one orphan or some helpless, elderly woman about whom no one cares. But flowers for a deceased are good form, they say; they meet the standards of propriety, and this is why they trailed after me . . .

I felt truly blessed.

Everything was going along like clockwork, of its own accord. Decently and mournfully, as befitted my merits and my person. Even I was beginning to feel better and better with every passing moment.

Yes, as I have said—my funeral did, after all, distinguish itself in some ways.

Many eyes looked upon me in life, and many looked at me during my funeral—but not a single pair of eyes was clouded by so much as a tear.

Not a single pair of eyes.

***

At last, they buried me, and the time came for dividing up my possessions.

And once again the room was overflowing with my friends, acquaintances, relatives, and others.

Once again there was pacing, cautious and respectful, and whispering, half-grave and half-nervous. It seemed as if I were still here somewhere, still among the living.

And truly, I was here; I was alive and saw what was happening. *That one* took away my valuable books; *another one* took some other priceless item; *this one* rummaged in a desk for something she simply had to have to remember me by; *those* were conferring how to divide up this and that between them; and *others* were scheming, wondering how they could come away with something without drawing any attention to themselves. Everyone hurried and gloated, and all were grateful to me that I had left them exactly what was most appropriate.

I felt truly blessed.

With every passing moment, I was feeling better and better—and I was reconciled to my death.

Good.

This was, probably, my best deed.

Finally, all the rooms were emptied. Had I not done the right thing by dying? The guests were preparing to leave, carefully holding on to whatever keepsake or treasure they had inherited from me.

Was there nothing left? After a moment, a voice, that seemed to be calling for order, replied: *"Nothing."*

And all eyes turned for the last time to search greedily all the rooms and nooks.

Was there truly nothing left?

"Nothing," a voice replied once again.

Then I glanced all around to see if everything had gone as it should have. Had anyone been short-changed?

Good.

They had forgotten nothing. They had taken it all, removed everything, made a clean sweep—the emptiness gleamed.

Only a tiny ray of sunlight, like a single thread of the most precious gold, crept into my study and sank timidly into a corner.

It was pointing to something.

My weary gaze dragged itself there.

What had been left behind?

Something remained there.

I drew nearer and peered into the corner.

They had left it! Without so much as touching it!

My cross.

The cross that I bore all my life, suffering and falling under it; *it* remained here now, untouched by anyone, forgotten—and it waited . . .

And I waited along with it.

Would none of those who had been here return to take *it* away from me?

No one returned.

All around me it was quiet . . . very quiet—and I was left all alone with my cross.

All alone—and a tiny ray of sunlight.

I felt truly blessed . . .

In the Vale
(1907)

Dedicated to V. and O.

A forest.

A forest of birches, chokecherry shrubs, oaks, and many other kinds of trees.

In the autumn, leaves turn yellow, rustle, and drift to the ground. At times, sparkling in the light with a profusion of colours, they blaze like flames in the sun.

Among them stands a solitary pine, forever green.

"Why are you green?" the trees attacked her one day. "We all turn yellow in the fall and shed our leaves. Do you want to distinguish yourself in the forest?"

"I am a pine," she replied in a dignified manner.

"What's a pine? Aren't you a tree like the rest of us? Don't you grow out of the ground? Aren't your roots in the ground? What is this!"

"I am a pine," she replied in the same dignified manner.

"All our lives, we've shed our leaves every year, and we aren't about to change our custom. You're the only one to play at staying green. It's a joke and a mockery! Impostor!"

Laughter rolled through the forest.

In late autumn, when snowflakes began to fly, settling on branches in a fine down, the trees were in an uproar, because the pine retained her apparel.

"You still aren't shedding your needles. It's time that you did! We've long since done away with our greenery."

"I am a pine," she replied once more.

Then they began to buzz: "Get away from here. You're not a tree—you're an intruder. You don't have an inherent right to be here; it's impossible for a genuine tree to remain green at this time of year."

The pine tree decorously lowered her branches to the ground. She had grown here for a long time and had always been green. Her needles had become sharp, inimicable to careless jostles, and her tip rose to the heavens.

She felt all alone in the forest. But, because she was the tallest, an eagle, flying back and forth, often rested on her uppermost branches. He enjoyed alighting amid her copious greenery. From her crown, he could view the entire forest.

He was a proud, austere bird that did not like the vale and avoided contact with birds that chirped in the oaks and trembling poplars. In a word—he was the king of the birds.

One day, the old chokecherry shrub spotted him on the tip of the pine.

"Look, an eagle is nesting on the intruder's tip!" she shouted. "Isn't this putting us to shame? Isn't it an insult to us? Come to your senses, everyone! Just look how many beautiful young trees there are in the forest—birches, aspens, chokecherry shrubs, beech trees, and alders. But no, he's made his nest on the intruder. Have you heard about it? What kind of a tree is she? Come on, let's chase the eagle away from the pine. She's stolen the king of the birds—she's robbed us!"

"Robbed us! Robbed us!" echoed through the forest.

"I am a pine tree," the pine spoke up.

"A pine tree? And what of it? What services have you rendered? What kind of lumber would you make? To last from today until tomorrow? All you've done is pushed yourself upwards. Hey, all of you out there, come to your senses; he was our eagle—she's robbed us!"

"Robbed us! Robbed us!"

"I am meant for eagles," the pine tree said.

There was a fresh uproar.

"For eagles? What do you mean? Don't we have anything on which nests can be built? Don't we have aspens? Don't we have elms? And beech trees?"

Once again, the pine tree explained that she was a pine.

***

A hunter was walking through the forest. The trees turned to him with their complaint.

"Transgressions?"

"Oh, yes! That one over there; the one that's pushing herself upwards."

A second voice: "She's stolen our eagle, the king of the birds; she's robbed us, robbed us!"

"She's robbed you of your eagle?"

"Robbed us, robbed us!"

"Where is this eagle?"

"Up there. On the intruder's tip."

The hunter was armed. His power surpassed even that of the king of the birds.

"Kill him?"

"No, that would be a pity. Perhaps we can tame him."

"Tame him, tame him!"

"And where will he live?"

There was another uproar.

"Look at all the aspens we have! And here's a young birch. And over there—a splendid, fragrant chokecherry shrub. And what about me? I'm thick and wide, and lumber from me would last a hundred years."

"Fine. We'll have to chase the eagle from her tip."

A shot rang through the forest. The crown of the tree shuddered. The eagle did not so much as stir a wing.

The hunter fell into a rage. He decided to set fire to the pine, so the eagle could never return.

He set the pine on fire . . .

Hey, hey, what a conflagration! How the pine blazed! In a flash, she turned into a martyr. Flames surged like banners through her spreading branches, and golden sparks showered in arcs over her crown. Smoke billowed with a desperate rush into the heavens, but there was no help to be had. Boiling resin streamed down like tears, and the pine flamed like an immaculate sacrificial offering. She burned down to a stump.

It grew still in the forest. Still and prosaic. The far-reaching rustle of the pine was heard no more.

No longer would she appear in her greenery in the winter, no longer would she lovingly gather eagles in her arms.

And what about the eagle, the king of the birds?

Angrily beating his wings, he flew away, never to return.

It was impossible to tame him.

Building his aerie high on a cliff, he guards his solitude.

His eyes blaze if anyone approaches him from the vale.

Proud and unassailable, he will never change. He has forgotten the ones he left behind—the aspens, the chokecherry shrubs, the beeches, and the oaks.

But in his faithful heart one thing will never be extinguished—the image of the splendid sacrificial offering that died in the lowlands . . . and his contempt for the vale.

Spring Accord
(1910)

My house.

Surrounded by linden trees and firs—the latter a memento brought from the mountains and planted by my grandfather—it looks out on a magnificent, far-reaching plain.

I imagine that the steppe spreads out like this—similarly to this plain of ours.

Away off in the distance, my eye can just make out a cluster of peasant cottages.

A long, long time ago, when I was still a child, an oak forest stood proudly on this plain. Then—I can see it as if were today—the oaks continued growing in circumference, and the forest thinned out. But when I returned as a greybeard to these parts, the forest, like my ancestors, seemed to have sunk into the ground and vanished. All that remained was a barren plain.

It is said that, in days gone by, when the first young oaks were growing, Sobisky fought here against the Turks and, from those ancient times, there still remains the occasional burial mound to serve as a reminder.

Now, as I have said, it is a plain that resembles the steppe . . .

It is spring; the fields are green. Somewhere on the horizon the song of a meadowlark rings out. In my mind's eye, I see the song as silvery translucent pearls cast into the air by an unknown hand and, *here and there,* pouring down as sounds that reach our ears.

Through the fields and green plains, a path winds its way.

I am not able to discern it with my naked eye, but it is there.

For example, right now, when I look carefully, I am able to distinguish, quite far off, a man, followed by his wife; they seem to be floating in the direction of my house. In half an hour or so, they will pass by my house at some distance from it.

It is scorchingly hot outside. He is in a sleeveless fur jacket; she is wearing a red kerchief and a black wool coat.

Today is the market day.

Farther down the road, about an hour's walk from here—they will be there, at the market.

Why?

They do not have anything to sell . . .

Still . . . and they themselves do not really know why . . . they are going . . .

Primarily, because it is a market day; because there will be an opportunity to see this person and that one, to chat for a while, and *to have a drink.*

And they float through the plain that is brimming with vitality and reawakening life.

"Did you take a few eggs with you?"

I can almost hear how the man, without turning around to look at his wife, shouts to her.

He is walking in the lead, and she, in keeping with the age-old custom, is following humbly behind him, carrying those "few eggs" in her colourful bag.

They continue floating down the plain; above them stretches the heavenly cupola and, beneath them—the ground . . . the greenery. And the working day is so enticing, so splendid, that it seems to be shouting: "Don't waste time; do something!"

They are indifferent.

It is thus every week. And then there is Holy Sunday, and the days pass by as if flowing into each other. And nothing changes.

At home, the children are alone, without supervision. Work is waiting for productive hands, but they just walk along and sink ever lower and lower—first in the level plain and, later, when my eye can no longer observe them, *at the market* and in the tavern.

They do not return until late in the evening and, sometimes, not until nightfall.

Time rolls on. It does not wait for even a moment.

During the day, and during the night that seems to conceal in its wake everything that has been created—and that which waits to be created—something presses ahead . . .

In the evening shade, the fields turn greener; the buds on the trees unfold more fully, the grass grows taller . . . ever quietly, ever pushing forward and farther, as if in accordance with an invisible plan, a contract—none of this stops, even for a moment.

Only a peasant never changes. Today he is the same as he was yesterday, and his life will be no different *tomorrow*.

Is it from *toil* that a murderous hand rises up against him?

Is it from the earth—that magnificent, green, fertile earth?

No.

It rises from him, from within. It grows out of his inner being. Out of the thicket of idleness and indifference in which he grows, but does not unfold. It rises from him alone.

He fears progress. Not with the clear consciousness with which he differentiates grain, but more as a matter of instinct. Progress reaches out for his traditions, in which he unconsciously finds support; it wants *to destroy him—to recreate him*. He senses this unclearly, instinctively—and he looks for help.

What will give it to him?

He does not know.

Education?

No.

He fears it.

It is difficult. His instinct holds him back. It will transform him and his children, and they will be ashamed of his coarse clothing.

No, not education.

The gods?

Perhaps.

They have hidden powers that his simple mind does not discern, but his feelings approve. He knows only his material existence—and nothing more. Where the finer, concealed paths and roadways of the gods lead—and whether they are good or bad—he does not know.

He is happy with things the way they are.

He is nature. He develops, blossoms, bears fruit . . .withers, sheds his autumn leaves . . . expires . . .

He *is nature* . . .

From on high, the singing of meadowlarks rolls like pearls through the air, and vanishes . . .

The power of life is in everything.

Oh, how wonderful. Almost overpowering.

Life is good—both for those who bow to the gods and those who bow to knowledge . . .

Spring blossoms for everyone. And everyone creates. *There*, something materially great . . . and there, something spiritual . . but the power of life is everywhere—it exists, it strives . . .

Where is its source?

No one knows. And it would not make any difference if they did.

When is its zenith, its end? This also is unknown.

It is as it should be. It does not change.

It is blind, mighty, great—eternal . . .

Sing on, O meadowlarks, sing on!

Old Parents
(1910)

Old Kostyn, or Konstantyn, as he was known in the village, kept his distance from the villagers, even though he himself was a peasant. He kept his distance, not only because he lived apart from them—his fields were quite far from the village—but also because there were very few people whose company he enjoyed. He did not like to visit the other villagers very often, nor did he like to accept visitors into his home. With respect to the latter disinclination, he had what he considered to be several important reasons.

First, even though he lived comfortably and harmoniously with his wife, she was a slovenly housekeeper, and he did not want other people to see that her cottage, unlike the houses of other village women, was in a perpetual state of disarray. And, secondly, he was superstitious; he thought he knew a lot of things which he could not talk about with the villagers, and which he preferred not to discuss with them; moreover, he did not trust them. And there were many such *things* that he knew.

For example, no one in the entire village knew the secret behind the droughts that oppressed and scorched the land, and it was only he, in his secluded home on his isolated homestead, who saw and knew a lot. He knew that a certain girl—she must have been immortal—was to blame, because whenever she wanted a drought to occur, she climbed to the highest peak of a mountain, took down the evening star from the heavens, and hid it for a time, and that was what made the drought appear. And it took a lot of pleading, magic incantations, and various other efforts to convince her to return the star to its proper place . . . And then the rain would come down . . .

He also knew all about cereal crops and had actually heard them *growing* out in the fields, because, as he assured me one time, while accompanying me through the deserted fields, he had lived with the land from childhood and, therefore, knew and understood it very well.

"We know everything, sir," he repeated loudly, referring to himself in the plural and taking me trustingly by the hand like a little child who enjoyed a special kindness and love. "We know everything. Because not everyone can know everything—only the one who loves the land, lives on it, and repays it with his whole heart. But not everyone loves the land, sir, even though it feeds everyone. I know for a fact that it's not everyone.

"I've lost everything that I've loved in this life.

"I had a son—and he's gone into the ground. I had another son—and that villain left the village to see the world, abandoning the *land*, and his father, and his mother. And so, in my old age, I'm all alone with my wife and my *land*. And that's why probably no one knows the land as well as I do.

"That's why I say—*once* I did manage to hear the grain growing. I'll tell you how it happened. One day in the summer, I had to spend the night out in the field, just when the corn was forming tassels. My main reason for going there was to find out, for certain, where wild ducks were flying from to my pond, and so I settled down on the ground among the cornstalks and lay there. And, at first, I wasn't thinking about the corn at all—neither about how it grows, nor how it ripens; I was puzzling over the wild ducks and a lot of other things that I can't even remember today.

"I lay there.

"It seemed that the heavens were being sown ever more thickly with silver flowers. But I'm a peasant. I'm used to these flowers, so I didn't give them much thought.

"I lay there.

"I lay and listened. But even though I listened, I couldn't hear a thing. Not a single duck, not a single rustle. All around me there were wide fields covered with grain. O Lord, what a crop we had that year! Cereal grains, corn, oats, clover, and all the rest of it—and I lay there. The air was filled with the fragrance of flowering clover—the clover in which, during the God-given daylight hours, my bees worked busily—and it was so still.

"Sir! Those of us who live like this in a village close to the land, who sleep on it, and give it the strength of our hands, we know, sir, what *stillness* truly is. The whole sky, scattered with stars, bends down to us at night, and whoever is not sleeping will hear its strength issue from it . . . It descends to the land and lifts the grain upwards.

"That's why I say, sir, that those of us who live like this in a village close to the land, who sleep on it, and who give it the strength of our hands, we know, sir, what *stillness* truly is. Because it is only then that you can hear the grain grow . . . how it rushes upwards. And I heard it.

"I was lying down . . . lying down just like this, and there wasn't even so much as a rustle nearby; not a footstep, nor a voice, nor a bird, nor a bee, nor any fly could be heard, because everything was resting. All I could see was the night and . . . the stars, like silver flowers, up there with God . . . And suddenly, in that silence, you could hear that something among the leaves *rushed up* softly . . . and stopped . . .

"It was quiet . . . so quiet, sir, as if the holy night had grown weary and fallen asleep and, along with it, the land and the grain on it. And then, all at once, it happened again—something seemed to *shoot up* among the leaves, and then it stopped. It was quiet once more . . . It was resting, sir; yes, it was resting. Then again, like the first time, something rushed up and fell silent. It was resting. And it continued like this, sir, until I realised that *it was the grain that was growing*, the corn cobs that were unfolding, and now I know.

"And a person should never complain that this or that is bad, because God never does anything bad; it's just that we don't know where it's all heading. We know our small business here on earth, but we don't know His business—and His business is big. That's the way it is, sir," and having said this, he stopped and thought a moment.

Then he added: "Now I can no longer spend nights on the ground under the open sky, and I can't work the way I used to. My hands shake, my spine bends all by itself, and I don't hear too well. And what is there for me to try to listen to at night! It's only my eyes that are still good, but it won't be long now before they won't be serving me too well. And it's a good thing that it's all happening in this way, that we move on by ourselves, and *it's not necessary to kill us as it used to be long ago*."

And when I glanced at him with a curious, questioning look, his eyes gazed back seriously into mine, and he continued: "Don't laugh, sir; what I'm telling you is no fairy tale. Now we die when we are to die, but in days gone by, old parents were killed. It's the truth—but not everyone knows it. But I know it, and that's why I'm telling you.

"Sit down and make yourself comfortable, and I'll sit down beside you. We'll take a short rest, and I'll tell you all about it."

After I complied with his request and settled down on the fragrant hay, he found a place beside me and began his story.

Long ago, the way things were, all old people were supposed to be killed; it didn't matter who they were, rich or poor. When they reached the fullness of their years, and their hair turned white, they were forcibly removed from this world.

And that's how it was in one village where a certain lord lived, and where there wasn't a single old person left, because they all had been killed off.

There was one son, however, who protected his old father from death by concealing him in a secret hiding place, a spot that no one knew about except the Lord God and he.

And the year of the famine came.

It was the seventh year that the land had been yielding poorly, withholding the grain. No matter how they ploughed it, no matter how they worked it, it appeared to have turned rusty and yielded less and less. And hunger was slowly beginning to come nearer. And before long, there would be no grain and no seeds left.

And the son was grieved by what was happening.

One day, as was his custom, he took some bread he had saved for his father's lunch, carried it to the hiding place, and said: "Here's some bread for you, my dear father; eat it in good health and continue living. But you should know that things are bad out in the world and on the land, and that hunger is drawing near. There's a shortage of grain, and I don't know if I'll be able to gather together enough seed for the sowing. We have to live, but there's nothing to eat. Tell me, what am I to sow the land with? There's not much land to begin with, but now I don't even have enough seed for the little that we have."

And the father replied: "Plough the land and the path, and then do the following: tear down the straw trusses with which our cottage is thatched and drag them over the field and the path. The seeds that are hidden in the straw are good, because they haven't been soaked. Every kernel will sprout, and the path, if it's ploughed properly, will also yield well; it has many different grains in it. And then, watch what happens."

The son obeyed his father and did everything he had told him to do. He ploughed the land and the path—in which more than one kernel was left from the years they had driven over it hauling various crops—and then he harrowed them with the sheaves of straw from his thatched roof and waited to see what would happen.

The people gathered; they watched him, wondered, and asked him what he was doing, but the son remained silent and waited to see what would happen next. And, before too long, the grain sprouted, lush and thick, and the son rejoiced, and the people envied him.

But then one day, the lord of the village—a powerful rich man—sent for him.

He went, and he stood before the lord.

The lord looked him over, sized him up and, piercing him with his eyes, finally asked: "Who instructed you to do what you did with the grain? Where did you learn to do that? It must be that your father is alive, and you have learned it from him."

The son became alarmed; he thought about his old father in his hiding place and replied: "The Lord God guided me, and I did as I was told."

The lord measured him with his eyes from head to foot, frowned, and said: "That's not true. It wasn't God who gave you this advice; your father must be living in hiding somewhere, and it is he who has advised you and told you what to do."

The son denied this accusation and stood firmly by his words. No matter what the lord said, he continued to say: "No."

Then the lord said: "If it's no, then go home, but come back tomorrow at this same time; and remember—you must come *neither clothed, nor naked*. And if you don't do this, I'll have you killed."

When the son heard these words, he turned cold with fear. Bowing low, he turned around, and went home.

When he got there, he went straight to his father's hiding place. "O, father," he said, "save me! My death is waiting for me. I was at the lord's home, and this is what he told me . . ."

And, sighing heavily, he told him everything that happened between him and the lord, and what the lord had told him to do the following day.

The white-haired father heard out his son, remained silent for a moment, and then said: "God is with you, my son. Do not worry; He will not forsake us. Tomorrow, at this time, take off your clothing, throw a fisherman's net over yourself, and go to see the lord."

When morning came, the son finished all his chores and, dressing as his father had told him to, went to see the lord.

The lord was waiting for him.

And when he saw the son, dressed so strangely, neither clothed nor naked, he yelled: "What is this?"

The son replied: "It is as you said, my honourable lord—I'm *neither clothed nor naked.*"

And he bowed down humbly.

Then the lord frowned and, after thinking deeply for a moment, asked: "Who instructed you to do this? Is your father alive?"

"The Lord God guided me, and I was able to think of how to do it," the son replied humbly.

And he bowed in the same manner as before.

"The Lord God!" the lord shouted. "And it wasn't your father?"

And he riddled the son so severely with his eyes, that the latter turned numb.

"Your father must be alive; it is he who has advised you to do this."

"I have no father, kind sir," the son found the courage to reply.

"You don't? You've hidden your father somewhere, and you're trying to outwit me? I'll teach you to learn from the wisdom of others. I'm asking you one more time—do you have a father?"

"I don't, if you please, sir."

"You don't? If you don't, then listen. Tomorrow at this same time, come to me,' the lord commanded him. 'But this is how you must come: *come neither walking, nor riding,* but simply appear before me. If you don't, remember—your death awaits you."

And, saying this, the lord turned furiously on his heel and strode into his house . . .

The son stood for a while beside the porch; he stood there, and then, lowering his head sorrowfully to his chest, sighed, put his cap on his head, and left.

As soon as he came home, he ran to see his father and told him everything.

"It's thus and so," he said. "The lord threatened me like this and like that, and then, for the second time, he ordered me to come to him tomorrow, saying: 'Come neither walking, nor riding, but simply appear before me; and if you don't, remember—your death awaits you.'

"What am I to do, father?" the son asked sorrowfully. "How am I going to get out of this alive? Now I most certainly will meet my death . . ."

And the poor fellow began to cry.

The white-haired father listened to what his son had to say, thought for a long moment, and finally said: "God is with you, my son. Do not worry; He will not forsake us. Tomorrow, at this same time, select a goat from your flock, sit down on him and, half-riding and half-walking, appear before the lord just as he ordered you to."

The son, heartened by this advice, returned to his work and waited for tomorrow to come.

And he did not eat, but neither did he go hungry; and at night he slept, but he also kept thinking that the lord was waiting for him. Finally, the next day arrived, and his waiting was over.

At the break of dawn, he selected a goat and, at the appointed time, sat down on it, like on a horse and, dragging his feet on the ground and supporting himself as if walking, went off to see the lord.

When he got there, he glanced at the porch . . .

The lord was already standing there . . . waiting for him.

The son took off his cap and bowed.

The lord was seething with anger.

"Aha!" he shouted menacingly, brandishing his fist. "You've come here to ridicule me again? Come closer!"

The son moved in closer. *Neither riding, nor walking*, he remained seated on the goat, moving his feet as if he were stepping along, until he appeared before the lord on the porch. He bowed down humbly—shivering with fear.

The lord's stern countenance did little to reassure him, and his gruff voice did not add to his courage.

The lord studied him silently. Then he yelled: "Who advised you to appear before me like this? Your father? Tell me! He has to be alive somewhere. It is he who told you what to do."

The son remained silent.

Then he said: "The Lord God guided me and helped me guess your lordship's will."

And, bowing down humbly before the lord, he waited for what would happen next.

"Where have you hidden your father?" the lord once again put the question to him.

"I have no father," the son replied.

The lord remained silent for a while, deep in thought. And then he said: "If you don't have a father, then listen. Tomorrow at the same time as today and yesterday, come and bring with you *a friend and an enemy*. Do you understand? Otherwise, I'm telling you for the last time—certain death awaits you."

The son bowed silently, turned around, put on his cap, and departed.

He walked home through the fields, feeling as if he were sinking up to his knees in them; that's how grieved he was by what the lord had said to him. If he did not carry out the lord's will, he would have to pay with his life.

At noon, he took some food to his father's hiding place, but he was so sad and worried that he could not say anything.

Noticing this, his father asked: "Well, how did it go, my son? Did you save yourself from death?"

"I fled from it this time, father, but it looks as if I won't come back to you tomorrow."

And he told his father everything that had happened at the lord's home, and what task he had been given for the next day.

"Advise me, father," he said, heaving a heartfelt sigh.

After hearing what his son had to say, the white-haired father remained silent, thought about it, and a moment later said: "The

Lord God is with you, my son. He will not forsake us. Tomorrow, at this time, go to the lord and take with you your dog and your wife. And we'll see what will happen."

The son calmed down when he heard his father's advice, and returned to his work.

Early in the morning, the son took his dog and, telling his wife to accompany him, set out at the usual time for the lord's house.

The lord was waiting for him on the porch. And when he saw him in the company of his wife and his dog, he turned livid with anger.

The son stopped in front of the lord, bowed, and waited.

"Who have you brought here?" the lord thundered at him.

"If you please, sir, *an enemy and a friend*."

"Who advised you to do this? Your father?"

The son remained silent; he did not dare to reply.

But then, mustering up his courage, he said: "The Lord God guided me and made it possible for me to guess your lordship's will."

"It was the Lord God, was it?" the lord shouted once again. "It's your father who is alive, and it is he who has advised you."

The son, frightened half to death, remained silent.

After thinking for a while, the lord commanded him: "Take a cudgel and beat your dog as hard as you can; but remember, don't show him any pity, or else you yourself will be beaten."

The son did as the lord ordered. He beat his dog so hard that it yelped and howled madly.

Finally, the lord ordered him to stop.

The son threw down the cudgel, and the dog, running a few steps away from its master, sat down and looked woefully at him.

"And now, take the cudgel and beat your wife," the lord shouted. "But remember, beat her hard!"

The son picked up the cudgel and began to beat his wife. He hit her with it once, and then a second time, and the lord shouted: "Harder!"

He had barely hit her a third time, when his wife lunged at him in a fury, screaming at the top of her lungs: "So! *You've hidden your father, and I'm to be beaten for it?* You're going to beat me?"

And she began to give as good as she got.

The son let the cudgel fall from his hands, and the lord burst out laughing and shouted: "So you see," he said, "who is your enemy and who is your friend."

"Go home," he continued. "Return to your father and keep on feeding him and looking after him; God will take him to Him when his time comes. He will not be killed, and neither will other old people . . . Let God take them when He sees fit . . ."

"And so, sir," the old man explained to me, "from that time on, old people leave this world on their own."

"And as for us," he added, "it's time for us to go down that road as well."

The Moon
A Novella
(1910)

I

It happened in the Bukovynian mountains, in the region between the villages of K. and P. in 18——. The forests then were almost impenetrable, and the few roads wending their way in and out of them were rutted and rough.

One day, a young theology student, Nykolay U., was on his way home to spend his summer holidays with his mother. He was the only son of a priest's indigent widow, and she was impatiently awaiting the day when he would complete his theological studies, get married, and perhaps—if God so willed—serve as a priest in the village where she had lived alone since the death of her husband.

Abandoning herself to endless dreams about her child, she envisioned him as a young priest in a long, dignified cassock, with a beautiful and rich wife at his side, and little children that she, their grandmother, looked after and loved boundlessly.

At other times, her imagination showed him to her as an archpriest with a red sash encircling his waist. She saw him driving a splendid carriage with handsome horses, occasionally entertaining the bishop himself in his home, and enjoying the respect and admiration of all the people. His home glittered with wealth, and his walls, wooden floors, and sofas were elegantly covered with beautiful hand-woven *kylymy [tapestries]* of the purest wool, some woven in the traditional geometric patterns of the region and others, more modern ones, with floral motifs featuring red, pink, and blue roses.

And all the presents and donations were from his parishioners who, in a word, worshipped him—her Nykolay—and, it could be said, had looked to him, from his earliest years, as their future priest and father.

Her Nykolay, in addition to being the best child in the world, showed signs of becoming an excellent householder as he matured. Even as a small child, when he came home for the summer holidays, he looked after everything on her little farm. She kept only one servant, an elderly woman with a limp, and so someone had to look after the outdoor work. He was her right hand man, especially during the haying season.

And this year, just as every summer at this time, she was impatiently awaiting his arrival. She could already see him in her mind's eye.

"He's probably sprouted a little moustache over his youthful lips," she thought.

After all, he was in his second year of theology. And he was probably dreaming in his heart about a young sweetheart, about marriage—even though he still had plenty of time to think about things like that.

All this must already be happening to her Nykolay, but he is not here, at her side, and she has not seen him for ever so long. She cannot see his youthful eyes that remind her so much of his father, nor can she caress him as her maternal heart would wish. She has to continue waiting, to count the weeks, the days, and the nights, and be satisfied with the letters she receives from him.

But now she did not have much longer to wait—just a few more weeks, just a few more days. And these weeks and days flew by and decreased in number until his arrival was only a day or two away. Well, it would not be long now. She was already waiting and watching for him.

The day before yesterday he would have left Ch., and yesterday he would have transferred to a hired wagon. Since the death of her husband, the priest, she had not kept any horses and could not send a wagon for him—he had to hire one.

So he was travelling on his own, and all she could do is wait.

And Nykolay actually was on his way.

After buying a few things that he and his mother could not get in the village, and getting all dressed up as if he were on his way to a feast day, he finally left behind the theological metropolis of Ch. Then, brimming with youthful exuberance and feeling like a bird released into freedom, he hired a wagon at the train station for the last leg of his journey.

His mother had her thoughts, and he had his.

He had been travelling since early morning, but it was only now that his eyes came to rest on mountains, cliffs, and forests, and, even though he was still far from his home, he felt he was back in his native land.

How delightfully the air embraced him, caressed his young chest, and stroked his cheeks! He felt unspeakably happy, and his soul was both laughing and crying.

He was finally going home; he was fortunate.

He had freed himself at last from the stone walls which, renowned though they were for their grandeur and splendour, held him like a prisoner, depriving him at times of his individual freedom.

"Drive more quickly, Uncle Georgi!" he begged the man who had agreed to drive him from the station to his mother's home with his strong Hutsulian horses.

"But I am driving, aren't I?" asked the owner-driver.

Hunched over on the wagon-box, he sucked on a pipe and only occasionally flicked his whip lightly at his fat, almost rotund, horses.

"I'm driving," he repeated.

At first they had talked and chattered animatedly, but after a while both had gradually fallen silent.

"Move over and let me sit next to you, uncle," the seminarian spoke up, just as the sun was declining in the west. "It's boring to sit all alone behind you. If I sit beside you, I can watch the horses, and time won't go by so slowly. Who knows what time we'll get home. It probably won't be until very late, in the dead of night."

The peasant shrugged his shoulders.

"It will be past midnight," he said gloomily. "As you yourself can see, the road is bad . . . stony, and one of my horses lost a shoe, and now his foot is sore, and I can't go any faster."

As he listened to the peasant, Nykolay pulled out his watch—an elegant gold watch with a gold chain that he had inherited from his father—and glanced at it. He examined it closely as if he could not see it too well, even though his eyes were still young and healthy, and finally concluded that the watch truly was showing the time to be quarter to one.

"What's this?" he cried in surprise, more to himself than to the driver. "Has it stopped?"

And he peered at the watch once again.

"But I wound it," he said, turning to the peasant.

The latter, not understanding the mechanism of a watch, evinced no interest in its workings, but, seemingly hypnotised by the splendour of the gold, stared wide-eyed and unblinkingly at the watch in the young man's hands.

"I remember very well," the young man continued, "that I wound it this morning before I left. So it shouldn't have stopped yet—not until tomorrow, either in the morning or at noon. But it's stopped at a quarter to one, almost five or six hours sooner than it should have. That's strange!"

"It's stopped exactly at the time that we'll be near your village, young sir," the peasant spoke up and, having said this, cracked his whip over the horses' backs and fell silent again.

A moment later, he glanced over again at the watch lying in Nykolay's hands. Just then, the young man gave it another look, closed it, and was about to slip it back into his pocket.

"Sir!" the peasant blurted.

"What is it, uncle?"

"Show me this watch of yours."

Nykolay let him look at it.

"Let me hold it."

Nykolay handed it to him.

"It weighs a lot," he said tersely.

"It's pure gold, uncle."

"Pure gold," the peasant repeated thoughtfully.

Looking at the young man as if he were listening attentively to him, he once again weighed the watch in his hand and then gave it back.

"Is it expensive?" he asked.

"I don't really know. I inherited it from my father."

"But how much can a watch like that be worth?"

"With the chain, about a hundred and twenty guldens . . . Or maybe even more. I don't know."

The peasant did not ask any more questions.

They both fell silent and continued their journey without saying another word to each other.

The peasant once again hunched himself over, and his back—clothed in a *keptar [sleeveless fur cloak]* that had the fur on the outside—jutted out powerfully. His face was overgrown with a thick beard and, as he rode along, his heavy black hair swung on his back. From beneath bushy eyebrows as black as coal, he occasionally cast thoughtful, searching glances at the young theology student.

Nykolay was riding along, gazing around in all directions.

It was so pleasant, so wonderful, to travel in these parts. Green forests stretched wherever you looked, and the occasional sheer cliff rose up like a wall before your eyes. And then there were the huge boulders that had thrust themselves out of the mountain and looked as if they might come crashing down at any moment, crushing travellers into dust.

All of this fascinated and intrigued the young seminarian, and he was no longer bored.

Suddenly the driver began reining in the horses.

"Why are you stopping?" Nykolay asked.

"It's time to graze the horses for a while," the peasant replied. "Before long we'll be travelling on a difficult road up the mountain and through the forest, so they have to have a short rest."

Having said this, he reined in the horses completely, and they stopped. Throwing them down some hay and pulling out a bundle with *mamalyga [cooked cornmeal]* and *brynza [ewe cheese]* from the depths of the wagon, he too took a rest.

Nykolay had nothing against having some lunch as well. The ride in the bare wagon over a rocky road, the fresh air, and his healthy constitution had given him a hearty appetite. He untied his bundle and, after enjoying a filling meal, got out of the wagon and lay down on the green grass near the bank of the Moldava River that flowed alongside the road.

Lighting up a cigarette, he watched the splendid, roaring mountain river that, gaining momentum as it coursed downwards, summoned up all its strength and moved forward majestically and, at the same time, swiftly and loudly.

It was so pleasant and so relaxing here, and he fell under the spell of the water that, taking on the green hue of the neighbouring forest, appeared to be infinitely deep.

On one side of the bank—the one that bordered on the forest—thrived thick clumps of willows, as if attesting to the deepness of the river beside them.

Nykolay tried to gauge the depth of the water, but its greenish beauty kept flickering before his eyes, and he could not tell how deep it was.

All at once he asked: "Uncle Georgi, is this river deep?"

"It's as you see," the peasant replied laconically.

"It seems to be quite deep in places, but over there, by the bank, it doesn't look deep at all," Nykolay observed.

"There are deep spots there, as well, especially over there, where it's overgrown with willows. On the surface it seems quite calm, as if its power is locked up in it, but just try to cross it, and it will suck you like a bubble into its depths."

"I feel like having a swim before we go any farther," the young man said, casting a look around.

The sun had hidden its last rays behind the ridge of mountains, and only a golden backdrop was left in the west where it had disappeared.

"Go ahead!" the peasant said, but an impatient look crossed his face.

Tying up the rest of his food in a bundle, he rose to his feet and turned to the horses. Then he added: "But don't take too long. I'll just water the horses, and we'll be on our way. I'd like to reach the forest while it's still daylight, so that we can come out of it before midnight. The road through the forest . . . is a long one."

Having said this, however, he did not begin watering the horses, because they had not yet finished nibbling at the hay; instead, he pulled a tobacco pouch out of his wide leather belt and slowly began filling his pipe. Tamping the tobacco, he approached the young seminarian, who was just finishing his second cigarette.

"Give me a light, sir," the peasant said. "I want to light my pipe. You go and have a swim and, in the meantime, I'll have a smoke; by the time you come out of the water, I'll have the horses watered and harnessed, and we'll be on our way."

"Fine," Nykolay said, casting one last speculative glance at the murmuring water.

The mountain river running alongside the forest was beautiful and alluring, and the young man's eye, skimming swiftly over its surface in search of a suitable spot for swimming, rested for a moment on a point not too far from the willows.

It was as if something were tempting him to swim there, as if a desire were growing within him to surrender himself to the water as to a mighty, enticing power. But only for a fleeting moment. The very next moment he shuddered in sudden dread and turned to the peasant who, standing stock-still, seemed to be waiting for something while looking at him inquiringly.

"I won't go for a swim today," the young man said.

And then, as if obeying some inner command, he took his watch out of his pocket, looked at it thoughtfully for a while and, after a long moment, spoke again: "It's almost half past seven; it's a little late to take a dip in a mountain stream. Don't you think so?"

"Whatever you say," the peasant replied indifferently, without moving or taking his eyes off the watch; indeed, he even leaned over Nykolay's shoulder to get a better look at the golden marvel.

Then he suddenly asked: "Sir, how do you tell time on a watch?"

Nykolay raised his eyes, looked at the man, and laughed merrily. "If you'd like to know how, then just wait a bit, and I'll teach you to tell time—it will take only a minute or two."

"Why not?" the peasant responded, and a look of satisfaction flashed across his face. "If you want to," he said, "then teach me. But speak slowly and show me a few times, so that I won't forget by the time I get home."

The young seminarian laughed once again. "Don't worry," he replied without looking at him. "You'll remember what I teach you for the rest of your life. Stand here, next to me, and pay attention."

"Fine," the peasant replied with a solemn, but excited servility, as he moved in closer to the shoulders of his young teacher.

"So—this is a little circle," Nykolay began his explanation, pointing at the face of the watch. "Do you see it?"

"Yes," came the reply in a voice deep as a bass string, but strangely dull and trembling.

"And do you see these two little arrows?" Nykolay continued, pointing at the hands of the watch.

"Yes."

"One is longer, and one is shorter. Look carefully—do you see them?"

"Yes."

"Now, pay attention."

After these instructions, Nykolay glanced seriously and questioningly at his pupil, who was bent down low over the watch. At that very moment, the latter looked up at the young man; their eyes met, and the expression in the peasant's eyes struck terror in Nykolay's heart. In all his life he had never seen such naked desire as he saw just then in his pupil's eyes.

"Uncle Georgi!" he cried in terrified astonishment.

The peasant started in fear.

Was it in fear of the candid blue eyes of his teacher? Without saying a word in reply to the seminarian's cry, he bent his shaggy head once again over the watch in the young man's palm and peered at it.

"Go on," he said. Breathing heavily, as if in the throes of an inner struggle, he stared at the watch as before.

Nykolay began all over again. He stood and explained clearly, earnestly, and patiently, in an even, distinct voice, the way things are explained to intelligent young children who we know can easily understand us.

The peasant watched silently and listened. He seemed to be listening with his whole being, without saying a single word.

Suddenly, Nykolay raised his hand—the one that was holding the watch.

"Where are looking, my good man?" he asked in surprise. "You aren't looking at the face of the watch, but at the inside of its top cover."

And it was true. The peasant's eyes were fixed, as in a hypnotic trance, on the underside of the cover. Made of pure gold, it shone brightly, drawing his eyes to it.

Looking as if he had been caught unawares in some evil deed, the peasant stared in alarm at the young man and then, scratching himself behind the ear, said in a confused voice: "From now on, sir, I'll look where you tell me to, and I'll pay attention. My mind wandered and, instead of looking at the little circle, I focused on the underside of the cover. But you shouldn't be surprised! It's so beautiful and expensive that even if you don't want to, it just pulls your eyes to it. Well, go on and teach me some more. I remember everything you've told me."

Nykolay smiled.

After explaining everything to the peasant for a third time—how to tell the hours, half hours, and quarter hours—Nykolay finally stopped. Having finished his lesson, he closed the watch and held it for a moment in his hands.

The peasant was still standing before him, looking at him with uneasy, glittering eyes from beneath his thick black eyebrows. He remained silent, as if he had been struck dumb.

For a moment, the two of them stared at each other in silence. Nykolay's gaze was earnest and serious, while the peasant's look was evasive and indecisive.

Nykolay was the first to break the silence.

"Now tell me, my good man, how do you know when the watch is showing the hour?"

The peasant thought for a while, scratched his head, and then, looking directly at the young man, replied: "When the small arrow is on nine, and the big one is on twelve, it's exactly nine o'clock."

"And when is it half past two?" Nykolay continued.

"When the small arrow is approaching three, and the big one is on six, then it's exactly half past two."

"Good," Nykolay replied, genuinely pleased. And then he asked: "*And when is it quarter to one?*"

The peasant once again thought for a moment, and then, as if obeying some inner compulsion, asked: "When? In the daytime, or after midnight?"

And, having asked his question, he waited for a reply.

But instead of replying, Nykolay burst out laughing, loudly and heartily. However, seeing the confusion on the peasant's face, he stifled his laughter, and cried: "It doesn't matter if it's day or night. But how do you tell that time on the watch?"

The peasant considered this for another moment and then, his eyes riveted on Nykolay, said: "When the small arrow is on one, and the big one is on nine, then it's quarter to one."

"Good," Nykolay answered with satisfaction.

Smiling warmly, he slapped the peasant on the back, shoved the watch into his vest pocket, and added cheerfully: "And now, Uncle Georgi, harness up the horses, and let's go! My mother is probably plucking chickens and preparing supper already, and we're still by the Moldava River."

"We'll be leaving the Moldava behind in a moment," the peasant responded hurriedly and, hunching down his massive powerful frame, he gathered up the few last wads of hay from under the horses' hooves, placed the halters on their heads, fastened the traces to the whiffletree, and took his place on the wagon beside Nykolay.

They continued on their journey, riding along in silence.

The thoughts of one were with his mother still far ahead in the mountains, with the city he had left behind, with his friends, and with young Aglaya, an archpriest's daughter he had met two months ago, and to whom he had taken such a liking that he had even written some poetry for her.

Just before his departure, he had met her in the residential park, greeted her, bowed to her, and then, after returning home, written a poem that very same evening. She had walked past him with her mother, a dignified woman with a kind soul, whose large brooch made of red beads stuck in his memory. And she, Aglaya, walked modestly beside her, and, when their eyes met, became so flustered that a vibrant rosiness flooded her face right up to her hairline.

At the time, he had not known that coming upon her so unexpectedly would fluster him as well. He had not anticipated such a reaction on his part. It was only later that he understood what had come over him. He realised that she had captured his heart, perhaps forever.

If only he could experience such happiness at least one more time! To see her and to feel, *together* with her, that their souls, attracted to each other, were blending into one.

And it was that single moment—the moment when they had greeted each other and looked into each other's eyes—that had given rise to this feeling.

He had only bowed low and respectfully, and she had thanked him. But still—this single, fleeting moment was *happiness*!

In the evening, when the park was almost deserted, he had gone there once again, supposedly for a walk, and his mind, which had been given to dreams from early childhood, had dictated a poem that he would now rework and send to her.

They drove up to the dense fir forest and, after arriving there, halted and looked back over the road they had traversed.

They were on the top of a mountain, facing a forest that stood before them like a dark world of deep silence. Behind them lay the white road, uneven and empty. Winding like a giant serpent, it nestled first against the mountains and then against the Moldava River, but it remained unchanged—deserted, white, and enticing to travellers.

"Now, with God's help, we'll go into the forest," the peasant said abruptly, looking inquiringly at the young man.

The latter, instead of sitting in the wagon packed with hay, jumped down nimbly and set out at a brisk pace down the forest road.

"Sir, why did you get off the wagon?" the peasant asked impatiently.

"I want to go through the forest on foot," Nykolay responded cheerfully.

"If that's the case, we may not get you home until early in the morning," the peasant called out in a surly voice.

"Then we'll get there in the morning, uncle. There's a full moon, and on such a night I want to walk through the forest. It's marvellous! Perhaps I'll see something wonderful . . . so why shouldn't I see it?"

"It will be wonderful for both of us . . . if some robbers attack us," the peasant stated belligerently.

Nykolay laughed.

"I wonder what they'd find to rob," he quipped cheerfully, striding evenly alongside the wagon crawling slowly down the forest road.

"It doesn't matter what they'd find; what's more important is what they might do to us."

"The worst they can do, uncle, is kill us," Nykolay replied in the same cheerful voice. "They can't do anything more than that. All of us—to the very last one—are in God's hands."

"Yes . . . all of us . . ." the peasant agreed reluctantly, peering from beneath his eyebrows first at the golden chain on the young man's chest and then at the spot where the gold watch was hidden in his vest.

"Well, you have a watch," he said with an affected carelessness as he tapped the horses' backs.

"I'm not afraid," Nykolay said. "Do you suppose I'm so weak? Just let someone try to attack me—my fists are young and strong!"

And as he said this, he brandished his fists at the depths of the dark forest and reached for his watch.

"How long do you think we'll be travelling in the forest?" he asked, turning to face the silent peasant who, hunched over on the wagon, his massive shoulders covered by his black furry *keptar*, resembled a gigantic, hirsute spider.

"It all depends on the horses . . ." the driver replied. "It can take two hours, or maybe three. This road is the best one, and that's why I prefer to use it, even though I do find it frightening to travel alone through the forest at night."

"The forest is wonderful!" the young man said more to himself than to the driver and, opening his watch, he lit a match and peered at the dial.

"What time is it?" the peasant asked, his glittering eyes fixed covetously on the watch in the young man's hands.

"It's ten o'clock."

"And when will you wind the watch?" the peasant suddenly asked, seemingly as fascinated by the watch and its workings as by a sweetheart.

Nykolay glanced in amazement at the peasant, and then drawled: "*Whe-e-n?*"

"Yes, to be sure. When?" the peasant repeated.

Nykolay considered the matter and then, as if still puzzled by something, replied thoughtfully: "I wound it when I was leaving this morning, and so, as I said earlier, I should wind it again tomorrow morning. But for some reason it stopped today, God knows why, at a quarter to one in the afternoon. That's when I wound it up again, so it should be wound tomorrow afternoon at the same time."

"At a quarter to one?" the peasant asked abruptly.

"Yes."

"At midnight?" the peasant asked, as if someone had prompted him to say the word.

Nykolay laughed and then fell silent. "No, uncle. In broad daylight. If God is willing, in broad daylight . . . and, moreover, in my mother's house, if I don't get the urge to do it at another time. But it doesn't matter."

And, whistling a happy tune, Nykolay continued walking ahead of the wagon, farther down the forest road.

The peasant drove slowly after him, without letting the youthful figure out of his sight . . . As he looked at the young man, he kept thinking about the wonderful, expensive gold watch on his chest. From the moment that he laid eyes on the watch and on the underside of its cover, from the moment that he touched the gold, held it in his hand, something had come over him. To have . . . to own such a watch . . . to touch it . . . to look at it seemed to him to be such a great happiness that just imagining it brightened his soul.

But how could he get the watch—how could he get his hands on it?

The young seminarian would not give it to him.

Steal it? But he couldn't steal it—how could he? *Take it away from him by force?*

The young man would struggle. There would be a fight; he would be put in jail for assault, and there would be shame, punishment, and God knows what else.

It simply was not working out. But he had to have this watch.

No matter what—*he had to have it*. He felt this clearly, as if a loud and distinct voice were speaking to him.

And, pushing his shoulders out still farther . . . he sank deep into thought, trying to think of a way to get his hands on the coveted gold.

In the meantime, Nykolay continued walking through the forest, and it seemed that he was sinking ever deeper into a thickening darkness.

It was a strange world—this forest of fir trees at night. Before him stretched a narrow road, a misty white path, and above him, high in the sky, the full moon sailed into view. Majestic, awe-inspiring, and blinding in its radiance . . . it waited. Sometimes the young man saw it in front of him, at other times—directly above him; and then there were times when all he could see was a red glow . . . way off in the distance among the trees.

It was strange to walk in the forest at night . . . The rumbling of the wheels and the clattering of the horses' hooves resounded so dully. It was scary and, at the same time, splendid . . . terrifying and peaceful.

But he was not afraid . . .

Even the fir trees had ceased their murmuring and were silent. Only the clip-clop of the horses' hooves was clearly audible. Up above, stars twinkled on the horizon; he caught glimpses of them through the trees.

Suddenly he wanted to enliven the stillness of the night forest with his voice, and he did so.

Something like a superhuman power distended his breast, and he shouted out a melodic church supplication: "Lord have mercy!"

"Lord have mercy!" the echo raced through the forest and then hid itself.

The peasant reined in the horses.

"Sir!" he cried in a terrified, agitated voice. "Sir, be quiet!"

Nykolay stopped for a moment; then he turned back and, approaching the wagon, asked: "Why? Why shouldn't I sing? After all, it's more cheerful than walking in silence. I don't feel as sleepy."

"Maybe you don't feel sleepy, but I got up at daybreak this morning," the peasant replied and, for no reason at all, cracked his whip loudly.

"But why shouldn't I sing as I walk through the forest—just because you feel sleepy?" Nykolay asked, irritated by the peasant's rudeness.

"Because you might call down some robbers or thieves upon us."

And he was right. Not a moment later, a shot rang out and echoed through the forest, as if scared off in the opposite direction from the travellers . . .

"Did you hear that?" the peasant asked, a menacing quiver in his voice.

"Yes . . . It's probably a forester," the young man replied in a calm voice and, grabbing hold of the ladder on the big wagon, climbed into the box and seated himself by the hunched-over peasant.

"Wait!" he said cheerfully. "Now, whether you fall asleep or not, you won't be afraid any more. It seems to me, Uncle Georgi, that you're afraid because someone about half a mile away from us fired a gun. Isn't that so?"

And, as he said this, the young man leaned forward to look into the peasant's face.

But he could not see it.

At that moment, the driver sank his head still lower on his chest and remained silent.

Instead of answering, he jerked the horses, lashed them, and drove off more quickly.

They both rode silently for a long, long time.

Nykolay felt no fear; he rode with a soul as peaceful as a child's—a soul filled with hopes and dreams, his mood bordering on the poetical. Sleep seemed to be avoiding him on this night.

Next to him was the peasant, a powerful mass doubled in half. All around, there was a profound silence, broken only by the rumbling of the wagon and the clip-clop of the horses' hooves. To the right and to the left, fireflies flashed on the moss.

Everywhere—sleep and silence prevailed. Everywhere—there was darkness and a holy peace. It seemed that the Lord Himself had lain down on the earth to rest.

Suddenly, the bulky mass next to Nykolay stirred, leaned over closer to his youthful face, and asked in a hoarse voice: "Are you finally sleeping, sir?"

"No, Uncle Georgi. I'm not at all sleepy. But why? *Did you think so?*"

"*Ye-e-s.* I did . . ."

"No. Will we be out of the forest soon?" the seminarian asked. "We've been travelling through the trees for almost two hours now."

"*What?*"

"We've been travelling in the forest a long time."

"Just a bit longer. Just a little longer, and we'll be out of it completely. I'm bored as well, and I'd be happy . . . to be . . . by the river . . . soon . . . like before . . ."

"The river's cheerful; it's always speaking to us with its murmuring and splashing," Nykolay said, attempting to bolster his spirits.

"Uh-huh," the peasant replied briefly.

He once again lashed the horses and fell silent.

In half an hour they finally drove out of the forest and, reaching a hillock, the horses came to a standstill, as if they had been reined in by an invisible hand. But they did not stay there long.

The peasant lashed them once more. The horses trotted off at a lively pace but, obviously very tired, soon slowed down, and then, given free rein, fell into a leisurely walk.

When they drove out of the forest, they found themselves almost on top of a mountain from which, in the valley below, could be seen the beautiful, winding white road that beckoned invitingly to travellers, and to which they were now supposed to slowly descend.

Feeling more clear-headed, now that they were out of the forest, Nykolay breathed deeply and, completely refreshed, took a look around.

A magnificent panorama unfolded before him.

The immense sky, like a holy cupola interwoven with a gossamer mist, embraced the mountain summits, whose contours were traced darkly against it. High on the translucent, bluish horizon, the giant moon flamed in its magnificent fullness . . . And farther on there were stars, incredible hosts of bright, flickering stars. The very tallest fir trees, looming out of the forest and silhouetted against the horizon, appeared to be woven into the moonlight, sinking and dissolving in it.

Nykolay stared ahead as if hypnotised by the beauty of the radiant night, by the majesty of this place, and his soul surrendered and melted away in the splendid, incredible, and elegant loveliness, merging with the incandescence of the silvery mist and the moonlight.

How marvellous he felt and, at the same time, how sad! Something was tugging at him, oppressing him.

Lowering his head for a moment and covering his eyes with his hand, he seemed to be listening to a poem he had known for a long time, and which, as if evoked by the beauty of the enchanting night, was surfacing from the depths of his soul and echoing in his mind.

It was a German poem:

> Eine stille monddurchleuchtete Nacht
> Betöret mir Herz und Sinn,
> Ergreift meine Seele mit Zaubermacht,
> Kaum weiß ich, wo ich bin . . .
>
> Ergreifet mich Sehnen und treibet mich fort,
> Hinaus ohne Pfad und Ziel,
> Als bärge die schimmernde Ferne dort
> Der süßesten Wunder viel.
>
> Als sollte ich wandern weithin durch Land
> Im flimmernden Mondesschein,
> Als säße draußen am Wegesrand
> Das Glück und wartete mich . . .
>
> [A quiet, dreamy, moonlit night
> Bewitches my heart and my senses,
> Its magic power grips my soul
> And I hardly know where I am . . .
>
> A longing seizes and spurs me on,
> And I drift aimlessly,
> As if the shimmering distance
> Were harbouring the sweetest wonders.
>
> As though I must wander far over the land
> In this glimmering moonlight,
> As if out there, by the side of the road,
> Good fortune were awaiting me.

Suddenly the horses stopped.

In his dreamy mood, Nykolay almost did not notice this, but the harsh voice of the peasant shattered his reverie and made him shudder.

"Are you sleeping?" the peasant called out. "What time is it?"

"No, I'm not sleeping," Nykolay answered.

Unpleasantly jarred and almost terrified by the voice of the driver, he reached hastily into his pocket to pull out his watch.

He pulled it out . . . opened it . . . bent over it . . . and peered at it.

"If I'm not mistaken," he said, "I think it's *quarter to one.*"

"Quarter to one," the peasant repeated and, jumping down from the wagon, he swung his arm and lunged at the watch and the golden chain.

"Give it to me!" he yelled, pounding the young man with his fists.

"Give it to me!" he repeated in a harsh voice. "Or I'll kill you and throw you in the Moldava, and not even a dog will howl to mourn you."

"God be with you, my good man," Nykolay shouted in terror. "Don't tug at me like that—you'll choke me!"

He tried to protect himself, to fend off the gargantuan strength that, seizing him like a colossal serpent, dragged him from the wagon, and threw him forcibly to the ground.

"Give me the watch!"

"It's a sacred memento . . . from my father. Have mercy! Don't sin . . . He-e-el-p!"

"So, you're yelling, are you?" the peasant roared. "I'm not afraid of sin. I want the watch . . . the watch!"

Breathing raggedly, he pressed down harder and harder on the young man's ribs, almost crushing him.

"Take it . . . Just don't kill me!" the seminarian pleaded as he struggled. "God will punish you!"

"I'm not afraid of God."

"Take it! Don't kill me!"

"Don't kill you?" the peasant repeated in a wild voice. "So you can turn me in later? No. You have to die. I won't be tricked!"

"I won't turn you in—I swear to God! Just . . . don't kill me!" the young man begged.

Stunned by the repeated blows, he summoned up the last of his strength to defend himself.

Hanging on to the peasant's knees, he moaned piteously: "I won't tell, I won't . . ."

"I don't believe you! Except for you, there are no witnesses!"

Breathing heavily, the peasant bore down with the full weight of his massive body on the chest of his almost unconscious victim. His enormous shoulders, heaving up and down, seemed distended, doubled in size . . . and they rose and fell . . . for a long time . . . choking the seminarian's throat.

"I wo-o-o-o-n't . . .!" the young man rasped, a heart-rending groan breaking from his youthful lips.

"I don't need any witnesses; hey, you—don't move," and, grunting in an almost inhuman voice, he bent his burly body even lower, and his shoulders pinned his victim's chest to the ground.

"*The moon . . . is my witness!*" The seminarian's final words bore into the murderer's ear. "*The moon . . .*"

And then—he fell silent.

For another minute or two, the hulking form straddled the inert body. For another minute or two, the murderer knelt, pressing his head to the young man's chest, listening for signs of life. He did not detect any—but still he waited.

Then he staggered to his feet.

His shoulders straightened, his murderous hand took the watch—and he stood dumbstruck.

His hand was still trembling from the exertion, his chest was still heaving with savage emotion, but his eyes stared with sheer satisfaction at the glitter of the pure gold in the moonlight.

The watch was not quite closed. Its owner's hand had not had time to shut it.

Bending his head, the murderer studied it closely.

"*A quarter to one . . .*" his lips whispered.

"A quarter to one." And then, as if obeying an inner command, he abruptly raised the watch to his ear. He listened. The watch had stopped. It was not going.

"I'd better wind it," he said to himself. He examined the costly watch from all sides, trying to remember how to wind it, even though he had seen the young man do it.

"*At noon, in the broad daylight, uncle . . .*" He heard in his mind the words of the unfortunate seminarian. "*At noon, in broad daylight!*"

And, once again, he raised the watch to his ear.

No. It was not going. It had stopped.

It should not have stopped yet.

Why had it stopped?

But then, without spending any more time on this trifling matter, he shoved the watch in his boot, returned swiftly to his horses, sat down in the wagon, and drove off. He glanced back briefly at the corpse, and then looked up at the moon. Fixed in all its blazing beauty on the silvery-blue horizon, it gazed down serenely from among the twinkling stars . . .

The murderer looked at it for a long, long time, and when the moonlight finally began to irritate his eyes, he hunched over double in his customary, comfortable position, lashed the horses, turned the wagon around, and made his way back to the forest.

Almost two years had gone by since that bright night suffused with moonlight. There were no clues to the murder of the young seminarian and, despite the keenest efforts on the part of the authorities, the unfortunate mother, and the entire community, the murderer had not been found.

Deep in the mountains, in a village neighbouring the one in which the ill-fated mother of the young murder victim lived, his killer made his home. His farm was quite impressive, his wife was good and thrifty, and he had several children. Everything was coming along as it should and unfolding in accordance with God's plan; it was only the master who was not the same as he had formerly been.

He had turned prematurely grey and, from time to time, he bowed down low and languished under the burden of a strange sorrow. Whenever a full moon, sailing out on the horizon, illuminated the mountaintops and peeked into every window with its enchanting silvery light, sleep fled from him, despair ravaged him, and he tossed from side to side on his bed, raking his hair with his fingers and wanting to hide . . . God only knows where.

"*The moon is my witness*," the voice of his victim echoed in his memory. "The moon is my witness."

And it was always like this, until the moon changed its face or half hid itself behind a cloud.

Yes, it was always like this . . .

At times he got up, seated himself on the edge of the bed and, dropping his head, with its long lank curls, deeply into his chest, sat numb and motionless, suffering, in pain, trying to guess the punishment that would be meted out to him on the Final Judgement Day, or pondering, until he almost went out of his mind, how the moon could bear witness against him.

"Yes, the moon will betray you, the moon will betray you," a sad voice—his whole being—spoke prophetically in the depths of his soul. Night after night, these thoughts swirled in his head, assuming an ever clearer form, giving him no peace, and depriving him of sleep.

At other times, he crept silently outdoors, walked about, wandered in circles around the house, and gazed—as if driven by an unknown power—at the moon; but it did not help.

There were times when he was overcome by a madness that drove him to the brink of suicide. To leave this world furtively by stringing a rope on this or that branch in the forest . . . And it was only the thought of his wife and children, who were good, and innocent of his terrible sin, that prevented him from ending his life in such a horrifying manner.

Day after day passed by in work, in grief, and in worrying about his daily bread. And when night fell, when he should have rested tranquilly to garner his strength for the next day—sleep shunned him.

The murder victim appeared before him, and he heard the words: "The moon is my witness."

He saw that same moon—a moon whose silvery light drove him to insanity—and he suffered hellish, secret torments. He had sold the watch, and only God knew who owned it now. Even the memory of the terrible crime seemed to have faded—and he was the only one in all these mountains who, on moonlit nights, suffered the torments of the damned and knew no peace . . .

In time, he began to grow grey, his health failed, and the laughter went out of his soul forever. But his wife and children, not knowing anything, remained warm and loving towards him, unconsciously supporting him and encouraging him to continue living.

On one such moonlit night, the peasant once again could not sleep. For at least the fifteenth time, he had turned over on the bed, unable to fall asleep, his mind and soul agonising over the question of how the moon might bear witness against him . . .

Finally, so as not to awaken his wife with his tossing and turning, he rose silently from the bed and went to sit on the bench by the window. Unable to abide the light of the moon, he covered his face with his hands as if hiding from it and, hunching himself over as usual, lowered his head, trying to fall asleep sitting up.

He had not been sitting for long that way . . . when he heard a rustle beside him. Raising his head in alarm, he saw his wife standing before him.

"You aren't sleeping again, old man," she said in a worried whisper as she sat down on the floor beside him. "You're being tormented once again by some illness, worry, or something else. What is it, old man? Tell me, for God's sake, and you'll feel better.

"I couldn't help but notice that, for some time now, you've been troubled; something's worrying you. And you can't sleep, especially on bright, divine nights like this one, and then you get out of bed and sit like this. Does something hurt you, my good man? Are you worried about something—something you don't want me to know about?"

She kept asking and questioning him, trying to look into his eyes, which he kept covered with his hands. But he remained silent, sighing and breathing heavily.

"Go to sleep, wife . . . and leave me in peace. I'll lie down right away, as well," he replied in a whisper, trying not to awaken the children. "There's nothing wrong with me; I just can't sleep."

"That's not true, my good man," his wife contradicted him, also in a whisper. "You're hiding something in your heart, and you don't want to tell me about it."

"If I am, then it's my worry, and you don't have to be concerned. You won't remove it from my soul. Go!"

"But maybe I can lighten your burden, old man. Have you got yourself into debt?" she asked in a troubled voice, crawling closer to him on her knees.

"Into debt," he repeated bitterly, and his smile was also bitter.

"Is it a big debt?" she asked, and she seemed to be a little happier now that she had found out the reason for his sadness.

"A big one . . ." he replied in a choked voice, pushing her away. "Leave me alone. Go to sleep, woman."

"No, I won't!" she responded, drawing still closer and embracing his knees in a pleading gesture.

That gesture made him lose all self-control.

He shoved his wife away and hissed fiercely: "Get away from me! Go to sleep, I said! Are you going to gnaw at my heart as well? Leave me in peace, I said. Get away from me! It looks like I'll have to go and hide myself in the ground!"

His wife did not budge.

"I won't go, old man," she said. "Now I most certainly won't go. You're worried about something—a big debt. None of us knows the hour of our death. God forbid that you should die, for I and the children would be chased out of the house. Tell me what it's all about, my good man; after all, I'm your good and faithful wife. Have I ever disobeyed you or betrayed you?"

And when she was done speaking, she began to cry softly.

"Don't cry, wife; go to sleep, and maybe I'll tell you some day," the peasant replied, touched by his wife's kindness.

"I won't go until you tell me, old man," she said, still sobbing. "I won't go. I won't stir from this spot, even if I have to sit here until morning."

The murderer, seemingly driven to despair by these words, raked his fingers through his hair and, sighing heavily, bent down over his wife on the floor, saying in a voice that was choked, bitter, and at the same time, disdainful: "If you didn't have the cursed tongue of a woman, I might tell you what's eating at me, what my secret worry is—the one that's burying me alive and taking away my sleep at night."

"I won't tell anyone; I won't say a single word, may God strike me dead!" his wife vowed and, swiftly bending over, she touched the floor with her forehead and kissed her husband's feet. "I won't tell; I'd rather fall dumb . . ."

"Remember what you've just said . . ." her husband whispered again. "If you betray me . . . I'll have to die."

"Lord!" the woman burst out in alarm, raising her hands. "May my tongue wither, may my eyes go blind, if I say even so much as a word. Just tell me what it is."

For a moment, the murderer seemed to be struggling with himself, as if he were deciding what he should do; then he said:

"If that's the case, then let's go outdoors. The children might overhear us . . . and then it would all be over."

Stealthily, like a cat, the woman rose to her feet and, just as silently, they both walked out of the house.

They walked out and came to a stop.

Outside, the night was clear and beautiful.

The sky seemed to be bathing in a mist illuminated by the silvery lustre of the moonlight, and the moon itself was glowing high in the heavens.

It was still all around . . .

The white village road ran in front of the house. Beyond it loomed a mountain covered with a forest and, high above everything, the cupola of the heavens was sown with trembling stars.

He looked around uneasily. "God forbid that someone should hear," he whispered fearfully, drawing closer to his wife.

"Don't be afraid. Everyone is fast asleep."

"I'm afraid," he whispered once again and, for a moment, stared at the moon with eyes that verged on madness.

"Don't be afraid," she repeated in a louder voice, but she herself began to shake as if she had the ague.

"*The moon!*" he blurted, turning towards her, his face white as a sheet.

"The moon is the only one, old man, who can see and hear us. It's the only one. Come, tell me . . ."

"Yes, the moon is the one . . ." the peasant replied.

And he staggered towards his wife as if he were drunk.

They sat down on the earthen ledge abutting the white wall of the house, directly opposite the moon, and he told her . . .

When he finished speaking, and she, sitting with her hands pressed tightly to her lips, was staring at the moon as if she had turned to stone, he said: "The moon threatens me, wife. Every time it sails out across the sky with its flocks of stars, it threatens me, and I suffer and can't sleep. I'm doomed, wife; if it reveals my secret, I'm doomed forever. And all of you as well . . ."

"You have to repent, old man . . . and pray to God. You have to pay for liturgies in memory of the poor deceased," she replied in a voice that did not sound like hers, as if she had just awoken from a terrible dream, "and maybe the moon won't reveal your secret. You have to repent. Ohhh!"

And, with a groaning sigh, as if she had taken on a burden that was far too heavy for her shoulders, she slowly dragged herself back into the house.

He followed her.

Now that he had passed his sin on to her, his soul was at peace.

She was a good wife.

He had done the right thing in telling her.

After his confession, he seemed to revive and, it seems, almost forgot what he had suffered during all those moonlit nights that had robbed him of his sleep.

He finally caught up on his rest and, regaining his former strength, attacked his work with his previous vigour. He also began to go more frequently, as he once used to, with groups of other village people, to find work for himself and his horses. He carted salt from K., and he also hauled building materials, lime, and other goods like that.

Making a trip almost weekly, he sometimes came home tipsy. Things went along like this for quite some time.

At first, when his wife attacked him for wasting, in the tavern, money needed for their children, he justified his drunkenness and then remained silent. Later, however, refusing to give up his drinking, he began to mutter when she reproached him, and then began to quarrel with her and utter threats.

"It's my money!" he yelled. "After all my hard work, I'm not allowed to have a shot of whiskey along with the others? Just look at my warden—just look at her! She's giving her husband a piece of her mind, she is!"

And he whistled in anger. "Keep it to yourself, woman, or I might give you a piece of mine. Just remember that!"

And that was that.

More time went by.

But it did not bring anything better with it.

The peasant did not give up his habit; indeed, with time, it fought to gain control over him.

Every month now, he gave his wife only a few *rynski [dollars]* from his pay. The rest sank as if into an abyss, as he drank it away in the tavern with his fellow drivers and other villagers.

His wife, who would have given her very soul for her husband and children, was increasingly pained and angered by his drunkenness.

The drinking bouts continued with growing frequency, and finally they occurred several times a week.

"I have to approach him differently," she finally decided, on the verge of despair over his squandering ways and his fits of drunken rage, during which he struck her and even threatened to kill her.

"For my work and my kindness, for my sincere heart!" she complained to her neighbours, wiping away her tears. "But, let it be!"

One time, when he came home drunk on the eve of an important holiday, and she found out that there was not even a penny in his purse, she raised such a ruckus that he, drunk as he was, sobered up as if he had not even so much as laid eyes on alcohol. However, having sobered up, her anger and reproaches whipped him into a terrible fury; he beat her and dragged her through the whole house, to remind her who was the master in the house and who had the authority.

"And I don't even have to tell you what I'll do the next time—you yourself know what will happen!"

Rescued by her children, she pulled herself to her feet.

White as snow, her eyes blazing with pain, anger, and humiliation, she tore out of the house.

When she returned—she did not come alone.

The neighbours came with her.

"The children saw it," she said in a hushed voice, her lips ashen. And she pointed at her husband: "They saw it. He swept the whole house with me, pulling me by my hair. The whole house! And just look at my arms . . . He's broken them, crippling me forever.

"He threatened he'd kill me, *just as he killed the son of the priest's old wife and took his gold watch.* And, as he told me himself, the murdered young man had no one to call upon—and so he asked the moon to be his witness.

"But I, my good people, am his wife, and I'm taking you—*living people*—as my witnesses."

Not even two weeks had gone by when, early one morning, two gendarmes appeared in the house of the peasant-murderer. They locked him in chains and took him away.

He admitted everything and did not protest.

When he was crossing the threshold of his house for the last time, his wife rushed up, wailed over him and, dragging herself along on her knees behind him, cried repeatedly: "Take me as well . . . I'm as much to blame as he is. *Take me and let me perish with him!*"

The murderer stopped.

Pale as death, he pierced her with eyes as sharp as a knife and said: "I'm sorry to leave the children, but not you. You're worse that I am."

And to the children, who were weeping and crowding around him, he said: "Pray for me. Pray for me on bright, moonlit nights, when the full moon rises. Pray. Maybe, in time, the Lord will forgive me. No one saw me; no one heard my sin. Only He saw it from on high—and all because of the moon. Pray . . . He will hear you.

"But I . . . I will never return to you.

"The moon has parted us forever . . ."

A Letter to His Wife
from a Soldier Sentenced to Death
(1915)

My dear wife, my beloved Mariyka!

By the grace of our Lord God, I am well, and I wish you the same good health.

There is nothing more I can say . . .

What I shall relate to you now is most painful, Mariya! I know that my words will cause you grief, but I must write you the truth, the whole truth . . . I am being ordered to do so by my conscience and by our Lord; He can see best what is happening now in my soul . . .

That's how it is, Mariya.

Not long ago, I dreamt that I was dead, and bullets were whistling all around me. I no longer remember clearly if they were coming from far away or from nearby, but it seems to me that this did not really concern me at the time.

I felt no pain, and no blood flowed from any wound.

I was dead.

But in my soul there was pain, such a deep, heavy sorrow, that even the din of the shooting could not drown it . . .

Oh, Mariya, you were to blame for that sorrow. You alone in all the world—for, as my dream continued, I saw that *I had been shot*—and, even in the midst of our seven children, you could find neither peace of mind nor solace in work. Instead, you cast about in all directions for a way to end your life . . . and all because I was dead.

In your despair, you once ran into the field to drown yourself in the pond, but my father followed you and prevented you from losing your soul. Another time, you stole away into the forest to hang yourself on a branch—I am filled with terror even today when I recall this. A third time, you went to the railroad tracks at night and waited for the train's red lights so that you could cast yourself under its wheels, but once again my old father rushed up and stopped you from killing yourself.

Mariya, my dear wife, how have our children harmed you that you would want to make orphans of them? They are still so tiny, just little specks, and there are so many of them, my dear wife! What would they do without you and without me?

Oh, my wife, do not lose your mind, do not lose it; for this is what happens here, in the midst of war, to some of our soldiers who have seen too much blood, too many blown off heads, arms, and legs, and can no longer put up with the horror of it all.

But don't you lose your mind, my wife! You have *seven* children!

That's how it was.

And I had to tell you all of this. Do not forget about this dream. And later, when our children are grown up, let them relate it to their children. Let it not be lost, even though their father has marched off their horizon . . .

. . . Did one of the children shriek just now, as if some phantom were approaching it? Is one of them ill? Perhaps the youngest? Is death sneaking up on it? Death is the master everywhere now, and a child senses this and screams . . .

Do not become ill, my wife, because then the little one who suckles your breast will follow its father. Perhaps it's a boy? I did not see it, this seventh one; I was marching farther and farther away from it when it came into the world.

Look after this child, Mariya; I fear for this seventh one . . .

Once more, and for the last time, I have been brought back from the military office to this prison, and once again I am sitting alone as before . . .

Never kill crickets, Mariya, even if they crawl on your breast or on your lips.

Back home, crickets chirp in our house when dusk falls, when a fire burns in the oven-stove, when people come home from working in the field, sit on the *pryz'ba [earthen embankment abutting the house],* and wait for their supper . . . It is then that they begin to chirp in some nook . . . where they are hidden, in deep crevices . . .

I have to cry, Mariya . . . My eyes ache so badly, it's as if I had balls of fire in my head instead of eyes . . . Oh, Mariya! The Lord sees everything . . . Do not kill them!

I still have two hours left to sit behind these stone walls, and the cricket that has crawled in here unnoticed chirps so plaintively from time to time that I see before me my native country, my fields, my home, and you and the children. It is the last comrade that I will hear. A cricket!

How wonderfully our grain rippled last year, Mariya! And it is rippling this year, my wife, oh, yes, how it *is rippling* this year as well. But am I reproaching it?

. . . The more tightly my lips are pressed together, the more the tears flow from my eyes. But I do want to write to you—and don't you cry!

It is so quiet in my prison cell—even the light creeps in almost furtively through the grate. And only the two of us are here—the cricket and I. It keeps track of me, and I listen to it, and tears fall from my eyes. No one hears me. I am a stranger here; I am what the war has made of me, for the judgement went against me.

"Chirp on, my comrade. Don't stop! Back home my seven children are chirping at their mother's knees as she cooks their food for them, and their father is in prison awaiting death . . ."

Death is not evil, my wife. Do not complain about it. Does it thrust itself on anyone? Does it come on its own? It is always some other misfortune that brings it.

"Oh, cricket, you are my last, my final comrade who reminds me of my native land . . . and of my death . . . But hush . . ."

It has fallen silent for a moment . . . I *had hoped*. Now, let death come, I am not afraid.

If only it were not for *one thing*, my wife. In my soul, a *question*, like a bucket full of blood, keeps emerging and coming to the fore, and then it sinks back down again—what am I suffering for? For what? Is it my *language* that is to blame, the distance from my native land—my fatherland? Or is it because God is the only witness of my innocence? I heard so often that our peasants were accused of betrayal, so often, but hush . . . It's all over. Together with my question, approaches my final destiny.

I still have two hours to live . . . I was able to secure *this much* by pleading with the gentlemen in the military tribunal, so that I could write some more to you before they *shoot* me . . .

And so I am writing, little by little, like that worn-out horse that pulls the plough with its last ounce of strength. The end has to come somewhere. Do you see it in me, my wife? Where is the dividing line?

I marched away with my regiment to Italy. Here, misfortune struck me. It comes and goes, but when you do not look to see where it is coming from, then others come and tell you what you are, and you stand and look, and you stand and think, but all the while, you are what you were before . . . a doomed man.

Yes, Mariyka. You should thank God that you're a woman. It takes a lot to be a woman, but it is still more difficult to be a man. A soldier.

When we had to retreat from—Lord forgive me, but I no longer remember the name of that place—I was left behind in the trenches. I was asleep, dead to the world. None of the ones who were retreating woke me up. Because at times like that it's as if someone had startled a flock of birds—everyone flees wherever his eyes take him, and no one thinks about anybody else.

I must have been sleeping on my knees, because when I finally awoke I was kneeling in the trench. It was the silence that woke me. Would to God I had never awoken!

Then I crawled farther along the trenches looking for my comrades. But I did not find anyone; it was deserted and quiet everywhere. I roared with grief, because they had left me by myself.

Oh, Mariya, Mariya, you don't know what it means to be a lone soldier in a war. What *grief* means . . .

I was left, as it seemed to me, all alone in the country of my enemy. Who was to be my comrade now? Can you not guess? But I'm not complaining. I finally crawled out of the trenches of the reserve army . . . But . . . you don't have to know everything, and I don't have enough time. I have a little less than two hours to live, and I want to spend my last two hours in this world with you.

I wandered around everywhere, without being noticed by anyone; I was searching for my regiment, for my comrades; I went without food, but I avoided the enemy, for I did not want to fall into their hands. But I was not thinking about my life then, just as I was not thinking about it when bullets fell like hail around me. I was accustomed to bullets; I walked about in them as one walks in the rain.

But that was nothing, my dear wife. When you were giving birth to our seven children—to our first, our second, our third, and then finally to that seventh one—did you think about your life? You did what you had to do, what could not be done differently.

The same is true of a soldier at war. A man does not think. He trembles, deafened by the roar of canons; he goes numb amidst the terrible roaring . . . shrieking . . . howling . . . and nothing matters to him. He only wants to push forward—ever faster and faster—the power that lies in the steel. Always more and more.

Here a man is not what he was at home, Mariya. Here, a man is . . . is—I know this only now, since I have been looking death in the eyes so often, without feeling any fear—*a man is nothing*, my wife. You don't know this.

Something other than us is at work here. Here steel is at work, and the soldier is nothing, and the man he used to be at home is nothing, and many hundreds and thousands—they are all nothing. And God . . .

Oh, Mariya! Was it I that screamed? Or was it your voice that found its way to my ear . . . that broke my heart? Mariyka!

Later, our soldiers found me in those trenches from which they had been forced to retreat. I was so weak from hunger I could hardly stand, because for all those days I had eaten almost nothing.

In my chest pocket I had a lump of my native soil; my father had tucked it into the bosom of my coat when we were parting for the last time, saying: "If you should fall in battle in a foreign land, this native soil will lie on your breast and lead you to God himself. It is holy."

Now they have taken my native soil away from me, pulled my weapons from my shoulders, placed me under guard, and brought me before a military tribunal. I did not know what I was guilty of. The hunger and the worry made me as weak and helpless as a child. Was it because I fell asleep when they were retreating from the trenches, and perhaps because, as a result of this, I saved myself from the enemy?

I wanted to defend myself, but I did not understand their language too well, just as they could not understand mine. A military tribunal is merciless, swift—like a blazing rifle. It does not ask questions; it only fires. It may strike you, or it may not; that's why it's a rifle. And I and my maternal language—we both suddenly felt the ground give way beneath our feet. Something happened; a few words were spoken in a foreign tongue—and both I and my language drowned . . .

Hush, Mariyka, hush!

I understood what they told me.

I will be shot for treason.

No one understood my language. It was so foreign and so neglected. But then, who even listened to it? It means nothing to foreigners. But did I mean anything to them?

I will be shot—for treason. I have nothing more to say. I'm prepared. It is a good thing that I will close my eyes.

It is your eyes and the eyes of our children that will see what the future will bring, for I have not lived to see anything, except perhaps, that I and my language have to die, that not even a bullet of the enemy ripped open my chest, but only a deep, dark grief that will return me to my native land with closed lips, a raised hand, and a dumb silence . . .

Mariyka, don't cry! Look here now, don't think about me. Think about the land I am leaving you. About the little green plot through which a stream gurgles, and where the spreading willow grows, the one from which we used to break off branches every year to have them blessed in church on Palm Sunday.

Keep our cow in mind; she feeds everyone in our home. And she lowed so mournfully when I pitched hay into her manger before I left for the last time. See to it that she never goes hungry.

Keep our children in mind; I am leaving them in your care.

Do not forget about my old father who is losing a son. It was only when I was leaving that I noticed his hair has almost all turned white, and his back is stooped. I am not asking what has become of him now. Respect him and take special care of him.

Do not lose your mind the way one soldier did during the war. Do not lose it, my dear wife!

Take care of yourself—it was to you I pledged my fidelity—and do not forget the years that we had together.

Gaze often at the sun, at God's sun that I now have to forsake at such an early age . . .

And from time to time . . . light a candle before the icon of our Saviour . . .

Your husband, Vasyl V.

Judas
(1915)

In the Carpathians.

He has left his ailing wife in one half of his small peasant hut, and his young daughter-in-law and little grandson in the other half.

His only son has gone to war, and now he has to look after everything.

It is hard.

His legs are weak, and the mountains demand the strength of the young. But he trudges everywhere himself.

O Lord, how had all this come about!

It was an inferno—such an inferno that even the mountains themselves were almost howling. The tranquillity of the mountains and forests heard what it had never heard before—the thunder of cannons and rifle shots fired singly and in unison, ricocheting off walls like a call for help. But when you go there—it is quiet; only a stream gurgles in the valley, or a frightened squirrel races up a tree like a flash of lightning. And the mountain forests seem agitated, as if questioning the propriety of continuing to rustle, dream, and sway.

He leaves the hut more often now, usually in the morning and in the evening, but, when necessary, at night as well—whenever he has chores to do, either for his family or his son's cattle.

Beyond the mountains there is a market where he buys whatever is needed. On the way there, or on the way back, he rests on a peak, smokes his pipe, thinks about his son, his meadow, and other things, and then continues laboriously on his way.

He prefers to go out in the evening, because then he does not waste any time. The nights are clear. It is often possible to count all the stars in the sky . . . this holy sky—the only thing left on which one can pin one's hopes . . .

It was dawning. The cattle simply had to have some salt. Oh, these cattle! Since Andriy went away, their condition had become pitiful, especially in the last while. His rick stands a long way off, high up on the mountain, and he has to haul the hay down from there; it is a difficult task for him.

And, as soon as he enters the barn, the cattle all turn their heads towards him and look at him as if to say: "Where is the one who brought us food to eat more often and in larger quantities than you? The one who herded us to the spring—to the spring that gushes out with a roar from the cliff—where we dipped our muzzles in the water's foam and drank . . . Oh, what a delight that was!"

At the beginning of December, in 1914, there was no snow on the mountains near the hut. It was only later that it began to fall slowly one frosty morning, as he was returning from the market, carrying some licking salt for the cattle, as one brings home treats for children.

It was here that a company of Russian soldiers stopped him. Terrified, he tried to avoid them, but it was too late. They detained him. One of them, probably the commander, asked him where the Austrian army was located.

He does not know; he truly does not know.

But the enemy soldiers insisted that he must know.

No, he does not know.

They laughed.

"You'll know right away . . ." threatened the one who seemed to be the commander. He was tall, and his face was grim.

"I don't know," the peasant contended, his fear of the enemy army beading his forehead with sweat.

How was he to know? He stays close to home, in the hut that stands abandoned like an orphan since his son left it. He works in his house and yard, and he tends the cattle and the sheep—he is both the owner and the servant. He does not even know where his son is now—how could he possibly know the location of the army. He is only a peasant who does not know how to read or write. He knows nothing . . . nothing.

Let the gentlemen leave him in peace. He has to go down the mountain and give his cattle the salt, for they had long been on edge without it, but they had to keep waiting for it, because he first had to buy other things that were needed.

Who can say whether they believed him or not. They surrounded him and offered him money if he would only tell them where the army was.

"What a stupid peasant you are," one of the soldiers from the middle rows shouted at him. "Why are you acting more stupid than you really are? Don't delay both us and yourself any longer; just tell us where the army is, and then—off with you! How dare you waste our time like this?"

With these words, the soldier broke rank, stepped forward, and pressed a few *rubles [dollars]* into the peasant's hand. The peasant did not resist and, without looking at the enemy soldiers, shoved the money into the purse on his leather belt.

"Gentlemen, have mercy on me; I don't know anything. I don't know where my son is, and I don't know where our army is located. Let me go home, and I'll be very grateful to you. I have a sick wife waiting for me at home, and cattle that are in such a pitiful condition that it breaks my heart, because ever since my son went away they do not receive the care that they used to get.

"I'm old already, but despite my age I have to do the hardest work around the home and in the barn. I can't call on my daughter-in-law to do anything, for, with God's help, she'll soon bring forth a son for her husband.

"Alas! Who can know my grief and my problems, who can know my heavy sorrow," he said, bowing humbly before the enemy.

"But you must know that your army had to go somewhere?" persisted a soldier, the one whose voice struck terror in the peasant's heart and seemed to identify him as the commander.

"Yes, sir."

"And do you also know what you were taught—how you are supposed to act towards us when we come into your country and demand something from you?"

"I don't know anything, sir! I live down below, across from the valley; I'm all alone with the two who live with me there and, as I said before, I don't know anything."

"Oh, so that's how it is! But you do know how to take money?" a hefty soldier exclaimed, threatening him with his whip.

"Take your money back and let me go!" the offended peasant cried, moving to take the *rubles* out of the purse on his belt.

"Look at him, just look! The son of a bitch wants to fool around with us! If you don't tell us immediately where your army is, we won't joke around with you. By the time we count to two—you'll be hanging from a branch. Do you understand? Put the money away and buy yourself some bread, because you look as if you haven't eaten for a month. So, you don't know how you were told to behave when we came to your country?"

The peasant gaped in fear at the speaker and did not know what to reply.

"You're supposed to obey us! Understand? Blindly, and without any objections," the speaker said impatiently. "To obey—do you see?"

And he pointed once again at a branch of a fir tree on the other side of the road that led over the mountain and which now, covered with snow, was known only to a few people.

"I don't know anything," the peasant moaned, and his thoughts flew to his wife and his daughter-in-law whom his son had left with him as a pledge of his return. "Father," his son had said, "you will have to answer for my wife in the next world if you don't do right by her, and for my child—if I don't return and it dies of hunger."

"No! Leave me alone, my good gentlemen. How am I supposed to know?"

The commander gave a signal to a few of the mounted men; two of them quickly dismounted, tore off the old man's sheepskin coat, and began lashing him with their whips. He screamed and sobbed. Falling at their feet, he pleaded and begged for mercy, crying over and over again that he did not know anything. Blood soaked through his shirt, and his face was bloody from the lashes.

"I don't know where our army is," he screamed. "No one has told me anything. I saw only a few soldiers—possibly four, or maybe six. They were going somewhere, and I saw them from afar. But I don't know anything else. As God is my witness, I don't know anything else."

"So. Four or six, you say. And it's only now that you're telling us this. Come with us, right this moment, and show us where this was. Here are two more *rubles* for you."

They shoved the money into the purse on his belt, while he wiped the blood from his face with the long sleeve of his shirt and struggled into his sheepskin coat.

"So. To the right, or the left?" barked the one who appeared to be the commander.

"My kind gentlemen, I have to get home. I'm carrying salt for my cattle. And I also bought a few things for the house. They're waiting for me there. My wife is sick—she's been lying on the oven-bed ever since our son went to war. Let me get on my way. O my dear God, surely You can see my grief!" And he tried moving away from the enemy, but his efforts were in vain.

Surrounded by the soldiers, he trudges along with them and, fearing new blows, turns blindly to the right into the forest. Occasionally, snow from the branches falls on their heads. The forest is so beautiful today that it seems to be enchanted. Silence reigns in it. It is as if its peacefulness and its depths are compelling the peasant to go ever deeper into it in order to lead the enemy astray.

Quite a bit of time passes in this manner. The men continue marching . . . tramping through the forest . . . breaking branches. Some of the soldiers swear and mutter profanities, but they all continue climbing upwards. The depths of the forest entice them, lure them on, and the bewitching stillness and serenity have a calming, almost mesmerising effect.

Suddenly: "Halt!"

They stop abruptly, in unison. A shot, but from where? Everyone looks around. All eyes turn towards the peasant. He stares at them, and they stare back at him. It seems that no one is breathing. It is quiet, ever so quiet. Inviolably quiet.

Suddenly, a cough is heard—from about five hundred feet lower down.

"Psst!" The commander places his fingers on his lips. "It's an Austrian patrol."

Six men are waiting in the snow. The shots all ring out at the same time. No one counts them. Four of the men fall to the ground; two leap up like deer and vanish.

For a moment there is dead silence, then—a din of voices a throbbing, like of bass strings. It grows in intensity and savagery.

Some of the soldiers run after those who escaped, while others examine the ones who are lying there. They are dead. Clearly dead. The commander is angry that more of the army was not found, only six men. The men regroup in their previous formation of two lines and, keeping the peasant with them, continue on their way.

"Liar!" The peasant hears the words directed at him. "You know where your army is. You speak well, but you don't speak the truth. March on!"

The peasant, guarded on all sides, limped along in the last row, deafened by terror and pain; escape was out of the question.

"Carry my spade!" one of the soldiers in the last row—all of them have spades—ordered the peasant.

He silently took the spade and carried it.

Oh that walk—may God spare everyone a walk like that!

They walked for about half an hour. Then a Russian patrol ran past them at full speed, shouted something at them, and kept on running. Terrified, the company turned around and marched back.

"And you, you son of a bitch, go back to where you came from," the commander shouted at the peasant once again. "But as punishment for taking money from us and deceiving us, go back where your patrol fell and bury its members. And you may be sure that if you don't do this, we'll find your home. Not a single soldier is to be left on the ground. You are not to leave that spot until you have completed your work, even if it takes you until tomorrow. And now—off with you!"

The tramping over the ground and the snow, and the tramping over the trees and dead branches receded, growing ever softer and less distinct. At last there was silence.

The peasant, following them with crazed eyes, leaned on the spade and shuddered. Crossing himself, as if some evil had passed him by, he turned around and continued on his way.

First he went into the forest where the four corpses were lying—the ones he had to bury before he went home. Well, there you had it! He had unwillingly become a murderer with four souls on his conscience. Hey, hey, father! Hey, hey, dear mother! Come and dig a grave for him. Four times deeper than the graves of those who had fallen doing what their sense of duty and loyalty demanded of them. They had fallen honourably. They would find peace here in the forest. He would bury them and, in time, place a cross over them. He—the only one who knew how this had happened.

He started digging, and the ground gave way. It was not yet frozen too solidly. At times, his movements dislodged the hoarfrost on the fir trees, bringing it down in soundless clumps. He worked hard. He should be happy that he had managed to get away alive. What would his wife, his daughter-in-law, and his grandson say when he appeared before them, his shirt bloody, his face swollen?

He had been beset by the kind of misfortune that, up to now, none of his ancestors and none of the villagers had ever experienced. So, praise God that he had been able to get away with his soul intact. But why, then, did his soul feel so inexpressibly heavy? After all, the danger seemed to have passed.

Yes, the danger had passed—but . . . had he in fact revealed something to the enemy—the question suddenly crossed his mind. He did not know. After all, it was only a patrol they had met up with—not the army, and it had happened only by chance, for, when he had left home very early that morning, he had spotted several Austrian soldiers at a distance, in almost the opposite direction.

Besides, the enemy had tortured and beaten him; his wounded face was burning like fire, and he was still bleeding in a few spots. And, as for those few rubles that they had pressed into his hand and which he had accepted, he would take them to the priest and ask him what to do with them; perhaps a memorial mass could be served for the four soldiers who had fallen in battle. Or perhaps he would ask the priest to be so kind as to serve a mass for his son, so that he would arrive home alive and not be crippled. He would tell the priest everything. Everything, to the last detail.

But now he did not dare leave this place until all four of the dead men were buried. Something told him that he owed it to them.

He wanted to place them in two graves; to be precise, two in one grave today, and two in another grave tomorrow. To do so, he would work without stopping, without resting; it just could be that the enemy might return tomorrow to check things out, and then . . . The thought of the *kozaks [Cossacks]* made him shake.

He glanced at the four corpses. Two were lying on their sides, one was lying face up, and the fourth, who evidently had been shot in the back, was lying face down.

Something seemed to be urging him to work faster. From time to time, he straightened his back and wiped his sweaty forehead with his sleeve. His chest ached sharply with a strange emotion. A feeling of distress. This distress would not leave him today. At home, his son's cattle were awaiting him impatiently—he could almost hear their lowing. Perhaps something had happened there, something he had not even dreamed of.

He had fallen into the hands of the enemy. He had said things that he would never have said of his own accord, at any price. Now he had the enemy's money—nice, shiny money that was beginning to torment him; and what was even worse, he had been forced to witness how four of his countrymen had fallen. And "as punishment" he had to dig graves and bury the corpses.

O God, O God! Why did You want this to happen? Why did this happen? What good would come of it? What good or evil? And even if . . . What kind of good could come of this? The fields and the meadows would be ruined. They were not accustomed to being watered with blood.

"*O meadows, O meadows! Hey, hey!*" something was screaming in his breast. "Whose hands will cultivate you now? What kind of grain will ripple on you now?"

It was with these and other despairing thoughts that he continued digging.

While working with his spade, he kept glancing at the four corpses, and his glance paused, for a longer time than he would have liked, at the one that was lying face down.

But because this one did not differ in any way in his outward appearance from the others, he continued digging. He was spading the earth in an almost feverish haste. The man who was lying face down was impelling him to hurry. Why? For what reason? The question flashed dimly through his soul. The enemy would not return to check things out today. It would soon be dusk. Yes, faster, faster; he had to work quickly, finish digging the grave quickly, bury the corpses as fast as he could, and then—go home!

So he dug feverishly. He put the first two corpses that were lying nearest to him in the grave . . . After placing them in the grave like brothers, and carefully crossing their arms on their chests, he covered them with soil. He felt as if he were united with God, or with something else. What it was, he did not know. In his heart, he felt as if he had done something good, but the feeling did not last.

After covering the first grave, he walked away to rest before setting out for home. His concern about the cattle took precedence over everything else that he was feeling. More than once it seemed to him that he could hear their lowing behind him. At first the sound seemed quite close, and then it came from farther away.

He had already risen to his feet in order to leave, when something suddenly made him turn his head. He did this, and without realizing it, as if obeying some inner, compelling voice, his eye sought out the newly dug grave among the trees. Without fully knowing why, he was struck by the feeling that he had to take another look at the grave. Even though he was sure that he would not be able to see it from behind the trees, from behind the branches covered with hoarfrost—he still tried to peer at it through the thickly intertwined branches.

No, he could not see anything. Let anyone who wanted to, try to find it—he would not be able to see the newly dug grave and the two corpses that lay in it.

He stood there, trying to make up his mind.

He had completed his work; in keeping with what he had decided earlier, two of the bodies were already resting in the ground. Tomorrow he would do the same for the remaining two corpses. So he could now return home with an easy mind.

He takes a few steps forward, and then stops once more. He cannot go any farther. Something is holding him back. Come what may, he has to take another look at the grave to make sure that everything is in order . . . if everything . . . He himself does not know what . . . Yes, if everything is as it should be.

Spitting far off to one side through his teeth, he turns around decisively and goes back into the forest. The quietness and peacefulness envelop him. A quietness that he had not noticed two or three hours earlier.

He walks into the depths, where he had left the fresh grave and the two corpses that were not yet buried. He has to look at them once more. It is only a few more steps. Looking in the direction of the grave, he draws closer and closer.

Yes—this is the freshly dug grave. In it lie the two young victims. He gazes at it for another minute. Then suddenly, unconsciously, his eyes fasten, as if bound by chains, on the two corpses lying nearby.

One of the fallen soldiers, the one lying on his side, has a peaceful look on his young face, but the other—the one that is lying face down—what about this other one? There is something about him—even though his face is not visible—something about his back . . . his hair . . . his neck . . . something that awakens grief and fear in his heart. All of this makes him tremble for a scarcely noticeable, fleeting moment. A feeling, in which grief and joy are intermixed, pierces him and, almost at the same time, he turns his gaze inward. This all happens in an instant.

A foreboding . . . a recollection . . . and, along with it, his thoughts fly to his barn, as if the appearance of the man whose face he cannot see is turning his thoughts in the direction of the cattle that dumbly wait and watch for him. Abruptly, he takes a step forward. He is unaware that he wanted to do so—but he does.

He walks up to the two corpses. His eyes run calmly over the one lying on its side, and then leap quickly to the one lying with his face to the ground. His gaze fixes on him, and there is a strange feeling in his soul. This back . . . this neck . . . this hair—all this reminds him of someone. Of whom?

But at this moment his feelings and senses are clouded. He is not aware of anything, not even of what has happened to him earlier in the day. He is not thinking about anything; instead, his eyes cling to the fallen soldier.

Should he turn him over and place him face up? No. He could do this tomorrow. Now he had to go. But . . . perhaps he was still alive. Oh, how could this possibility not have occurred to him even once—that he should look at him. Even now he cannot make up his mind. Something is drawing him to the corpse and, at the same time—something is pushing him away.

He is seized by terror, as if he were to meet the gaze of a living person. Suddenly, something in his heart begins to boil so furiously that he raises the dead man's hand and looks at it. Wound around a few times with a brass chain, it is cold and stiff. He shivers, overwhelmed with dread, and stares, like an insane man, at the corpse. His hair stands on end.

Unthinkingly, desperately, he seizes the corpse, lifts it quickly in his strong arms as if it were a child, and—*his gaze falls on the face of his son.*

The dead body dropped to the ground, and along with it, the living one . . .

It was not a human being who was screaming, it was not a father—it was a fatally wounded wild animal.

His one and only child . . . dead.

His head fell on the breast of his son, but he did not cry.

He lay thus for a long time. Then he pressed the corpse to himself . . . shook it, and shouted at it—all in vain. His shouts were lost in the forest.

"Get up, my son, lift your head, open your eyes, open your lips and say: 'Father, I'm alive. I haven't died. I'm—your son, your only child!' My son!" he shrieked like a madman. And he wiped the face of the corpse, ripped its clothing, and sucked at its wound. He scarcely knew what he was doing.

Perhaps he had not died yet; perhaps he had just turned numb. Oh, no! He was dead. Dead.

And it was he, his father, who was to blame. It was because of his evil doing. Why had the enemy not shot him? But was it not he who was lying there—had the shot not hit him in the back?

"O God! Answer me! How could You allow it to come to this—that human beings go mad, and a father turns against his son! Kin against kin . . . or is this, perhaps, the Final Judgement Day?"

The forest was quiet.

Its depths were peaceful and enticing.

He once again raised his head from his son's chest and, almost out of his mind, glanced deep into the forest.

Could he see anything? Was anyone circling around him?

No! Everything was still the same. Only large clumps of snow were falling from above—carefully, deliberately, almost without a sound, as if they did not want to disturb the surrounding tranquillity. It seemed that a portent, an omen of some kind, was passing through the forest. And then a gentle breeze blew over the branches. Hoarfrost was falling, as if pelted by an unseen hand; it washed the son's face and buried the father's head. Then everything became still, motionless. But not for long.

A roaring noise grew louder and louder. It roused the father, and he lurched to his feet.

Something had happened. Something. Something overwhelming. Monstrous. He was to blame; he did not have the strength to carry the burden that he had to bear from this moment on. He would not go back to the village now. Let the cattle all die, let them bellow themselves to death.

He now had another task—his son, his child was waiting for him. He could not abandon this one, and if what he had to do got done before the moon rose—so much the better. He had to finish his work.

It was all the same now. No matter what he did, he would be condemned by all.

But this was not what was occupying his mind.

The main thing was that his child was no longer living, and he was to blame.

He picked up the spade and began digging a second grave. But not over here, immediately beside the first one, but farther over there, next to the tall fir tree. Its interwoven branches were so strong, so wide, and so huge that—like a house—they would protect his child from everything.

Yes, yes!

Weeping as he dug, he talked to his son as if he were standing next to him. He talked to himself. About his misfortune. He talked about his wife, about his daughter-in-law whom his son had left in his care, and how he had guaranteed her happiness and promised to be the peacemaker if a quarrel ever arose between her and the mother. He talked about his grandson—he was to teach him his prayers if his father fell in battle in a foreign land, or if some other misfortune struck him.

He was to do everything.

"It's me!" he cried out despairingly between sobs. "It's your father, my child, your father. I gave you your life, blessed you as you set out on your difficult road, and brought you your death! It's me!"

The second grave was ready, and he placed both corpses in it. First the stranger, and then his own child.

"May the ground lie like a feather on you, my child!" he whispered through his tears as he covered the grave. "Sleep, my son, sleep; your father has made a good bed for you. Your mother will sing you a lullaby, and your young wife as well."

He interrupted himself abruptly, rose to his feet, and stood straight as a candle.

A shudder ran through his body; then he picked up his son's knapsack, placed it on his back, glanced once more at his son's grave, and walked away.

Stepping quickly, he moves farther and farther away from the grave, claps his hands from time to time, stops and looks around, but sees nothing. He does not even see the Austrian sergeant who appears at his side as if he had risen from the ground. He had been following him for a long time and now came up behind him.

"Halt!" he shouts.

The peasant shudders, looks at him, and stands dumbfounded. The sergeant puts his hand on his back.

"What's wrong with you?" he asks sternly. And then he points at the knapsack on his back. "Where did you get this?"

At first, the unfortunate peasant remains silent. He wants to say . . . he wants to say . . . but it is too much. He is almost out of his mind. The death of his son . . . his wife . . . the young daughter-in-law . . . the punishment, the cattle. Everything!

"I . . . I . . ." This is all that he can manage to gasp, and then he falls silent.

"Yes?" the sergeant says questioningly, giving the peasant a stern look. "Where did you get the knapsack?"

"The knapsack?" he asks, as if in a stupor. "What knapsack?"

"Why, this one—the one that you have on your back. Did you put it on by yourself? You! You!"

The peasant howls, covers his face with both his hands, and shakes his head.

"Yes, yes," he stammers, "the knapsack, I took it with me. It's from him, from him. I took it for myself, for his mother, his wife, and his child. Oh, sir!" and having said this, he begins to wail.

"Tell me, my good man, what happened? Has your son fallen in battle? If that's the case, then you do not have the right to keep it. Do you know that you could be punished for this? Take it and put it back where it belongs. Right now. Do you understand?"

"Oh, sir!" the peasant replies, raising his hands as if he were praying. "I'll tell you everything, I'll confess to everything as I would before God, even though He knows everything and saw everything. I'll tell you the whole truth, because I know that I must die. I have to, sir!" he almost shouts. "I have to!

"My misfortune has cleared my vision, because up to now I didn't see anything. But now my soul has eyes, and you must look into them. Prior to this my soul was locked. No one had the key to it . . ." he speaks haltingly. "Until my misfortune crawled up behind me. Step by step . . .

"O sir, step by step," he hisses shrilly in a mournful, furtive whisper. "Quietly, like a shadow in the moonlight, until it caught up with me and sucked out my mind. Because I did not will any of this. I went to buy some salt for my son's cattle, and my thoughts did not even so much as search for the footprints of misfortune. They were back home with the cattle, with my problems, with my work, with my wife, and with them . . ."

He breaks off abruptly and slides down at the feet of the armed man. "I'm confessing to you, I'm confessing everything to you. Perhaps God has sent you to me on the road, for I don't know what to do; I only know that I must die."

And he confessed everything. Breathing heavily, sobbing, and tearing the hair on his head, or raising his arms to the sky—he told him everything. From the very first step that he made when he left his home that morning; about his chance meeting with the enemy; about everything—up to the very moment when he met the sergeant.

He told it all truthfully and in great detail.

"For I know that there is nothing but death awaiting me," he repeated the words twice and completed his confession.

"Why did you tell them about the patrol?" the sergeant asked him.

"Ask me instead, sir, why I did not let them whip me to death. Was I thinking then? Does a person know anything? Can you foresee what is going to happen? Why!" he added, pounding his chest with his fist until it resounded.

And he stared straight ahead for a long moment, silently, without saying anything, as if he saw something beckoning to him.

Suddenly he turned to the sergeant and said: "Where is this holy being that the priest tells us about—the one that the Saviour gives every person for his protection, so he would take care of that person, teach him what he should do, and what he shouldn't do? Perhaps he would have warned me about my misfortune . . ."

Smiling bitterly as he uttered these words, he gazed into the distance as he had gazed before.

"He must have fallen as well, for otherwise a father would not go against his son, a Christian against a Christian. Would he have done this?"

The sergeant listened silently and let him talk himself out. Then he ordered curtly: "Forward march!"

They walked in silence.

The peasant in front of the armed man.

The snow did not stop falling. The old man took off his cap, and the snow melted on his head.

Suddenly he stopped.

He threw his head back unexpectedly, as if he were completely exhausted; his gray hair fell on his shoulders, and he closed his eyes.

After a moment, mustering his strength, he said: "Please, sir, go to my home later and tell them about me, about Judas; let them be on guard about becoming what I have become."

And, after another moment, during which the armed man looked at him as one looks at a person sick with a fever, or at a madman, he continued: "There are *two* who will not forgive me my misfortune. One is the soul of my son, and the other is our meadow.

"Perhaps I'll meet my son in the other world, and perhaps he'll forgive me for what I've done. Perhaps. But my meadow—this small piece of land that has come down to me from my ancestors, that the hands of my son have tilled—I'll never meet up with it again, and it will never forgive me for orphaning it and taking away from it the hands that cared for it. Then there's my little grandson . . ."

But at this point he abruptly stopped speaking, and his entire body shuddered as before.

Then he halted and asked: "Will they hang me, or shoot me? What do you think, sir?"

"Perhaps they will have mercy on you."

"How's that?"

"Perhaps they'll sentence you to life in prison."

The peasant was struck dumb with fear; he turned so pale that it seemed the last drop of blood had drained from his face, and he spoke as if the core of his being had died: "Then I would not die all at once, but I would have to die bit by bit, until my end finally came."

"What do you mean?"

The peasant did not reply.

"My meadow will not permit me to die all at once," he stated briefly and firmly after a little while.

"What are you talking about?"

"Just this. It will torture me every spring because of my hands and his. Oh, you do not understand this, those of you who are not peasants and do not work the soil. It waits for hands to care for it with the rising of the sun and in the moonlight; it waits for us when the grain is green and sways most beautifully in the wind. It waits for us all the time, until we come and give it what we have given it since the beginning of our lives. We give it our toil, sir!" he says, and then he stopped, bowed down low, respectfully removed his winter cap and, with the back of his hand, touched the soil as if paying it his last respects.

"Sir!" he exclaimed. "I've confessed everything myself, I admitted to everything, and, just as I'm walking with you, I know that I will never again walk down this road . . . that death awaits me. Could you grant me my request?"

"What do you want?"

"I want to go once more to my son," he said with a decisive calmness. "No one has ever escaped his fate. You can remain here, or go back with me—it's all the same to me. It's about one hundred steps . . . then there's the forest, and in it, under a fir tree, lies my son . . .

"Alas, my son, my son!" he called out, as if he were all alone. "My feet are taking me to you for the last time. They will not walk over this road again. Will you let me, sir? This is my final request."

His large, wild, anxious eyes were fastened on the lips of the armed soldier.

What should he do?

He nodded his head.

After the peasant moved off and vanished in the forest, the sergeant also turned his footsteps in that direction. He followed the footprints that attested to the peasant's quick pace. His final, broken steps.

There was a gentle rustling in the forest.

The sergeant stood at the edge of the forest, peered into its depths, and listened. The depths did not betray anything. There was a monotonous rustling, and the snow slid down to the earth without a sound. The snow was soft and gentle.

After some time went by, and the peasant still could not be seen, the sergeant walked farther into the forest. Here he found two graves. On one of them—the one that was standing apart, under the protection of a noble fir tree—lay a sheepskin coat and a cap, and from one widely opened pocket protruded a large piece of salt; next to it there was some Russian money. The peasant was dead. His long, colourful wool sash and a branch of the noble fir tree had performed a final service for him.

Silently, without haste, and evenly—like someone breathing—the heavy wads of snow continued to fall. Then they stopped.

Everything was hushed, expectant, waiting . . .

A forest . . . the solitary trees at its edge . . . And, far away from this spot, over there, in the depths of the valley, a lonely peasant hut with brightly lit tiny windows rimmed with plaster . . . a gate opened wide . . . and the gaping door of a barn . . .

When the twilight faded, night descended.

A silent, moonlit night . . .

A Dream . . .
A War Sketch
(1917)

(A harbour with men whose voices are carried in uneven waves, first higher, then lower . . .)

We are not on the way back; our work is not done. We are still on the move. At times, up—and at times, down. Can't you hear us? Some crawl up the cliffs like ants, stand guard, and sow the seeds of cannons. And in the valleys, some mingle with the horses, others with the lacerated earth. Some, nestling in a bloody heap, are no longer rising. Still others have hidden themselves, like badgers in holes . . . among the forest trees that, when they are hungry and cold, lull them with their everlasting whispering and, shaking down on them festal garments of white hoarfrost, breathe into them eternal sleep, turning them rigid as they stand sentry in the early morning or in the midnight frost. Here, under a fir tree white with hoarfrost, and there, in a small group, straggling with difficulty through the snowy haze to meet the enemy face to face . . . to look at each other with ferocious, hate-filled eyes . . . and then . . . But why do you need to know all this?

In a word—we are not yet ready.

But—we will return, we will return.

When everything quiets down, a white horse without a rider or a saddle will fly in among us, its nostrils torn and bloodied by its desperate flight and frantic breathing and, lifting its head up high— will neigh . . .

We will return . . .

How many of us? You will see.

And not all of us will come at the same time.

And we will not have the same stride. Nor will we be on the same road.

Alas, not on the same road, and not with the same stride.

***

When we bade our farewells and departed, the earth felt our power, our courage, our eagerness, and our even strides; it heard them as if they were a *single* stride. All of us were as *one*; *one* wholeness, *one* worthiness. And at that time the earth was still black or green, covered only with golden or green rugs and tapestries. It was fed with our hands, caressed by our solicitude, and warmed with our love . . .

But we will return, we will return; it is just that we are not ready yet.

We still have a remnant of strength; it is still alive in us—do you not hear us?

Do you not hear us?

Listen most attentively, strain your eyes to the utmost, and you will ascertain how many of us there still are.

Be patient—do not disturb us; stifle your crying. And do not send your sighs and yours prayers in pursuit of us. They get in our way and roll away the stone from the sepulchre of the heart.

But no, pray for us . . . pray . . . Christ is . . . somewhere . . . He drags himself like an exhausted shadow . . . There is too much work . . . Perhaps His holy feet are giving way under Him . . . or . . . or . . . He is carrying bullets from rifles—forgive us, O Lord—straight to the *heavens*.

The earth is slashed and gouged! It opens wide its jaws . . . It wants to drink . . . *It is waiting for . . . the white horse . . .*

***

(A harbour with women and children who are waiting expectantly for their husbands, fathers, and brothers.)

All are shading their eyes with their hands, for they are dazzled by a bloody brightness. Emaciated, weak, ragged, and aged figures are illuminated by the blood-red light of the sun that is sinking in the west and, at any moment now, will disappear from the horizon, replacing itself with a fog that, as usually happens here . . . will shroud everything in grey veils.

Are they still not returning? Their lips, their hearts ask . . . How much longer must they wait for them? Once, twice, and even a fourth time, the trees have lost their leaves and turned green again, and once more a snowy whiteness has covered everything. But *they* still are not here . . . they are not here . . . not here.

And they have prayed and pleaded, paid for scores of liturgies in the churches, waited silently, comforting themselves only with nocturnal dreams, with apparitions of husbands, fathers, and brothers, who seemingly, from afar . . . from fields, from trenches, from among cliffs, crawled towards them with gaunt faces, with insane eyes maddened by the gory terrors of war . . . as if gnawed by wild animals, with gaping wounds on their bodies, some without arms, others without legs, limping, stumbling, falling, and rising to their feet once more . . .

"Who will cultivate the fields and sow them for us? Even the ploughing has not been done!" they lamented, casting the words among themselves, firmly and dully, like stones, and smiling eerily, as if they were smiling their last smile.

"It is already ploughed and watered—that black earth," a strange rumble reverberated hollowly in the air, "without the hands of your husbands, fathers, and brothers . . ."

And, leaving behind a trail of terror and wailing among the women and children before it vanished into the distance, the thunderous voice of an invincible power roared over their heads: "You can already gather what has been sown. Do you not know what that means?"

"Yes, yes, we know . . . They have taken the clothing, and black ravens have flocked to the bodies like flies, but the bones, and only the white bones . . . are left for us. For the widows, the orphans, and the earth as well . . ."

(After a time, the same people once again, the same pleading.)

"Return at long last!" a cry resounded in unison from all the breasts. "Return!"

And at the same time, children, forcing their way through to their mothers, began shoving, timidly over here, wilfully over there—

and they were all crying, demanding bread. Rubbing their eyes with their tiny, reddened, frozen fists, they struck their mothers in the back and called them insulting names, punishing them for the hunger, the suffering, the unheated houses.

"We'll tell father, we will!" some threatened, cursing and glowering at their mothers, who turned away from them and searched the distance determinedly with their eyes. "Oh yes . . . we'll tell them *everything* . . . We're not like you think we are—we know *everything*.

"Even that about which you are silent.

"It doesn't matter that you're waiting for them from *that other* side.

"Your eyes are turned upwards, as in icons, and you fill the churches . . . locking us up at home, hungry and cold, so that we would not run after you—and not know anything. *We'll tell them everything*."

***

(The harbour of the men, enveloped in clouds of smoke, shrouded in a darkness sporadically rent by flashes of fire . . . approaching and receding from the harbour of the women.)

Are you overcome by impatience?

Because ours also has been eroded by rust.

Is it *we* who create time? What are we? Once we *were*, there was a past and a present, there *were* the fairy tales of peace, not life itself.

Now we are being swept up like scattered debris . . . and where will they put us? But you do not have to know this. Yes. You do not have to know where they have herded us . . . what a *distant* road means. They drive us first into one corner, then into another . . . And they throw bones of discord among us, so we would poison ourselves on them . . . so we would be tormented by our thoughts about you and about what we will find when we return home. They are undermining our faith in our cause . . .

Chained together by *words* and an oath into a wholeness—we console ourselves.

Do you not hear our songs from afar? From afar . . . from afar, where wolves circle around us . . . When they toss the earth upon us and cover us with boards, so that others can cross over on them.

We are not ready yet.

And how could we be, so soon?

The white horse has not stopped beside us yet; he has not neighed joyfully nor brought us good tidings.

We are not winged birds, to flock on high. And the land here is not like ours back home. On one side, red poppies grow on it, filling in the trenches, adorning the graves—on the other side, it is covered with eternal snow. And this is where they send us, so that we will fill the steppes . . . hey, hey, women . . . and fill them well! Not one of us will return . . . if we ever get to where we are going . . .

And whoever does return . . . will stand before you like an apparition. He will come to you to lay down his bones . . . to show his white hair . . . He will lose his speech. A word will fall like a frozen snowflake before it reaches your ear . . .

We, who are awaited by you, cannot yet return. Many of us are walking with a *new* stride. Slowly, slowly, on *one* leg, with the dull thud of crutches and wooden legs, traded in for our marvellous, shining weapons.

With a new stride . . .

We will not return soon.

Do not wait for us as yet.

The leaves have not fallen off the tall trees for the last time.

The eyes of the young fighters are still bright, and their lips are not twisted in disillusionment. They have not yet seen what we, the prematurely old, see and have seen—but *you* do not have to know this. *You*, you know something else. You, the loyal mothers of sons—your heroes—the impatient sisters, young wives, and girls in full bloom!

Wait for us! You are no worse off, and we are no better off. Wait!

Listen to the roar of the cannons and to what follows immediately afterwards. It fills the air.

It is strings that are snapping.

The ones that bound us to you, and those that drew you to us.

And you be silent, O poet-birds! Turn to the heavens and kiss the earth. Let it not weigh heavily on our wounded breasts . . . for we will return to you, we will return. Just wait for a short while longer . . .

***

(A harbour with women, children, and old men. In the air above them there is the din of cannons, while in the streets of the town silence has hidden itself.
A fragmented breath of fear is flying.
Choked tears gush from eyes, and the white lips of women and children open almost unconsciously to let loose a shriek of fear and despair.)

They thought the end would *finally* come, because once more the trees were turning green—but the earth was shaken again and again.

But what was happening *there*, on the opposite side—who could know that?

Thoughts were circling like black questions in their heads.

"Children, be quiet! Stop your whining and don't keep asking for bread! Where are we to get it? Wait. Your fathers will return one day!"

"Our fathers are not returning! We don't want to wait so long! Bread! Mother, give us some bread! And if you don't, we'll hire ourselves out to them."

"Damned *traitors . . . traitors from conception . . .* Is this why we fed you with our own blood? Come to your senses!"

(Crying and wailing.) "Mother, bread! All we want is bread!"

Old men, once tall, but now bowed down, threateningly raise their bony arms with thick fists, like hardened lumps of black earth, and brandish them at the horizon: "Come back, O sons and grandsons! Come back, our heroes, so that you may leave a trace of *yourself* on *your own* land!"

And then, bunching together into a tight little group, they listen as one of them speaks softly.

"Once, a long long time ago," he narrated, "there was a famous tribe. And it is said that they had a strange custom. Once a year, every woman or girl had to go to the market place—some say that they went to the gates of the city or to the temple of a goddess—and she had to stand there and wait until some stranger who desired her threw some gold into the lap of her skirt. And she *had* to go with him.

"That golden money was sacred and given later to the goddess. And afterwards she could return home.

"My brothers," he added gloomily as he finished his story, "We are not a famous tribe, and as for our women, do they sacrifice themselves for the *temples*?"

And turning his face to the distant male harbour, he called out, together with other voices: "Come back, O sons and grandsons, come back, O brothers and heroes, so that you may leave a trace of yourself on your own land!"

"On your own land."

A faint echo was scarcely heard, and then it vanished, dissolving like a wave in the expansive sea.

***

(From the harbour of the men.)

We will return, O dear fathers and friends, our former guardians, our teachers of virtue and of love!

We will return—but we are still blind and not able to see the path that leads to our home; we are still groping our way . . .

It is hope alone that is leading us.

We are not dead.

We will live on.

He Lost His Mind
A Sketch from Real Life
(1923)

The night of June 10, 1915.

A clear and starry night.

On all the streets of the town of Ch., a deathly silence reigned. Everything was *listening intently*. Everything was breathing deeply and heavily; everything was solemn, with tightly closed lips. Everything, as has been said, was listening intently.

Not far from the town, just across the river, a battle was raging. The Russians were fighting the Austrians. A heavy hail of rifle bullets fell incessantly. Amidst that noise, cannons roared from this side of the river where the town was situated, and from the other side. From our side, the noise sounded louder, and from the enemy's side it was weaker, but finally the din and the roaring fused together, and an inferno was set ablaze. Whoever found himself on the street stepped along very carefully, trailing his shadow behind him.

The moon, like a silver grindstone, swam out into the starry heavens. Nothing assailed it. It poured forth its enchanting light and looked on in amazement.

Very few people ventured out of their homes, and anyone who dared to, did so stealthily. No one was thinking, because everyone was listening with his entire being. Some people, especially the women, returned home in the company of their shadows, tears rolling from their terrified eyes. The throats of others were choked with emotion. It seemed that bodies without souls were prowling the sidewalks and streets. The sidewalks rang with the clicking strides of passersby and fell silent after the footsteps had passed.

An invisible funeral was taking place. Instead of tears—blood was flowing. Someone's arms, raised to the heavens, pleaded for mercy. There was none. The Saviour was nowhere to be seen. He was performing miracles. Over there, in the midst of a stream of artillery fire, He protected, with His breast, a widow's poor son. There, He turned aside, for a moment, the face of an only son—and the bullet pierced his cap. Here, by raising His holy hands, He repelled a bullet, and the steel plunged into the ground. There, He fell like a cross to the earth, sheltering from horses' hooves the body of a father surrounded by his children. And over there, He leapt on a horse, guiding it so that the horse reared in a wild rage and jumped to one side with its rider, while a bullet tore through the banner.

He did not stand idly by. His white garments were soiled, and with every passing minute He closed more and more eyes . . .

Grief had descended from the heavens to stagger among the living. It was only insensate bodies that roamed the streets; minds and souls were turned to where the battle was blazing.

The hellish moments passed with agonising slowness, and over there, where voices were ringing to the heavens, death rushed about, miring life in eternal crippling and corpses. Strong young men toppled like sheaves, blood pouring from their temples . . .

Madness, shrieking, bullets in hot pursuit, the roar of cannons—everything was forcing its way upwards to the heavens, searching for justice.

There was no justice . . .

God's wide and deep cupola, having adorned itself with stars, embraced the earth. The desire to bargain did not come from the heavens, but from the earth—*it* alone was accountable.

It is true that some of the stars strove to glimmer more brightly, as if startled out of their appointed places by the wailing and carnage below, but not one of them flew down to help. A few broke loose and, feigning speed, plummeted downwards. But where they fell or whom they saved, no one ever knew. There, one may have saved an *orphan* . . . And over there, perhaps, another decorated a noble young breast, endowing it with even greater virtue . . . or a brave, fearless old breast that led the way, setting an example.

Was there anyone who knew?

Everything had descended into chaos.

"Yesterday," people were saying, "an inferno raged beyond the river; the roar of cannons—those iron beasts—rang out, but today . . . it's as if nothing had happened."

And truly, yesterday and today were like day and night. The sky was now calm, a silver-blue—it was June—and filled with sunshine; silence reigned. The trees by the road, attired in their green finery, appeared to be guarding the tranquillity—a tranquillity that, having shunned this vicinity for such a long time, was now in joyful ascendancy.

The road, long and straight as an arrow—known as the tsar's road—was empty. Here, among the fields, it looked like a coiling snake; over there, it once again was a straight ribbon, and everywhere it was clean, white, and hard, for it was well built. Sturdy and agile hands had fashioned it at one time, marking its length with wooden stakes and placing telegraph poles, strung together by wires, to stand guard over it.

The meadowlarks, those tiny creatures of God, that alone can fly into the blueness of the sky—where the eye, trying to follow them, loses its way—poured forth their sweet pearly trills, sowing them in the air. Their song was all that could be heard on this heavenly morning; the fields were empty, deserted, and peaceful.

A truly divine day.

But no. Not a divine one.

The eye can find no peace.

Somewhere, far off on the white road, it espies a black speck. This black speck is moving and pushing itself forward. And it is not alone. In its wake, others come forth, like beetles crawling out of the ground; the first ones followed by others . . . Growing numbers of these specks creep down the road and, gradually, a convoy comes into view . . . a ribbon of medical coaches interspersed with ordinary wagons.

The wounded are being carted to hospitals—some into the city, others to the field hospitals, and still others to be lowered shortly into the black earth. Mournful, rhythmless music that tears at the heart issues from this moving ribbon. The closer the wagons approach, the louder the rhythmless music becomes. Soon, the wagons themselves can be seen. The eye closes, because the scene is unbearably painful; the ear receives the grief, carves it up, and twists the lips in anguish.

The wagons are carting fragments of hell.

Victory wanders somewhere over the empty fields . . . and vanishes. No one is laying claim to it . . . It has benefitted no one.

Hey, hey there, horses! Hey there, oxen! Keep on going, step carefully ahead, do not sway your heads, do not lower them. Are you intoxicated with the voices of those who went forward bravely to fight for "their own" land, and whom you are now carting back to it? Possibly it—that singing that tears at the heart—has intoxicated you and is confusing your feet, for you are stepping very uncertainly.

Hey, hey there, horses . . . Hey, hey there, oxen! Hey there, ha! Carefully now!

Past the forest moves still another medical coach, but it is not a real one—there are not enough of them; so a simple wagon, spread with straw, is hauling two badly wounded men. The wagon skirts a pile of corpses that, if time permits, will be buried today; the driver is moving along very carefully, when a painful cry for help reaches his ear. This cry, that is more like a shriek, seems more sorrowful than all the previous ones; it begs permission to enter the driver's ear and soul.

A soldier, his head leaning against a tree trunk at the edge of the forest, is beckoning to him with his hand.

What is this?

He is already hauling two men, and his wagon is small. Nevertheless, he reins in his horse—or rather, the horse stops of his own accord, as if he knows that he should stop where there are shrieks, and turns his head to look at his master. Will he be given a still heavier load to haul? No, nothing more will be added to his load, and what he is carrying now is barely stirring on the wagon, except for an occasional groan . . .

The driver hurriedly leaves the wagon and, just as hastily, approaches the wounded man. What is wrong with him? At least he can ask who he is.

He takes a look, and falls back in horror.

The stomach of the wounded man is ripped open; he has no clothing, just a gentleman's shirt drenched in blood . . . His left hand has been shot—he is hopelessly wounded, almost a corpse.

A single step away from him, a revolver peeps out from under his cap, revealing that this is no ordinary soldier. His face is young, but who knows whose it is . . . His eyes are burning, and his waxen face is covered with red blotches. He is lying there, and only his head is leaning against the oak, while his chin, with its sparse growth of hair, touches his chest . . . and because of this, his dark eyes, looking upwards from under his brow, are terrifying. Only his right hand is whole and unharmed.

The driver draws nearer and bends over the wounded man.

"His soul is gazing out of his eyes," the driver thinks. And he asks: "What do you want, soldier?"

"Take me with you. I have a blind father . . . Have pity on me; otherwise they'll throw me in a hole along with the others . . . Quickly," he pleads desperately. "They took the live ones, and left me . . . It's clear to me . . ." he breaks off what he is saying, and his head sags helplessly to one side, "there is no hope for me. Perhaps you have a soul . . . a father or a mother," he moans these words between pauses. "To the very last moment . . . I bared my chest . . . thinking . . . *it's for Ukraine!*" he groans with great effort . . . as if he had no strength left.

But no!

There is still a drop of life in him, there is still a vestige of energy. He lifts up his head again—it keeps slipping to one side—leans it, as before, against the tree and, looking up at the driver with those terrifying eyes, adds: "Now I'm lying here like an abandoned dog on a dunghill . . . And I'm waiting."

His eyes search for the driver . . . And a moment later, without moving his head, he turns his eyes to the right and points in that direction with his good hand.

"Give me . . . My revolver's over there, it's still loaded . . . It's my defender . . . I want to die with it . . . but . . . but," and his eyes fill with tears.

"But all the same, take me with you; I've waited so long . . . Night is coming . . ." and he breaks off what he is saying.

The driver looks to the right, and the revolver is lying there, on the ground . . .

He picks it up and gives it to the dying man.

"On the wagon," the dry lips of the fighter groan . . . as if for the last time.

"I can't, my dear one . . . I can't! There's no room . . . and those two unfortunate fellows," the driver blurts out in terror. Confronted by the eyes of the dying man, he feels as if his hair is standing on end. He would like to flee from those maddened and impassioned eyes which, like beautiful stars, blaze from under his arched dark brows, reflecting the very depths of his soul.

"It's as if he were burning," the driver thinks. And then he says: "There's no room, my dear one; I wasn't told to remove wounded men from this place, no matter who they might be; perhaps the wagon coming after me will be able to take you, but even if I wanted to . . ."

As he bends over, the mortally wounded soldier grabs him by the edge of his coat.

"You weren't told to? There's no room for a *Ukrainian*? Where will there be room? I'm still alive . . ."

The driver sees that the soldier has only moments left to live. "His head is healthy," he thinks, "but his body is no longer meant for this world."

Troubled because he can not take him—there is room for only two wounded men on his wagon—he says: "Perhaps . . . when I finish driving those two on the wagon, but," he excuses himself, "I'm not guaranteeing it."

And he steps back.

Something breaks loose from the soldier's breast, and his chest is ripped open by pent-up tears. He gestures hopelessly, lifts his head higher, then drops it back against the trunk of the oak. Something akin to a smile twists his lips.

"Thus ends a soldier's life . . . Go then, if that's the case," he barely croaks. "But when *she is resurrected*—the one that I went to fight for—then . . ."—he stretches out his hand, and his eyes pierce the terrified driver—"inform me about it!"

"In . . . in . . . form you?" The driver stares at him with bulging eyes.

"When *she is resurrected*, so that I may rise to my feet, *see her*, and lie down once again."

"See whom?"

The dying man has no strength left.

"Go," he gasps. "It's not death . . . that's frightening, but . . . but . . ."

The driver bends over once again. His lips want to say something to the unfortunate man, but his eyes fill with tears, and he only repeats after him: "But . . . but . . ."

" . . . but the *ignorance* . . . of our people."

Convulsively holding the revolver in his good hand, the soldier waves the driver away and closes his eyes.

As the driver moves off, he looks down for the last time at the unfortunate young man and, turning away, walks towards his wagon where he has left the wounded men. He has taken just a few steps forward when something seems to strike him in the back like a fist, and the sound of a shot causes him to recoil. He stops dumbstruck and looks back in horror.

There, under the oak tree where the soldier is lying, a thin wisp of smoke curls in the air.

Terrified out of his wits, he goes back.

Blood is gushing from the heart of the dying man. His chest is heaving. His lips whisper: "I'm dying. But *she* will not die."

"Who?" the driver asks sharply.

"U . . . U . . ." his lips rustle, but the word remains unfinished.

The driver, rooted to the spot, crosses himself three times.

Then, wiping away the tears trickling down his moustache, he picks up the revolver that has fallen from the hand of the dying man and looks at it. There are no bullets left.

Lifting his shoulders in bewilderment, he says: "In the final moment, the poor man *lost his mind*."

Then, looking around fearfully, he adds: "It's terrifying! U . . . U . . . U . . ."

But . . . The Lord Is Silent
(1927)

When Kalyna Maystryukova, the indigent widow of Mykhaylo Maystryuk, spent her hard-earned money on a heifer that she called Blackie White-Spot—she was black as a raven, and only her forehead was white, as if covered by a lady's dainty white handkerchief—no one would have expected that in four or five years she would become a sturdy, impressive cow with a chest that even the best bull in the communal herd would not have been ashamed of. But who else would have known how to pamper and take care of cattle as Kalyna Maystryukova did.

In the early dawn, she would throw on a coarse wool coat, secure her door with a big wooden lock, circle the hut a few times to make sure she had not left anything of value on the *pryz'ba [earthen embankment abutting a cottage]*—a little bucket or a small hempen cloth—and let out into the yard the few chickens that she kept in a side porch. Then, without taking along even a scrap of bread for a noon meal for herself, she would tie a rope to Blackie's young horns, pat the cow all the way down her back and flanks, and set out to graze her somewhere. But where?

It was quite far to the common pasture from her house, and she was afraid to let this creature of God go there by herself, for fear she would damage someone's property, and it would be she, Kalyna Maystryukova, who would have to pay for the harm done by her voracious Blackie's mouth.

It was better that she keep Blackie on a rope while grazing her. Roving through the countryside in search of feed, she occasionally dared to go as far as the lord's forest. The grass grew there in wonderful abundance! And, entangled in it was a profusion of brilliant tiny flowers and healing herbs: wormwood for weak legs, madwort, fall-out-hair, forget-me-not, wild thyme, and other wonder-working herbs that, being sought after by well-to-do city folk, enabled a poor person to earn a bit of extra cash.

Oh, that wonderful forget-me-not! The forget-me-not that grew on the hayfields or in the forest, the forget-me-not in which people with paralysed hands and feet were bathed. And the madwort—an herb that only a few people knew where to find, for it did not grow everywhere. It was used to cure a child or adult possessed with fear, or with—it was best not to utter the words, for it was terrifying even to think of it—the falling sickness; and this was why it was called madwort.

It was these herbs that caused her to almost lost her mind one day and flee from the forest in excruciating pain.

She had been grazing Blackie and had crossed over the boundary of the forest by just the slightest bit. As the cow sank her muzzle into the lush forest grass and pulled up so much of it that huge handfuls were hanging from both sides of her greedy mouth, a gadfly, confused by the bright sunlight on the flowers, bit the poor old woman. And she, poor thing, forgot not only about the madwort, but even about Blackie, who, jerking the rope out of her hands, wandered off some distance into the forest in search of more grass.

It was fortunate that the forester had not come by just then, for he would have given her so many "madworts" on her spine that she would have completely lost her taste for picking herbs. And it was all because of the cow and that black gadfly that circled above the flowers as if intoning a liturgy over them.

That time, instead of walking home, she had run all the way, tugging and pulling the young cow that did not have the slightest inclination to leave the pasture. And all the while, the pain was almost driving her mad. The vicious fly had bitten her just above her right eyebrow. The bite had swelled instantly—she could feel it with her finger—to the size of a dove's egg, or, God only knows, maybe even bigger, and it was making her rush home at a frantic pace in order to put something on the throbbing spot—a knife or anything else made of metal, or at least a wet rag.

It had not been easy for her to raise her Blackie. Oh, not easy at all! She lived through a long and difficult time as she watched her heifer grow into a cow, for she did not have much land, just a couple of small patches—no more than a poor widow could hope to have. And that was why she often grazed her cow on neighbours' boundaries, and why she was frequently cursed by them and other people, may God forgive them. And sometimes she drove her cow on the stubble belonging to fellow villagers, and her feet got pricked and scratched—but that was not so bad yet.

It was worse when the Heavenly Ones got the urge to fill the air with a mist or a fine rain, and you had to stand around for hours on end with a soaked hempen wrap on your back, waiting wearily and staring endlessly at the mouth of the cow, which—no longer pestered by summer flies—seemed to be filling a bottomless pit.

O Lord!

No, it had not been easy to raise her black pet, the rambunctious, disobedient Blackie. But the Lord had made it possible for her to raise her, and to get one calf from her, and then a second, and a third. And when the third one turned out to be similar to Blackie—they were like two peas in a pod—she decided to sell old Blackie and keep this third calf as a cow for herself.

The roof needed to be rethatched; the old straw was almost completely rotted, and the rains came through it in God's summer, and again in the fall and spring, drenching almost everything in her hut: the cornmeal flour; her dyed, home-spun blankets; the variegated beans and the plain ones; the broad beans; a few dried apples, and some nuts—these were for Christmas—and other things like that with which the Lord rewards people for their labour.

And so she decided in her own mind, without discussing it with anyone, to sell the "wet nurse" that had kept her alive in this world with its milk—for who else would have cared for her after her husband died? She was going to sell her on the market day held on the Feast of Saints Peter and Paul—or maybe later.

She would take the cow to town and sell her to some good householder. And with the money she got for her, she would fix up her hut and rethatch the roof, because you cannot know how long you are fated to walk about on this earth. Perhaps it would not be for too much longer, but then again, what if she lived until she was very old?

She had no family.

There had been two children once—two infant boys—but they both caught colds and died within a week of each other. Only God and the Heavenly Mother knew ... On evenings when the heavens were strewn with stars, she would look up at the sky and recall her little sons. That was where they belonged, and they blinked down at her from on high. She would look up, cross herself, and go back inside her hut.

Some day they would all meet up there.

The two little sons, their father, and she.

And so she was left alone. All alone.

For could you count as family Maftey, her dead aunt's son, who lived in the neighbouring village? He was a hard-working man who visited her only rarely. True, he had invited her to his wedding; both he and his bride had come and asked her most warmly to attend. And she had been in the bridal party, both in his home and hers. They had treated her very well at the wedding, giving her the place of honour reserved for a mother. This is why she does not forget about him.

When she closes her eyes for the last time, she will leave Maftey everything.

First of all, he did not drink; moreover, he was as industrious as a bee, did not get involved in law suits, and would appreciate and take care of whatever was left to him. And he would see to it that she had a grand funeral; he would give the priest money to preach a fine sermon and, together with his wife, host a funeral dinner for the repose of her soul.

She should go and see them sometime. He had passed on a message to her that a child had been born to them—it was probably a few months old by now.

Sometime . . .

And so when the Feast of Saints Peter and Paul came and brought good weather with it, she led her "wet nurse" out of the barn. She washed the cow's udder as she always did and then, after scrubbing her all over, rubbing her down, and currying her—just as you would prepare a sacrifice for the Lord—she led her to market.

She sold her to a fine, upstanding householder.

And, having pocketed a tidy sum of money, she started out for home.

She set out in the company of some acquaintances.

Then, when she came to a country road that led to the home of her dead aunt's son—if you took this byway it was not too long a walk to his village—she politely parted company with her travelling companions and set off down the trail.

She walked for quite some time, conscious of the fact that she was all alone—there was no one else in sight.

But she continued on her way. Yes, she was a little tired already, but her feet were still strong. Wearing only a sleeveless jerkin and a coarse wool coat, she walked along, holding in her hands the stick she had used with Blackie.

Accustomed as she was to spending her waking hours in work, the day seemed very long to her, very long indeed. The sun set, and the early evening arrived, just as it was supposed to. Now she could spot the cottages of a small village, but they were few and far between, and she still had to walk through a goodly number of fields.

In the distance, an old man, supporting himself with a cane and carrying a bag slung over his shoulder, slowly approached her, followed by a woman. They exchanged greetings with her and kept on going. Unconsciously patting her ribs on the side where the money she had received for the cow lay knotted in a sturdy piece of cloth inside her shirt, she too continued peacefully on her way.

If only God were willing to let her find Maftey at home and in good health. If only!

She did not have much farther to go, just one more hayfield to cross, one on which a man appeared to be mowing. From there it was not far to Maftey's house. And then, it suddenly seemed to her that the mower was Maftey, the son of her deceased aunt. She relaxed.

Before long, she came up to the man, and it truly was Maftey. He was sitting on his haunches, sharpening his scythe.

They exchanged greetings. He invited her to sit down on the grass and then asked what was new with her—where she was coming from. His wife had been talking about her quite recently.

"She said she just had to go to see you and show you our little Zahariy. And when I said there was no time to do this now, because there's no end to the work, and no one else will do it for us, she said we would go on a *feast day*—the Feast of the Virgin Mary in the fall—because, as she herself said: 'Something is telling me to go and see Aunt Kalyna.'"

Kalyna sighed piously.

"And I felt drawn to come and see you," she picked up on his words. "Ever since I decided to sell my Blackie."

"Who?" the young man asked, and he turned his large, grey, penetrating eyes questioningly at her.

"Well . . . my old cow. You know, that spotted Blackie; I've left myself one of her calves that's almost three years old now. And so I decided to drop in and see you when I was returning from town, to find out if you're healthy and to see your little son. My neighbour Herasymykha says he's a fine little boy."

"For how much did you sell your cow?" he asked, his piercing grey eyes riveted on her lips.

She stated a rather large sum and, as before, struck herself on the side where she had secreted the money.

"They paid you well for it," he said seriously, and went back to his work.

She watched him silently for a while. Then, rubbing her feet, tired and dusty from her long walk, she inquired: "Will I find your Dokiya at home?"

The young man appeared not to hear her question and, instead of answering, asked: "What are you planning to do with your money?"

"What? I'm going to rethatch the roof, buy a few things I need, and put away some hay to winter over the cow that's still left at home. I'll buy a fur jacket if it isn't too expensive, because my old one no longer keeps me warm in the winter—it's so tattered that it's only good for blocking a hole in the pantry wall. And, as for the rest, I'll take it to the priest. He'll either put it away to earn interest, or tell me what to do with it."

Having answered his question, she fell silent for a moment.

"You wouldn't, by chance, lend me a thousand or so?"

His eyes fastened searchingly on her face. The old woman beside him was well over the hill already, yet she still wanted to put away her money "to earn interest."

Kalyna Maystryukova turned around abruptly, almost in alarm. "To you? Why do you need it? What do you want to buy?"

He scratched himself, lowered his head, and set to work on his scythe once again. "Just for a year or two, auntie. I might buy a horse . . . It's hard to be without a horse. I have one, but if I had the money, I'd buy another one to have a pair. It could even be an old nag. That is, if you wouldn't charge me too much interest," he said, and he gave her a strange look.

"I don't know," Kalyna replied, suddenly wary. "I don't know yet; I'll tell you when you and your wife come for the feast. I can't say either yes or no today, because I myself don't know. I'm just happy that, praise God, I managed to get this money; and as for buying a horse, well, the horse's mother hasn't died yet." And she laughed.

The young man pushed his cap to the back of his head, wiped his forehead with the palm of his hand and, looking straight ahead, said: "We'll talk about it some more. But now, go to the house, to Dokiya; don't wait for me here. I'll finish up the mowing and some other work . . . and then I'll catch up with you later. I have to go to the village yet, so I won't be back soon. Tell Dokiya this. Have some supper and go to sleep. Tomorrow is Sunday; we'll talk then."

With these words, he nodded to her and walked away

She rose to her feet with a painful groan and, rubbing her backside with her right hand, as if it had gone numb on her, glanced back at him. At that very moment, he also turned around and looked at her.

Their eyes met and then, as if caught in some evil deed, quickly turned away.

She looked up and saw that the sky had clouded over, while he, flinging his scythe over his shoulder, strode off heavily in the other direction.

She thought long and hard . . .

After greeting Dokiya and chatting with her, she found out that for some time now the young woman really had intended to visit her—she felt drawn to her as if Kalyna were her own mother—but something always came up and prevented her from doing so.

The two women ate their supper and, even though Kalyna was tired, they both continued moving about the house.

"Do lie down, auntie," the kind young woman urged the older woman.

Kalyna glanced around the hut, trying to find a spot to sleep and, so as not to be in the way of the householders, chose a corner of the cottage.

"You'll sleep on the bench, auntie; I'll give you a pillow for your head and a blanket or something, and I'll crawl up on the oven-bed with our little son. He's used to sleeping there. You're going to sleep on the bench, auntie, not on the floor, and that's that. Whoever heard of such a thing!"

"What about Maftey?"

"He . . . if he said that he had to go to the village, then he'll be home later. Maybe he went to the barber for a shave, or to the smithy with his axe. He begrudges the daylight hours for tasks like that. He's so hard-working that at times he's in no hurry to come home to eat. I scold him sometimes, but he doesn't even reply. So now I no longer say anything."

Just as she was saying this, her husband unexpectedly walked into the house and asked for some food.

He had a light lunch, thirstily gulped down some water, and left.

Before he went out, he stopped for a minute on the threshold and glanced back at his wife: "Make up a *comfortable* bed for Aunt Kalyna—she's tired."

"I will, I will . . . I'll make it on the bench, and I'll even put a fur coat under her."

"Remember to do that. And don't wait for me. When I come back, *I'll lie down in the porch*—it's not cold now."

After a while, both women lay down to sleep.

Night descended. A dark, very dark night.

The moon must still have been low in the sky, for no one saw it.

Did Kalyna Maystryukova sleep? She herself did not know; it was only when she awoke that she realized she had been sleeping. Tired from her long trek, she had fallen asleep instantly, as if she were dead, but now she was awake.

She lay quietly, so as not to awaken the young woman and the baby. Moreover, it seemed to her that someone was walking around outside the house, and that this person had stopped momentarily by her window. Perhaps it was only a dog. She involuntarily pressed the money in her shirt closer to her body and tried to fall asleep again.

It might have been midnight . . . It was still a long time to daybreak; there was still time to sleep, get up in the morning when the sun rose, and go home to tend to the cow and everything else dear to her that she had left behind . . .

Her cottage was locked, and the key to the lock was in her shirt.

The Lord would help her.

Once again someone seemed to pass by her window. She felt cold, engulfed by a chilling wave of fear. She wrapped the blanket more tightly around herself and lay perfectly still.

"Aunt Kalyna, are you sleeping?" Dokiya asked suddenly in a distinct whisper.

"No."

"Why not?"

"For some reason, I can't fall asleep. I feel cold; shivers are running up and down my spine."

"You're overtired. You're not up to a long walk like that anymore. And I'm too hot. I haven't slept at all yet. I heard Maftey come into the house and then go out again. I dozed a little, and now I'm so hot that I feel like getting up and dousing myself with water. But I can't move for fear of waking the little one. He's sleeping so soundly."

"Sleep, my dear Dokiya, sleep. Sometimes that's the way it is at night. I'm also trying not to move around too much, so that I don't wake up completely."

Once again it became silent. The silence merged with the darkness.

After a minute: "Aunt Kalyna . . ."

"What is it, my daughter?"

"I just can't sleep. It's too hot for me. I've pushed the little one off to one side, but I still can't fall asleep. You take my place up here, and I'll lie down there, and we'll both get some sleep."

Kalyna agreed to this, and the two women exchanged places. The young woman had scarcely lain down when she fell into a deep sleep; clearly, she was exhausted.

But old Kalyna could not sleep. She was afraid that if she fell asleep, she might smother the child . . . And the little one was breathing so evenly.

It was quiet in the house—not even a fly was buzzing. There was only darkness. If you gazed into this darkness, it seemed to dissolve; it must be midnight already. It might even be past midnight.

But Kalyna could not sleep.

All at once she not so much heard, as saw, that the door in the wall across from her was opening. It seemed to be opening all by itself, and a dark pole appeared to come through it. This pole stood motionless in the middle of the house for a few seconds, and then it disappeared—and only darkness remained in the doorway.

The old woman was frightened. Could this apparition be of this world? Why did the door not shut? Beyond it was the porch, and there, in the porch, Maftey lay sleeping.

Maftey is sleeping?
He is digging a grave.
A little ways off, behind the barn.

In a short while, the black pole once again rises from the threshold of the porch.

The old woman trembles, and her teeth chatter. The child next to her moans and turns away to the wall. The dull thud of an axe rings out on the neck of the woman sleeping on the bench. The black pole bends down over her and, as if merging with her, vanishes from the house.

Lord!
But . . . The Lord is silent.

The old woman does not walk; she flies like a phantom, her hair streaming behind her, to get help—from the neighbours, the watchman . . .

They come. They appear before the sun rises over the earth. They come upon Maftey burying his wife in a pit in the manure pile.

"Hey you! Why did you murder your wife?"

He howls.

He howls for a long time, breaking occasionally into demonic laughter.

When the people take him into their midst and lead him away in chains, he finally stops howling and laughing.

Lord!
But . . . The Lord is silent.

And Maftey is led away. He does not utter a word to anyone, and his eyes—his large, grey, piercing eyes—are now devoid of expression, exposing the eternal darkness of his mind.

Yevheniya Yaroshynska

1868-1904

Biographical Sketch

Yevheniya Yaroshynska spent her short life in a constant struggle to educate herself and ameliorate the living conditions of the peasants among whom she lived and worked in her native province of Bukovyna in Western Ukraine. Born into the family of a village teacher, she was unable to receive a higher education, as her father believed that his first responsibility was to secure the future of his two sons. After completing her elementary schooling, she satisfied her intellectual curiosity by reading widely and intensively, and embarking on a systematic program of self-education.

At that time, the Ukrainian province of Bukovyna was part of the Austro-Hungarian Empire, and German was imposed on the local Ukrainian population as the official language. The books that Yevheniya read, therefore, were all in German, and when she began writing she wrote in that language. Her first stories were published in a Viennese periodical when she was eighteen.

Just when Yevheniya was beginning her literary career in German literature, the first Ukrainian-language newspaper was established in Bukovyna under the editorship of Yuriy Fedkovych, one of the leading Bukovynian writers of the day. The articles published in this newspaper were pro-Ukrainian and promoted unification of Bukovyna with the rest of Ukraine. Drawn to the ideas expressed in the newspaper, Yevheniya began to correspond with its editor.

Under Fedkovych's influence, Yevheniya Yaroshynska began to read the works of Ukrainian authors from other parts of Ukraine, and to collect and study the folklore of her region. Becoming aware of the richness of her literary and cultural heritage, she decided to start writing in Ukrainian, and to devote herself and her talent to her people.

Assiduously applying herself to the task of collecting folklore materials, Yaroshynska wrote down 450 Bukovynian folk songs. For this notable collection, she was awarded a silver medal and a sizeable monetary prize (500 karbovantsi) from the ethnographic section of the Russian Geographical Association. In 1888, she began writing articles for Ukrainian, German, and Czech periodicals about Bukovynian embroidery, Easter egg designs, and wedding rituals.

At this time, as the daughter of a village teacher, she seized the opportunity to assist in the local school, where she taught young girls many practical skills and traditional arts. This program proved so successful that other parents asked her to instruct their children as well.

By 1890, she was publishing stories written in Ukrainian, literary translations, and articles about contemporary issues in Bukovynian society. In addition, inspired by her young pupils, she began to publish stories in journals for children.

In 1891, she travelled to Prague with Nataliya Kobrynska and other cultural leaders from Western Ukraine (Bukovyna and Halychyna) to see an exposition of Czech artifacts. She was greatly impressed by the work done by senior citizens and the mentally challenged, and by the fact that these people were integrated into Czech society

In 1892, Yevheniya began an apprenticeship as a teacher and, after writing a qualifying examination in 1896, received her teaching certificate. In conjunction with her teaching career, Yaroshynska contributed articles to pedagogical journals, began developing new curricula for village schools, and supported the idea of creating a teachers' association.

During this time, Yaroshynska became deeply involved in the women's movement in Ukraine. Encouraged by Nataliya Kobrynska and Olha Kobylianska, she wrote numerous articles and delivered speeches on the role of women in society. She participated in publishing the almanac *Nasha dolya [Our Fate]*, edited by Kobrynska, which was devoted to fighting for equal rights for women in education, in the workplace, and as full-fledged members of society.

Yaroshynska also worked tirelessly on a practical level to improve the lot of peasant women. In 1889, after completing a weaving course, she began instructing peasant women in this craft, thereby hoping to provide them with an additional source of income. She also established reading clubs in which she read newspapers to peasants to inform them about contemporary political and cultural issues.

In 1904, Yaroshynska attended a teachers' convention in Chernivtsi with her father and presented a lengthy paper outlining an innovative curriculum for public schools. The response was enthusiastic, and she was asked to submit it to the district Board of Education. Unfortunately, her untimely death later that year prevented her from pursuing this goal and cut short her selfless efforts on behalf of the disadvantaged peasantry.

In her works, Yaroshynska expressed the view that the Ukrainian intelligentsia had an important role to play in educating the masses and improving their quality of life. She is remembered today as a prose writer, folklorist, pedagogue, and community activist.

All levels of society are reflected in Yaroshynska's works. Complementing the writings of other Bukovynian authors, they provide a realistic and sympathetic picture of life in that region of Ukraine at the turn of the twentieth century.

The Brothers
A Folk Tale
(1891)

They say that during the heyday of the *kozak [Cossack]* era, the large farmstead of Semen, the *koshovy otaman [chief leader]* of the *kozaks,* was not too far from the Dnipro river. That *otaman* had two sons, Oleksa and Marko. They were handsome young men, bold and fearless, the joy of their father, and the hope of their motherland Ukraine, which they had already defended more than once from Tartar attacks.

One fine spring day, the two young men galloped off to hunt. They rode into the forest and, hearing a faint voice calling for help, sped swiftly as arrows in the direction from which the calls were coming.

A moment later they saw that two bandits had waylaid a carriage travelling through the forest. The driver had been killed, and the bandits were dragging away a beautiful young lady. She was struggling to break free—crying, cursing, and pleading with them to let her go. But the bandits responded to her pleas with raucous laughter and gestured scornfully at her governess who, lying on the ground, bound hand and foot, was calling for help.

Oleksa and Marko flung themselves at the bandits, chased them away without further ado, and set free the wondrously lovely young lady and her companion.

As it turned out, the young lady was the daughter of a rich Polish magnate who lived not far from there. She was on her way home from Warsaw when the bandits attacked her carriage, and she would have died at their hands, like her driver, if it had not been for the *kozaks*. With tears in their eyes, the two women gratefully thanked their saviours.

The beauty of the young Polish woman enchanted both *kozaks*, and their hitherto calm hearts, strangely stirred, began pounding in their chests.

And the young lady, her flaming eyes fixed artfully on the two brothers, spoke very charmingly and sweetly. Finally, she asked them if they would be kind enough to accompany her and her companion to her father's palace.

The proud magnate, hearing that he owed the life of his only daughter to the bravery of the two young *kozaks*, received them warmly and graciously. He did not know how to thank them enough and, when they were leaving, invited them to visit him as often as they could.

The two brothers returned home in a pensive mood. It did not even occur to them to sing the happy songs that always issued from their lips. They now eyed each other stealthily and shook their heads. A new, unfamiliar feeling took possession of their souls, and they could not even begin to guess what would happen because of it.

From that day on, the brothers were frequent visitors in the elegant palace where the exquisite Wanda lived. And their love for her blazed ever more vigorously in their *kozak* hearts. They became gloomy and morose, but they never talked about the anguish that filled their hearts.

No one knew the reason for their dejection, and it was probably only the beautiful Polish girl who guessed it. Wanda's heart beat more quickly whenever she looked at Oleksa; she was smitten by his dark brows, brown eyes, and tall, lean *kozak* build.

Did Oleksa know that the comely Wanda loved him as much as he loved her? He probably did, but this knowledge did not offer him much comfort, because he understood only too well the great chasm that divided him from the daughter of a Polish magnate. And there was no hope that this chasm could ever be bridged.

One time, a truly wonderful Ukrainian night descended on the earth, and the gentle moon illuminated the gleaming paths in the Polish magnate's orchard. Silence reigned supreme, disturbed neither by the rustle of a breeze, nor the swaying of a leaf.

In the depths of the orchard, however, on the banks of a magnificent man-made lake, soft whispers could be heard. There, under two spreading linden trees, sat Oleksa and Wanda. Caught up in their conversation, they forgot about time, and it was only when dawn began to break that Oleksa realised he should be on his way.

"Oh, stay for just a moment longer!" the girl whispered, nestling against the chest of her dear one. "Everyone in the palace is still slumbering; no one will see us; no one will interrupt our conversation."

Oleksa sighed heavily, gently removed her white hands from his neck, and clasped them in his own.

"No, Wanda," he said sadly, gazing into her enchanting eyes. "We were not fated to live together . . . What would your father say if he found out that you loved someone of another faith? He'd send me away at once and lock you up in a nunnery."

"No, my darling, my one and only!" the young lady replied, passionately kissing the *kozak's* red lips. "Don't talk about such sad things! O Oleksa, my beloved Oleksa, I beg of you, do what I ask of you, do it because of my love for you. Renounce your faith and accept mine, and then I'll be yours!"

Oleksa's eyes flashed as if they had been struck by lightning. He leaped to his feet, shoved the temptress away, and exclaimed: "How dare you say this to me! You, whom I love more than life itself, are asking me to renounce the faith of my fathers, to disown my people, and to accept yours. No, my dear young lady, if such an idea could occur to you, then you've never really loved me."

Oleksa wanted to walk away, but Wanda, flinging herself at him, began kissing him and exhorting him in soft whispers: "Don't leave me, Oleksa! Hear me out, my dearest. I'll take the place of everything in your heart—your father, your nation, your family, and your faith. Look at me—aren't I beautiful, young, rich, and powerful? Listen to my plea, and you'll be happy forever. Of what use to you are your father, your nation, your faith? Abandon them! Join your life with mine forever."

Oleksa stood as if in a trance. The kisses and the passionate pleading of his beloved set his blood on fire. He could hear her racing heart and feel her soft, trembling arms twining around his neck. He was on the verge of yielding to her powerful spell, but, at that very moment, the bells in a nearby church rang out, signalling the end of the all-night liturgy begun on Whitsunday eve.

Like a madman, Oleksa tore himself free from the temptress, and stated resolutely: "Get away from me! No one will live to see the day when a *kozak* renounces either his faith or his people.

I don't want to pay for your love, your wealth, and your gentility with my betrayal."

And Oleksa vanished in the dense thicket.

The young lady stood dumfounded; however, after a lengthy pause, she regained her senses and pressed her hand to her heart. Her eyes blazed fiercely, and from her coral lips burst the words: "Just wait! You'll see who it is that you've scorned . . ."

A few days went by . . .

A magnificent ball was being held in the illustrious magnate's palace. The brightly-lit rooms were overflowing with guests. Marko, Oleksa's brother, was among them, but Oleksa was not there.

The beautiful Wanda spent the entire evening conversing only with Marko. The gracious attentions of the lovely Polish girl intoxicated the young man and filled his heart with paradisiacal happiness.

After supper, Wanda led her companion into a small room illuminated by a rosy light and ensconced herself with studied casualness on a sofa.

Marko, stunned by her exquisite beauty, dropped before her on his knees and, kissing her white hands, uttered passionately: "I'll do anything you want me to do, anything. I'm prepared to bring down the biggest sin on my soul to gain your love."

"You have to swear that you'll do what I tell you to do," the young lady said, taking his hand.

Marko, feeling as if he were in a trance, whispered tremulously: "I swear."

She laughed, and her eyes flashed with a strange flame. Putting her rosy lips close to his ear, she said: "Bring me the head of your brother, and I'll be yours."

Marko turned pale from fright and wanted to flee, but white arms clasped him closely, and ruby lips kissed his, taking away his reason, his courage . . .

The moon slowly began sending forth its pale light from behind the mountains. On the shore of the lake, trees whispered mysteriously among themselves, and a light evening breeze groaned in the reeds, as if fearing to disturb the prevailing silence.

It seemed as if all of nature had fallen silent and become mute; as if it were waiting for something dreadful to happen, and as if the waiting was making it hold its breath.

The slim figure of the beautiful Polish girl emerged from among the trees, and she softly drew near the shore of the lake where she and Marko had agreed to meet. Her heart was beating violently, her eyes were burning, and her body was trembling with fear. It seemed to her that the trees were flinging curses at her, that the moon was drenched in blood, and that the wind was carrying to her the screams of the dying Oleksa.

On the lake, a small boat appeared; Wanda closed her eyes so she would not see it. She heard the boat as it approached the shore, and then someone stepped out of it and began coming towards her. Reluctantly, she opened her eyes and saw Marko standing before her. His face was pale, his hair was dishevelled, and his eyes were staring vacantly.

In a quivering, fainting voice, Wanda asked: "Well?"

Marko extended his hand and showed the stupefied Polish girl the head of his brother.

And then, something completely unexpected happened.

With an insane cry, Wanda tore Oleksa's head out of Marko's hands and began kissing it, lamenting grievously and berating herself. And the pale lips of the murdered man parted, and a bloodcurdling laugh awoke all of nature. The wind howled mightily, the calm lake churned in agitation, trees rustled ominously, the moon fled behind a cloud, and night birds emitted terrifying shrieks.

The din woke a fisherman who lived near the lake; stepping outdoors, he saw a strange red flame rise fleetingly from the lake and instantly vanish.

Marko and Wanda disappeared without a trace.

The next day, a boat and a silk kerchief were found on the shore, and that night, the magnificent palace of the Polish magnate caught fire and was reduced to ruins in a matter of hours.

The old *otaman* had avenged his sons.

And, since that time, on the anniversary of Oleksa's murder, an ephemeral blood-red flame appears on the surface of the lake. People say it is Oleksa's soul, searching for its murderers . . .

On the Banks of the Dniester
Novella
(1895)

Dedicated to the eminent
Omelyan Popovych
as a token of the author's
great respect for him

I

It was Sunday—a fine, clear summer's day. The sun was already declining, but the sweltering heat, far from dissipating, seemed to be intensifying. In the shady green forest, the sultriness was less oppressive, and the air was pleasant and refreshing. The chirping of the birds and the fragrance of the grass and forest flowers pervaded the mellow air and enticed passersby, as if saying: "Come, rest for a while in the cool, sweet-scented forest."

On a twisting, well-worn path that wound its way through the middle of the forest walked a young man. About twenty-five years old, tall and broad-shouldered, with beautiful dark eyes and curly blond hair, he wore a lightweight grey suit and a finespun, snow-white shirt trimmed with a collar embroidered in two colours. In his hand he carried a wide-brimmed white straw hat.

The expression on the young man's face was artless and inexpressibly charming. His eyes radiated intelligence, his high forehead attested to his intellect, and his slightly pursed ruby lips bespoke his energy and a certain degree of wilfulness. Even though it was evident that he was slightly tired, he sang cheerfully as he made his way through the trees. Pulling a white handkerchief from his pocket, he mopped his perspiring forehead.

"What a heat wave," he thought, "and I'm tired, but at least it's not in vain. I'm truly glad my sister told me to go across the Dniester river to the province of Bukovyna. What a beautiful country this is! In a whole day of walking I haven't come across a single unattractive spot; all the landscapes are incredibly lovely, as if an artist had arranged them. Why, take even this path—how aesthetically it wends its way amidst the greenery and the flowers.

"People can say what they wish, but there is nothing more beautiful than blessed nature, especially for those of us who were born and raised in a village. Whenever it's possible to escape from the cursed city, you flee like a child to the village, and you simply can't get your fill of it, because everything there is so natural, so pleasing, so dear . . . The cottages thatched with straw and ringed with verdant orchards, the fields flourishing with rye and wheat, and the people who work on them—the people who are so dear to my heart, and whom I would be so glad to help, devoting to them my life and my work."

Caught up in his thoughts, he continued on his way until he unexpectedly came upon a wide meadow surrounded by lofty green pines that filled the air with their intoxicating aroma. A narrow streamlet, its banks adorned with a host of forest flowers, gurgled its way through the middle of the glade. Transfixed, the young man gazed in awe at the wondrous scene spread before him. Then, he approached the stream and began picking the flowers that grew in profusion near the water.

"I'll pick my sister a bouquet in memory of my trip to Bukovyna," he said with a smile.

Just then, he heard cheerful voices and ringing laughter coming towards him.

"Let's go to the stream; there are cartloads of flowers over there."

He heard these words distinctly and, a moment later, several young women dressed in traditional folk attire emerged from behind the pines. Two young men, one wearing clerical garments, and the other in a uniform, stepped out after them. The whole group created an idyllic scene in the glade illuminated by the bright rays of the sun. The young women's white shirts, richly embroidered with silk thread, filaments of gold, and sequins, glittered and appeared whiter and more sheer amid the encircling greenery. The sequins and the golden filaments, sparkling in myriad colours in the sun's rays, imbued the surrounding greenness with life and lustre.

The sturdy young men acted as a foil for the beautiful young women; standing beside them, the girls appeared to be smaller, more slender, and more delicate than they actually were. The wayfarer regretted that he was not a painter who could capture this delightful montage on canvas.

Not noticing the stranger, one of the girls dashed out ahead of the others and, singing a merry song, headed straight for the stream. As she drew nearer, she slipped on some damp moss and would have tumbled into the stream if he had not caught her.

"Watch out, young lady, or you might end up taking a bath," he said, smiling at her.

"Thank you for saving me," the girl said cheerfully to the young man. "See what luck I have," she added, turning to her friends, who by now had arrived at the stream. "I had every intention of drowning, but this guardian angel appeared out of nowhere and saved me."

After saying this, however, she blushed furiously. It suddenly occurred to her that it was not proper to joke in this way with a stranger, and that he could well be offended by her words.

"I've always maintained, Miss Mariya, that you have more luck than you deserve," the man in clerical garb said. "And even though I'm not very happy that it was someone else, and not I, who caught you, I would still like to express my gratitude to him for saving your life."

Turning to the stranger he said: "I'm Denys Goretsky, a theology student, and I'm eternally grateful to you."

"And I'm Orest Martyniv, a law student, and I'm honoured to accept your gratitude," the stranger said, extending his hand to Goretsky.

"Since the two of us are now acquainted, permit me to present the rest of our group to you. The young lady you saved is Mariya Liskovska; these two ladies are Miss Emiliya Radoska and Miss Halya Radoska, and this gentleman is Volodymyr Halytsky, a forester."

Orest bowed to everyone.

"Forgive me for being so bold," Halytsky said, "but you must be the son of the priest in the village of D. in the province of Halychyna. I'm employed not far from your village, and I've heard a lot about you."

"You're quite right," Orest replied. "I came to Bukovyna to rest in the fresh forest air and to become acquainted with the Bukovynian countryside, and I'm very grateful to the god of chance for granting me the good fortune of meeting all of you."

"You'd do better to thank Miss Mariya, she's the one who dragged us here today—it's as if she knew that we'd find a new acquaintance here," Denys said half jokingly, half mockingly.

"On this occasion, chance has chosen to assume the guise of a goddess," Orest said, looking at Mariya.

And this young woman truly deserved the title, for she was astonishingly beautiful. Her thin, supple figure alone would have appealed to anyone, even before seeing her exquisite, rosy complexion, large, sky-blue eyes, fine eyebrows, and coral lips that smiled so appealingly, revealing small pearly teeth. Luxuriant blond hair crowned her comely head.

Upon hearing Orest's compliment, Mariya blushed to the tips of her ears. "You must have met some goddesses in the forest—and now you're now comparing every mortal woman to them," she said uncomfortably.

"I truly did meet some, but none as beautiful as the one I'm looking at now," Orest replied, gazing directly into her eyes.

"And you must have lived among them for quite a while to have learned how to pay such compliments," Denys observed, enviously noting the witty manner in which Orest spoke.

"There's no need to live anywhere or to learn anything; beauty itself teaches us to bow down before it," Orest replied passionately.

Denys smiled ironically. "Well, let's either proceed farther into the forest, or go home," he said. "You can catch a cold, standing around on this damp ground."

The girls laughed loudly. "It's obvious you're from the city if you're afraid of catching a cold in the middle of summer," they chimed in chorus.

Denys flushed with anger. "The philosophers of old were right," he said, feigning a joking tone, "when they said that women have no logic. When this gentleman talked about goddesses, which do not exist, you listened attentively, without laughing, but when I began to speak about reality and something that's practical, you immediately started to laugh."

"Oh, God forbid—don't start in on your philosophers again," Mariya said, covering her ears with her hands. "We've heard quite enough about them at home—and there, at least, it didn't seem out of place to talk about them, because it was quiet, gloomy, and somewhat solemn. But here, in the forest, no one wants to hear about them; here there's only joy, and happiness, and freedom for the heart."

"Bravo, Miss Mariya," Orest exclaimed. "That's the way I like to look at things as well! In the forest, everyone's thoughts ought to delight freely in the beauty of nature—without disturbing the reigning tranquillity with philosophical theories."

"I'm happy that you acknowledge the veracity of what I'm saying, because Master Goretsky claims the forest is for philosophising, Volodymyr insists it's for hunting, and my father says it's for firewood. And even though Emiliya, Halya, and I keep saying that it's for taking enjoyable walks, we still can't convince them. Now that you're on our side, perhaps we'll be successful in our efforts. This is why I'm going to be bold enough to ask you not to pass by our home, but to stop in to see us; we'll be very happy to receive you," Mariya said with an enchanting smile.

Orest bowed. "Thank you most graciously for your invitation; I'd be very happy to have the opportunity of making the acquaintance of your parents."

Denys, listening to this conversation, heard Mariya invite Orest to her home and clenched his fists. Her politeness to the stranger first irritated and then infuriated him and, when they set out for Mariya's home, he trailed silently after the other young people, who were chattering happily and animatedly.

Halytsky was walking arm in arm with the older Miss Radoska; she was his betrothed, and their wedding was to take place in a month. The forester was a native of Bukovyna; however, after completing a course in forestry, he had not sought government employment in that province because he was offered a very good private position in Halychyna on the estate of a count with whom he had gone to school. Enjoying a special friendship with the count, he lived very well and had everything he needed.

He had met Miss Radoska, the daughter of a forester, quite by chance and, without thinking about it too long, and after only a few visits to her home, he proposed to her, and they became engaged. They were truly in love, and there was no opposition to this engagement from the parents on either side. Now, as they walked along together, they appeared to be in seventh heaven.

Mariya's father was a relative from Halychyna. Having inherited a large estate that included about a hundred *morgy [acres]* of land, Mr. Liskovsky had set himself up to manage it; however, a few years after he married the sister of Emiliya's father, a variety of misfortunes, including crop failures and fires, forced him to sell his property. With the assistance of his brother-in-law, he was able to locate and purchase a smaller property of about fifty *morgy* in Bukovyna, and now he was better off than he had been on the larger estate. He was an intelligent man, a university graduate, and he saw to it that Mariya, his only child, received a good education.

After completing her studies in the school for girls in the capital of Bukovyna, Mariya returned home, but she was not permitted to remain idle. A governess was hired to polish her piano playing skills, and to teach her French and German. The governess was a Ukrainian woman from Halychyna and, in addition to providing instruction in music and languages, she taught Mariya to call herself Ukrainian, to wear traditional Ukrainian clothing, and not be ashamed to speak Ukrainian—as is often the case among the upper classes.

Emiliya and Halya also attended the lessons. And so, when the governess departed from the Liskovsky home two years later, she could be assured that her work had not been in vain, for she had taught at least three girls to love their people and preserve their womanly dignity.

As she walked beside Orest now, Mariya told him about her governess, saying that it was due to her that she knew what her nationality was. And this woman would have taught her even more if she had not moved on to another position. Mariya especially regretted that there had not been enough time to become acquainted with Ukrainian literature and history. She would be only too happy now to read Ukrainian books, especially the works of the great poet Shevchenko and the writings of the prose writer Kvitka-Osnovyanenko, but she could not borrow them anywhere.

"If you will permit me, I can lend you books like that; I have a large number of them," Orest said.

"Oh, I beg you most fervently to do so, if you would be so kind," Mariya responded.

"There's no reason to beg me; I'm very happy to find a woman who is interested in our Ukrainian literature. A woman like that is a rarity in Halychyna. Our women prefer Polish, French, and German novels to the works of their own writers."

"That's true, and it's a sad situation," Mariya said. "I think that one should know one's own literature first, and only then go on to read foreign works. But I must admit with great shame that although I've read many Polish, German, and French works, I do not, as yet, know the literature of my own people."

"Well, now the literary works of your own people will seem all the better for it, because they have an unfathomable charm about them, the charm of something that is native, one's own."

"I'm very interested in them," Mariya continued. "And I'm confident that you won't forget the promise you've made me—to help me become acquainted with these writers."

"If you will permit me, I'll bring you some of those books later this week."

"I beg you to do so," Mariya said, blushing faintly. "But here we are—we're almost home," she added.

The entire group walked out of the forest and stopped for a moment on a small rise, from which the whole village could be seen. It was a picturesque scene; in the centre stood a large brick church surrounded by white cottages and green orchards. Lively music, the boisterous singing of young men, and the laughter of girls spread far and wide.

The young people on the hillock were reluctant to go any farther; the village, sparkling in the magical light of the sun, dazzled their eyes.

"How beautiful your village is!" Orest said to Denys, whose silence he found surprising.

"I don't see anything beautiful about it," Denys replied. "You'd have to be a great idealist to find something engaging in those thatched roofs, green orchards, and simple people. I've often wondered how an educated man can live out his life in a village."

"A love for one's people and a passion for work ought to guide the life of every educated man who lives in a village, sweetening any moments of bitterness and boredom. When one is engaged in work, one forgets about a life of luxurious amenities and frivolous diversions," Orest replied in a dignified manner.

"Ah, yes," Denys responded sardonically, "I can see that you belong to the apostles of work and national enlightenment. I did not expect this from what you were saying."

The mocking note barely concealed in Denys's voice incensed Orest. Blood rushed to his face, but he replied calmly: "I do not belong to those people who display the entire program of their lives on their foreheads."

And he started out after Mariya, who had turned into a street that led to her home.

Now it was Denys's turn to blush; he did not want to appear as an uncouth person before the stranger, and so he said amicably: "I did not wish to insult you with my words, but I can see that you were offended. I assure you that I did not harbour any evil thoughts when I spoke them."

Orest could not reply, because they had reached the gate of Mr. Liskovksy's estate, where the owner was waiting for them.

II

Mr. Liskovsky was a tall, robust man with grey hair. "Where have you been tarrying so long?" he asked Mariya affably.

"We've made a new acquaintance, father, but we had quite a time convincing Master Martyniv that you would want to thank him for the great service he did me. This is Master Martyniv, father; he saved me from drowning, and this, Master Martyniv, is my father, who is grateful to you for what you've done."

Liskovsky, a troubled expression on his face, extended his hand to Orest. "You saved my daughter from drowning?" he asked.

"Miss Mariya is attaching far too much importance to as trifling matter as the small service I did for her," Orest replied, smilingly.

"A trifling matter!" Mariya picked up on his words. "So you consider my life to be so unimportant?"

"God forbid! I most certainly do not consider it to be unimportant, but your life was in no danger," Orest said. "It happened like this," and he began telling Liskovsky what had transpired. "Miss Mariya slipped and would have fallen into the stream, but I didn't let that happen."

"Thank you for what you did," Liskovsky said, "and, please, do come in. My wife has lunch ready for all of you."

They entered a wide yard encircled by various buildings. To one side stood a fairly large house, in front of which flourished an attractive flower garden. Everything in the yard was maintained in an orderly manner, and it was evident that the estate was in good hands.

Mariya led her guests to the house through the flower garden. Among the many flowers growing in it were some exquisite roses.

"Miss Mariya," Orest said, "you know what I'm going to ask of you? If I've really done you as great a service as you've been saying, please give me one of the roses from your garden."

Mariya walked up to a rose bush, selected one of the finest flowers, and turned to pass it to him.

"Oh, no, not like that," Halytsky and Emiliya chimed in unison. "It's a reward—you must pin it on him yourself."

"Do you want me to?" Mariya asked Orest.

"If others insist, then I certainly won't refuse," he replied, laughing.

"Yes, that's how it should be done," Liskovsky added. "I remember reading, when I was younger, that damsels of yore bestowed roses on knights as a boon, or favour."

Mariya drew nearer to Orest, holding the rose in her hand. As she pinned it to his coat, she glanced up at him. Troubled by the strange way he was looking at her, she blushed, and her hand trembled faintly.

Noticing this, Orest also flushed, and his heart began pounding in his breast.

"If you know, my good sir, how ladies, in days gone by, bestowed favours on knights," Orest said to Liskovsky, "then you must also know how knights expressed their gratitude; and so I'll thank the lady in the same fashion."

And, saying this, he raised Mariya's hand to his lips and kissed it warmly. Everyone laughed; only Denys remained silent, his eyes fixed balefully on the ground.

"And now let's go into the house," Mariya said, her face as crimson as the rose she had given Orest.

As the guests entered the first room, they could hear someone in the adjoining one. Mariya opened the door to it and invited the guests into the parlour, a room that was quite large, but a trifle dark. On the walls, decorated with blue wallpaper, hung two large mirrors and three paintings in gold frames. Sheer white curtains draped the windows. A walnut sofa, covered with blue fabric, presided in one corner; in front of it stood a masterfully crafted table and a grouping of blue armchairs. A piano dominated the other corner.

The hostess was ensconced in one of the armchairs, and an older lady was seated on the sofa. A young lady was leafing through sheet music on the piano. Seeing the guests enter the room, she lowered her head and waited until it was her turn to greet them.

"Mummy, allow me to present to you Master Martyniv, a law student," Mariya began the introductions. "Master Martyniv, this is my mother, and these other two ladies are the wife and the daughter of our priest, Father Goretsky."

They all bowed and invited the new arrivals to be seated. The hostess, before going to the kitchen, asked Mariya to set the table.

Orest sat down beside Miss Goretska and struck up a conversation with her. The young lady's appearance was not prepossessing; a swarthy, but pale face with protruding dark eyes, thick wide lips, and a nose that was out of proportion to her face, did not conspire to create an attractive image. In addition, she carried herself haughtily, and the expression on her face was arrogant. When she engaged in conversation, however, she tried to appear friendly and congenial.

Just now, Orest was telling her what a favourable impression the traditional folk dress of the young ladies had made on him.

"As for me," the young lady said, "I don't like wearing traditional clothing; it doesn't appeal to me at all. It seems to me that if I wore it, the peasants would treat me with far too much familiarity."

"It seems strange to me that, growing up in a village, you not only don't like your own people, but even scorn them," Orest said.

"Oh, pardon me, but I didn't grow up in a village; my cradle stood in the city, and I grew up and was raised in the city. It was only two years ago that my father got the urge to move to a village, among the peasants," Miss Goretska countered.

"So village life doesn't appeal to you?" Orest asked sarcastically.

"I don't know how it could appeal to anyone! It's so boring here; if it weren't for my books and my piano, I would most certainly fall ill from boredom."

"My sister lives in a village; she reads a lot, but she doesn't play the piano, and yet I've never heard her complain about being bored," Orest said pointedly.

"*Hier hört alles auf [I've heard everything now]*! What does she do there?"

Even though Miss Goretska was Ukrainian, she did not speak the language well, and so whenever she ran out of Ukrainian words, she borrowed some from German. In doing so, she was like most young ladies in Bukovyna who, accustomed to conversing in German with their fathers and mothers, failed to learn their native tongue.

"She's taken it upon herself to enlighten the village girls by teaching them how to read, sew, embroider, knit stockings, and even tat lace. And she does all this voluntarily, just so she'll be at least of some use to her people," Orest replied.

"*Mutter, hören Sie es? [Mother, did you hear that?]* And she's become accustomed to associating with the peasants?"

"Why not? She adheres to the principle that you should not shun those who provide you with your livelihood. Besides, she's like me—she loves her own people, their language, songs, customs, and traditions," Orest stated emphatically.

Miss Goretska bit her lip. This *Galizianer [a man from Halychyna]* dared to try and impress her by saying such things? She had never even dreamed of anything like it. Not knowing what to reply, she fell silent.

"It's very sweet of your sister to work among the common people the way she does," Madam Goretska picked up the conversation. "I've often heard that the peasants are much more enlightened in Halychyna than they are in our province, and that they are more apt to like the intelligentsia."

"The common people are the same everywhere, my dear lady," Halytsky interjected. "I know this from my own experience. They are basically good people, no matter where they are, but their attitude towards the intelligentsia depends on how they are treated by it. If the members of the intelligentsia try to assist them, then they will repay them in their own coin."

"But it's a well-known fact that our peasants are ungrateful, and that it's no use trying to work among them," Denys interjected.

"I've heard this statement more than once," Liskovsky spoke up. "But I don't understand what kind of gratitude the intelligentsia wants from the peasants. And what, exactly, is it that they're supposed to be grateful for? Let's look into our hearts and speak the truth for once—who is it that's ungrateful? It is we—the intelligentsia who are ungrateful, because the common people could get along quite nicely without us, but we couldn't manage without them."

Orest could not restrain himself; rising to his feet, he walked up to Liskovsky and fervently shook his hand. "Please accept my most sincere gratitude for your words," he said, deeply moved.

Listening to this interchange, Madam Goretska smiled as if someone had poured vinegar on her lips. Her daughter stared fixedly in another direction, and Denys frowned angrily.

Mariya interrupted this difficult moment for the Goretskys with an invitation to lunch.

The tasty coffee and lunch changed the tenor of the conversation to a happier note. Orest said he would have to be leaving soon, because he still had a long walk ahead of him; Halytsky responded that he would be pleased to drive Orest home because he had to go right past his village—and this meant they could enjoy themselves for a while longer.

Denys shot Halytsky an annoyed look, but pretended not to have heard their conversation.

After lunch, Orest was anxious to converse with Mariya, but Miss Goretska kept intruding into their conversation. Finally, Orest asked the interfering young lady to play the piano.

Miss Goretska seated herself at the piano and started pounding out an ear-splitting piece of music. As she played, she cut a very comical figure—bouncing on the stool, tapping her feet, and nodding in time to the music.

At first, Orest listened attentively; however, unable to determine what she was playing, he turned to Mariya and engaged her in an animated conversation.

After she finished playing, Miss Goretska lifted her hands ostentatiously from the keyboard and then dropped them in her lap, as if expecting applause.

Noticing this gesture, Orest applauded her generously and thanked her for the pleasure her playing had afforded them. "Even though I scarcely heard what you were playing," he thought as he clapped.

Emboldened by such praise, Miss Olha began to play a second, even louder piece. Orest, without listening even to the beginning of it, continued his interrupted conversation.

"And now, Master Martyniv, ask Miss Mariya to sing us some folk songs," Halytsky said, when Olha finished playing and rose from the piano. "In all my life, I've never heard anyone sing folk songs as beautifully as Miss Mariya."

"Is it true that you sing folk songs?" Orest inquired joyfully. "Please, sing at least one."

"Oh, Volodymyr is making things up about how well I sing; you'll soon find out for yourself," Mariya replied and, rising to her feet, she walked over to the piano.

The first chords of a prelude spread through the room, and then a tender, melodious song flowed from Mariya's lips:

> 'O maiden fair, like a cherry bright,
> Why didn't you come out last night?'
> 'O dearest, how could I meet with you?
> Our enemies sleep not—much harm they can do.'
> 'Let them spread rumours and scheme in stealth,
> I love you, my dearest, as I love my own health.'
> I love you my dearest, I'll love you forever,
> As long as we live, I'll forget you never.
> And even if I do, I'll recall you betimes.
> O God! How dear is this beloved of mine."

Mariya sang beautifully; her mellow voice spread through the room and touched the hearts of the listeners.

Orest's heart beat rapidly when she sang the strophe:

> "I love you my dearest, I'll love you forever,
> As long as we live, I'll forget you never."

Enraptured by the lovely young woman, he felt that a hitherto unknown force was overpowering him, and that any word that might be uttered would be an offence against the mood created by Mariya's singing.

"How did you like the song?" Olha intruded.

This question jolted him back to reality.

"I don't know how to say what I feel, because my soul soared with this song into unseen worlds," Orest responded with a heartfelt sigh.

"Oh, you must be a great *Schwärmer [dreamer]*, if such an *einfaches [simple]* peasant song can *aufregen [move]* you like that," Olha said, giving him a coquettish look and expecting to hear a compliment from him about her not so simple playing.

But Orest remained silent and listened to the melody of another song that Mariya had begun singing at Halytsky's request.

Olha sat down beside her mother, and the two of them began to speak mockingly, in German, of course, about the populist tendencies espoused by Orest.

Mariya sang a little while longer; then Emiliya took her turn at the piano; and, before long it was time for the evening meal.

Father Goretsky arrived; he shook Orest's hand heartily when the young man introduced himself, and invited him to sit beside him at the table. But Orest excused himself, saying that the ladies had not yet been seated, and then tried to occupy a spot as far away from Olha—and as close to Mariya—as possible.

His manoeuvring proved successful, and he was able to spend the entire dinner hour conversing with Mariya. He asked her where she had learned such wonderful folk songs and praised her for singing them, observing that other young ladies were ashamed of everything associated with the common folk. Mariya replied that she learned the songs from their neighbour's daughter, and that she sang them for her father, who loved folk songs dearly.

This lively conversation was like a slap in the face for the Goretskys. Madam Goretska, upset that the young gentleman showed no interest in her daughter, barely answered the questions put to her by the hostess. Olha was jealous of Mariya, and Denys could hardly stay seated—he was so incensed by the words "populist, the people, idea," that Orest kept using. And so all the Goretskys were waiting for the meal to end, because they knew that Halytsky would leave as soon as it was over.

Before long, Halytsky and Orest began saying their goodbyes.

Orest held out his hand to Mariya. "I'll see you soon," he said. "Don't forget about the books," she responded.

A few minutes later, the carriage carrying Halytsky and Orest rolled out of Liskovsky's yard.

III

It was a clear, calm night. The moon, bathing the entire countryside with its chimerical light, swathed it in a mysterious, fabulous veil. A fog, so thick that even the moon's rays could not penetrate it, billowed above the river.

Intoxicated by the beauty of the summer night, Orest was overcome with a desire to burst into song, and he began to sing softly the first folk melody with which Mariya had entertained her guests. Halytsky joined in, harmonising with him, and the song flowed gently through the warm, bright night. The alluring charms of nature that surrounded the young men put both of them in a lyrical mood, and they poured their feelings into the sad, melancholy melodies.

After travelling about an hour and a half, they reached Orest's village. Orest stepped down from the carriage, invited Halytsky to visit him the next day, and walked slowly down the street towards his home.

Everyone was sleeping when he arrived. Not wanting to wake his family, he slipped quietly over the gate and knocked on the barn door; the young male servants let him in, and he climbed up to the loft to sleep in the hay. But various thoughts kept him awake, and he could not fall asleep for a long time; it was almost morning when he finally dozed off.

When he awoke, he realised it was quite late, because there was no one left in the barn. He came down from the loft and went directly to the kitchen, where a maidservant was already rinsing the glasses that had been used for the morning coffee. After splashing some water on his hands and face, he walked into the adjoining room. His father had left, but his mother and sister were embroidering by the table.

"Good day!" Orest said cheerfully, kissing his mother's hand.

"Where were you gallivanting yesterday that you came home so late?" his mother asked.

"I can't even begin to tell you where I was and what I saw," Orest replied melodramatically, "because I saw more beauty than I have ever seen before."

"Go on, get away with you, you mischief-maker! You want to fool us once again," his mother said, glancing with pride at her handsome son.

Orest sat down beside his sister and examined her work. She was embroidering a traditional folk costume.

"Your costume will be pretty," he observed, "but it won't be as beautiful as the one I saw yesterday on a certain young lady. Hers would suit you very well, Melanya."

"You're assuming that because you liked it, everyone would," Melanya replied. "I'm not even going to ask you who the young lady was, because I know you won't tell me."

Their mother got up and went into the kitchen.

"Dear sister," Orest began. "My dear sister, I've always been fond of you and respected your wisdom, so I'm going to tell you now what happened to me yesterday."

And he told her about the unexpected meeting in the forest glade, Mariya's invitation, her conversation with him, her singing, and the fact that he had promised to lend her some Ukrainian books.

"Watch out, little brother, that you don't get caught in a net. I'm afraid you might fall in love with her, and what will you do then?"

"I'll marry her, if she agrees to have me."

"So it's gone that far, has it? Oh, my little brother, I hope things turn out well for you."

"I'd really like you to get to know her, because then you'd agree that I most certainly would find happiness with her."

"I'd like to meet her as well; I want to see who has managed to melt my ice-cold brother with her charms."

"When I go there, I'll try to find out who their friends are, whom they visit; perhaps we can meet them on a feast day, or at an evening social."

Their confidential conversation was interrupted when their mother re-entered the room.

Towards evening, Halytsky came to visit Orest. As he walked into the yard, he looked through the fence into the orchard and saw an attractive young lady sitting on a bench, surrounded by a bevy of peasant girls; they were all busily embroidering.

Orest came out to meet him, saying: "Come, I want to introduce you to my sister; I want you to see her engaged in her work."

He opened the gate and led his guest into the orchard. Catching sight of them, Melanya rose to her feet and responded politely to Halytsky's greeting.

The three of them were soon engaged in a discussion about the enlightenment of the common people. Halytsky, hearing how courteously the peasant girls replied to every question put to them, could not find the words to express his amazement at Melanya's success in teaching them.

After Melanya dismissed her pupils, she invited their guest into the house to meet her parents. Halytsky impressed both the priest and his wife so favourably that they asked him to visit them whenever he could.

It was late when Halytsky bid his hospitable hosts farewell. Orest walked with him part of the way and nonchalantly asked if there was something he would want him to say to his betrothed the next day.

In reply to Halytsky's astonished look, Orest informed him that he was going to Mariya's tomorrow to take her the books he had promised her, and that he just might have the opportunity to pass Miss Radoska a greeting from her fiancé.

Halytsky smiled knowingly, but did not say anything; he simply passed his warmest greetings to Emiliya.

IV

The next day, Orest dressed with care.

Seeing that he was putting on his best necktie, Melanya asked him where he was going.

"To seek my fortune," Orest replied in a jovial tone.

"Oh, my dear brother, it's dangerous to play with fire," his sister said seriously. "Be careful that some misfortune doesn't befall you."

"Melanya, my dear sweet sister, please don't scare me! If you knew what was transpiring in my heart right now, you wouldn't say things like that."

"There's something different about you, brother, but you're old enough to know what you're doing," Melanya joked, throwing her arms around her brother's neck.

Orest kissed her on the forehead by way of farewell and, tucking a bundle of books under his arm, picked up his walking stick and left.

He was so happy to be on his way to see Mariya that his feet flew over the ground. His only worry was that he might find Denys or Olha there; both the brother and sister had made a very negative impression on him—the sister even more so than her brother. He was irritated by Denys's consistently sarcastic tone, and felt that this young gentleman would one day cause him grief. And he was repelled by Olha's use of German, the airs she put on, and the way she pounded the piano.

Caught up in his thoughts, Orest arrived on the banks of the Dniester river. There was no one in sight who could ferry him across to the Bukovynian side—everyone must have been working in the fields.

Peering intently all around, he walked along the riverbank until he spotted a pretty young woman dipping a large wooden bucket into the river.

"Would you mind calling your father to ferry me over to the other side?" he asked her.

"Daddy isn't home, but I can take you across, if you want me to," she replied.

"Do you know how?"

"Well, I guess I must know how, or else I wouldn't have offered. Sit down in the boat, and I'll go fetch the oar." The girl sped away with the bucket and returned a minute later holding an oar.

Gracefully pushing the boat away from the bank, she steered it out over the water.

Orest was amazed at her strength and at the assured and confident manner with which she handled the boat.

"Oh, I often ferry the son and daughter of the priest. They aren't at all worried about crossing the river with me," the girl said, boasting about her skills.

"Where do they go?" Orest asked.

"To Mr. Liskovsky's," the girl said. "There's a very nice young lady there, and I ferry her quite often as well; she dresses so beautifully in our folk dress, and she's such a good person; she talks with me the whole time that she's in the boat."

Orest could have kissed the girl for what she had said; it seemed to him that the praise was being directed at him.

A short time later they were on the other side. After paying the young woman ten times as much as the trip was worth, Orest set out for the Liskovsky home without really knowing which way to go. The previous time he had approached their home from the forest, and now he could not get his bearings as to where their house was. It was true that, on his way home, he had travelled on the road leading to the Dniester river, but that had been at night, and now he could not recall the countryside.

Coming across a young boy, he asked for directions, and the little fellow showed him the shortest way of getting there.

It was scorchingly hot; the sun was searing the earth with its flaming rays, and the air was becoming oppressively close. Drops of perspiration trickled down Orest's forehead, and he was glad to finally catch sight of the Liskovsky house. He walked through the gate and crossed the quiet, deserted yard. Even the dogs did not announce his arrival—they were seeking refuge from the sun in their kennels.

When he suddenly showed up in front of Mariya, she was startled.

"Oh! How did you get here that I didn't even hear you?" she asked, turning scarlet.

"Through the gate, through the yard, through the door, and here I am. Or do you suppose I crawled in through the chimney?" Orest asked in jest, holding out his hand to her.

"Please, sit down," Mariya invited him. "You must be tired if you walked in this heat wave."

"If I knew that you would be happy to see me, I'd walk even a hundred miles," Orest responded.

"I'm happy to see everyone who comes to our home," Mariya, not looking at him, said a trifle coolly.

"So that includes me."

"It includes you and everyone."

Seeing that Mariya was confused and embarrassed, Orest stopped his bantering. To help her regain her composure, he inquired about her parents.

"Father isn't home—he's out in the fields with the workers, and mother lay down to have a nap, but I'll go and wake her right now," the girl replied.

"Please, don't wake her," Orest begged. "I don't want your mother to miss out on her rest because of me."

He pulled a handkerchief out of his pocket and began mopping his damp forehead. Seeing this, Mariya hurried into the kitchen and asked the servant to bring him some fresh water. Then she went to the cupboard, removed two jars of preserves, and placed them on a tray.

After drinking some water sweetened with the preserves, Orest untied his bundle and passed the books to Mariya. She flushed happily, jumped to her feet, and began thanking him for not forgetting his promise.

"I've brought you Shevchenko's *Kobzar*; you should read it first; then the writings of the woman writer, Marko Vovchok; and, finally, the stories and plays of the male author Kvitka-Osnovyanenko. When you've finished reading these books, I'll gladly bring you some others. It would make me happy if you developed a liking for our Ukrainian literature."

"I'll love it with all my heart, just as I love our folk songs," Mariya said.

"Which you must now sing for me, Miss Mariya . . . I've earned this reward, haven't I?"

"Oh, you've earned an even bigger one," the girl replied, but then her face flamed, and she fell silent.

"What kind of a reward, for example?" Orest asked, smiling happily.

But Mariya's mother saved her from having to find a reply to his question—a question that truly troubled her.

Madam Liskovska had taken a liking to Orest when she first met him, so she greeted him warmly.

"I trust, Madam, that you won't be angry with me that I've been bold enough to visit your home again," Orest said, bowing respectfully.

"On the contrary, we're very pleased to welcome a wise man in our home," Liskovska responded.

"I promised Mariya that I would bring her some books to read, and so I brought them today."

"You took the trouble to do this in such sweltering heat? I don't know what Mariya can do to thank you for your kindness. She loves to read, and I like listening to her read; but it's too bad that I don't understand German, just Ukrainian and Polish."

"These are Ukrainian books," Orest said.

"Then I too am grateful to you. You see, I was born in Halychyna, and so I didn't learn any German; but here, in Bukovyna, everyone babbles in German, no matter where you go, and all I can do is sit and look on, without saying anything," Liskovska complained.

"I know from the last time I was here how well Miss Goretska speaks Ukrainian," Orest said.

"Oh, that was one of her better days, because she at least did speak it a bit; there are times when she refuses to say a single word in Ukrainian," Liskovska added.

"I find that strange, because her brother speaks Ukrainian fairly well," Orest commented.

"He's begun learning the Ukrainian language since he entered the seminary," Mariya said.

"Oh, say it as it is—he's begun learning it since you insist on speaking to him in Ukrainian," her mother said, smiling.

The blood rushed to Mariya's face.

"But his father speaks only Ukrainian, as well," she interjected hastily.

"Because he's a Ukrainian by birth, but his children grew up in the city, and now they shun their own people," Liskovska said with a laugh. "It's happened here more than once that Ukrainian people turn into either Romanians or Germans."

Orest and Mariya both laughed.

"Let them be whatever they want to be, but you have to sing me some folk songs," Orest said to Mariya.

She did not have to be persuaded; seating herself at the piano, she sang a few songs in her charming voice.

Mariya's singing was casting an ever-stronger spell on Orest. He could not take his eyes off her comely face, which seemed to have a hint of sadness on it—perhaps because of the mournful melody of the song.

"Please, sing me that song once again: 'I love you, my dearest,'" Orest pleaded.

She fulfilled his request. When she finished the song, she folded her hands, leaned on the piano, and did not begin a new one.

"Mariya, why aren't you singing?" her mother inquired.

"For some reason, I can't sing any more right now," the girl responded in an agitated voice.

"How thoughtless I am!" Orest leaped to his feet. "I didn't stop to think that you might be getting tired, and I asked you to go on singing . . . But you yourself are to blame, because you shouldn't sing so wonderfully—one could listen to your singing for the rest of one's life."

"Do I truly sing well?" Mariya asked somewhat sadly.

"If it were Miss Olha who asked me such a question, I would assume that she was fishing for a compliment. I don't know how to answer you, except to thank you once again for your exquisite singing," Orest said with feeling.

Mariya rose from the piano.

Her mother suggested that she take a walk and show the young gentleman their fine orchard. Orest and Mariya strolled through the flower garden and entered the orchard, in which a large variety of trees flourished, flaunting their ripe fruit.

The pleasant coolness and the aroma of the fruit had a soothing effect on Orest, calming him down. Somewhat refreshed, he resumed his conversation with Mariya. He was more than pleasantly surprised to learn that she was familiar with almost all the best works in world literature, and this fact increased his admiration for her.

Intoxicated with delight, he listened avidly to her engaging conversation and marvelled at her mature judgement of various writers. Except for his sister, he did not know another young woman who was so enlightened. In addition to being well-read, she was poetical and innocent, like a rose in May, while his sister had a more practical nature and was more prosaic, possibly because she was older than Mariya.

As for Mariya, she enjoyed listening to Orest's ideas and opinions, and admired his enthusiasm for the common people. She compared his thoughts to those of other young gentlemen she knew, and Orest came out the clear winner. This was why she spoke more frankly and sincerely with him than she would have otherwise.

Over coffee, Mr. Liskovsky engaged Orest in conversation and was pleased to find a young man with whom he could discuss serious matters, because other young gentlemen took notice only of Mariya and ignored him completely.

During their discourse, Orest learned that, in exactly one week, the Liskovskys would be crossing over to Halychyna to celebrate the Feast of the Virgin Mary in the parish of a priest that his family knew very well. This information gladdened Orest; he was determined to have his parents and his sister attend this feast as well, so that they could meet Mariya.

Liskovsky walked Orest home as far as the Dniester river and invited him to visit them again. Orest promised that on Sunday he and Halytsky would come to see them.

V

During the days leading up to Sunday, a Ukrainian folk song kept going through Orest's mind:

> "O Lord, let me live to see Sunday sublime,
> I'll go to my dear ones to have a good time."

His sister inquired how the books he had taken the young lady were received, and he told her how friendly Mariya and her parents had been. He also entreated his sister to join him in asking their parents to attend the Feast Day in the neighbouring village. The parents, not knowing the reason for the request, acquiesced; his mother was especially pleased to have the opportunity to show off her son to the other priest's wife.

A couple of days before Sunday, Orest visited Halytsky to make arrangements to travel with him to Bukovyna. Halytsky was delighted to see him, received him most hospitably, and was very happy to learn that he would have a travelling companion.

Orest told Melanya that on Sunday he would once again visit the Liskovskys.

"I can see that you're looking for trouble. Why are you going there so often?" she asked.

"If you only knew, my dear sister, what it means to me—how my heart is fainting—then you wouldn't say that, because you would know, even before you said anything, that all your words are in vain," Orest replied.

"But I fear for you, because I know how sensitive you are; I dread the thought of what might happen should you experience a disappointment."

Orest turned pale. "I don't know how I would live through something like that," he said, "but there can be no question of a disappointment here. I can tell that Mariya likes me."

His sister gave him a look filled with such love and sympathy that he came up to her and pressed her hand.

"Don't worry, dear sister, it will all work out somehow," he said emotionally. "And, after all, even if I should be disappointed, I still have you, my ideal of what a woman should be."

On Sunday afternoon, Halytsky drove up and took Orest away with him. They travelled swiftly and, before they knew it, reached the Dniester. After crossing the river, they made their way into the forest where Emiliya's parents lived.

The forester's house, standing on a hillock in the forest, looked very appealing. The entire yard was encircled with a hedge, and the charming cottage, with its carefully plastered white walls, gleamed from behind the green shrubbery. A large orchard and garden stretched behind it.

As the young gentlemen drove into the yard, the dogs set up a terrible racket. Hearing the barking, Emiliya and Halya rushed out of the house and, seeing the young men, smiled joyfully.

Orest fell in love with the forest abode; it seemed to have been created expressly for a quiet life, one that was not to be disturbed by any tempests. A blessed peacefulness permeated the rooms, and the very air seemed to be saturated with dreams and forest tales.

The hosts greeted the guests very warmly. They were rustic people and, living in isolation, delighted in having visitors. They expected every guest to bring them some news, something that would amuse them, for at least a short while.

A lunch immediately appeared on the table; the hosts invited the guests to enjoy it and ate along with them.

Orest was hoping that someone would say something about Mariya, but it did not seem to occur to anyone to do so.

Finally, Halytsky, who knew that Orest had come along expressly to see Mariya, said: "Perhaps we could pay uncle a visit?"

"Mariya invited us to come over," Halya said, "so if you want to, we can go."

As Orest rode through the forest alongside Radosky, he savoured the aroma of the forest grasses, deeply inhaled the fragrant air, and took great delight in the singing of the birds. He could not fathom what was happening to him; he had never before been in the kind of mood that possessed him today. Although happy and lively by nature, he was engulfed by a strange sadness punctuated by moments of ecstatic happiness.

Chaotic thoughts raced through his head, searing his heart and stirring his blood. He laughed at himself for being so preoccupied with a young woman whom he hardly knew and had seen only twice; but these ironical thoughts did not provide him with any relief.

On the contrary, he tortured himself with the worst possible scenarios as to how Mariya might greet him. He imagined that she would receive him haughtily and coldly, and would not even look at him. This thought troubled him greatly, and he would have been happy to have it all over and done with in order to convince himself of the veracity of his suppositions.

Well, his wish had finally come true; here he was, standing before the young woman who had preoccupied his thoughts during the entire trip. She was holding out her hand to him, and there was an indescribably lovely smile on her lips—it was obvious she was happy he had come.

After exchanging greetings with everyone, Mariya invited all the guests into the living room. They had barely taken their places, when Madam Goretska appeared in the doorway with Olha and Denys in tow.

Seeing them standing there, Orest's face assumed a sour expression, and the Goretskys, catching sight of him, looked equally displeased. Olha, however, quickly recovered and smiled sweetly, and Denys shook Orest's hand in a show of apparent heartiness.

Everyone appeared to be confused by the arrival of the Goretskys; no one seemed able to find a topic of general conversation. Madam Goretska inquired about Madame Radoska's health, and then the two of them began to talk dispiritedly about household matters.

Denys focused exclusively on Orest, asking him innumerable questions which, caught unawares, the latter had to answer. Orest knew full well that Denys was doing this to prevent him from talking with Mariya, but he had enough presence of mind to remain patient and answer seriously the questions put to him by the jealous seminarian.

Mariya was engrossed in her thoughts and only occasionally added a word or two to the conversation between Halytsky and Emiliya. Radosky and Liskovsky went off to have a look at the apiary; the hostess was busy in the kitchen. Orest could not free himself from his tormentor; there was no one to interrupt their conversation.

Finally, after what seemed an interminably long stretch of time, just when Orest's patience was beginning to wear thin, the hostess rescued him by entering the room and inviting the guests into the adjoining one for afternoon tea.

Orest managed to occupy a seat next to Mariya, but, as luck would have it, Denys sat down on her other side. There was no point in trying to have a serious conversation; Orest did not even ask her if she had read the books he had lent her. He wanted to ask her about this matter when they were alone, in order to hear her frank assessment of them.

Denys was trying to be amusing; he related funny anecdotes that made his mother and sister laugh heartily, even though they were probably hearing them for the umpteenth time. Observing Denys's aggressive pursuit of Mariya, Orest remained silent, a woeful expression on his face.

Mariya became aware of his silence.

"What's wrong? Why have you suddenly become so quiet?" she asked him.

"Why should I talk, if Master Goretsky is doing such a fine job of amusing everyone? Isn't his discourse enough?" Orest asked.

"Oh, that's true—it's more than enough," the young woman said softly, so that Denys could not hear.

Realising from her words that Denys did not pose a threat, Orest's good humour returned.

After tea, Olha suggested they should all practise dancing in preparation for Emiliya's wedding. And, turning with a sweet smile to Mariya, she said: "As the hostess, Mariya, you should play the piano, so that your guests can enjoy themselves; and then, when one of us gets tired, we'll take your *Plaz [place]* and you can dance."

Mariya immediately did as she was bid.

Orest looked angrily at Olha and, instead of inviting her to dance, as she had expected, he went up to the hostess and asked her to dance the first set of waltzes with him. She refused at first, but then gave in to Orest's persistent requests and twirled around the floor with him a few times.

After thanking Madam Liskovska, Orest asked Madam Radoska to dance. Madam Goretska fumed; she had expected him to ask her next, but he had snubbed her and asked the forester's wife. She silently pursed her lips; she had never seen such impertinence—to give precedence to a forester's wife over the wife of a priest.

When Orest later asked her to dance, she haughtily refused him. After dancing with several of the other young ladies, Orest decided that he did no want to dance any more; he sat down beside Mariya, who was still playing.

Denys, however, had other ideas.

Running up to Orest, he said: "Why aren't you dancing? Look, the ladies are sitting. Surely you aren't tired after just a few short sets?"

And so Orest had to continue dancing, even though his heart was not in it. No one was taking Mariya's place, and Orest finally asked Halya to take over the piano playing because he wanted to dance with Mariya.

When Halya complied, Orest circled Mariya's slim waist with his arm and began dancing with her. Never before had he danced with such enthusiasm; his feet barely touched the ground. It seemed to him that he was flying into faraway realms overflowing with happiness and love. His eyes shone with happiness.

Denys watched him and ground his teeth in jealousy.

When the set was over, Orest could not remain in the house any longer; the closeness of the air was choking him. Stealing out of the house, he went into the orchard, sat down on a bench and, leaning his head against a tree, fell deep into thought. His soul felt heavy, and he almost regretted having met Mariya when he realised how deeply his love for her had taken root in his heart. What if she did not return his love? He knew that if this were to happen, he would be terribly unhappy for a long, long, time.

He looked back with regret at the time when he knew only one love—the love for his poor nation. It was true that the love he had for his country had not faded in his heart, but now, finding itself positioned next to his ardent love for a young woman, it had tucked itself away in the darkest recesses of his heart; it was ready, however, to burn again with a mighty flame, with beauty, tenderness, and selflessness, if the love of the girl should prove to be untrue.

Orest did not know what was happening to him; the passionate excitement that consumed his soul was new to him. But he gave his feelings free rein and waited to see where they would take him.

"Where have you disappeared to, Master Martyniv?" Halytsky was standing right next to him. "The ladies are very bored without you, and here you are, sitting quietly, philosophising."

"I felt a sadness come over me," Orest replied softly, "and so I came out here to think for a while."

"And you've left the object of your thoughts in the house with your rival! I must tell you that it's not the best thing to do," Halytsky said in jest.

Orest seized Halytsky by the hand and dragged him into the house; the words he had heard were very unpleasant ones for a man in love.

"Where have you been you so long?" Mariya asked, and she sounded distressed and offended.

"I wanted to regain my composure after experiencing the great happiness of dancing with you," Orest replied.

"It must have been a really great happiness if you won't even try it a second time," Mariya's tone was jocular now.

"Are you sorry about that?" Orest asked, looking intently into her eyes.

"You're fishing for a compliment. No! I won't tell you," Mariya responded with laughter.

Miss Olha vigorously attacked a polka on the piano.

Orest looked pleadingly at Mariya; she smiled and nodded her head, and a moment later they were flying away on the wings of music.

During the entire evening, Orest did not have a single opportunity to speak to Mariya alone. As he said his goodbyes, he was angry at the whole Goretsky family for making it impossible for him to converse with his beloved.

VI

This time, Orest did not return home in the same good spirits as he had the previous two times. Melanya noticed this and tried to find out the reason for his ill humour. He was not forthcoming with an answer, and so she guessed that his pursuit of the young lady was not going smoothly.

She waited impatiently for Tuesday to arrive so that she could see the girl who had so drastically changed her dear brother. Orest also was waiting for this day; he wanted to hear what his sister would think about Mariya.

Tuesday arrived. Father Martyniv's family prepared to leave for the Feast Day in the neighbouring parish served by Father Biletsky. At one time, the two families had been on close terms but, because of a misunderstanding, they had not seen each other for several years. Now, Father Martyniv was happy to yield to the urging of his children to go and see his old friend.

They arrived after the liturgy. Father Biletsky greeted them with obvious delight and led them into a large reception room. Melanya, spotting a tall, slender, and exceptionally lovely young woman in a bright pink dress standing near the doorway, instantly guessed that it must be Mariya. After greeting a few acquaintances, she approached the young lady.

"If I'm not mistaken, I think I have the honour of speaking to Miss Liskovska," she said with a smile.

"Yes," Mariya replied, "but I haven't had the pleasure of meeting you, and I'm puzzled. How did you recognise me?"

"From the description of you by a certain person," Melanya smiled, looking at Mariya's confused face.

"Who could have described me so well?" Mariya inquired, peering at Melanya.

"A certain person," Melanya continued.

"Are you, by chance, the sister of Master Martyniv?" Mariya asked.

"You see, you did guess who it was."

"You bear a striking resemblance to your brother," Mariya said, blushing.

"So that's how you knew who I was?" Melanya laughed. "I'll have to tell him that it is through her brother that a sister is recognised."

Mariya answered wittily, and a lively conversation sprang up between the two young women.

Orest watched them from a distance; he would have been happy to join them, but the host had engaged him in a discussion, and it would not have been proper to walk away from him.

Because Father Biletsky had two marriageable daughters, he had organised a gala feast day and, taking advantage of the fact that it was during the summer vacation when there were a lot of young people around, he had arranged for a social with dancing. In the fall, the young gentlemen would leave for the towns and cities, and his two daughters would have only each other to dance with.

All the young people were impatiently awaiting the arrival of the musicians, who apparently had been detained en route. The young gentlemen were doing their best to amuse the young ladies beside whom they were sitting. And they must have been successful in their efforts—the young ladies were laughing and chattering like magpies.

It was very warm in the house, and someone suggested a walk in the gardens. Everyone rushed outdoors, like bees zooming out of a hive. Mariya and Melanya were among the last ones in that flight, and Orest joined them, greeting the goddess of his heart for the first time that day.

The three of them, carefree and chatting happily, strolled down the neatly trimmed paths. Then they gradually became more serious, and Orest inquired whether Mariya had read the books he had lent her.

Mariya nodded her head animatedly. "Yes, I did, and they revealed to me a hitherto unknown world—a world whose beauty inspired me with hope. I read them with great pleasure; and I was amazed at the perceptiveness that, limiting itself to the confines of shorter prose works, could endow them with so much beauty and unaffectedness.

"Take, for example, the story 'Marusya.' It's written so artlessly, but it had the greatest impact on me, because everything in it is so natural; there's nothing artificial about it."

"It moves us because the author knew the people well and faithfully depicted peasant love," Orest stated seriously.

"Oh, I know only too well from my personal response to the story 'Marusya' that it speaks directly to the heart; I wept my eyes out over the plight of the poor parents and of Vasyl, the unfortunate young man. I've never cried with such heartfelt sorrow as during the scene when the father bids his only daughter farewell as he accompanies her to her grave," Mariya said in a trembling voice brimming with emotion.

Melanya pressed her hand.

"What a pleasure it is for me to hear such sincere, guileless words," she said. "It proves that you have one of the greatest treasures—a kind, sensitive heart."

Orest gave his sister an affectionate look. He surmised that her words were a mark of approval of his choice.

"I also read Shevchenko's poems, but, O my God, I must shamefully admit that I do not yet have the knowledge required to comprehend the lofty ideas presented in his works. I struggled to understand his words, his every thought, but I was not always able to do so.

"And then there's the added problem that I don't know the history of the Ukrainian people, and so Shevchenko's political poetry was incomprehensible to me. For example, I put aside the poem 'Haydamaky' with tears in my eyes, because I did not know who Gonta, Zaliznyak, and the other heroes in the poem were, and why they treated the Poles so harshly."

"It was in revenge for the hundred years of captivity and poverty that our poor nation had to suffer," Orest replied. "But you're right when you say that it's impossible to understand a poet's works without knowing the history of his people. As one German aptly put it: *'Wer den Dichter will verstehen, muss in des Dichters Lande gehen [Whoever wants to understand a poet must live for a time in his country].*

"I'll give you the History of Rus-Ukraine and, after reading it, you will understand the passages that were unclear to you in the works of our greatest national genius."

"You have no idea how grateful I am that you are giving me the opportunity of becoming familiar with the literature of our people. I always think of you as I'm reading," Mariya said.

"How nice it is to hear that! I'm on the verge of becoming conceited, knowing that you think about me," Orest said merrily.

"Your conceit would work against you, because I can't tolerate conceited people," Mariya said jokingly.

"I wonder what our two young Goretskys are doing now," Orest asked with feigned innocence.

Mariya glanced at him, but seeing the happy, untroubled look on his face, she responded laughingly: "She's pounding away at Beethoven's sonatas, and he's digesting the philosophy of Kant. And when they come to see us, they'll torment us with their playing and their philosophising."

"Don't you like piano playing and philosophy?" Melanya asked.

"I like good playing, but I don't understand philosophy, so I can't say if I like it or not," Mariya replied.

Orest laughed mischievously. "More than likely, there isn't a single mouse left in the Goretsky home," he said.

"Why is that?" both young ladies asked.

"Because by now all the mice must have fled to the neighbours to escape from Miss Olha's playing—such playing is unsettling even for the nerves of mice."

Both girls laughed heartily.

Melanya wagged her finger remonstratively at her brother: "How can you make fun like that of someone's playing? That's not very nice of you, my dear little brother."

"But I'm saying that her playing is wonderful, and she herself is convinced of this fact; isn't that true, Miss Mariya?"

"Yes, it is. She plays very badly, but she wants everyone to praise her. Even though we live in the same village and get together quite often, I'm not a close friend of hers, because our characters are so different."

Just then, some young gentlemen ran up and invited the young ladies to dance. The musicians had finally arrived, and the young people were drawn to the music.

All the young gentlemen breathed a sigh of relief that they no longer had to amuse the young ladies and talk to them in detail about "white birches and withered oaks," because in the course of discussing these matters, the young men had become unbearably bored. "White birches and withered oaks" can entertain you for only so long, but without a serious topic to discuss, you can become so bored that even a feast day no longer appeals to you. This was why everyone, with the exception of Orest, Melanya, and Mariya, welcomed with unabashed joy the music that was like a saviour to them.

The fathers sat down to play cards; the mothers settled on the benches against the walls and, watching proudly as their daughters danced, kept tabs on which young gentleman danced the most with which young lady. The host's daughters had the most young gentlemen circling around them—it was hard to tell whether it was because they were thankful for the wonderful hospitality, or if they had caught scent of a hefty dowry. Melanya and Mariya also were very popular—their pretty faces attracted everyone's eye.

Around midnight, supper was served, and many toasts were raised. After the meal, the young people danced with an even greater enthusiasm.

Many a candid word, which would not have been spoken at any other time, passed between the young ladies and gentlemen—words that filled more than one young lady's heart with joyful optimism. But this joy lasted only until morning, because the gentlemen, realising they had been overly zealous, turned cold as stones and tried to disappear like smoke into thin air. For now, however, all the ladies were still cheerful and happy, and not a single thought about their uncertain futures clouded their optimism.

The guests began to disperse in the morning. There were furtive handshakes, and many a tear fell into the young ladies' hearts, but most of the young gentlemen paid no attention to the feelings they had evoked with their behaviour and departed with unencumbered hearts and souls.

After conversing the whole night and getting to know each other, Madam Liskovska and Madam Martynova were now exchanging invitations.

Orest and Melanya were greatly surprised to hear this, because their mother rarely invited anyone to visit her. Melanya, assuring Mariya that she was very happy to have met her, added her words of invitation as well.

Orest pressed Mariya's hand and said softly: "Until our next meeting."

Mariya could not refrain from asking: "When?"

Orest's eyes sparkled. "I'll try to ensure that it's as soon as possible," he replied with a happy smile.

When they arrived home, Melanya and her mother, weary after the sleepless night, lay down to rest. Before falling asleep, however, they discussed Mariya's beauty and concluded that she would be a fitting partner for Orest. Father Martyniv also dozed for a while.

Only Orest did not lie down—he went for a walk in the fields to share his happiness with all of nature.

Towards evening, he sat down beside his sister in the orchard and asked her what she thought of Mariya.

"You're luckier than you deserve to be, Orest, because I've never met a girl like Miss Liskovska."

"So you don't have anything against her?" Orest asked.

"No, and if I formerly said: 'Don't go, be careful,' now I'm saying: 'You'll be happy with a wife like Mariya.'"

"Melanya! You're the best of sisters! How happy I am to hear you say that."

"It's not difficult to be a good sister with a brother like you," Melanya said, smiling.

"What do you think—will she love me?"

"It seems to me that she already loves you, but you should ask her about that yourself."

"Good evening," someone said, and Halytsky's sturdy figure appeared before them.

"Good evening," Orest responded joyfully. "How are things with you?"

"For someone who is soon to be married, everything's fine," Halytsky replied. "But you know, I've come to you with a request."

"I'll do whatever you ask of me, unless, of course, it's something impossible," Orest said.

"It's not impossible, because I'd never ask something like that of you. I hope you won't be angry with me that, after knowing you for such a short time, I have the audacity to ask you to be the best man at my wedding," Halytsky said.

Orest held out his hand to him. "You should know how happy this invitation has made me; I'll gladly be of service to you," he said sincerely.

"Who are the bridesmaids?" Melanya inquired.

"Miss Liskovska and the sister of my betrothed; the second groom's attendant will be Master Goretsky, the son of their priest," Halytsky replied.

"You're going to have an attractive bridesmaid, Orest," Melanya remarked, looking at her brother.

"So you know Miss Liskovska?" Halytsky asked in surprise.

"Yes; I made her acquaintance yesterday, at a feast day. She's a lovely and wise young lady."

"And she sings so beautifully," Halytsky began saying, "if I weren't already in love with my betrothed, I'd most certainly fall in love with Miss Liskovska."

As he finished what he was saying, Halytsky glanced obliquely at Orest.

"How fickle you gentlemen are!" Melanya said, laughing. "Your wedding is just around the corner, and here you are—attracted to another young lady."

"Every beautiful young lady may be deified," Halytsky said jokingly, "because beautiful girls live to be loved by us, isn't that true, Master Martyniv?"

"Yes, it's true, and Miss Liskovska is one of those who can cause more than one man to lose his mind."

"Yes, as she's already made Master Goretsky lose his. We'll probably live to see the day he takes his own life because of her."

Orest turned red. "Are you saying he's so deeply in love with her?"

"Yes, like a fool," Halytsky said. "I often laugh at him, because he tells me all about his great love."

Orest's heart pounded; he could hardly speak. "And what about her?"

"She doesn't know anything about his love, because he doesn't have the courage to propose to her. And even if he did propose, it wouldn't help him too much, because Mariya would refuse him. I'm positive about that."

Orest felt somewhat relieved when he heard this.

This conversation was not to Melanya's liking.

"When is your wedding?" she asked Halytsky, trying to change the direction of the conversation, so that he would not guess Orest's feelings.

"A week from this Sunday," Halytsky replied.

"That's very soon!"

"If only the time would pass more quickly," Halytsky sighed.

"If only . . ." Orest echoed.

VII

Intensive preparations for the wedding were underway at the Radosky home. The bride's trousseau was ready; now they had to decorate the rooms and prepare the food and drinks.

Three days before the wedding, the cries of the geese, ducks, piglets, and chickens that were being led to slaughter spread through the forester's home. And so the old adage once again proved to be true: for some it may be a wedding, but for a chicken—it's death.

Emiliya, Halya, and two village girls were tidying up the rooms. Tapestries and pine boughs festooned the walls, and a few large mirrors, borrowed for the wedding from the neighbours, peeped out from among them. In the room designated for dancing, rug-covered benches lined the walls, and additional lamps adorned the decorated walls. The floors were washed and then waxed to make it easier to dance on them.

By Saturday evening everything was ready; all the rooms were fragrant and sparkling clean. And the cook, having baked mounds of bread, buns, tortes, and cookies, was chopping up the fowl for boiling and baking.

Everyone was satisfied with the way everything was coming along, but Mr. Radosky was not in a good humour.

Coming into the kitchen and seeing everything that had been prepared, he said, only half-jokingly: "If I had to put on a wedding every week, I'd surely die of hunger. Just look at all this food, but I haven't had a decent dinner for the last four days! With all the cleaning and the preparations, you've completely forgotten about me."

His wife chuckled, went to the pantry, and brought him a chunk of fresh ham. Regaining his good humour after eating the ham and drinking some beer, the master of the house walked through all the rooms, praising his daughters for the fine job they had done.

On Sunday morning, Emiliya and Halya went to church in the village. Emiliya met Mariya and Olha there and asked them to come over early to help her get dressed. The girls chattered away cheerfully, but Emiliya seemed preoccupied. As she stood in church, she thought about the happy, carefree life she was about to leave and the responsibilities she was about to assume. Even though she would be leading her new life with a husband she loved, she still regretted leaving her family, her home, and her girlfriends. Immersed in her thoughts, Emiliya wept silently, dabbing at her tears with a white kerchief.

After returning home, Emiliya was so sad that her mother asked her if she was ill. In the afternoon, she stole out of the house and ran into the forest. She wanted to be alone, to bid farewell to those beloved places that were a part of her very being, and that she now had to leave. Weeping bitterly, she sank down on a little green bench under a tall, spreading oak tree; it was here that she liked to sit with her embroidery in her hands and a song on her lips. Then, sobbing loudly, she ran to bid farewell to her favourite clearing, with its sparkling stream.

Gazing at her beloved haunts and the green, shady forest, she realised that her happy times here were now a thing of the past, and her heart almost broke. Forcibly holding back her tears, she looked around one last time, and silently took her leave of everything: "Farewell, oh, farewell, all you dear witnesses of my childhood, of my happiness!"

Completely lost in her thoughts, she slowly made her way home.

At the forester's house, they had been looking for her everywhere.

Her mother, seeing her teary, inflamed eyes, clapped her hands in despair. "What in God's name is wrong with you, my child, that you're all teary-eyed? How can you appear in front of the guests with such red eyes? Why are you crying? Don't you want to marry Volodymyr, or what?"

Halya took one look at her sister and began crying as well.

"There you have it!" the mother exclaimed. "What's to be done with them? Calm down! Are you children, or what?"

"If I'd known that I would be so unhappy to leave you, I wouldn't have agreed to get married," Emiliya sobbed.

"But you're not leaving us forever," her mother comforted her. "After all, you'll come to visit us with Volodymyr, so we'll see a lot of each other. We can't always live together. God be with you, my child, settle down and stop crying; you're going to make yourself ill."

The mother comforted her daughters for a long time before she calmed them down. Finally, they started dressing.

When Emiliya donned her white gown and her myrtle wreath with its long veil she looked like innocence personified; her pale face became comelier, and her eyes took on a soft lustre and shone with a sad, melancholy glow.

Halya was also wearing a white dress; she had regained her composure and was now looking forward eagerly to all the dancing she would be doing as a bridesmaid.

Before long, the Liskovsky's carriage arrived. Madam Liskovska who was the *matka [matron of honour]* was dressed in an expensive silk dress. Mariya, attired all in white, looked incredibly beautiful.

Almost immediately, two other carriages pulled up. It was Halytsky with his family and Orest. The hosts heartily greeted their family-to-be and led them to a table laden with appetisers.

Orest went up to Mariya right away, saying that he deserved the best wedding corsage. Smiling and blushing, she pinned on him a corsage of myrtle tied with white ribbons. The guests, arriving now in a steady stream, did not let them talk for long, as Mariya, with Halya's assistance, had to pin corsages on all of them.

In a short time, the house was filled with animated, elegantly attired people. They sauntered through the rooms, chatting gaily.

The Goretskys also came. Denys rode up in his own wagon and brought with him several male friends that Halytsky had asked him to invite. Other young gentlemen, school buddies of the groom, also arrived, and they at once began to fill up the dance programs of the girls.

At dusk, carriages drove up to take everyone to church for the marriage ceremony. The bride sat in the first one with her *matka* and the best men. Halytsky sat in the next one with the bridesmaids and Mr. Liskovsky, the *bat'ko [honorary father and master of ceremonies]*. The rest of the wedding party settled into the remaining carriages.

After the ceremony, the young couple climbed into the first carriage along with the *matka* and the *bat'ko*. Orest, who was leading Mariya by the arm, helped her into the next one and, without waiting for Denys and Halya, who were supposed to ride with them, told the driver to go full speed ahead. The night was dark, and two horseback riders, holding huge lanterns, rode alongside the carriage of the newlyweds.

"How happy I would be if we were the ones who were now returning from our marriage ceremony," Orest said, pressing Mariya's hand.

Mariya trembled violently and tore her hand out of his. "Why are you saying this?" she said in an offended voice suffused with tears.

"Why are you making me suffer?" Orest asked. "You know that I love you—I love you more than life itself, more than my own happiness, and every unfriendly word of yours causes me inexpressible grief. Mariya, my dearest, my love, tell me: do you feel at least a tiny bit of affection for me?"

The darkness did not permit him to see her flustered face, on which joy and happiness, mixed with uncertainty, were breaking through.

"You aren't answering me," Orest sighed sadly. "It's clear you don't love me . . . You hate me; I did not expect this."

"I don't hate you," Mariya whispered softly, giving him her hand.

"Then you love me, my dearest, my happiness, my joy!" Orest exclaimed, passionately embracing the supple figure of his beloved.

She bent her head on his chest, and the emboldened young man kissed her ruby lips.

She tore herself from his embrace.

"My God! What are you doing?" she cried, terribly upset. "What if someone saw us? What would people think?"

"They would think that we're very happy," Orest replied cheerfully. "But Mariya, sweetheart, you haven't told me that you love me. Tell me, my darling, tell me that you love me; otherwise I won't believe in my good fortune."

"I love you, my dearest, and I'll love you forever," the bashful girl said, nestling against him.

Orest embraced her with one hand and stroked her head with the other one. He was too deeply moved to speak.

A moment later they arrived at the forester's house. The mother came out with bread and salt to greet the young couple and bless them as they entered.

Orest, leading Mariya by the hand, also went up to her to be blessed. "Bless us as well," he said light-heartedly, but his voice was choked with emotion.

Madam Radoska took his words at face value, but Halytsky surmised that they had a deeper meaning.

The remaining guests drove up, and everyone sat down to eat. The young couple were seated in the place of honour; the *matka* and the *bat'ko* sat beside them and, next to them, were the more important guests.

The wine was poured. Mr. Liskovsky rose to his feet and drank a toast to the newlyweds. The boisterous singing of *mnohaya lita* [we wish you many years of health and happiness] filled the house. Then the host toasted the health of the *matka* and the *bat'ko*, thanking his sister and brother-in-law for agreeing to do his children the honour of performing this service. Many other toasts were proposed and, after each one, the young gentlemen thundered *mnohaya lita* in chorus.

Seeing that the older people, wearying of the orations, were about to conclude them, Denys rose to his feet and raised a toast to the bridesmaids. It was an elaborate toast, replete with compliments and interspersed with fragments of poetry, in which he compared the young ladies to stars and roses who, with their radiance and their beauty, adorned the entire gathering.

He had composed his toast with Mariya in mind, as Halya meant nothing to him. Knowing Mariya's poetic nature, he was confident that his flattering words would win her heart.

During Denys's speech, Orest watched his beloved carefully. She was listening to it with a disinterested air, as if the toast had nothing at all to do with her; but, seeing Orest's keen eyes fastened on her, she blushed furiously.

Denys assumed that she was reacting to what he was saying. He was sure that Mariya was flushed with joy because he was singing her praises so highly.

After supper, the dancing began. Orest did not leave Mariya's side, talking to her, joking, and dancing with her.

Denys watched from the sidelines and, when he danced the quadrille with Mariya, warned her not to spend too much time with Orest.

"These young gentlemen from Halychyna are all great deceivers," he said, as if in passing. "They make a girl's head spin and then abandon her."

Mariya acted as if she did not understand what he meant, as if she did not have the slightest idea that he was directing his words at her.

"But are our Bukovynian young men any better? I've heard more than once that 'they love and adore, then head for the door,'" she said merrily. "Come on, admit it—even you have promised eternal love to more than one young woman."

"There's only one young woman that I love—only one," Denys said, "but I've never told her of my love."

Mariya felt uncomfortable and did not respond.

"You're not asking me who she is," Denys said. "Aren't you curious?"

"Other people's secrets are of no concern to me," Mariya replied frostily.

"But more than likely you would be interested if that secret concerned Master Orest," he said sarcastically.

Provoked by Mariya's cold demeanour, he did not stop to consider what he was saying.

"I don't know why you keep mentioning Master Martyniv to me! Please don't do this, because I find it most unpleasant," Mariya said, drawing herself up haughtily.

"Forgive me, I did not think that a joke would offend you so greatly," Denys apologised, cursing, with all his soul, his stupidity in having angered Mariya.

After the quadrille was over, Denys sat down beside Mariya and, when the next dance began, he once again asked her to dance. She could not shake him and had to listen patiently to what he was saying, because she did not want to arouse his suspicions regarding her feelings for Orest.

Finally, a young gentleman rescued her by calling her into the next room to have a word with her.

At dawn the guests began to disperse to get some sleep. The Goretskys and Liskovskys, giving their word that they would return by eleven in the morning, left together.

Olha was not in a good mood. The young gentlemen had not paid much attention to her, despite the fact that she smiled sweetly at them and tried to hold their interest by telling them about all the household duties that she performed.

She was, of course, an intelligent young woman who could talk about more than household matters, but it is common knowledge that even though young ladies may be well-versed in many different areas, they try to conceal this fact for fear that their intelligence will prevent them from attracting a suitor.

And nowadays it is true that men, especially seminarians, fear a wise woman as they fear fire, saying that such a woman will not be a good housekeeper. But they overlook the fact that present-day wives—who are neither overly educated nor overly intelligent—are also not the greatest of housekeepers, preferring to scurry from one ball to another where, because of a dearth of intelligent matters to discuss, they pass the time slandering their dearest friends.

And so, Olha, who was not pretty, was forced to talk about household matters if she wanted to find a suitor. But even this ploy did not attract anyone. The most foolish statements, as long as they issue from beautiful lips, entice men, but even the wisest words, if they are spoken by unattractive lips, will not succeed in holding a young man's attention.

And truly, Olha did not meet with any success. Envious of the attractive girls, especially of Mariya, she resolved to give Denys a good dressing down for the flowery speech he had given in honour of the bridesmaids.

But she could not do this just yet, because Denys had stayed behind at the forester's home where, along with the other young gentlemen, he lay down to sleep in the huge barn which had been spread with straw, blankets, and pillows.

Morpheus, the god of dreams, accepted all the young men into his embrace and, filling their heads with delightful, tantalising visions, kept them there for a long time. It was only when he saw that the images he was conjuring up no longer held sway over them that he freed them from his powerful grasp.

Denys was the first to awaken, and he inadvertently jabbed Orest and woke him as well.

"Good day," Denys said, yawning protractedly. "Have you slept enough?"

"Why yes, I feel completely refreshed," Orest replied.

"Oh, but I don't; towards morning I peered too deeply into the eyes of Miss Glass, and so, as they say, I'm not all that bright this morning."

"Which Miss Glass?" asked a high school student, probably no more that eighteen, who had just awoken from a deep sleep after dancing the whole night away as if he had been paid to do so. "Was she the one in the white dress?"

Orest and Denys laughed so loudly that the other young gentlemen woke up with a start, as if they had been scalded.

"What is it, what's going on?" they asked.

"Nothing. Master Goretsky said that he peered into the eyes of Miss Glass, and I asked if she was the one in the white dress," the high school student answered naively.

"No, *edler Jüngling [noble youth]*, her dress may be white, or yellow, or red, or, at times, it may be, as they say, *schwarzbraun [dark brown]*," a law student said phlegmatically as he stretched himself out on the straw once again. "Wait until you enter university, then you'll also have the good fortune to become acquainted with Miss Glass."

Everyone was weak with laughter, and the high school student, feeling ashamed of his stupidity when he realised what Denys had meant, hid his head under his pillow to hide his embarrassed face.

"Ugh! It's so awful to get up after such an event!" one of the young men said. "All my bones ache, and my head feels as if a billion rats are nesting in it."

"Mice maybe, but not rats; are you sure they're rats?" another young man entered the conversation.

"There are no rats and no mice in the heads of those who interrupt the speech of others, only straw," the first one replied apathetically.

The second one pretended he had not heard the remark that had made all the others laugh until the barn shook.

"It's time to rise and shine, my little brothers," another young man said. "More than likely the young ladies got up long ago and are impatiently awaiting us."

"It's fine for them to wait—they didn't pass as much *stoff [stuff (liquor)]* through their throats as we did! It's really done us in," a third one piped up.

"You know what," Denys suggested, "the Dniester river isn't too far from here. Let's go for a swim, and maybe the water will chase the rats out of our heads."

"What a wonderful idea! Wonderful!" the young gentlemen chorused and, hastily leaping to their feet, began pulling on their clothes.

They returned an hour later, freshly washed and combed, and neatly dressed. No one would have recognised them as the same young men who, with pale faces and sunken eyes, had lain in the barn. They attacked breakfast with wolfish appetites and, after eating their fill, lit up cigarettes before looking around to see where the young ladies were.

The ladies had already gone for a walk in the forest. Seeing their bright dresses gleaming among the trees, the young gentlemen set off after them.

A moment later, the air rang with singing, jokes, and happy laughter.

Orest did not go into the forest, because Halya told him that Mariya and Olha had not yet arrived. He sat beside Halytsky and Emiliya, who was looking very dignified in her black dress, and waited for his good fortune to arrive.

And arrive it did. Mariya, knowing that Orest liked to see her in Ukrainian folk dress, had dressed accordingly. Orest's eyes shone with delight; he guessed why she had chosen to dress this way.

"Mariya, my dear, please go and ask everyone to come back from the forest. Now that the *matka* and the bridesmaid have arrived, we should dress the bride in the *ochipok [married woman's headdress]*," Madam Radoska said.

"I'll go with you," Orest piped up. "It's only proper that the best man accompany the bridesmaid to invite the guests."

He gave her his arm, and the two of them set out for the forest.

"Tell me, do you still love me?" Orest asked, after they had walked a few steps away from the house.

He had no intention of hurrying to invite the guests.

"I said that I would love you forever," Mariya replied, blushing, "so why wouldn't I love you today?"

"I find it hard to believe; it seems too good to be true that you love me—it's like a dream from which I'm afraid I'll awaken."

"It's not a dream; it's the truth, the wonderful, delightful truth, my dearest Orest," Mariya said, looking into his eyes.

He took her hand and kissed it. "What will you say when I ask your parents for your hand in marriage?"

Mariya turned crimson. "I'll agree, with all my heart," she said tenderly.

"And your parents?"

"When they see that my happiness depends on it, they'll also agree."

"But will you want to wait a year for me—because I need that much time to complete my studies."

"Of course. I'm willing to wait even longer, but take care that you remain faithful to me."

"Until the day I die," Orest stated resolutely. "This is how it will be," he continued. "I won't say anything to your parents now, because there's too much noise and confusion here, but when I return home, I'll write a letter asking for your hand in marriage. You'll show this letter to your parents and tell them about our love for each other, and you'll write me a reply. Then I'll come over with my family to celebrate our engagement; and, in a year, we'll be married."

Mariya listened raptly, as if she were hearing wonderful music and, when he finished speaking, warmly pressed his hand.

"Fine. I happily agree to everything," she said with a smile. And she no longer was upset when he kissed her.

Drawing nearer to the guests, they assumed a more serious and aloof mien as they invited all of them to the house. The young ladies were not too happy to comply with this request; they were enjoying themselves here where, unlike in the house, the young gentlemen were uninhibited, charming, and quick to offer compliments; and so they reluctantly followed the older ladies out of the forest, deeply regretting that they could no longer listen to the highly inflated words that the young gentlemen were showering upon them.

Arriving at the house, they all gathered in the main room and sat down on the benches. A large mirror had been placed in the middle of the room, and Emiliya, still wearing her bridal wreath, was seated next to it. The best men carried out the *ochipok* on a tray and began dancing around the bride with it.

In the meantime, the *matka* unpinned Emiliya's bridal wreath, placed it on the tray, and covered it with a kerchief, so that the bride could not see it. She then pinned the *ochipok* on the young woman's head. The best men turned the mirror around, and the new Madam Halytska saw herself in an *ochipok* for the first time. The *matka* took her by the arm and led her to the groom. As she handed over his wife to him, she admonished him to respect and look after her.

After this part of the ceremony was concluded, the young ladies took turns dancing in the bridal wreath.

As Orest danced with Mariya, he whispered softly to her: "In a year I'll see you wearing the same kind of wreath."

Mariya smiled blissfully.

Now the best men had to dance, holding aloft the gifts that the *bat'ko* and *matka* had brought the young couple. The best men also did not come up empty-handed; they received lovely embroidered kerchiefs from the bride and, from the groom, silver tobacco cases engraved with their names.

When the entire ceremony was over, dinner was served. After dinner there was more dancing, but now the older people joined in as well. They danced until midnight and then, completely exhausted, went their separate ways to get some sleep.

In the morning they all had breakfast together, and only then did they begin to depart. Denys, under orders from his mother and sister, invited all the gentlemen to their house. Orest excused himself by saying that he had to wait until evening to see the young couple off.

After crying to her heart's content, Emiliya prepared to leave her home. Her dowry was already piled into two wagons, and Mr.

Radosky sent the wagons and Halytsky's carriage ahead to the ferry crossing, because the young couple wanted to step in to the Liskovsky home in the village to say their farewells.

Orest was glad to have the opportunity to see his beloved once more, but they did not stay long at the Liskovskys, because Halytsky was in a hurry to go home, and the wagons were waiting for them at the crossing. Weeping loudly, Emiliya bade a final farewell to her relatives who had accompanied her to the Dniester river.

As they parted, Orest said to Mariya: "You'll receive my letter no later than a week from today."

"Don't make me wait too long," Mariya replied, and tears welled up in her eyes.

VIII

Melanya impatiently awaited the return of her brother. Her mind was not on her work, and she could not interact with her pupils in her usual warm manner.

On Tuesday, after dismissing them towards evening, she walked in the direction from where Orest would be coming. As she went along, a faint trace of sorrow settled on her attractive lips. Recalling the past, she remembered how she had given her passionate young heart to a young teacher.

He had come to their village on his first teaching assignment and, seeing her, the comely daughter of the priest, had fallen head over heels in love with her. But this rustic idyll did not last too long; her parents, seeing their daughter's affection for the young teacher, did everything in their power to have him removed from their village.

He left and took Melanya's heart with him. From that day onwards, Melanya became a quiet, serious young woman whom love had elevated and ennobled. She did not give in to grief; instead, she devoted herself to helping the common people that her beloved loved so dearly.

Her brother knew the reason for her selfless work among the people, and he encouraged her in it. He pitied his sister, because he knew that her love for the young teacher would never fade. But he never mentioned him to her, and he never encouraged her to marry the various seminary graduates who sought her hand in marriage.

Melanya's parents were annoyed with her for refusing all her suitors, among whom there were quite a few who would have made a suitable husband. Melanya did not respond to their reproaches, but there were times when tears filled her lovely eyes. She did not know what had happened to her beloved; he had vanished from her circle of friends and acquaintances.

As she walked down the road, Melanya was preoccupied with the thought that her life would flow by in unabated grief for her lost beloved.

"I'll never be happy," she grieved, "but I'd like at least those who are dear to me to be happy; if only my dear Orest could find happiness—I'd forget my own sorrow and find my happiness in his good fortune."

The rumbling of a wagon broke into her sad reverie. In the distance, Melanya could see her brother travelling with the Halytskys.

When the travellers drew nearer, Orest and Halytsky jumped down from the carriage, and the latter introduced his young wife to Melanya.

Shaking Emiliya's hand, Melanya wished her all the best in her new life, and Emiliya thanked her sincerely and expressed her delight in making a new acquaintance. Melanya then invited the young couple to visit them, and Halytsky replied that they would take advantage of her kind invitation in the very near future. After talking for a few more minutes, they parted, and Orest was left with his sister.

"Well, how did things go for you, Orest?" Melanya asked as she took Orest's arm and started walking back home.

Orest smiled joyfully: "My dear Melanya, it all turned out much better than I had dared to hope. Mariya loves me; Mariya is mine."

"Glory to God! Orest, you don't know how happy your good fortune has made me!" Her voice trembled, and her eyes filled with tears.

"My dear sister," he said sympathetically, pressing her hand. "I will know true happiness only when I succeed in seeing that you are happy, as well."

Melanya blushed.

"Don't talk about it, brother," she said reluctantly. "You know it's impossible. You'd do better to tell me how Mariya confessed that she loves you."

"It cost me no end of trouble before she admitted that I'm dear to her heart, but because of it, my happiness knows no bounds."

"You asked her to marry you, didn't you?"

"Yes, but so far I've only talked to her about it, and not to her parents. I said that I would write to her, and that she could show my letter to her parents, and then give me their reply. I have to talk with our parents, as well."

"Yes, you do. But I know that they won't say anything against Mariya—because she's considered a highly acceptable match," Melanya said, a hint of bitterness in her voice.

"Soon Mariya will be my betrothed," Orest said joyfully, "and when that happens I wouldn't trade places with the richest man or lord. I truly don't know how I got so lucky that I won the heart of a girl like Mariya."

"How humble you've become, my dear brother," Melanya laughed. "It must be love that has changed you like that. But Mariya is also fortunate, because she'll have my brother for her husband, and my brother is no ordinary man."

Orest was not able to respond, because when they reached their yard, his father addressed him.

"Welcome home, my son. Tell me, did you enjoy yourself at the wedding?"

"Yes, I did, and I even received a present," Orest replied, showing him the silver tobacco case.

"Well, well! So it was worth being a best man there; but tell me—do the Bukovynians know how to enjoy themselves *comme il faut [as it should be done]*?"

"Of course. It seemed to me that I was at one of our socials. But there's just one thing—they speak German a lot."

"Just as we speak Polish. We Ukrainians seem to be fated to use the languages of others. Every nation uses its own native language, and it's just our Ukrainian people who are ashamed of their own tongue and so, as soon as they're out among other people, they latch on to their language."

"I don't know whose fault that is," Orest said, sitting down on a bench in front of the house and mopping his high forehead.

"Hm, as if you don't know," Father Martyniv responded. "It's our own, because we wouldn't forgive ourselves if we didn't speak in Polish to a Pole, but he wouldn't forgive himself if he spoke to us in our language."

"Then we should do what they do, and speak only our language," Orest said laughing.

"Yes, we should, we really should; but find me even one person who would dare to do anything like that."

"So this means that we lack civic courage and, because of this, we don't even use our own language," Orest said with a smile.

"Oh yes, you say things beautifully. But then, all you young people have a lot of flowery phrases—the trouble is, you don't do anything."

"I assure you, father, that when we take our turn, no one will hear a foreign word in our company."

"Well! I'd like to live to see that day," Father Martyniv said, also smiling. "But in the meantime, tell me about the wedding which—according to you—went off *comme il faut*." Father Martyniv liked to use this foreign phrase in his speech.

Orest smiled and began describing the wedding in detail.

The next day, Father Martyniv went to an assembly of priests, and Orest could not speak to him about his plans. It was only on the third day that he was able to tell his father about his intentions with respect to Mariya.

His father, wanting to assert his authority as a parent, replied that he would have to think about such an important matter as his son's marriage before he gave his blessing—which he gave him two days later.

After receiving some advice from his sister, Orest sat down to write Mariya a letter.

"My highly respected Miss Mariya!

"As you already know, my heart belongs to you and will belong to you forever, and there is no need to try to describe the feelings that you have aroused in my heart, because I would never succeed in doing so. I love you, and I will love you forever—I said it then, and I am saying it now.

"Because of my great love for you, I am asking you and your parents for your hand in marriage. Make me a fortunate man and unite your life with mine. You will never regret it, because my love will strive to imbue your life with happiness.

"Having received your promise, I am asking your parents most humbly to accept me as their son, and I beg you, my dearest, to support my plea. My parents greeted the news of our love with great joy; they are delighted that they will be able to call you their daughter.

"I beg you to reply as soon as possible, because these last few days that I have spent apart from you have seemed interminable to me. Please end my waiting and grant me the happiness for which I will always be grateful to you.

Your *Orest*."

After reading the letter to Melanya, Orest sealed it and wanted to send a special messenger with it right away. His sister stopped him, however, saying that he ought to send Mariya a bouquet of red roses. They went together into the flower garden where the last roses—the queen of the flowers—were still blooming. Picking a few dozen roses and tying them with a pretty ribbon, they gave the bouquet to a servant, telling him to deliver the roses, along with the letter, into Miss Mariya's hands.

IX

Madam Goretska and Olha were hard at work. The seminarians they had asked Denys to bring home with him from Emiliya's wedding were due to arrive at any moment.

Olha was in high spirits—she hoped that one of her brother's friends would propose to her. Piling her hair up high on her head and putting on a bright pink dress that clashed with her dark sallow face, she rolled up her sleeves, tied on an embroidered apron—that she passed off as her own work, even though it was actually done by a young peasant woman—and rushed around the kitchen, pretending that she was helping her mother; she wanted the young men to see her working busily when they arrived.

Both the mother and the daughter led Father Goretsky around by the nose. Mild and taciturn, he was a close-fisted man who often had to loosen his pockets to satisfy the whims of the two women. He was renowned as a true patriot and Populist, and, even though everyone knew that his patriotism was limited to speaking Ukrainian and reading German newspapers, and his Populism to fleecing the peasants, these facts did not seem to detract from his reputation. And he, too, viewed himself as being very patriotic, especially when he made excruciatingly long toasts in old Church Slavonic, exhorting all patriots to close ranks in solidarity.

After arriving in the village from the city where Father Goretsky had been a catechist, his wife and daughter wanted to establish themselves as leaders in their social circle. Olha, of course, could not count on her looks to attain this position, so she attempted to do it by being the most fashionably dressed. Whenever she appeared in public, she wore a new dress sewn in the latest style—a luxury that she, as an only daughter could afford, but which earned her the animosity of the less fortunate daughters of the neighbouring priests.

Both the mother and daughter, seeing themselves as grand high society ladies, derided the other priests' wives and daughters, scoffing at their speech, their attire, and their manners which—lacking the affectations and artificiality of their detractors—truly were quite simple at times.

In public, the two women acted politely with everyone, and the older lady, in her attempts to increase their popularity, paid compliments left and right. This ruse of hers was partially successful and, in certain quarters, she was viewed as a highly educated and elegant lady. In private, however, she and her daughter laughed at the people with whom she ingratiated herself with the express purpose of having them sing her praises.

At home, Madam Goretska never troubled herself with running the household; she would hurriedly prepare something to eat and then devote herself either to reading German novels—the source of all her enlightenment—or to listening to what she considered to be Olha's admirable piano playing. But whenever anyone came visiting, she talked endlessly about household matters and about her industrious daughter, implying that Olha spent hours in the kitchen tending the pots and pans.

And Olha, to prove her mother's words true, immediately disappeared into the kitchen whenever guests arrived. By putting on a show of domesticity and stifling her antipathy to cooking, servants, and household concerns, Olha hoped to find herself a good suitor—one who was, of course, a seminarian.

As the two women awaited the arrival of the seminarians, they chatted in the kitchen, where the mother was overseeing the preparation of an elaborate dinner.

"Olha, my dear, go and tell daddy to order a keg of beer from the tavern. It's simply impossible to get by without it, you know," the mother said.

"He won't want to—he'll just yell at me."

"Don't worry, he'll agree this time. If we tell him it's for seminarians, he won't mind buying even two kegs."

"But, mummy, haven't you told him yet that we're expecting seminarians?"

"No, what for? To have him start quarrelling about the extra expenses that have to be incurred to receive them properly? People must know that we are capable of putting on a proper reception, that we aren't as poor and as simple as other priests."

"Oh, mummy, you really know how to manage daddy. You say he's the master of the house, but actually he has to do things your way."

The older woman laughed.

"Just see to it that you institute the same kind of order in your home; pretend to yield to your husband and do as he wishes in trifling matters, but when it comes to the bigger decisions, make sure that he listens to you. But now run along and tell daddy that guests are coming, and that we must have some beer for them," she said

Olha dashed off to her father's study. "Daddy, mummy wants you to order a keg of beer, because some seminarians are coming to visit us."

Father Goretsky gaped in stunned astonishment at his daughter. "Seminarians are coming here? Well, no doubt it's going to cost me a pretty penny, because you'll want to put on a count's reception for them," he started saying, but stopped abruptly when his wife appeared in the doorway.

"Listen, dear," she began speaking with a sweet smile on her face, "the seminarians are visiting our home for the first time, and we have to receive them properly so that our home will have a good reputation; if we do, there's a chance that someone will come along who will marry our Olha."

"Just stop and think how much money the good reputation of our home has already cost me! It's always about a good reputation—but I'm telling you that if one's pockets are empty, then a good reputation doesn't mean a thing."

"But, my dear, I'm begging you to do this; you don't want the young gentlemen to criticise our home," the priest's wife entreated.

"The devil take them, those young gentlemen!" Father Goretsky shouted angrily and, taking a *pyatka [five-dollar bill]* out of his pocket, he threw it on the table. "Here! Take it! Give them as much to drink as you want to!"

Clutching the *pyatka* in her hand, his wife walked triumphantly out of the room with Olha.

At that very moment, a parishioner came to see the priest about some matter. The priest redirected his wrath at the poor, unsuspecting man and tried to recoup from him the money he had been forced to spend on entertaining the seminarians.

The peasant backed out of the house, crossed himself, spat, and thought: "I wouldn't advise anyone to go and see the priest today, because he's in such a state that God forbid!"

Just before noon, dogs began barking in the yard, youthful voices rang out cheerfully, and a crowd of young gentlemen came through the gate with Denys. Olha glanced out the window and, scarcely able to contain her excitement, rushed elatedly to inform her parents about the arrival of the visitors who were so dear to her heart.

Before Father Goretsky could make his way to the door to greet the guests, they were all in the house. A round of introductions began, along with a renewal of acquaintances made at the wedding.

The young gentlemen inquired how Olha felt after such an exhausting event as a wedding, and she replied that she was ready to dance again.

As the guests began complimenting her on her good health, they became aware of the delicious aromas drifting out of the kitchen and, wishing to earn their dinner, laid the compliments on thick and fast.

The table was set, and Olha, fluttering about like a fly that had fallen into boiling water, hastened to demonstrate how efficient she was.

The seminarians were given the seats of honour. The law students jabbed one another with their elbows and smiled without saying anything; they were accustomed to being treated with less respect in priests' homes. It went without saying that none of them would marry a priest's daughter, and so it was only proper that the seminarians were given the best places, while they were relegated to less important positions.

The table was groaning under a sumptuous dinner that would have sufficed to feed all the parishioners on a feast day. It was clear that Madam Goretska had perused the pages of her cook book very diligently indeed, in her hopes of pleasing the young gentlemen.

Some of the guests were delighted by such a display of hospitality, but others just turned up their noses and laughed mockingly in their hearts, because they knew that they were being feted in this manner so that one of them would become engaged to the host's daughter.

After two hours of eating and drinking like rooks, they rose to their feet and asked Olha to do them the favour of playing something for them. She seated herself at the piano, and her ensuing performance evoked a sober thoughtfulness and a jangling of nerves in more than one musical soul.

The young gentlemen stayed on for two days, entertaining themselves very well indeed. Then Denys drove them to the home of a neighbouring priest who had several children and could not afford to put on a reception like the Goretskys. It was Olha and her mother who had convinced Denys to take the young men there, so they would see for themselves how differently they would be treated in that home.

After two days there, Denys returned with the sad news that even though the neighbouring priest had not hosted the young gentlemen as grandly, one of the seminarians had become engaged to his daughter.

Olha burst into tears when she heard this and flung accusations at her brother that he did not care about her happiness, because he had not encouraged any of his friends to propose to her. Denys shrugged his shoulders and, to avoid further attacks from his mother and sister, walked out into the orchard; he sat down and pondered how he might propose to Mariya.

He was about to embark on the fourth year of his theological studies, and so, in a year, he could get married. In view of the dangerous threat presented to him by Orest, he thought it would be a good idea to become engaged before then. He did not have the nerve to propose in person; he had high aspirations and felt he would not know how to behave in the event that he might be refused.

"It would be better to settle the matter in writing," he said to himself, "and put an end to my suffering. I never dreamed that I could become so obsessed by love for a girl."

He went to the house and, without further ado, began writing a letter to her that reflected his poor knowledge of Ukrainian:

"Esteemed Miss Mariya:

"You must be aware that my heart is on fire with love for you. For the longest time I have deferred admitting my feelings for you, fearing your refusal, and having no indication of your feelings for me. In the last while, however, having become aware of your affection for me, I am hastening to confess my feelings for you, and I sincerely beg you to respond to them.

"I love you, Miss Mariya, I love you with my entire soul; I think only about your happiness. This is why I am making bold to ask you and your esteemed parents for your hand in marriage. You may rest assured that I would value greatly the good fortune of owning you.

"With the fond hope that my proposal will be approved by you and that you will not deny me the happiness of owning you,
 "I remain

"Sincerely yours,
Denys Goretsky."

Calling his mother and Olha to him, Denys told them that he was proposing to Mariya; he did not consult his father in this matter.

His mother praised his intentions, but Olha pouted. She was jealous of Mariya.

After dispatching a servant with the letter, Denys waited impatiently for his return. Finally the servant came back and told him that the young lady would send her reply later.

Denys was beside himself, and the taunts of his sister, who was laughing at him, drove him to distraction.

Shortly after lunch, a servant of the Liskovskys delivered a letter to Denys.

He tore open the envelope and read:

"Dear Sir:

"Thank you for the honour you have bestowed upon me by asking for my hand in marriage, but I cannot give it to you because I wish to give it to the one to whom my heart belongs. I have already made my choice, and I am not able to renege on it now.

"As for the signs of my affection that you mention in your letter, be assured that I deeply regret any thoughtless behaviour on my part that may have inadvertently given rise to hopes which I am unable to fulfil.

"I would like to think that my refusal will not sever the amicable relations that have existed between us.

"I thank you once again for the honour you have shown me, and I ask for your forgiveness if I have caused you any pain; in matters of love, it is impossible to command one's heart.

"Respectfully yours,
Mariya Liskovska."

As he read this letter, Denys turned deathly pale. His hands shook, and his lips twisted sardonically.

"I know who your choice is!" he hissed, grating his teeth. "But as long as I'm alive, I won't let you belong to him."

When his mother and sister came and heard about the refusal, they began speaking ill of Mariya, stressing her pride and arrogance, saying that she was reaching very high, but could end up falling very low.

Denys did not reply, because he knew that Mariya was not like that. Her refusal pained him, but his sense of justice would not permit him to agree with what his mother and sister were saying.

He went to his room, where he sat sorrowfully at his desk, trying to think of a way to come between Mariya and Orest. To give him time to be by himself, Olha set out for a walk to the Dniester river.

She had hardly crossed two streets when she heard a voice call out to her.

"Miss, if you please."

Turning around, Olha saw a stranger with a wonderful bouquet of roses in his hands. By his clothing, she could tell he was from Halychyna.

"Glory to Jesus Christ," the man greeted her. "Could you, by chance, tell me where Mr. Liskovsky lives?"

"Glory forever," Olha replied. "Where are you from?"

"I've come over from the other side of the Dniester; I'm supposed to give Miss Liskovska this bouquet and a letter."

"It must be from Master Orest."

"Uh-huh."

A strange idea occurred to Olha; she felt flushed, and her heart pounded, but she replied calmly: "Give them to me; I'm Miss Liskovska."

"Really? It's fortunate that I met you then, because our young gentleman instructed me to give them only to you."

The man took the letter from his belt and passed it to Olha. She turned pale and then flushed, wavering as to whether or not she should take the letter. But evil triumphed, and she boldly reached out her hand to accept the letter meant for someone else. She even took a couple of small coins from her pocket and gave them to the messenger, telling him to thank the young gentleman for the bouquet.

"But, you see, I was told to wait until you wrote your reply," the messenger said.

"Tell him I'll send it in the mail, and give him my best wishes for his continued good health."

"Fine, fine. I'll tell him everything."

The man headed back to the Dniester, and Olha raced home with a pounding heart.

"Do you know why Mariya refused you?" she asked Denys as she entered his room. "I just intercepted a letter from Orest to her."

"How? Where? What?" Denys exclaimed, leaping from his bed.

"I was on my way to the Dniester, when I saw a man carrying this bouquet. He inquired where the Liskovsky house was, and said that he had a letter for the young lady there. And I tricked him into thinking that I was Miss Liskovsky, and he gave me the bouquet without the slightest hesitation."

"How could you do something like that?" her indignant brother shouted.

"And how could she make you so unhappy?" his sister shouted back at him.

"That has nothing to do with it. Have you already opened the letter?"

"No."

"Then send someone with it to Mariya."

"Not likely! I want to see what he's written to her." And, swiftly tearing open the envelope, she read Orest's letter and then laughed gleefully.

"Here, read it," she said, passing the letter to her brother. "These are the words of a fortunate love."

Denys grimaced, but he read the letter, and his face assumed a demoniacal expression.

"You know what, Denys?" his sister said, as she watched him. "Orest is also asking for her hand in marriage, so you should send him the letter she sent you, and he'll think she's refused him."

"What devil prompted you to think such a thing?" Denys asked in a shaky voice. "The very same thought occurred to me. It must be a sign that I am the one who is to part them."

And he no longer opposed his sister, who insisted that he send Mariya's letter to Orest. Denys knew that this was a vile deed, a dastardly deed, but his passion, inflamed by his sister's words, succeeded in corrupting him.

Denys placed Mariya's letter in an envelope. Forging Mariya's handwriting, he addressed it to Orest and dispatched it to the post office.

He was not the least bit troubled that, by doing so, he would be causing two people a great deal of misery for a long time.

X

When he returned, the messenger conveyed Mariya's regards to Orest and said that she would send him a letter by mail. The fact that his beloved would make him wait so long surprised Orest greatly.

"This doesn't bode well," he said to his sister, "but maybe she wants to find out if I'll have enough patience to wait for her letter."

"Why would she want to torment you, Orest? It would have been better if she had replied at once," Melanya said.

"Well, what's to be done; I'm sure of her love, so I'll wait patiently for her reply." Orest said this lightly, hoping to hide from his sister the bad mood he had fallen into after the messenger's return.

She saw that he was upset and did not pursue the matter.

The next three days went by in a daze for Orest, as if he were in a fever. On the fourth day, just as he was about to go and see Mariya, the postman brought him a letter. The address had clearly been written by a woman.

Seizing the letter, Orest dashed into the orchard to read it. Melanya, seeing him rush past the windows, hurried after him.

Tearing open the letter, Orest began to read. He could not believe his eyes as he read the cold, formal refusal that Mariya had written to Denys.

"This . . . this was written to me?" he shouted insanely. "She dared to toy with the most sacred of my feelings; she encouraged my love with her own sweet words and looks, and now she tells me that I should forgive her foolish behaviour. Oh, the damned coquette! She's struck me in the very heart with these words! I won't forgive her as long as I live!"

Seeing her brother in such turmoil, Melanya became alarmed. "What's wrong, Orest? O my God, what's wrong?" she shrieked, staring at his deathly pale face.

"Here, you read it, and see for yourself how she mocks my most sincere love. And then she comes right out and says that she's committed to someone else. It's probably Goretsky who has elbowed me out of this lady's favour," Orest said with bitter sarcasm.

"If she can write you such a letter after what has transpired between the two of you, she isn't worthy of your love. Orest, my dear brother, calm down and find comfort in the thought that she isn't worthy of you." Melanya embraced her brother and pressed his head to her breast.

"Rest here on my heart—it too is unfortunate," she said tearfully. "It looks as if neither one of us is ever to know any happiness—as if we are fated to live solely to discharge our responsibilities."

Orest clasped his sister to his heart. "O my dear guardian angel, if I didn't have you I don't know what I'd do to myself now. Oh, it's hard, so hard, to be on the verge of bliss, only to plummet into an abyss of despair."

"I've lived through it, my dear brother, except for one difference—I didn't live to see the one I loved become unworthy of my love."

Melanya sobbed softly, and Orest looked at her sympathetically. He sensed that her soul was undergoing a struggle no less painful than his.

"You know what, Melanya," he said after a lengthy pause. "Let's vow never to mention the past, to forget all about it. We'll strive to make life easier for each other and find meaning in our lives by honouring our responsibilities. Let our people be everything to us; let their happiness be our happiness and our purpose in life."

His forehead cleared, and his face regained its healthy colour, but he could not force a smile to his tightly clamped lips. This hour of grief bound the brother and sister still closer to each other, and transformed Orest into a man who, renouncing his quest for personal happiness, was ready to adopt a life of service to his nation and his people.

In the few days that Orest remained at home before returning to the university to prepare for his doctoral exam, neither his parents, nor his sister, said a word to him about Mariya, and he never mentioned her.

Pondering his and Melanya's tragic fate, he cast about for something he could do to make her happy. As they parted, he said he would find out where her beloved lived and, if he was convinced that the young teacher had remained faithful to her, he would take it upon himself to ensure that his parents did not oppose their marriage.

"You'd have the best possible opportunity to work among the people," he said, as he seated himself in the buggy that was to take him to the train station, "and I could visit you once in a while and find respite in your home."

Melanya watched her departing brother for a long time. Then, sighing heavily, she returned to her pupils, cursing Mariya for spurning a sincerely loving heart like Orest's and filling it with bitterness and grief.

Three months went by without a letter from Orest.

Then, just as they were beginning to be truly worried about him, they received a letter replete with wit and humour. Melanya could tell he had written it that way to allay her worries. Replying by return mail, she asked him to come home for the Christmas holidays, but he responded that his studies were too demanding. This news saddened Melanya; she was accustomed to having her brother home for the Christmas season.

During the holidays, many guests, including Halytsky and Emiliya, came to visit Father Martyniv. Melanya welcomed them warmly, hoping to hear some news from them about Mariya. But there was no opportunity to speak to them in private, because the other guests demanded Melanya's attention. The Halytskys departed before she had time to exchange more than a few words with them.

Orest did not come home during the long winter, nor did he write Melanya anything about her beloved.

"Perhaps he's forgotten about him, or maybe he wants to spare me any more grief if he found out that my dear one has married," Melanya thought. "But regardless of what the situation is, it would be good to know; my heart would be eased."

Keeping up her acquaintance with the Halytskys, she visited them a few times with her parents, and they repaid the visits. But whenever Melanya mentioned Mariya, Emiliya broke off the conversation and replied in monosyllables. When she asked if Mariya had already married Goretsky, Emiliya replied that her cousin had never entertained such an idea. This news surprised Melanya, because Orest had identified Goretsky as the cause of Mariya's refusal.

When Orest arrived home for Easter, his appearance was noticeably altered. When asked about his lack of colour and sunken eyes, he blamed his studies.

He informed Melanya that he now knew where her beloved lived; he would speak to him and bring her some news when he came home for the summer holidays.

The change in Orest was striking. Formerly talkative and vivacious, he was now uncommunicative and deliberate in his movements.

His reserve suited his pale face and made him very intriguing to the ladies. But he ignored the fact that all the priests' marriageable daughters fastened their eyes on him when they came visiting at Easter time; instead, he carried on serious conversations with their fathers about improving the lives of the common people.

His bold words appealed to some of the priests, but others shrugged their shoulders and whispered: "It's really too bad—he's going to ruin his career with his radicalism."

Seeing Halytsky and Emiliya among the guests, Orest greeted them heartily and engaged them in a lengthy conversation. He did not, however, even as a matter of courtesy, inquire about Mariya, thereby incurring their strong disapproval.

When Orest departed after the Easter break, he looked somewhat happier. He had presented his views to a number of his educated acquaintances and succeeded in persuading them to take up the cause of bettering the lot of the masses; this realisation filled his heart with joyful pride.

A short while later, Melanya drove over to the Halytskys for a visit. Halytsky was not at home. Emiliya greeted her in a somewhat troubled manner and, after tea, engaged her in an earnest conversation.

After some time, Emiliya said: "Excuse me, Miss Melanya, but I simply have to ask you something; I would not do so if I did not feel so sorry for poor Mariya. Why is your brother angry with her? Because he is angry—I could tell he was, because he did not even inquire about her."

Melanya flushed. "Mariya herself is to blame that he's angry with her. She promised him her hand in marriage and then she refused him. You can see how he has changed because of the grief she caused him."

"It's true; he has changed. But you should see her—she's just a shadow of her former self," Emiliya said. "But how can you say that she promised him her hand in marriage and then refused him? That's not possible. If she had been able to keep him at her side, she would have done so—instead of grieving for him now."

"I'm giving you my word of honour; my brother sent a letter asking her to marry him, and she replied that she didn't want him; she loved someone else."

"I don't understand that," Emiliya said. "I only know that Mariya is very unhappy because of your brother."

"And my brother is unhappy because of her! There seems to be something more to this; we'll have to solve this puzzle."

"I just hope it isn't too late. I know that Mariya loved your brother and still loves him; it seems strange to me that she would refuse him."

"Ask her yourself; my brother can show you the letter she sent him."

"I've already said that I don't understand this, but I'm not going to get involved if things are the way you say they are."

"In that case, we can't be of any assistance," Melanya said, as she prepared to leave.

On the way home Melanya mulled over what she had heard, but she could not figure it out. She resolved to await the return of her brother, at which time she would tell him everything she had heard from Emiliya. Perhaps he would find a way out of the labyrinth.

XI

After Emiliya's wedding, Mariya waited daily, hourly, for a letter from Orest. When she received Denys's proposal, she refused him without hesitation. She had never liked Denys and would have rejected him even if she had not fallen in love with Orest. He had written that she had displayed affection for him, but she knew she had never given him any reason for false hope.

Having sent Denys a letter of refusal, Mariya anxiously awaited a letter from Orest. Unable to work or read, she paced the rooms like a body without a soul. She spent a week like this, thinking that, at any moment, a messenger would arrive with a letter from her dear one. But no one came.

Wandering aimlessly through the orchard, Mariya sat down on a bench and thought: "Maybe he was making fun of me?"

The moment this idea occurred to her, she shuddered, remembering what Denys had said to her at the wedding about men from Halychyna. Tears poured from her eyes, and she was unable to restrain them.

"But no! It can't be," she said to herself. "He probably doesn't have time to write to me. Or perhaps his parents have not yet agreed to our marriage. He isn't like the others; his eyes radiate honesty, and he vowed to me that only I could make him happy."

Troubled by such thoughts, Mariya did not sleep all night. The next day she got up looking weary. Her face was pale, and she had dark circles under her eyes. Her mother asked her why she had not slept, but Mariya did not say anything. She still had hope, even though that hope was fading.

This day passed as well, and there still was no news from Orest.

Mariya lay down to sleep convinced that Orest had been mocking her, and that he was not worth thinking about. But this was easier said than done; Orest's image had embedded itself deeply in her soul and, only time, in addition to a firm resolve, could root it out.

For Mariya, the days passed by slowly and dully; nothing interested her, and all she could think about was Orest and his despicable behaviour. She could never have imagined that a man with such noble ideas could behave so reprehensibly. Her sorrow transformed her lovely face, making it pale and thin.

Her grief was all the harder to bear because she could not share it with anyone. Emiliya, her best friend, was now far away, and Halya was still too young to offer any comfort or advice. Her parents were very worried as they looked at the gaunt face of their only child; they were convinced that she was ill, even though she assured them that she was perfectly fine. Her mother may have guessed at the reason for her daughter's sadness, but she never even hinted at it, not wishing to add to her sorrow.

Mariya said nothing to her parents about Denys's proposal, and so the Liskovskys had no way of knowing why the Goretskys no longer came to visit them. And they were astonished that Denys had not come to see to them as he always did before leaving for the seminary.

"Why are the Goretskys avoiding us?" her mother asked Mariya one day. "Do you have any idea?"

"No, I don't," Mariya replied. "In any event, their good will means very little to me."

"To me also, but I'd like to know why they're angry with us."

Mariya did not respond. She suspected her refusal had angered the Goretskys, but it did not matter to her one way or the other.

One Saturday, well into autumn, Madam Liskovska and Mariya decided to attend evening vespers. When they arrived at the church, they took their usual places and began to pray.

A moment later, Madam Goretska entered with Olha, and, seeing the two Liskovsky women, they deliberately positioned themselves well behind them.

When the service was over, Olha and her mother hurried out of the church so as not to encounter the Liskovskys. The latter, taken aback by this affront, stared at each other in amazement and, when they came home, related how the Goretsky women had publicly insulted them, fleeing from the church to avoid the customary exchange of greetings.

Madam Liskovska kept speculating about possible reasons for this show of bad manners, until Mariya finally told her what had happened.

"You did the right thing, my dear," the mother said. "But it's still no reason for them to be snubbing us and insulting us in front of everyone."

Father Goretsky had no idea why his wife and daughter were angry at the Liskovskys. They told him that visiting the Liskovsky home would compromise the honour of a priest's family, and, being the meek soul that he was, he complied with their interdiction and stayed away from his old friends.

For Mariya, the winter was filled with grief and sorrow. Her only comfort lay in reading Orest's books and occasionally singing his favourite songs. She could not forget him, nor did she want to, because she did not believe him capable of deception. In her heart, she was convinced that some strange twist of fate had forced him to break his promise.

Spring finally arrived; the orchards bloomed. The air, filled with the fragrance of fresh grass, reverberated with the songs of birds returning home from southern climes. Everything seemed to be caught in a strange, mysterious spell—the spell of revivifying nature—and Mariya's grief intensified, for she knew that never again would she see her beloved and delight with him in the pristine charms of nature.

One evening Mariya was sitting in the fragrant, blossoming orchard where the pale light of the moon was veiling the fresh greenery of the trees. From the distant bushes by the Dniester, came the tender warbling of nightingales. Transfixed by the magnificent beauty of spring, she fell into a deep reverie.

A short while later, she became aware of the sound of grievous crying.

Springing to her feet, she ran in the direction of the weeping and, by the fence that divided their property from that of the neighbour's, found a young woman sobbing bitterly.

"What's wrong, Hanya?" Mariya asked her sympathetically. She knew this girl and really enjoyed talking with her and listening to her happy ditties and jokes.

Hanya lifted her head. "Oh, my dear lady, how can I help crying? Today, my Dmytro was drafted into the army for three years."

Hanya was overcome with tears, and Mariya was deeply moved by the poor girl's plight.

"Hush, Hanya," she said kindly. "What good are your tears? If God grants it, Dmytro will serve his three years and return to you."

"Oh? Do you suppose they'll let me wait for him? They're all happy that he was taken away, because now they can force me to marry someone else." And Hanya wept even harder.

"If there was some way I could help, I would gladly do all that I could, but no one can do anything about this," Mariya said softly.

"I know. I know no one can help me. I've lost my Dmytro forever, forever!" Hanya wailed.

"But maybe your parents will wait until he comes back?"

"Oh, no, they won't! They're waiting for the fall as they'd wait for God, because that's when he'll have to leave. And what, oh woe is me, will I do then?"

Mariya comforted the weeping young woman, telling her that not all who fall in love get married, and that you have to bear the fate God sends you. Little by little, she succeeded in stemming Hanya's tears. Feeling satisfied, Mariya went home, happy that she was able to bring solace to at least one human being.

From that time on, Mariya began to take more of an interest in Hanya. As she sat with her embroidery in the orchard, she would call Hanya, talk with her, convince her to sing, and even sing along with her.

The destiny of Hanya, who would have to obey her parents and marry someone she did not love, seemed as harsh to Mariya as her own sad fate. And so she felt an attachment to the young peasant woman and even considered pleading with the parents to allow their daughter to wait for Dmytro.

But Hanya assured her that no amount of pleading would convince her parents.

"Sing, Hanya," Mariya said one day as she sat embroidering on the grass in the orchard.

"If you knew how heavy my heart was, my dear lady, you wouldn't ask me to sing. The only time I manage to forget my troubles for a while is when I'm here with you, but when I'm at home, I wish the ground would open up and swallow me."

"God be with you, Hanya; perhaps things will work out for you. Come on, sing!"

"I know a new song now."

"Then go ahead and sing it."

Hanya began singing softly.

> "No one ever asks me
> Why I shed bitter tears.
> It's because my beloved
> Has gone for three years.
>
> No one ever asks me
> Why I weep and pine.
> It's because I don't hear
> His voice so divine.

> Oh, my dear little fish,
> I'll go down to the sea;
> All the lads are revelling there,
> But my beloved I don't see.
>
> Oh, I'll go to the Danube
> And I'll bitterly weep,
> Because nowhere can I see
> My beloved so sweet.
>
> I'll go back home
> And lament like a dove.
> My beloved's gone!
> Who am I to love?"

"It's a very nice song," Mariya said.

"I made it up myself," Hanya replied. Then, glancing at Mariya, she started singing again:

> "O dear friend, dear friend,
> My young lady so fine,
> Do you miss your dear one,
> The way I miss mine?
>
> I miss him, my dear friend,
> I miss him, as you can see.
> Why can't things be now
> As they used to be?
>
> I used to have someone
> With whom I could talk.
> Now there's no one at all
> To share my sad thoughts.
>
> My beloved said he loved me
> And vowed it was true.
> But he's gone, he's vanished,
> Like the wind that once blew.
>
> So I weep and I sorrow,
> But he cares not, alas.
> He's enjoying his freedom
> With another young lass.

> O God, dear God,
> Only this I ask of You—
> Let my poor soul
> Find some joy anew.
>
> Return, O dear God,
> My beloved to my arms,
> So I won't weep or grieve,
> Longing for his charms."

When Hanya finished her song, Mariya broke into tears. The image of Orest rose before her, and the utter hopelessness of her love was revealed to her in its true light.

"Why are you crying, dear lady?" Hanya asked. "It must be for that dark-eyed young gentleman who visited you last summer in this orchard. He didn't let you out of his sight."

Mariya blushed.

"Who told you this?" she asked.

"No one. I figured it out myself, because when he stopped coming you turned pale, and you know what they sing:

> 'Why have you grown pale
> Like white linen, my dear?'
>
> 'Oh, my heart is aching
> Aching for you, my dear.'
>
> 'Why have you grown pale,
> Like a white kerchief, my dear?'
>
> 'Oh, my head is aching
> Aching for you, my dear.'

"And I felt very sorry for you, because you're so kind! But that young gentleman also seemed like a good person; he had such a twinkle in his eye."

Mariya looked at Hanya. She wanted to thank her for praising Orest, but then, remembering the grief he had caused her, she did not say anything.

"Don't worry, Miss; that dark-eyed young man will come back to you, I swear. He's so handsome—the perfect partner for you."

"No, he'll never come back; we'll never see each other again," Mariya said, her voice trembling.

"Never, never . . . O merciful God, why? Won't your parents let you marry him?"

Mariya remained silent; she did not want to reveal the secret that lay in her heart—the secret that only Emiliya knew.

"So that's how it is," Hanya said. "I thought that gentlefolk were lucky and could marry the person they chose, but it turns out that it's the same for them as for us. I'm crying for my Dmytro, and you're weeping for your young gentleman. If I'd known you were so sad, I wouldn't have sung that song."

"It's nothing, it's nothing; I'm not annoyed with you for singing it," Mariya said. "But I beg you not to say anything to anyone about what we've talked about here."

"Oh, I swear I won't tell anyone—not even Dmytro."

Mariya found comfort in her discussion with the peasant girl whose native intelligence she truly admired.

And in this way, time went by.

During the Pentecost, Emiliya and her husband came to see their relatives in Bukovyna.

While visiting the Liskovskys, they invited Mariya to spend a few weeks with them. Mariya was delighted to receive the invitation, and her parents did not oppose it—they hoped their daughter might recover some of her former zest for life in her friend's home.

Mariya felt less restrained at Emiliya's. She could speak freely about what lay in her heart and be comforted by the words of Halytsky and his wife, neither one of whom could understand what had made Orest—about whom everyone thought highly—behave the way he had with respect to Mariya.

"There must be some kind of misunderstanding here," Halytsky said.

But Mariya shook her head doubtfully.

When Emiliya mentioned the letter of refusal Melanya had told her about, Mariya smiled ironically, saying that she could not have written such a reply, as she had not received a letter from Orest.

For Mariya, the days flowed by peacefully in the forester's home. She began to grow more animated and cheerful. Her thoughts about Orest became less painful, and she felt that her love for him was slowly receding. Her eyes no longer gazed so sadly at the world, and in her heart a glimmer of hope was beginning to break through.

When her parents came to get her, they saw that she was happier here than at home and agreed to leave her at Emiliya's for a while longer.

The summer holidays arrived.

One Sunday, Halytsky came home and announced that they would have a guest that evening.

"Who?" Emiliya asked curiously.

"A new teacher arrived in the village yesterday; he's an old acquaintance of mine, so I invited him to come over," Halytsky said.

"What's he like? Is he young, old, married?"

"He's young, unmarried, and very handsome," Halytsky replied. "He lived in the village of D. once before for half a year or so."

"Where the Martynivs live?"

"Yes."

Emiliya ran to tell Mariya about the guest.

XII

After completing his studies and brilliantly passing his exams, Orest returned home. He had acquired a new dignity, and his eyes, although still melancholy, looked at the world confidently. His lips were tightly closed, and the energy and will power that last year had been only faintly outlined on his face were now etched indelibly on it.

Orest greeted his family cheerfully.

Presenting his doctoral diploma to his father, he thanked him sincerely for all the sacrifices he had borne in order to provide him—his son—with an education. His mother and sister embraced him and, wishing him happiness and continued success in the future, almost smothered him with their kisses.

"What do you intend to do now?" his father asked, after the initial moment of joy was over, and the mother had seated her son at a table laden with food.

"I plan to become a lawyer, because I'll be able to help our people most in that way; I'll get to know the injustices being perpetrated against them, and then I'll defend them from their abusers. A government position would also be good, but I prefer to have my independence."

"I agree with your views," his father said graciously. "Our people don't have enough defenders, and so they're fleeced from all sides."

"That's why I want to be a peasants' lawyer," Orest said. "I'll stay here a few more weeks and then enter the fray with fresh vigour."

"That's good, my son, very good." Father Martyniv rose to his feet and placed his hand on his son's shoulder.

"And I can see you're no longer thinking about that young lady," he added gently, as if he did not want to bring up an unpleasant subject.

"No," Orest replied, turning red. "I'm not thinking about her, or about anyone else. I'll never marry; I have enough people to live for . . ."

"Your goal is noble and beautiful, my son, but I regret that you had to experience such suffering before you decided upon this life of self-sacrifice."

Orest did not reply; he did not want to reveal to his father the wounds that still had not healed in his heart.

Father Martyniv nodded his head and began asking about the latest news and about the social and political life of Ukrainians in the capital.

Orest spoke enthusiastically about the new ideas—the striving for a new life, a better way of life for the common people—that gripped him and his friends.

Father Martyniv, looking at his son's eyes, blazing with fervour, was confident that these ideas would in the future gain ascendancy, if all those who were fighting for them were as inspired as his son. He firmly believed that these new ideas had to be better than his outdated views, because he could see that his son was prepared to sacrifice his life for his convictions, whereas in his day, such a thought would not have occurred to anyone.

Orest had not been truthful when he told his father that he no longer thought about Mariya; he thought about her constantly and imagined how happy he now could have been. But evil fate, instead of allowing him to attain such happiness, had dictated to his beloved the letter of refusal she had sent him.

It was with this letter in his hand that Melanya found him in the orchard.

He tried to hide it, but his sister stopped him.

"You still haven't forgotten about all that, Orest?" she asked, looking into his eyes and pointing at the letter.

"Have you forgotten?" Orest asked in turn. "So you of all people ought to know that I too can't forget that quickly. But I'll tell you something now—something that you've probably wanted to hear for some time, but did not dare to inquire about. Your Dubrovsky was appointed to a teaching position in H."

"What are you saying? Here? In the neighbouring district?" Melanya blushed like a rose, and her lips and hands began to tremble slightly.

"Yes, and he'll most certainly come to visit us, because I've invited him to do so. I spoke with him in Lviv, and he's just as handsome, good, and sincere as ever.

"When he saw me, he turned beet red—as you did just now—but after we talked for a while, he said: 'Miss Melanya has probably been married for some time now.' When I told him you had not married, he became deathly pale and then flushed again, and became so agitated that I thought he'd have a stroke. So you see, my dear Melanya, your chances for finding happiness are now greater than mine."

Melanya rushed up to him and began hugging and kissing him.

"Now, now, that's enough. You're kissing me as warmly as if I were someone else," Orest joked.

Melanya covered her face with her hands, so her brother could not see the confusion his words caused her. "Since you've given me such wonderful news, I'll tell you something concerning your matter.

"A few weeks ago I was visiting the Halytskys and, one day, when Volodymyr wasn't home, Emiliya and I had a frank talk. She told me that Mariya is withering and dying of grief for you. I told her that Mariya herself was to blame because she refused your proposal of marriage, and Emiliya said that was impossible, because Mariya truly loved you and certainly would have accepted it. I didn't want to write about this, but now that you're here, we can go to the Halytskys and clear this matter up."

"Are you saying that Mariya is grieving for me?" Orest asked in disbelief.

"Yes, very much so. Emiliya said that Mariya is only a shadow of her former self."

Orest turned pale.

"So why did she send me that haughty reply?"

"I'm saying that we should pay the Halytskys a visit, and find out more about it."

"Well, let's go."

"It's too late to start out today, but tomorrow is Sunday. We'll leave right after lunch."

Melanya felt very happy, but her brother's sorrow cast a shadow on her happiness—for it is impossible for anyone, no matter how happy that person is, to be so selfish that another person's sorrow does not temper that joy. She waited impatiently for the moment when she would see her beloved, because after hearing what her brother said, she was confident that he had not forgotten her.

With a contented smile on her lips, she was imagining her future with her dear husband at her side. It was true that it would be a life filled with work, but in their free moments they would enjoy complete happiness and true harmony. Melanya had no doubt that her parents would now allow her to marry the teacher, because she had her brother on her side, and he could win them over.

The next day, immediately after lunch, Orest and Melanya got into the carriage and set off for the Halytskys. Orest was besieged with doubts; he wanted to hear with his own ears that Mariya was grieving for him.

They drove through the lush green forest, and as they approached the home of the Halytskys, Melanya said to her brother: "Let's leave our carriage here and go the rest of the way on foot; I want to walk for a while."

"Fine," Orest said.

They stepped down from the carriage and walked side by side in silence.

A short while later, the forester's house came into view. They passed through the gate, but did not see a single soul in the yard. Fragments of a conversation drifted in to them from the orchard, and they set out in that direction. When they were halfway there, they stopped, not knowing if they should go on or turn back.

Emiliya was sitting on a bench with Mariya and, next to her, was the young teacher Dubrovsky. Halytsky was lying on the grass. He was the first to see Melanya and Orest, and jumped up to meet them—thus making their decision for them.

"Oh, greetings, greetings, Master Martyniv!" Halytsky said amicably.

At his words, Mariya lifted her head and, seeing Orest, turned white. Orest was also confused; he did not know how to react in this situation, but he overcame his confusion and politely greeted the host. He extended his hand to the young teacher and then led him to meet Melanya who, after greeting Emiliya and Mariya, was all rosy with joy and excitement.

Melanya greeted her old friend with a loving smile, and then they looked shyly at each other; after such a lengthy separation, they did not know how to initiate a conversation. But their hearts prompted them and, after a few awkward moments, they were talking about the days gone by that had been such a happy time for both of them.

Orest bowed low to Mariya, but did not extend his hand to her. She glanced at him with strange eyes, in which a quiet despair was brewing. Seeing that he was talking freely with the hostess and paying no attention to her, Mariya rose, walked into the house, and then fled into the forest.

Seeing her bright dress flash among the trees, Orest assumed she wanted to hide from him. He noticed she had lost a lot of weight and felt sorry for her, but her flight angered him. Why did she not want to look him straight in the face and explain why she had written him the letter of rejection? Why was she running away?

Emiliya, thinking that Mariya had gone into the house to prepare lunch, followed her. When she did not find her there, she asked a servant where the young lady was.

"I don't know," the servant replied.

Emiliya became alarmed.

"Where can she be?" she asked herself. Troubled, she called out: "Mariya!"

No one answered.

"What is this?" she thought, and she went to tell the others that Mariya had disappeared.

"Perhaps she's gone into the forest," Melanya said. Busily engaged in her conversation with Dubrovsky, she had not observed Mariya's departure, and now she silently reproached herself for ignoring her and not speaking more warmly to her.

"Perhaps she has," Emiliya said. "Well, someone should go and find her. Perhaps you, Master Martyniv, can find your former bridesmaid."

"Fine," Orest said unwillingly and, rising from where he was sitting, he went down the path where he had spotted Mariya.

It was awkward now for him to be alone with her. What had happened once could not be undone, could not be changed; he had become somewhat reconciled to the situation, but now he had by chance been reminded of something that had caused him many a sleepless night.

And the young woman—with an expression of quiet sorrow on her face, and eyes replete with grief, longing, and melancholy—looked even more attractive to him now.

"Why did I have to meet her again? Was it so that my heart once more would experience great suffering? Because it's quite clear that she doesn't spend any time thinking about me. Why did she run away from me? She must be grieving for the one to whom she gave her heart—as she herself wrote in her letter. Perhaps he abandoned her, and now she's yearning for him."

Orest clenched his fists. He was convinced that Mariya was grieving for someone else, and he was jealous of that person.

"I'll have to ask her who he is; I'd at least like to know to whom I lost out," he thought, quickening his pace. "The sooner the better," he added, explaining his haste to himself.

Before long, he found Mariya.

Lying on soft moss under a spreading oak tree, she was crying her heart out. Her face was covered with her hands, and her body was heaving convulsively.

"Miss Mariya," Orest, deeply moved by her grief, began in an emotional voice. "Why did you run away from us? I was sent to find you; I know you don't like me, and that's why I won't trouble you for long; I'll just walk back to the house with you, and then I'll leave you alone."

Mariya rose from the ground, uncovered her face, and looked at him with tear-filled eyes. "Why did you follow me here? Do you want to ridicule my grief?" she asked in a reproachful tone.

"No, God forbid, but I would like to know who it is that you're grieving for. Who is the lucky man who forced me out of your heart?" Orest asked, looking at her.

Mariya wept even harder. "You say you don't want to laugh at me, but you're laughing right in my face, because why would you ask me about the reason for my grief, when you yourself are best aware of it."

"I swear by all that is good, I don't know! I only know that because of you, I've been very, very unhappy."

"You, because of me? What did I ever do to you?"

"You said you loved me, but when I sent you a letter asking for your hand in marriage, you said you couldn't marry me because you'd given your heart to another."

"I? I wrote that to you? No, I never wrote you anything," Mariya said with great astonishment.

"I can show you the letter, because I carry it with me as a reminder of both my ecstasy and my misery."

Orest pulled a small notebook out of his pocket where he kept Mariya's letter.

"Here you are. Please take it," he said, passing her the letter. "Now tell me, aren't you the one who wrote it?"

Mariya took the letter, read the salutation, and shrieked.

"Well, what do you have to say about it?"

"That you've been duped, fooled!" Mariya exclaimed. "I wrote this letter not to you, but to Denys Goretsky on the very same day that I expected to receive a letter from you."

Orest turned as white as a wall. "And you didn't get a letter from me?" he asked in great consternation.

"No, I waited and waited, but all my waiting was in vain."

"But I sent you a letter along with a bouquet of roses. The messenger said that he gave them to the young lady herself," Orest protested.

"I didn't get any letter, nor any bouquet . . . It's probably someone from the Goretskys who intercepted your letter and then, to take revenge on me, sent you the letter they received from me," Mariya said in a trembling voice, her eyes filled with tears.

Orest stood dumbfounded. He could not fathom such a despicable deed. "So Goretsky asked for your hand in marriage?" he asked after a moment.

"Yes, he did; I wrote him that I could not accept his proposal because my heart belonged to another."

"Oh, how contemptible they are! How many heartaches, how much anguish and suffering they've caused me! Oh, Mariya, my dearest, my love," he said, taking her hand, "if only you knew what torment I've lived through, you wouldn't be angry with me; you'd look at me as kindly and as lovingly as you once did."

"I'm not upset any more," Mariya replied, "because I can see that we've both been duped, but up to now I was very angry with you, Master Martyniv; I was very angry, so angry that I didn't want to speak to you."

"Really, my dear Mariya?" Orest said mischievously, as he used to in the past.

"I never lie," Mariya replied. "And I would have thought that you knew this."

"I do know. So tell me, my dearest, do you love me as much as you loved me then? For I've never ceased loving you."

Mariya blushed and lowered her eyes.

"Oh, God, I've suffered so much because of you—it's terrible to even think about it—but in all that time, your image never left my heart."

"Oh, my love, my joy!" Orest said, overcome with emotion. "Now come with me. Let me introduce my betrothed to everyone; and we'll have the wedding very soon, so that no one can ever again come between us and destroy our happiness."

"Oh, now that I know that you were faithful to me for a whole year, I'd never believe anyone again," Mariya said with feeling.

She used the familiar form of "you" in addressing him; not knowing how to thank her for this, he kissed her.

Mariya blushed and wanted to free herself, but he clasped her still closer to his heart, covering her rosy lips with passionate kisses.

"Please, that's enough," Mariya said, smoothing down her ruffled hair, "or I'll be annoyed with you."

"Well, in that case, I apologize," he said cheerfully, and kissed her once more.

Mariya wagged her finger at him. "You haven't changed a bit! You always know how to talk your way out of things. I can see that I'm going to have more than enough trouble with you."

Joking merrily, they forgot the anguish that had oppressed their souls for a year—a youthful, pliant nature rebounds quickly.

Melanya and the Halytskys were more than a little surprised when they saw Orest and Mariya, their faces happy and radiant, walking hand in hand.

Their astonishment grew when Orest came up to them and presented Mariya as his betrothed. But, hiding their amazement, they showered them with heartfelt wishes for their future happiness.

"And now listen to what lengths some people went in their attempt to part us," Orest said, and he described in detail the intrigue that had transpired with the letters.

The indignation of the listeners knew no bounds, but they were appeased when they saw that, despite the intrigue, everything had turned out well.

It was late in the evening when Orest and Melanya, after giving Mariya their word that their family would pay her parents a visit the next day, set out for home. The Liskovskys, seeing their daughter happy and carefree once again, were overjoyed when they heard that she was engaged to Orest. The vile machinations of the Goretskys angered Madam Liskovska to the quick.

But there was no time now to discuss the matter; she had to prepare for the arrival of the guests. They immediately began tidying up the rooms, sweeping and dusting them, even though there was no need to do so, for the highest standards of cleanliness were adhered to in the Liskovsky home.

Mariya robbed the flower garden and placed a bouquet of fresh flowers in every corner.

Before dinner, a carriage drove into the Liskovsky yard. Smiling happily, Orest leapt to the ground and ran into the house, where everyone was prepared to greet him.

Father Martyniv and his wife ran a well-trained eye over the entire household and smiled at each other with obvious satisfaction.

The future in-laws were received warmly, open-heartedly, and without excessive formalities. Melanya could not stop talking to

Mariya, who looked absolutely charming in her Ukrainian traditional dress.

After dinner, the two young ladies walked out into the orchard with Orest. Mariya told them about Hanya, and how the young peasant woman had made her days more bearable.

Suddenly, Hanya's dark head peeped out at them from behind the fence.

"Hanya, come here," Mariya called her.

Hanya ran to the stile and, a moment later, blushing and confused, stood before the young people. After a few words from Orest and Melanya, she felt at ease and, smiling happily at Mariya, said: "You see, I told you, my dear lady, that this young gentleman would come back to you, but you didn't want to believe me."

"How did you know I'd come back?" Orest asked, and Mariya lowered her eyes.

"I just knew you would; I was so sorry for the young lady, because she wept and grieved for you so much."

"You cried, Mariya?" Orest asked, taking her by the hand. "You grieved so much for me?"

"I'll tell you how she grieved for you, because she may be too shy to say anything," Hanya replied boldly and cheerfully. "I sang her a certain song, one time, and she almost died crying. It was then that I told her not to grieve, because the dark-eyed young gentleman would most certainly come back to her."

Orest gave the attractive peasant girl a look of gratitude for having cheered up his beloved.

After repeated requests, and urging from Mariya and Melanya, Hanya agreed to sing. Her sorrowful, moving voice and the words of her song touched their hearts:

> "'Why do you bend, O cranberry red?
> O girl, so young, what do you dread?'
> 'It's the wind that makes me bend so low,'
> 'My beloved is leaving—and I worry so.'
>
> He went o'er the mountain and forgot his love.
> 'Oh, I'll die of love—come back, my dove.'
> 'Oh, dear girl, you must not yearn,
> He's found a new love and won't return.'

'No, no, he'll never have another love,
He pledged his love by the stars above.'
'And you, dear girl, won't grieve too long,
You'll find another—and to him belong.'

'Oh, I won't love another, I love only him.
As long as I live, I'll grieve for him.'
And the girl grieved, she grieved and raved
Until a high mound covered her grave.

He returned from the army and fell on the mound:
'Oh, grave, release my beloved from the ground.'

'Oh, I won't give her up, for now she's mine,
She waited, O unfaithful one, for a long time.'

He sought a beloved in other lands,
But died all alone on foreign strands.'"

"Where do you learn these songs?" Melanya asked.

"I just make them up myself," Hanya replied.

"Yourself? How?"

"Oh, I just mull things over, and mull them over, and then I put some words together—and the song is ready," Hanya said.

"You're a very wise young woman," Orest exclaimed, fascinated by this revelation of talent among the common people. "Do you know more songs?"

"I know the ones that I sang to the young lady, and I'll soon have more of them, because whenever my heart feels heavy, I put words together into a song," Hanya replied.

"Let me know when you have songs that are ready, and I'll write them down and have them printed in the newspapers," Orest said.

"You mean in those newspapers from which the young lady read me those wonderful songs about Kateryna and the woman servant? How can my songs be good enough for those papers?" Hanya asked blushing, referring naively to poems written by the renowned Ukrainian poet Shevchenko.

Orest smiled. "I'll put them in the newspapers so that people will realise that village girls know how to compose songs."

"As if anyone, other than girls and women, compose songs; men sing about war and whiskey, but women sing so movingly about a beloved, about orphans, and about absolutely everything," Hanya said.

This peasant girl, whose confidence Mariya had been able to win, appealed greatly to Orest and his sister; they talked with her for a long time, amazed at her quick wit and the self-assurance with which she spoke.

After Hanya left, Orest said: "Just think what a pearl this young woman is, what native intelligence and natural talent she has. But what will become of her? She'll wither like a flower in the sun, unsprinkled by droplets of dew. I've come to realise that there are women among the peasantry who deserve a better fate, and that educated ladies ought to do all they can to help these women recognise their potential."

"But that is something that many of these ladies are unable to do, my dear Orest, for how many intelligent women are there among us with the requisite appreciation of their own potential?" Melanya asked.

"A recognition of one's potential leads to independence and equal rights," Orest said, "and that's why women ought to strive to improve themselves. At the same time, they should remember about their lesser sisters, because so many of them are perishing in vain."

"That's true, but if only someone would tell us how to work for the good of the peasant women," Melanya observed.

"You've made a good beginning, sister," Orest replied. "You're teaching young girls and gaining their confidence. Now you must teach them the practical skills they'll need in life.

"And since theoretical conclusions can be drawn from your work with them, you should make your observations available to the public, thereby encouraging other women to work among the peasantry in the same fashion."

"Orest is right," Mariya said, squeezing his hand.

"I also recognize the truth in what he is saying," Melanya said, "but he knows very well that I'd be laughed at for making such observations, just as I'm ridiculed now for running my village school."

"I didn't realise you were so sensitive to the laughter of others. Why does it concern you? Even if someone laughs at you, you should go on doing what your heart tells you to do."

"And my heart tells me to follow the advice of my dear brother," Melanya said with a smile. "As soon as I have the time, I'll write an article about the experience that I've gained in my work with the girls and about the success of my school. Perhaps in this way I'll succeed in encouraging a few other enlightened women to undertake similar projects.

"Women have to help each other like this, because I think a lot of water will flow under the bridge before we gain equal rights with you men, before we can be seen as being equal to men."

"I also think that a lot of time will pass before women enjoy the same rights as men, the lords of creation," Mariya said, turning to Orest.

"It just seems like that to you, my dear; but in this age of electricity, steam, and gas, nothing is impossible. Many ideas that, at one time seemed strange, are now taken for granted and are universally accepted.

"The same holds true for the women's question; it was unheard of a few years ago—indeed, it was even ridiculed—but now it has come to the fore, because it is of growing interest to various segments of society. In due course, it too will be taken for granted."

"May God grant it," Melanya and Mariya said simultaneously.

***

Orest and Melanya stayed on at the Liskovskys for a few days. The engaged couple was intoxicated with happiness which, to them, in their youthfulness, seemed unending.

The wedding was to be held in two months. Orest wanted it that way, and the Liskovskys did not oppose him, even though they were sorry to part with their only daughter.

The news of Mariya's engagement spread rapidly through the village, but the Goretskys did not hear about it.

The following Sunday, Denys, who had come home after completing his theological studies, went to church with Olha. He still had hopes that Mariya would marry him and so, after hearing how his mother and sister had treated the two Liskovsky ladies in church, he became very angry and called his sister a jealous monkey. He now took it upon himself to make peace with the Liskovskys and decided to go and visit them that very day.

But things turned out differently.

As Denys was considering what he should say to apologise to the Liskovskys, he became aware of people whispering. Turning around, he saw the older Liskovskys entering the church, followed by an attractive, tall young woman; behind her were Orest and Mariya. Denys stood and gaped until they were halfway into the church. Orest and Liskovsky remained on the right side, while the ladies moved to the left.

Orest noticed Denys and could not refrain from smiling gloatingly at him. Denys turned around to avoid looking at his rival.

Olha, seeing that her perfidious plan had failed, and that Orest and Mariya were united despite it, turned red as a beet.

After the liturgy, when people started leaving the church, the elder Liskovsky met Denys by the gate.

"Good day to you, young sir!" he said, purposely delaying him. "Congratulations on the completion of your studies."

"Thank you, thank you most sincerely," Denys replied, without really knowing what he was saying.

Just then, Orest walked up with Mariya, and Liskovsky said to Denys: "Well, I've congratulated you, and now you can congratulate me on the engagement of my daughter to Master Martyniv."

Denys, his face chalk white, felt as if he were standing on hot coals.

Orest came up to him.

"You see, Master Goretsky, truth, like oil in water, always rises to the top. You wanted to deprive me of my good fortune, and that is why you yourself do not have any. May this serve as a lesson to you."

Saying this, he bowed to Denys and Olha who were standing dumbstruck and, giving Mariya his arm, headed for the gate. The Liskovskys and Melanya followed them.

The brother and sister, their scheme foiled and their conniving revealed, were left behind, humiliated and furious.

The Liskovksys accompanied Orest and Melanya home where their mother, usually a somewhat reluctant hostess, received the guests in a most hospitable manner—a fact that in itself spoke volumes.

In the afternoon, the Halytskys arrived, bringing Dubrovsky with them. Initially, the hosts were not too happy to see him but, observing the great joy of their daughter, they gave in to Orest's persuasions and permitted the union of the two hearts that had remained faithful throughout their long parting.

"Now we're all happy," Orest said, embracing both his betrothed and his sister, who was weeping with joy.

"We had to struggle hard for our happiness, and our hearts suffered great anguish, but fate was on our side, and we have prevailed."

The Linden Tree on the Boundary
(1897)

It was the day before I was to leave the place that I called home. This circumstance had a depressing effect on me, making me feel sad and out of sorts. I felt deep regret at the thought of leaving the area where I was born and raised, and where I had experienced some of the most bitter and the most sweet moments of my life.

The entire day slipped by as if in a fog.

Towards evening, I set out for my usual walk to visit, one last time, those places where I had spent such joyful, happy moments, where I had dreamed and fantasised about an ideal, utopian existence.

Here are the trees that grace the pathway leading to the ravine; they have seen me any number of times in many different moods, sometimes happy, more often melancholy. But nature, holy nature, heals all wounds, for who could remain sad while gazing upon the beautiful vistas that my eyes are feasting on now? How could these enchanting scenes not serve as a healing potion, especially since they belong to one's beloved native land?

I am standing on a high hill and, down below, the broad Dniester river flows gently by. Off to one side, on the opposite bank, extends a village, while in the other direction lies a dense forest, that, caught in the rays of the setting sun, takes on the appearance of a soft, velvet coverlet. The forest is alive with the sounds of birds trilling, cattle bells ringing, and shepherds singing and playing their flutes.

To the right lies my beloved village, with its tall church standing in the middle, surrounded by clusters of neat cottages that peep out from lush orchards, as the sun peeks out from behind the clouds. In those cottages live the people that I know and love—the people whose sad, mournful song is embedded in my heart, whose grief, joy, and destiny I shared.

Now I must leave these people . . . Just the thought of it restricted my chest and made my soul feel heavy. A lump rose in my throat, hot tears welled up in my eyes, and then, at that very moment, the sound of workers singing filled the air:

> "It's as hard to live in a foreign land
> As to lift a boulder with your hand.
> I'll lift the stone, and then I'll rest,
> But in foreign parts, I'll die unblessed."

I continued walking, farther and farther, to bid farewell to all my favourite spots.

Engrossed in my thoughts, I did not notice the encroaching twilight and the threatening dark clouds approaching from the west. It was only the echo of distant thunder that jolted me back into the present.

I had to return home, or the rain would soak me, and everyone would laugh at the outcome of my romantic walk. I wanted to carry out this most laudable intention at once, but something interfered with my plans.

I was on the boundary of two fields that had been marked by a large, hewn stone. Immediately next to it stood a tall cross and, at the foot of the cross, I saw a peasant girl on her knees. I was intrigued. What was she doing so far from the village? I stopped and waited until she finished praying.

After a few moments, she prostrated herself a few times and rose to her feet. Catching sight of me, she blushed furiously and greeted me softly, saying: "Good evening."

She was not from our village, so she must have been from the neighbouring one, which was closer to the spot where I was now than my own.

"Oh, it's so wonderful that you've come here," she continued, with a slight stammer. "You'll advise us and tell us what to do, won't you?"

I was taken aback.

"What can I advise you about?" I asked, looking intently at her attractive, flushed face.

"About everything, everything. She said that the one who crossed the boundary at sunset would advise us."

"Who said this?"

"Well, she did—the fortune-teller," the girl replied, lowering her eyes in confusion.

I smiled. "So, you went to a fortune-teller. But you know, don't you, that it's a sin to go to one? All they do is dupe people; they don't really know anything."

"I know it's a sin, but when people are in trouble, they'll turn God knows where to rid themselves of it."

"What kind of trouble are you in? Tell me about it."

Loud thunder accompanied my words.

The girl gave me a pleading look. "Come to our place, lady; we're right at the edge of the village, so it's not very far from here. Besides, it's going to rain, and you'll get soaked."

This advice did not seem at all inappropriate to me. "But how will I get back later?"

"We have horses; we'll drive you back."

"Well, fine. I'll go with you, but tell me what kind of advice you need."

Along the way, I found out from Vasylka—that's what my guide was called—that her father Mytro Zahirny was a very wealthy man, and that his neighbour Nykolay Fenyuk was equally rich. Nykolay had a son Onufriy, and so the parents thought it would be a very good idea to consolidate their land holdings by uniting their children in marriage and leaving them the biggest farm in the village.

Onufriy and Vasylka, having been in love for a long time, did not oppose the idea, and the wedding was in the offing when something happened that broke up the agreement between the neighbours and threatened to part the young couple.

On the boundary that divided the farms stood an old, spreading linden tree. The stately tree caught the eye of a carpenter who was passing by and, as he needed some linden wood, he asked Zahirny to sell him the tree.

At first, Zahirny did not even want to hear of it, but when the carpenter offered him a sum of money that he never would have even dreamed of receiving for it, he allowed himself to be persuaded and made a deal.

The following day, the carpenter brought a few people to help him bring down the tree. As they were winding ropes around the branches, Fenyuk came by. Sorry to see the tree come down, he strode up angrily and stopped them from carrying out their plan.

"Don't be angry," Zahirny tried to mollify him. "I'm getting good money for the tree. And if you feel that you have some rights to it, I'll give you your share."

But the infuriated neighbour shouted: "I don't need a share. I won't allow them to fell this tree—a tree that shaded our grandfathers as they rested under it."

Zahirny scratched the nape of his neck. "You're right about the tree, in-law; I didn't really want to sell it, but that man went on and on about it, and I couldn't get rid of him. But now that I've taken the money for it, I can't go back on my word."

"That's some deal you made," Fenyuk mocked him. "You can do with your property whatever you want to, but the tree belongs to me as much as it belongs to you, and I won't allow so much as a leaf to be torn off it. And that's my final word."

The two neighbours began to quarrel in earnest. Intemperate words and curses began flying from both sides, and it would have ended in a fight if the wives and children had not intervened between the enraged owners. But the involvement of Onufriy and Vasylka in the dispute worked to the young couple's detriment, for their fathers, in order to drive home their point more forcefully, gave them a tongue lashing and forbade them to see each other.

"I'll break your bones if you so much as speak to his daughter," Fenyuk shouted at Onufriy.

"And I'll cut your braids off if you so much as look at him," Mytro screamed at Vasylka.

As he strode away, Fenyuk yelled out a parting shot: "I don't care if I lose all my property defending that tree; just let someone dare come near it with an axe!"

And Zahirny shouted back: "And I'd be just as likely to inherit a kingdom, as to let that tree stay there!"

From that moment, a great hatred consumed the two neighbours. They sued each other, hired lawyers, and spent money liberally to make life miserable for each other.

The other villagers enjoyed the situation. Making up the wildest stories, they told Zahirny that this was what Fenyuk was saying about him, and then they told Fenyuk that Zahirny was destroying his good name with slanderous stories.

It was Onufriy and Vasylka who suffered most because of the rift. The fathers, refusing to budge from the stand they had taken, began looking around the village to find more suitable partners for their children.

"And so they want to drive Onufriy and me apart," Vasylka finished her story. "My mother and I have tried everything: we've paid for liturgies and gone on pilgrimages to Suchava, Dalesheva, and Vovkivtsi, but nothing helps. And so we were advised to go to a fortune-teller.

"She said she couldn't change things, because the matter had gone too far. But she told me to go and pray at the boundary every evening, and she said that the first person to walk by me when the sun was setting, would advise me. And I've been coming here for two weeks already, but you're the first person to come by. Please tell us what we should do."

Just then we reached her yard, and this fact spared me from having to come up with an answer—a task I found intimidating. The farmstead had an aura of prosperity; the yard was large and, at the far end, a stately linden tree proudly spread its branches.

By now the clouds had drawn in closer, and lightning flashes were flying one after the other. I was glad I would be able to view this spectacle put on by nature from a dry nook instead of out in the open field.

A woman, still fairly young, came out of the house and, thinking that I was simply seeking shelter from the rain in their yard, politely invited me in. But after Vasylka told her that I was the first person to cross the boundary when the sun was setting, she spoke to me with great deference and could not do enough to ensure my comfort.

I have to admit that the idea of being a medium of sorts, one that was supposed to provide sage advice, did not sit too well with me. I was on the verge of informing the women of their mistake and telling them that they were wrong to believe the foolish words of the fortune-teller, when the door opened and the master of the household walked in. He was tall and handsome, and you could see by looking at him that he was not the kind of man to give in easily to the will of others.

Greeting me, he sat down on the bed that stood next to the bench where I was seated between the two women.

"It looks like God will give us some rain," he said to me. "I only hope it's a gentle rain, but with the lightning and thunder it doesn't look too good."

"How could we expect anything good when people are so evil that they rise up against each other, and all there is now is hatred, quarrelling, and curses," his wife said boldly, as if I had given her courage.

He wrinkled his brow. "Even a worm wriggles when you step on it, so why shouldn't a man seek justice when another man wants to ride roughshod over him. It's like this, my lady," he said turning to me, as if to explain the brief interchange with his wife, "I'm suing our neighbour, and my wife is forever giving me a bad time because of this."

"Why are you suing him?" I asked, acting as if I did not know anything.

He gave me all the details about the incident with the linden tree. "The process has been going on for more than half a year, but my lawyer says that the way the matter stands, I'm sure to win the case."

"Why is that?"

This brief question disconcerted him.

"Because the roots have spread on my land," he said hesitantly. "But maybe the law doesn't say that?"

He looked at me with such an expression of fear and expectancy in his eyes that I did not have the heart to say a single word that would destroy his hopes.

"Well, what do you say about all this, my lady? I can see that you know something, but don't want to tell me."

"I'll tell you that it would be best if you made peace with your neighbour, because you're bound to lose; as I understand the matter, it looks as if you can't win this process."

My words appeared to crush him; a moment later, however, his peasant stubbornness awoke within him, and he said somewhat defiantly: "That's what you say, but the court may decide differently."

"I feel sorry for you, my good man; the court can't say anything different, because the law says that it's the trunk—and not the roots—that indicates ownership; if the trunk stands on a boundary that is shared in common by several neighbours, then the tree belongs to all of them. So, your neighbour has the same right to the tree as you do; and if the lawyer is promising you the moon, well, that's part of his trade—to deceive people.

"I'm giving you good advice; it would be better to make peace with your neighbour, abandon your hatred, and live as you've lived up to now, in friendship, instead of making German lawyers wealthy with your money.

"And aren't you sorry for your child who will waste her life, not for honour or glory, but for nothing?"

Hearing these words, the two women began wailing, and the stubborn peasant appeared to soften.

"But I swore by the Kingdom of God that I'd chop down this tree; I can't break my vow and leave it standing where it is."

A bright flash accompanied his words. It seemed to me that the lightning bolt struck right next to me. It was bright as daylight in the house.

A terrifying peal of thunder resounded in the room, and the smell of sulphur filled the air.

We all ran out of the house to see what was causing the brightness that lasted long after the thunder was gone.

Outside, people were screaming that lightning had struck the old linden tree on the boundary, and that it was engulfed in flames.

Old Fenyuk, standing by the tree with his wife and son, was trying to put out the fire.

To me, this seemed like an opportune moment to reconcile the neighbours, while they were still in a state of shock over this disastrous turn of events.

"Leave it; don't extinguish the fire. Let this tree that has given rise to hatred between you burn right down to its roots. God must have willed this to happen, to release you from your vow. Apologise to each other right here, and then celebrate the wedding of your children as soon as possible; it's a good thing that the Lenten season is almost over."

The feuding neighbours exchanged glances. They must have been wanting to make up for a long time, because they approached each other without hesitation.

"Forgive me, dear in-law; may our hatred burn up along with this tree!" Fenyuk said.

"May God forgive you; it's all past history now, and may God grant good health to the lady who put in a good word at the right moment."

In the meantime, their wives pressed close to me. "It's God who has sent you, my lady, holy God Himself; how can we ever repay you for coming to us?"

"The best way for you to repay me is to stop believing in fortune-tellers and convince others to do likewise."

"Stay here with us, lady," they begged me, as I prepared to leave. "There are a lot of people who need good advice, but there's no one to help them; and . . . they wouldn't want to get it for nothing."

It was impossible to explain to them that I had not contributed in any way to the fortunate resolution of their dispute, and that it was strictly chance that had led me to them. They believed that I had been sent to them—and could not be convinced otherwise.

Her Story
(1897)

Spring. How much magic there is in this word, how much poetry! It instantly brings to mind fragrantly blossoming orchards, bathing in the pale light of the moon and flooded with the trills of nightingales.

As we recall these hauntingly beautiful scenes, a half-mournful, half-poetic feeling envelops our hearts; but how much more powerfully they affect us when we are actually experiencing them, when we are surrounded by the magic of spring! All these enchanting images of nature merge and excite even the most prosaic person, for they have an unsettling, not calming, effect on one's nerves.

In one such orchard, two young people were sitting in a charming arbour. While the moon was still pale and the nightingale was silent, they engaged in quiet conversation; but when the voice of the feathered songster poured forth from the thickets, the young man leaped to his feet, drew nearer to the young woman and, taking her by the hand, began to speak.

"My dear, precious Miss Halya, would you be my . . ." and he suddenly cut short what he was saying, for he could not believe his eyes.

The composed, dignified face of the young woman had taken on a soft, radiant expression, her eyes shone with happiness, and her demure lips were ready to break into a blissful smile—it seemed her whole being was overflowing with a powerful feeling of love for him.

The gentleman looked at her helplessly; an exquisite flower, whose beauty he had never guessed at, had come into bloom before his very eyes. He began to tremble. What he saw before him was love—a generous, sincere, and passionate love—that he could never reciprocate. He felt sorry for the unfortunate girl whom he admired and respected as a sister. And he hurried to complete his unfinished sentence.

"Would you be my sister, my confidante? I'm in love with Malyna; please speak with her and ask your father to allow us to marry."

He spoke slowly, as if trying to give her an opportunity to regain her composure.

Upon hearing his words, a deathly pallor replaced the excited flush on Halya's face. It looked as if she might faint at any moment, that she might scream out in pain—but she mastered her feelings.

Casting a stricken look at the man standing in front of her, she lowered her lashes, as if desiring to conceal the unspeakable grief emanating from her eyes, and spoke in a casual tone of voice.

"You may be assured, my good sir, that you could not have found a better mediator; I know you and respect you as an honourable man; therefore, I am prepared to entrust my dear sister to your care."

She spoke calmly, but the corners of her mouth twitched convulsively, and her right hand, which he held in his, trembled as if she had a fever.

"Farewell for now. I must speak with Malyna, and tomorrow I'll convey to you the results of my conversation."

He bowed and left.

She flung herself face down on the green grass and began to weep inconsolably.

"At last," she thought. "Oh, at last I'm alone with my anguish, my grief. One more word, one more moment—and I would not have been able to restrain myself. I would have fallen at his feet and admitted that it is I, I who love him.

"O God, my God, does it have to be like this? Must I be the one to tell her he loves her? Must it be me?

"But what if I don't tell her? And what if I tell him that Malyna doesn't want to marry him? What then?

"Malyna wouldn't grieve over him; she doesn't love him. Her heart wouldn't break, as mine is breaking now, because she isn't in love with him. She wouldn't have been crushed if he had chosen me. No, not in the least!

"But he doesn't want me—he's chosen her.

"O God, do not permit evil feelings to take root in my heart; do not allow me to be jealous of my own sister. I must go to her at once! I must do my duty!"

With these words, she rose to her feet and slowly made her way to the house.

"Let Malyna decide her own happiness," she thought. "And let whatever is to happen to me, happen."

When she reached the door of their shared room, however, she paused momentarily, suddenly feeling incapable of persuading her sister to marry the man she herself loved.

But then, pressing her hand to her violently beating heart and forcing herself to overcome her agitation, she stepped into the room.

"Why are you so pale?" Malyna asked her when she entered. "Are you ill, perhaps?" The voice of the younger woman quivered with concern.

"No, Malyna, but I have something very important to say to you."

"What can it be? It can't be anything good, because you look very sad."

"It only seems that way to you, my child. I have a slight headache, and that's probably why I look like this. But what I have to tell you is not at all sad. Come here and sit down beside me, so I can look into your eyes."

"Why are you speaking to me in such a solemn manner? I feel as if I'm in church."

"I'm glad you feel that way. Now, tell me the truth—do you love Roman Maletsky?"

Malyna stared in astonishment at her sister, who turned red as a cherry under her intent gaze.

"Malyna," Halya continued. "Do you love him more than everything else, more than life itself? Could you forsake your father, and me, and your home for him? Could you see yourself finding happiness in his happiness? Answer me truthfully, as if you were speaking to our mother, who left you in my care."

Malyna, terrified by her sister's words, flung herself into her arms and whispered: "Yes, I love him. He appeals to me more than other men; he's so handsome, and he treats me so kindly."

Halya, stroking the thick, dark hair that cascaded in long waves down her sister's back, thought to herself: "Of what significance are the tender, bashful feelings of this child compared to my passionate love—a love that is bound to destroy me?"

Malyna raised her comely head: "Yes, I love him; I even think that I love him very much."

At these words, Halya's heart contracted painfully.

"But tell me, my dear sister," Malyna continued, "what is the meaning of all of these questions? What will happen now that you know my secret?"

"My dearest Malyna, Roman wants to ask for your hand in marriage."

"Me? He wants to marry me? What's come over him? The two of you are such a perfect couple. You're always talking and having such good times together, and father was delighted that he'd be asking for your hand. Halya, my dearest, I myself was happy that the two of you would be getting married; and now it seems he's courting me. Are you sure you've understood him correctly?" Malyna had no idea how her words tore at Halya's heart, already bleeding with mute pain.

"No, my dear Malyna, I haven't made a mistake. He loves you; he talked only about you—there was no mention of me."

"And are you advising me to marry him? It would be ever so nice—I'll get married, and you'll come to visit us, and father will be pleased, and we'll all be happy." Malyna was jumping for joy around the room.

"You'll be happy with him. He's a good and honourable man; you can entrust yourself to him without any qualms. But now, please go and give father his supper, for my head has begun to ache in earnest. I'll lie down for a while, and we'll talk more about this tomorrow."

A short while later, Malyna came back into the room and found her sister in bed. Not wishing to disturb her, she quickly undressed and, falling asleep, dreamed the happy dreams of youth.

"Daddy," Halya said to her father the next day, "Roman Maletsky wants to marry our Malyna."

"Malyna? Malyna? Surely the time hasn't come for her to get married, has it? She's still so young. Can't he see that?"

"He loves her, so let them get married," Halya said, and a forced smile crossed her lips.

"Well, I have nothing against it, but I was under the impression that he was courting you. Didn't you think so?"

Blood rushed to Halya's head, and she thought: "So, everyone assumed he'd marry me, but it never even occurred to him."

"I didn't think about it," she said out loud. "It's better that he marry her. How would you ever manage without me?"

"My good, sweet child," her father said tenderly. "God will reward you for your kindness. People rarely appreciate the true worth of a person—that's the way it always is in this world!"

At that moment there was a knock at the door, and Roman walked in. He greeted them, and then turned with a pleading look towards Halya.

"I've already spoken with Malyna and my father. They both agree to your request," she said quietly and evenly.

"Call her here, that little imp," the father said affectionately. "Let me scold her for daring to steal the heart of this wise, learned lawyer behind my back."

Halya walked out, glad to have completed her difficult task.

Malyna, blushing shyly, entered the room. She was too modest to raise her eyes until her father, after a long jocular speech, asked her if she wanted to become the wife of the man called Roman who was standing in front of her.

At that point, she boldly lifted her eyes and stated: "Yes, I do."

Forgetting all about the time, the engaged couple conversed merrily. During their discussion, Malyna said to her fiancé: "You know, my dearest, I often thought that you loved Halya."

Roman was completely shaken. "Why did you think so, sweetheart?"

"Why? I really can't say why, but both of you are so wise, and you always spent so much time talking together, and, and . . ."

"And what?"

"I don't know; you've made me all confused. Don't ask me anything more about this." And, placing her hand on his shoulder, she added with a smile: "Because I'm very happy—so very, very happy."

After a while, she began to wonder why Halya had not rejoined them. Going in search of her sister, she found her in the kitchen, helping to prepare the dinner to which the newly-engaged fiancé had been invited.

It seemed that Halya, having reconciled herself to the inevitable, kept her feelings in check and suppressed her love. She took care of the household as she always had, and she read, sewed, and did not complain to anyone. She smiled at the engaged couple and conducted serious conversations with her father; it appeared that she was completely contented.

But Roman could see that she was doing all this mechanically, that she lacked enthusiasm for everything, as if her body were without a soul.

The pallor did not disappear from her face, and it was evident that she was not well. At times, she pressed her hands to her chest as if she felt a great pain there, but when she noticed the eyes of others upon her, she smiled cheerfully.

This smile of hers pierced Roman's heart and poisoned his happiness; he pleaded that the wedding not be put off for too long. Halya gladly acquiesced in this request and threw herself headlong into the preparations for the upcoming celebration.

Indeed, she was in such a rush to expedite matters that one time Malyna stated half angrily: "You're doing everything in such a hurry—as if you can't wait to get rid of me."

Halya deflected her words with a casual joke.

It was a quiet wedding.

After the happy young couple left for their new home, Halya walked into the room she had shared with her sister, folded her arms, and stated: "And now, everything has come to an end . . ."

Malyna was standing in the middle of a room choosing a fabric to upholster the furniture in her new living quarters. Roman was not at home, so she had plenty of time to think about it.

Suddenly, her father's servant ran in with the distressing news that Halya had fallen seriously ill during the night. The young lady dressed quickly and rushed, weeping, to her father's home.

Her father met her on the threshold.

"For the love of God, what's happened to Halya? Is she really ill?" Malyna was shaking as if she had the ague.

"She had a hemorrhage; it's all over for her," the poor father lamented.

"How? When?"

"Yesterday evening she was exceptionally pale. I asked her why she was looking so poorly, and she replied that she was tired. This morning she was cheerful and talkative. We had breakfast, and then she suddenly said she had a pain in her chest. I glanced at her and saw that she was as white as a sheet. 'Go and lie down immediately,' I said to her.

"She got up, stumbled, and blood gushed from her lips—once, twice, and then a third time. I became alarmed and carried her to bed. First, I sent for the doctor, and then, for you. Go to her. The doctor is with her; but I beg you to remain calm, so that you don't make her condition any worse."

Malyna approached her sick sister. The latter was lying as if she were dead, and her hands were as cold as ice.

Halya opened her eyes and, recognizing Malyna, smiled at her. "I'm glad you've come. I'm very ill. Don't abandon father, comfort him. Perhaps I'll get better . . ."

The doctor forbid her to talk anymore, saying that she had to be completely quiet. After prescribing some drugs, he walked out of the room to see the father.

"Well, what can you tell me, my dear friend?" the father asked.

They had known and liked each other for a long time, and it pained the doctor that he had to be the bearer of sad news.

"A vein has burst. This in itself is not a grave danger—if this were to be the only attack; but I fear that there may be another one, and then . . ." the doctor passed his hand over his eyes as if something had fallen into them, and looked sympathetically at the distressed father.

"What could have caused this?" the latter inquired.

"Who knows? The illness could have taken root quite some time ago, or it could have come on quite suddenly, as a result of some traumatic event that caused a terrible shock to the nervous system, to the entire body. One can never pinpoint accurately the cause of something like this. We don't know enough about these cases, and we don't have a cure for them as yet."

"So there's nothing that can be done to save her?"

"Not if there's another attack. But let's not lose hope."

But their hopes were dashed, for there was another hemorrhage.

Halya, who had been feeling somewhat better after the cold compresses and the ice tablets, began to complain during the night of a terrible pain in her head and a constriction in her chest, and she stated fearfully that the attack was recurring.

Before dawn, another stream of blood gushed from her lips, and she lost consciousness. The doctor's efforts to save her were in vain, as were the helpless tears of Malyna and her father. In a few hours, Halya was no longer among the living.

The despair of her father and her sister was beyond words. The father could not believe that she was gone; Malyna sat in a state of shock by the deceased. Roman tried to comfort her, but his words were futile. He had a suspicion as to what had driven Halya to her grave, but he did not dare to put it into words; he did not want to admit it even to himself.

After the funeral, the father moved in with the young couple to avoid living alone in the now desolate house that only recently had echoed with the laughter and singing of happy young women. He asked Roman to take charge of selling his furniture and putting his books and papers in order.

Roman spent an entire afternoon in the deserted house sorting through books, letters, and documents. Finally, he entered the room that had been occupied by the two sisters. On the desk lay the last books that Halya had been reading. They were the works of Fedkovych—books that he had once brought her.

Glancing down, Roman saw that one book was opened on the page where the poem "To Her" was found. The following lines were underlined:

> And when you find her and are about to wed her,
> Come to my grave and pick some nuptial periwinkle.

Roman felt uneasy.

He opened a desk drawer and saw some quarto paper covered with writing. The handwriting was Halya's. A wonderful scent of violets wafted from the paper on which Roman's eyes were now fastened.

At the very top were written the words "My Story."

February 2. Today has been an important turning point in my life, and so, from now on, I want to keep track of everything that happens to me; I shall write my own story.

I never could have dreamt that any man could bring about the kind of radical change in my life as the one that has now occurred. Nevertheless, it has happened; it has happened, and it cannot be reversed.

Today, I met the one to whom my soul, my entire being—willingly or unwillingly—has attached itself forever.

It seems to me that I am like the traveller who, becoming lost in a desert, follows a flickering light that lures him on, farther and farther, until he tumbles into an abyss. It is in the same way that I, disregarding everything else, must follow this new feeling, for it is the light that has illuminated my soul which, until now, has lived in darkness.

I was sitting at home with my sister when someone knocked and *he* walked in and introduced himself as Doctor Roman Maletsky, the son of one of father's old friends. He planned to open a lawyer's office in our little town and wanted to consult with our father about this matter.

Malyna went to call father, and our visitor began conversing with me. I said little, for I found it very pleasant to listen to his soft, even voice. Father invited him to stay to dinner, and he spent the entire day with us. My fate was sealed.

A new feeling—half joyous and half painful—has filled my breast. I tremble when I recall his charming words and the affectionate look he gave me when we were parting.

February 18. I saw him again. I came home from town this morning and found him conversing with Malyna. It was as if something stabbed my heart when I saw Malyna's lovely, smiling face turned towards him. For the first time in my life I almost felt something akin to jealousy towards my beautiful sister. It was the first time that I felt envious of the charm that graces only a youthful face. But when I extended my hand to him and felt his eyes upon me, I forgot about everything else. I was once again swept up by that powerful, exciting feeling that I experienced when I saw him for the first time. I predict that he will be either my heaven or my hell . . .

March 5. We are well acquainted now. We go for walks together, and we read. He brings me various books, advises me which ones to read first, and then we discuss them. I'm so happy in his presence that I forget those hours filled with heartfelt suffering that I live through when he is not with me. At those times, I don't know what to do; I'm full of hope and bliss, but then I fall into despair and weep.

Am I not ridiculous with my hopes, my memories, my expectations?

He brought me Fedkovych's poems; well, at this point in my life they do not appeal to me, for they are replete with sorrow, grief, pessimism, and woe, while my soul desires something that is cheerful and uplifting, something that would rid it of this agitated waiting and calm it for at least a moment.

My whole being has fallen under the sway of the enchanting spell cast by his voice and his manner.

My cold, serene heart—that up to now has belonged only to my father and my sister, that has prayed for them and worried about them—has begun to awaken. The block of ice in which my heart was encased is beginning to thaw. I tremble when I stop to consider the chaos that now reigns in my heart.

Just like ice floes that break up under the pressure of the spring sun and, flowing ever farther and becoming ever more threatening and dangerous, stir up the water, rise up to the heights, and then crash with a roar into the depths, so do my mind and my dream of an ordinary life seethe and struggle against my love and against my intent to admit all of this to him.

April 12. Overnight, spring has arrived. Spring has come to nature, and an even more beautiful spring fills my heart. The waiting and the anxiety have retreated far away from me. Just as the trees have come into bloom almost in a single night, so have hope, joy, and peace blossomed in my heart.

How wonderful it is when the bright sun looks down upon the tender young greenery—just as wonderful as when the eyes of one's beloved gaze at the luxuriant flowers in one's heart!

Oh, to live like this forever—in happiness and with love. I boldly say with love for—Oh, my dear God! Oh, my great joy!—I think Roman loves me!

I've observed how he sometimes forgets about everything and gazes pensively into the distance. More than once, I've intercepted a look from him which uncovers the heavens to me.

It seems to me that there is a magic word on his lips—a word that would disperse my melancholy in an instant . . .

May 1. Roman asked my permission to speak to me in private tomorrow. O God! What does he want to say to me? But don't I know? Does he perhaps want me to prepare myself for my great happiness, so it won't overwhelm me?

Oh, my dear one, my one and only—I am yours with all my heart. I belong to you, for you have awakened me to a new life. I am your slave; I will follow you wherever you wish to go, because for me there is light and sun only where you are.

May 3. My fate is decided. I have lost him, lost him forever; I am ashamed. My feelings are in turmoil and my heart refuses to accept this fact. Alas! He loves Malyna, not me!

For one moment I thought the conversation was about me. And it was then that he glanced into my soul, into my trembling, hopeful, soul that was brimming with happiness. And he read it— if only for a second, but he did read it—as if it were an open book.

My God, why has this grief befallen me? Why has this shame come down upon me? If he had chosen me, my sister would not have been as unhappy as I am. She does not know as yet what love is. Nonetheless, he has chosen her and rejected me.

O darkness! Cover me and conceal the suffering that my poor heart must bear. My beloved! You brought paradise so close to me—paradise! I saw it in your love! And then you cast me into an inferno of despair.

How difficult, how painful is the transition from happiness to grief! How horribly my heart aches, how it shrivels under the oppressive weight of its suffering.

I am not the first whose love has not brought her happiness, nor am I the last to experience such grief. Since the beginning of the human race, everything alternates in this world—weeping with laughter, happiness with grief. So be still, my heart—do not curse, do not break, do not flutter so violently. Nothing will help you; you must ache!

What does this cramp in my chest mean? It seems to me that my blood has stopped flowing.

Oh, if only I could forget!

If only I could banish the happiness and the grief of the last few days from my memory!

May 8. It seems to me that all life within me has congealed. I walk around, I work, but I am indifferent to everything.

It is only now that I'm beginning to understand Fedkovych; it is only now that his sad, mournful poetry appeals to me, because now a sympathetic string responds in my heart.

I weep over his poem, "Prayer," for I too can no longer pray; my heart is not able to lift itself up in prayer, and I am not yet able to utter the words: "Thy will be done."

More than once I feel within my heart the snake that, inciting the sisters in his poem "Yuriy Hinda" to rise up against one another, thrust poison into their hands. I hear the voice of jealousy. I struggle against it so that I won't curse my sister and her alluring beauty which has taken from me what was dearest to me.

Forgive me, my sister; forgive me for these wicked thoughts; forgive this alien feeling that has possessed me and come between us!

Oh, if only I had never laid eyes on Roman!

Of what use are all my resolutions when I still love him? But my love, instead of uplifting me, ennobling me, is making me evil and jealous; it is poisoning my heart and my soul, and embittering every hour of my life.

Is he to blame that I misread the soulful looks that he gave Malyna as an answer to my love? Is he to blame that I was attracted to his proud, imposing figure? Is he accountable for the fact that I interpreted his words in my own way, that my hand trembled when he shook it? It was only that one time that he was able to read what was in my heart and eyes, but since then—never!

Malyna often gazes sadly at me—can it be that she guesses something?

Oh, what torture it is to mask your feelings, hide them from those who are dearest to you, and pretend to be happy when your heart is bursting with grief.

Moreover, I'm not feeling well. I'm exhausted by a pain in my chest that is growing worse every day, but I'm remaining silent about it. Why should I grieve my sister—and then he would grieve along with her . . .

May 15. Day or night, I have no peace. Tossing about in my bed, I weep and count the hours that separate me from daybreak.

Malyna sleeps soundly. I close my lips tightly to prevent her from hearing my groans; I do not want to cry, but my tears flow in torrents. Springing out of bed, I want to fall at Malyna's feet and beg her to give him up—to give up my beloved, my one and only—to me.

It seems to me that I must beg her for my happiness.

She would not be as devastated as I am.

But could I beg her for a love that she received without asking? I would sooner die than do so!

And could Malyna give it to me? He loves her; he does not want me!

Did I not pray a thousand times for Malyna's happiness? Did I not ask that good fortune be hers? And now, when that good fortune has appeared, when she—at the cost of my happiness—is going to be happy, why does my sacrifice seem so painful? Do I now want to be unfaithful to the vow I made to our dying mother—to look after and care for her youngest child?

What has happened to me? Where has my passion driven me? And what if she had refused him—what would I have benefitted from that?

He does not want me; I could never belong to him. So hide yourself, my insane thought, in the darkest corner of my heart, and do not ever come out, because I will not listen to you; but the struggle with you is very painful—oh, very painful indeed!

At times there is such a coldness in my chest that I am terrified, and I clutch at my heart, thinking that it has stopped beating.

I am not able to live with this open wound in my heart; there is no cure for it, and I must perish because of it. And to make matters worse, I must live with the pain of seeing him happy, and being tender and loving towards her, my sister.

More than once he turns to me with cordial words that fill my heart with an even more bitter potion. I fear for myself. If only all this would finally end, so that my soul, like a boat that nears the shore after a terrible storm, could find peace . . .

June 2. How much longer will I be able to live like this? Their wedding will take place in a week, and I've become accustomed to the idea.

He is pitiless—he is taking everything away from me. He will also take my sister who was my only joy, about whose welfare I was so concerned. Without her cheerful voice these walls will become still gloomier.

What is this shivering that spreads over my entire body? Why do I feel so terrified? What is this pain that I feel in my chest? What is this dizziness in my head? What is this sweetish taste in my mouth?

Oh, it's blood! Warm, red blood—perhaps I'll feel better now. I must hide the handkerchief so that Malyna won't see it; she'd worry, and I don't want to cast any gloom over her last few days in her father's home.

June 8. Poor father, he will be bereft of both of his daughters at the same time. I feel very weak, but I'm not giving in to my illness. Malyna is so dear, so kind; praise God that at least she is happy. As he gazes upon her good fortune, father will forget about his elder daughter. The wedding is tomorrow; I only pray that I'll have the strength to get through it.

June 10. It's all over. Malyna has gone to her new home with her husband, and I'm left all alone, completely alone. A fear of the unknown is enveloping me; I'm trembling—it must be my illness that's doing this to me. Dear, kind Malyna, may all that is good descend upon you. I now am completely calm, because I see that you're in the care of a good, honest man. Now, I can say with true humility: "Thy will be done," for I sense that my story is drawing to a close.

Roman, deeply moved, gazed for a long time at the writing that professed such a deep, passionate love.

"Poor Halya," he said softly. "So this is how her story ended. She concealed the first outburst of blood; perhaps a cure could have been found then. But she is better off this way. She is at peace. Her fiery, passionate heart, which could not reconcile itself with the inevitable, had to stop beating."

Roman lit a candle.

"Malyna must never find out how Halya's story ended; it would ruin our happiness. Let the flame destroy what her proud lips concealed."

The paper was reduced to ashes, and a gentle breeze, drifting in through the open window, scattered them throughout the room.

"I will do whatever I can to compensate Malyna for the harm I unwittingly did her sister," Roman vowed.

And he walked out of the room in which Halya's poignant struggle had taken place, the struggle that had ended in her death.

The Addressee Is Deceased
A Miniature
(1902)

An old woman who was not a beggar, but on whom the signs of poverty were clearly visible, approached a wicket in the post office and timidly asked the clerk if there was anything for her.

"Nothing this time either," the clerk replied.

"It can't be!" the old woman's voice trembled. "There has to be something for me!"

The clerk was obviously a kind man for, instead of shouting at the old woman, as is usually the case, he looked in the drawer once again and then stated quietly: "Really, there's nothing."

The old woman shook her head in disbelief and stepped aside. Her wrinkled face reflected the anguish of her soul, and so the clerk, out of pity, repeated his assurance once more.

He then turned his attention to the other people who were waiting. When everyone else left, the old woman once again stepped up to the wicket.

"Don't be annoyed with me, sir . . ."

"But you see, my dear woman, I can't do anything for you, except, perhaps, take another look. And I've done that twice already."

"Yes, I know. Thank you for everything. But what can it possibly mean that there's no letter? I wrote to my daughter well over a month ago. She usually replies immediately . . . and sends me money as well . . ."

After a moment, she added: "Maybe she's left the place where she was working?"

"Then they would have forwarded the letter to the place where she was staying."

"It wasn't a letter. It was a postcard."

"I can take a look to see if the postcard has been returned."

"If you would be so kind, sir."

"To whom was the card addressed?"

"To my daughter."

"You have to give me her name and the place where she is staying."

The old woman told him, and the clerk opened a thick book in which undelivered and returned letters were registered. He moved his finger down the long list of names, and the old woman anxiously followed every movement of his hand.

After a lengthy moment, the clerk paused.

"Did you find anything, sir?"

"It appears that her place of residence hasn't changed. I'll look for the card right now."

He went up to a big cupboard, pulled out a large bundle of mail, and began to sift through it. Ah yes, there it was.

"Is this your card?" the clerk asked.

"Would you read it to me, please? I don't know how to read and write, but I know what was in it because I told the neighbour's boy what to write."

The clerk hesitated.

"Please, if you would be so kind!" the old woman pleaded.

The clerk began to read: "My dear child! I beg you not to leave your work. You have a job that isn't too bad; they pay you well, and so you can help me a bit too. You know that you're the only one who can help me. I can no longer earn money, because I've grown old and sick. I live only on what you send me. So, I beg you, do as I say. I wish you all the best a hundred times over. Your old mother."

"Yes, yes, that's my card. The boy must have written down the wrong address, and so my daughter did not get it."

The clerk read out the address to the old woman. It was correct. But next to the address there was a note in someone else's handwriting.

"Why didn't they send the card there? Something's wrong!"

"It was sent there, my dear woman, but it says that . . ."

The terrible words did not want to pass through the clerk's lips.

"It says here that . . . the addressee is deceased."

He passed the postcard to the old woman, and she reached for it in a daze, staring with bewildered eyes at the clerk, who could not hide his agitation. Holding the ill-fated postcard in her hands, she slowly dragged herself to the door. Four words—so short and official—but they had shattered her heart. No, no! This could not be true! It was impossible! Her daughter was her only mainstay in her old age . . . Her dearest daughter, her whole world . . .

"Please, sir," she said to a young man who happened to be passing by. "What's written on this card? Here, at the top."

The young man took the card and, seeing the trepidation in the wary eyes of the old woman, said sympathetically: "The addressee is deceased."

It was only now she believed that the terrible news was true—her only child was no longer alive. She was no longer alive, she had died . . . She had died far away from home, among strangers. There had been no one to care for her in her illness, no one to hand her a candle when she was dying, no one to prepare her body for burial . . .

"She's dead . . . dead . . ." her pale lips whispered, and tears streamed from her eyes.

Her feet stepped forward mechanically and, before she knew it, she was on the road that led to the place where her child had lived. She had only one thought—to see the place where people had buried her dearest treasure.

The sun sank behind the hills, and twilight blanketed the earth, but she walked on and on without stopping. Finally, exhaustion forced her to rest. She sat down by the side of the road and, almost instantly, sleep closed her weary eyelids.

The darkness of night descended, autumnal fogs rose above the hayfields, and frozen droplets of dew coalesced on the yellow leaves of the trees . . .

The sun rose in a flash of glory. It vanquished the fog, and the frozen dew glittered like diamonds on the withered grass. But this beauty of nature was frigid. It did not delight human hearts, for it foreshadowed the ebbing of life.

The old woman lay lifeless in the ditch. The postcard was still in her hands and, in the bright sunlight, four words shimmered under the frozen dew: "The addressee is deceased."

In the Forest
(1903)

It was very early. Pearls of morning dew trembled on tall trees, and the stillness of the forest was not yet disturbed by the blows of an axe. In the pale morning light, slender beech trees glimmered, soaring proudly upwards, flaunting their great height that reached into the sky. The first rays of the sun, slowly breaking through a rosy curtain, shone shyly and timidly, shimmering in the morning mist.

On a narrow path winding through the proud beeches, hobbled an elderly woman, groaning under a bundle of brushwood balanced precariously on her back. The beauty of the early morning did not move her; the singing of the birds did not enchant her; and the invigorating air did not refresh her. She was preoccupied with a single thought—how to avoid meeting up with the forester.

It was still dark when she got up and went into the forest to gather brushwood. She dreaded the winter; she feared the fierce frosts that pierce to the bone when there is no firewood left to heat a cottage. And so she was stocking up on dry brushwood before the winter set in and caught her without a supply of fuel. Her store was growing daily.

Limping along and glancing furtively in all directions, she was thinking that she would not have to make many more trips into the forest.

A distant rustling jolted her out of her reverie. "It's the junior forester," she thought in panic.

She was right. A minute later he was standing in front of her, anger flashing in his stern eyes.

"So, it's old Nastya again!" he shouted, stepping closer to her. "How many times have I told you that I don't want to see you here! Am I talking to the beech trees? Or do you think that my mercy knows no bounds?"

"But it's just dry, useless brushwood, if you please, sir."

"That may be, but it isn't lying around for thieves to take. Do you understand?"

Nastya fixed her eyes on the ground.

"This brushwood belongs to the Kaiser's forest, and whoever takes it from here is stealing. And I don't want to let you commit such a great sin. Untie your bundle!"

"Sir, I'm poor, and old, and crippled . . ."

"That makes it all the worse! Older people should set a good example for younger ones. What will become of children who see that their mother is stealing and doesn't consider it a sin? Untie your bundle!"

"I must have bent over a hundred times before I gathered together these branches. It's not easy at my age! And by doing so, I've already done penance for these few sticks of kindling wood. Pity me in my old age, sir!" She looked at him pleadingly with her sunken, rheumy eyes.

"Untie your bundle!" A threatening note was creeping into his voice.

Nastya's eyes filled with tears, and her body, racked by heart-rending sobs, began to shake uncontrollably. The forester pulled a knife out of his pocket and slashed the bundle a couple of times, cutting the rope that held the brushwood together. The dry branches tumbled to the ground; he gave them a good kick, and they flew in all directions.

Nastya stood dumbstruck, staring in disbelief at the scattered branches.

"And now, move on!" His menacing voice drove itself into the depths of her soul.

Her heart pounded, her chest heaved, and her lips quivered. "God will punish you for trampling a poor, helpless worm!" she began saying.

"So you're talking back, you old witch!" the forester yelled. "Now I'll treat you according to the letter of the law!" And, in a sweeping motion, he removed from her back the patched coarse wool cloak that had protected her from the cold for so many years.

She did not try to stop him; she just stared with despairing eyes at her only protection from the elements.

"You can get your cloak back from the village office!" the forester spat disdainfully as he walked away.

She could get her cloak back from the village office where it would be kept as security against a fine. If she could redeem it, then she would get it back, and if not, it . . . would stay . . . there. She stopped crying; her agitation subsided and, at the same time, her strength failed. The entire world became blurry; a tremor born of fear pulsed through her legs, and she sank silently to the ground.

The rising sun was gilding the forest with its rays. Birds were flitting from branch to branch, pecking at the leaves, singing their cheerful songs, and looking in surprise at the old woman lying motionless on the ground.

From around a bend, there appeared a heavy wagon loaded with wood. A driver was walking ahead of it, and the senior forester was bringing up the rear.

"There's a woman sleeping here!" the driver shouted as he approached Nastya. "Aha, it's old Nastya; she must be sleeping off a hangover."

"Oh, no, not Nastya—she never does anything like that!" the senior forester responded, stepping up closer to her. "Hey there, get up, granny!" he said, taking her by the arm.

She raised her head and looked around as if she were awakening from a deep sleep. Then she slowly raised herself to her feet.

"How did you get here? I thought you were dead," the senior forester said with a smile.

"Dead . . . If only God would let me die! Then my heart wouldn't break from grief . . ."

"What's wrong? Is there something you need?"

"Oh, no, sir, I have too much of everything! Too many years and too much poverty, and a person who has all this has no need to live . . ."

He once again asked her what was wrong, and she told him about her encounter with the junior forester. She spoke slowly, holding back her grief, and making no reproaches against the young official. And when her glance fell on the scattered brushwood, she said tearfully: "But I'm not a thief, sir; no, no, I'm not a thief!"

"Don't cry, Nastya! The junior forester knows only the letter of the law, but how it's applied is a totally different matter."

"Winter doesn't know any 'law or its letters,' sir! It comes, and I have to rack my brain how to get by without my old cloak if it stays in the village office, and I don't have the money to buy it back . . . God! I used to wrap myself up in it, and it didn't matter if a blizzard raged, or if the rain poured down . . . It served me for so many years, and now . . ."

"And now you can once again wrap yourself in your cloak. I'll sin against the letter of the law—just don't cry any more. Come to the forestry office in the afternoon, and we'll return your cloak. And as for the brushwood, you can take it with you now . . ."

"Can I, my good sir?" the old woman exclaimed, and joy squeezed a few more tears from her eyes.

She wanted to take the forester's hand and kiss it, but he stopped her.

"But don't come here anymore, Nastya! If the two of us meet, there's no problem—old people understand each other, but if the junior forester should come across you, then you know what will happen . . . You'd do better to come to me when you need something, and I'll ignore the law and give you my personal permission. Well, goodbye for now."

"May God reward you for your kind heart, my good sir!" the old woman said, crying and laughing at the same time; and she followed him with her eyes as he vanished into the thickets.

"O my poor cloak," she said to herself as she gathered up the scattered brushwood, "we'll see each other this afternoon! I'll put on my warm old cloak again today . . . My heart's ready to burst in my chest! I was about to lose my one piece of warm clothing because of some kind of 'law and its letters' . . ."

In the thicket a bird began to sing.

Turning to it, Nastya said: "How cheerful you are, my little bird! And you have the right to be happy; no one can harm you; there are no 'laws and letters' for you . . ."

A Woman's Happiness
(1904?)

Little Slavko slipped his school bag on his back, bowed politely to his parents, and walked quickly out of the room. His mother watched wistfully as he left. Every time they parted, her mind conjured up all the infectious childhood diseases he had not yet contracted.

At one time, she had not been so fearful, but since his bout with scarlet fever, she was filled with fear that, even though he was healthy and happy when he left home, he would return—as he had on that occasion—deathly ill. An invisible force compelled her to run after him now; she wanted to hug him one more time.

"Slavko!" she called out. "Are you still there, in the porch?"

"Yes, mummy. Did I forget something?"

"Yes, my darling!"

Now she felt embarrassed about her boundless love for her son and, suppressing the feelings in her heart, refrained from hugging or kissing him.

"Here's some money for a pencil," she said, and she gave him some small change, wanting him to think that this was why she had called him back.

"Thanks, but I don't need a pencil."

"Are you sure? Take the money!"

He took it and started to leave, but she stopped him once again: "Just a minute, your cap has slipped to one side."

She straightened his cap and made the sign of the cross over him. She did this silently and covertly, so he would not notice and become soft because of her softness.

But he did notice, and he kissed his mother impetuously, sensing that she was blessing him to protect him from evil. Then he tore down the street.

She walked slowly back into the room, where her husband was sitting at the table reading a newspaper, and sat down.

He glanced over at her, stopped reading, and said: "You seem to cry whenever he leaves for school."

She blushed and, without answering, picked up a newspaper and began reading.

"In our day, mothers weren't so sensitive," he continued grumbling.

"Probably not," she said. "But do you find it surprising? You know very well the boy is all I have."

Was this a reproach? No, there was neither blame nor reproach in her grave eyes; she was beyond that. No rebuke had crossed her proud lips from the day her husband had ceased caring for her and transferred his affections to another woman.

How could anything like this have happened? After all, he had courted her so passionately, truly loved her for several years, and continually assured her that she was the only woman for him—that he would love her forever.

She had believed him. It seemed to her she had the right to believe him, to rely on his word. In her pure soul, she had never suspected he could deceive her. He was much older, but she loved him, worshipped him, and thought he was superior to everyone.

The change in him did not escape her attention. She saw that the flaming fire was slowly dying down, and even though at times it still flared up for a moment, it finally turned into grey smoke. She accepted this with dignity, thinking that her husband, as a serious older man, no longer took any pleasure in foolishness.

At the same time, she noticed that he was going out in the evenings. And then her acquaintances told her that he was involved with a young widow, the most beautiful woman in the city.

She did not believe them. It simply could not be. How could he have changed so much? How could his heart have been emptied of all his desire for her, when her love for him still burned so ardently, so passionately? Could his assurances of eternal love have drifted away like so much smoke?

No, it was impossible! But the uncertainty was tormenting her soul, and she resolved to ask him if what people were saying about him was true.

Frankness was one of the basic qualities of his character. With unmitigated cruelty, he readily admitted that a new love had taken root in his heart and that he was not about to deny himself its delights.

After learning the truth, her outward appearance remained completely calm. Her nature was such that she never revealed her profound grief. But because of that, the storm within her raged even more fiercely.

At the height of her rage, she wanted to leave her husband, but she could not abandon her only child. So her sense of responsibility towards the child kept her in her husband's home. She stayed there with death in her heart.

Even time, which heals all wounds, which cures all ills, brought her no relief. It is true that, in the company of her child, she momentarily forgot her despair. But when she was alone, she became despondent once again and, whenever she looked at her husband, the wounds in her aching heart reopened.

She never said anything, but he sensed her suffering and felt annoyed with her and, indeed, with himself.

"What do you mean—the child is all you have?" he picked up on her last words. "Have I left you? You're my wife, Slavko's my son, and the three of us constitute a family which will exist as long as we live. Don't forget—the faithfulness of a husband can never be like that of a wife. In a man, faithfulness means that he will never desert his family, that he will feed and protect it. Am I not doing this? I even feel the most sincere amity towards you, Marta. Does all this not mean anything to you?"

With genuine feeling, he extended his hand to her across the table: "Friendship in exchange for an unconditional, ardent love!"

She remained silent and did not touch his hand.

"I feel sorry for you, very sorry," he continued, withdrawing his hand, "but I can't help you. I'm not to blame for the situation; I didn't actively seek it. Unfortunately, I'm the kind of person who is ruled by his emotions."

"Let's drop this topic and move on to something else," she said. "Can you come with me to meet Slavko today? He would be so happy to see you."

"No, I don't have time; I have to go to the office right away."

She knew he had no office work in the afternoon, but her serious face did not betray any emotion. She simply inquired quietly: "So Slavko won't see you until this evening?"

"That also won't be possible. I have some important matters which will keep me away until late. That's why I would like to have the key to the apartment. I don't want to rouse you from your deepest sleep."

Her deepest sleep! Did he really think she could sleep, knowing as she did, that he was enjoying himself with his mistress?

She silently gave him the key.

He dropped it into his pocket, picked up his hat, and said: "Goodbye!"

He wanted to kiss her, but she turned away from him.

She did not want his friendly kisses. No, she did not want any kisses from those profaned lips; she felt that this would be an affront to her dignity as a woman.

He left, but she stood in the same spot for a long time, pondering her fate.

There was a knock at the door.

In response to her invitation, an elderly doctor, a longtime friend of her parents, walked into the room.

"Good day! How are you? Not too well, I see, eh?"

Depositing his hat and cane in a corner, he sat down opposite the young woman, but did not look at her.

She replied: "Slavko is very well."

"But, as for you and your husband, things are not going all that well. I met him out on the street, and he was bounding away like a rabbit."

"Bounding away to meet his happiness," she bitterly completed the doctor's thought.

"That may be, but don't take it to heart, my child. This will pass. Every love passes, and affairs on the side pass most quickly of all. Don't spend too much time thinking about it; instead, devote yourself to your true happiness. There is something a woman has over a man—a love for her children which can bring her great joy.

"We, as men, have won a lot of privileges for ourselves, even ones that don't rightly belong to us. We know how to find fleeting pleasure and enjoyment, but we are prohibited from knowing the pure delight, the blissful joy, the comfort that a mother finds in her children. A man's foot cannot cross the threshold into this paradise. That is why I'm saying that a woman who has the joy, the good fortune of having a child, has not lost everything."

"You're right, doctor," she said, rising to her feet and offering him her hand.

"It will soon be four o'clock. We'd better move along, or you'll be late to meet Slavko," the doctor said, warmly pressing her cold hands.

Remembering what the doctor had told her, she felt twice as happy when she caught sight of her little son whose happy, smiling cheeks were glowing with health.

The two of them went for a walk beyond the city limits. How happy the mother felt as she responded to the questions of her only son and identified for him the flowers, the butterflies, and the birds. He listened to her with shining eyes, and they both had a wonderful time.

They returned home late in the evening, carrying armfuls of flowers.

Slavko felt tired and went to bed immediately. His mother sat at his side, arranging the flowers into a bouquet.

It was fresh and quiet in the room, and the mother could hear the even breathing of her child.

Suddenly he asked: "Mummy, why doesn't daddy ever come with us now? All my friends go for walks with their dads."

Her heart began to beat violently, and a painful expression came over her face.

She forced herself to speak calmly. "He doesn't have the time, my darling; he has lots of work in the office."

"Oh, mummy, you're so kind, and you go for walks with me so I won't be bored. I love you very, very much!" And he hugged his mother and cuddled up to her.

And, feeling his little arms wrapped around her neck, she concluded she had no reason to complain, as long as she found such great joy in her child, as long as she felt such an unutterable happiness when she was with him.

The Guest
(1904)

She told him how many eggs the hens had laid, that meat had gone up in price again, that the vegetables were terrible, and that the wash was giving her no end of trouble—it had been hanging on the clothesline for three days now without drying.

He heard her out with his customary consideration. This was the report he had to listen to every day when he came home from school and sat down to have dinner with his wife.

After they finished discussing every item in detail, she finally asked him how things had gone for him in school that day.

Oh, he had more than his share of problems as well! The young Mykhaylovych lad was sorely trying his patience. He was very mischievous and disruptive, but could not be dealt with strictly because he was the principal's son.

"Just imagine this, if you can! He drew a caricature of me on the board today and then wrote under it: 'The teacher, wearing a coat altered by his wife.' I think it would be better if you didn't try your hand at tailoring—your alterations are making me the butt of the youngsters' jokes."

While saying this, he glanced over at his coat. Its overly long coat-tails and foreshortened sleeves truly did not inspire any feelings of awe or betray an elevated aesthetic sense.

But his words got him into deep trouble! They were cause for real indignation!

Things even went so far that his wife accused him of reproaching her for her hard work.

"I've always said the Mykhaylovych boy was a mischief-maker, and now, because of him, you're not going to wear the coat I worked so hard to alter? You want to discard it? No, Vladyk, I never expected anything like this from you. Whose business is it if it's a trifle too long? We can't afford to buy new clothes every year."

Fearing her tears, he did not dare to reply. Perhaps she was right. He had never concerned himself with such matters as fashion and clothes. He had no time for that. Schoolwork and lessons consumed all his attention. He worked for days on end without ever once worrying how his coat fit. Besides, the coat was comfortable. He was being ungrateful. It was the first time he had ever criticised his wife for her tailoring efforts, and he should not have done so.

She was so kind and took such good care of him, tending to his needs and trying to please him. It was a sin to be angry with her. And she spent nothing on clothing for herself; she scrimped and saved their money, so they could buy a modest little cottage in the village when they retired. All she wanted was to live in it for a year or two before she died.

He was deeply moved when he stopped to think about how good she was.

"Don't be angry. I won't stop wearing my coat," he said, as he prepared to go back to work.

A knock at the door interrupted his plans.

Alarmed, they both glanced at the clock. Who could it be? Who would come to see them at such an hour? Guests at such an hour? It could not be! Who would dream of going visiting at one o'clock?

But it was not a guest. It was the postman, and he handed them a registered letter.

Both of them were apprehensive. With trembling hands, Vladyk opened the letter and began reading it. But the longer he read, the more confused he looked. Finally, he glanced up hesitantly at his wife.

"My dear Malvina, just think, Doctor Lomnytsky . . . Do you remember him?"

"The one who had a suite in your sister's house?"

"That's the one. He's written to say that he'll be passing through our town, and he wants to know if he can spend the night at our place. If it's awkward for us, he'll try to make other arrangements for accommodation."

"Is that what he's written?"

She completely lost her presence of mind. A young gentleman from the big city was to be in their home? What was she to do with him? Where would he sleep? They had only two rooms and a kitchen; but there, in the city, he had two rooms all to himself.

And her sister-in-law had said that he was very demanding. How was one to host him, so he would be pleased and not make fun of their provinciality?

"Do you think he'll really come?" she inquired timidly.

Vladyk was convinced that he would. Bowing her head in resignation, Malvina cleared the table.

And then she immediately started changing the whole house around. She tidied up, scoured everything, and rearranged the furniture and all the pictures.

When the time drew near for the guest to make his appearance, both the host and the hostess, dressed in their finest clothing, anxiously awaited him.

The guest arrived.

And he was so pleasant and so gracious, that both the teacher and his wife reproached themselves for having felt so little pleasure when they read his letter.

At the table, the young doctor initiated a conversation: "So, my lady, do you go out for walks quite often?"

She blushed and looked in alarm at her husband. "Oh, no. There's nowhere to take walks here. There are only Jewish market streets."

"Well then, my lady, you must have some good friends in this little town with whom you often get together for parties, picnics, socials . . ."

"My husband has so little time. We don't get together with anyone."

"Then, obviously, the two of you must take delight in nature and travel frequently through the countryside. Perhaps you ride a bicycle, sir?"

The teacher glanced at his wife and smiled. "No, I haven't attempted that as yet."

He said this so naively, that the guest almost laughed out loud.

"Well then, what do you do? Do you go hunting?"

"No."

"Then you must be excellent card players."

"No, doctor, I don't play cards."

"Then, what do you do in your free time?"

"I . . . work, I read, I write . . ."

"And what does your good lady do?"

The teacher and his wife exchanged glances. They did not know what to reply to this. The good lady did not have any leisure time, because all the household duties fell on her shoulders.

"But this is terrible! How can you tolerate living like this? Why, you must be dying of boredom!"

These words lingered in their thoughts. Both of them had a very bad night; they hardly slept at all.

They thought about the young doctor who was so full of life, and something like envy began to awaken in their hearts.

How engagingly he had talked about all the wonders of the big city. Had his stories not transformed their lonely apartment? Had they themselves not become happier and more talkative with every passing hour? Had they not thought they had never spent a more pleasant evening?

How fortunate he was! But what about them? They remained in the same place year after year, with the same worries, the same aggravations!

What did they really know about life? Only disagreeable incidents with school children and discussions with parents, who invariably blamed the teacher for the naughtiness and laziness of their children.

In the winter, they worried about the stove that smoked. In the summer, they had to cope with the dust that drifted from the road into their living quarters. And there was always one unending problem—a lack of money. This was the life they had led for a long time now, and which they would continue leading to the end of their days.

Concluding his sad reflections, Vladyk heard a muffled sobbing at the other end of the room. So, she could not sleep either. She was also thinking about her life and weeping for her lost years. He held his breath, trying not to betray the fact that he too was besieged by unhappy thoughts.

In the morning, they saw their guest for a only moment; in the evening, he returned to the capital. It seemed to them that he took back with him all the joy from their small apartment.

Malvina fixed things up the way they were before the arrival of the guest. They sat down in silence to have their supper. He was in his old coat, and she was wearing a huge apron which she had taken off while the guest had been there. They sat at the table, and it was unpleasant for both of them. Everything seemed so boring, so mundane. It was as if grey shadows were hovering over their chairs.

She began to tell him how many eggs the hens had laid, that the clothes had finally dried, and that she had bought some milk, because there was none left over from yesterday.

He glanced at her with a look of bewilderment on his face, and she fell silent, feeling ashamed, very ashamed, for having tried to catch his attention with such trifling matters—matters which up to now had seemed so all-important to her.

In desperation, she racked her brain, trying to think of some way of intriguing her husband the way the young doctor had succeeded in doing yesterday. She wanted to make him cheerful and talkative, but nothing came to mind. It was always only the hens, the neighbours, and the school.

Tears welled in her eyes. She hated herself.

He saw her tears and felt sorry for her.

"Come," he said. "The moon is shining. Perhaps we could go for a walk?"

She rose from the table, and something akin to a smile flitted across her troubled face.